The
PARADISE
PROBLEM

*Audiobook only

CHRISTINA LAUREN

The
PARADISE
PROBLEM

GALLERY BOOKS

New York   London   Toronto   Sydney   New Delhi

G

Gallery Books
An Imprint of Simon & Schuster, LLC
1230 Avenue of the Americas
New York, NY 10020

First Gallery Books hardcover edition May 2024

GALLERY BOOKS and colophon are registered trademarks of Simon & Schuster, LLC

Simon & Schuster: Celebrating 100 Years of Publishing in 2024

For information about special discounts for bulk purchases, please contact Simon & Schuster Special Sales at 1-866-506-1949 or business@simonandschuster.com.

The Simon & Schuster Speakers Bureau can bring authors to your live event. For more information or to book an event, contact the Simon & Schuster Speakers Bureau at 1-866-248-3049 or visit our website at www.simonspeakers.com.

Interior design by Kathryn A. Kenney-Peterson

Manufactured in the United States of America

10 9 8 7 6 5 4 3 2 1

Library of Congress Cataloging-in-Publication Data
Names: Lauren, Christina, author.
Title: The paradise problem / Christina Lauren.
Description: First Gallery Books hardcover edition. | New York : Gallery Books, 2024.
Identifiers: LCCN 2023053120 | ISBN 9781668017722 (hardcover) |
   ISBN 9781668017739 (paperback) | ISBN 9781668017746 (e-book)
Subjects: LCGFT: Romance fiction. | Novels.
Classification: LCC PS3612.A9442273 P37 2024 | DDC 813/.6—dc23/eng/20231117
LC record available at https://lccn.loc.gov/2023053120

ISBN 978-1-6680-1772-2
ISBN 978-1-6680-1774-6 (ebook)

Dedicated to the things that keep us sane:
group chats, Bangtan, Harry, and Taylor

The
PARADISE
PROBLEM

$\mathcal{P}$rologue

ANNA

The day my husband moves out of our apartment is also the day *Resident Evil Village* releases for PlayStation, and you might be surprised which of these things lands with a greater emotional impact.

But given that I am not a monster, and that we have indeed enjoyed this apartment together for two years, I do what any woman who's been given the couch and TV in a divorce would do: I watch with a supportive smile as West and his two well-muscled and newly minted PhD bros carry box after box, dining chair after dining chair, suitcase after suitcase, and the remaining ninety percent of the furniture and decor out to the moving van parked at the curb. I now have hardly any earthly goods to my name, and I guess that's a little sad—I've made great use of West's stuff over the past two years—but this moment was inevitable.

At least I take comfort in knowing that packing my own belongings in two weeks will be significantly easier than this.

Out at the curb, West emerges from the back of the truck and hops gracefully down to the street, gazing up at what I'm sure is a highly organized packing job. You should have seen our pantry: truly a work of cataloging genius. My meticulous ex is twenty-eight, infrequently verbal, and one of those incredibly capable men who make complicated things like doing taxes and fixing holes in drywall look easy. I admit, beyond the sexy capability vibe, West is also a fox. He's that perfect combination of height and muscle, though I have no idea how tall he is. Is it weird that I've never asked? I realize that most tall women are obsessed with how tall other people are, but I've never had that itch. I've known lots of men—men who are taller, men who are shorter, men who are exactly my height. All I know is that West is chin-at-eye-level tall. At our wedding he had to bend to kiss me.

I haven't thought about that day in ages, but I guess it makes sense that I'm thinking about it now. That kiss feels like it happened a lifetime ago. Two years into this adventure, and I'm better acquainted with the couch he's leaving behind than I am with him.

Now, standing on the sidewalk, he turns and looks at me, our eyes meeting and giving me a weird, wavy feeling in my stomach, a touch of lightheadedness. It's not low blood sugar; I ate half a bag of jalapeño chips while I watched him pack. And it's not the heat; May in LA is the very definition of temperate. I think, strangely, it's *him*.

West's eyes are the color of sunlight passing through a glass of whiskey. His hair is that exact same color, but with more sunlight streaking through, and so thick I suspect it alone has ruined me for other men. I tried to paint it once, mixing Transparent Oxide-Red Lake with Old Holland Yellow-Brown but it wasn't quite right, and as soon as I realized how much it annoyed me that I couldn't get the correct color of his hair down on canvas, I immediately wondered why I'd become so invested in the first place.

With that intense eye contact still happening, West walks over and stops barely a foot away. For a weird, fevered beat I wonder if he's actually going to kiss me goodbye.

"I think I'm all set here," he says, and lol of course he isn't going to kiss me. "But if I forgot anything, you can have Jake come pick it up."

Jake: younger brother to West (and only slightly less good-looking) and that type of college friend who knows everything about my life at UCLA but has never met my father, who lives only an hour away. Jake introduced me to West; now Jake will be my sole remaining connection to West. The thought makes me a little sad, but then I remember I have the couch and T-virus zombies waiting for me inside.

"Sounds good," I say.

"You've got copies of the papers?" he asks. "My attorney looked over everything, and it should be sorted, but his phone number is there in case there's any issue." He pauses, eyes searching mine in a way I honestly don't think they have before, like he's trying to see me for the first time. "My number will be the same, of course. Read through everything and call me if you have any questions."

"Of course. Thanks for handling that."

He smiles, and his face absolutely opens up when it happens. I wonder why he doesn't do it more. Maybe he does, actually. I barely ever see him. He's up before sunrise to go for a run and spends every waking hour at class or the library before hitting the gym around midnight. By contrast, I live at the art studio, or on his—now my—couch.

I'm not sure what else there is to say, so I try to wrap this up: "Congratulations on finishing, West. You must be so happy."

"Absolutely," he says, digging his hands into the pockets of his jeans. I've mostly seen him in basketball shorts and free marathon T-shirts, so the worn Levi's and cozy gray T-shirt combo is a surprise this late in the game. I feel a little cheated to only be seeing it now. A tiny strip of his boxers waistband is visible and I work very hard to keep my eyes on his face. "Congratulations to you, too," he adds. "On to new, big things."

"Right," I say, laughing. "The world breathlessly awaits my next move."

He laughs, too, and the sound sends electricity scratching down my spine.

An awkward silence blankets us, but he's staring directly at me, and I feel like I can't look away. This is, like, *eye contact* eye contact. Like staring-contest eye contact, like studying a series of numbers to be memorized in a spy movie eye contact, and I force myself not to fold first.

"Well," he says finally, "I guess that's it, then."

"I hope you have a good life." It sounds trite, but I do mean it.

"You, too." West smiles that eye-crinkling smile again, and damn, I really wish I'd seen it more. "Bye, Anna."

"Bye, West."

We shake hands. He turns, walking to the curb to meet his friends, who squeeze beside him into the truck's cab. One of them rolls down the window, waving at me. I happily wave back, even though I have no idea what his name is.

I feel a body come up beside mine and turn my head to see our neighbor Candi in her bathrobe. She's always in her bathrobe so I've long wondered what she does all day. But she makes a killer key lime pie and has loud sex with her husband, Rob, around midnight every day like clockwork, so clearly she's crushing it.

"Are you moving?" she asks, looking behind me toward the mostly empty apartment.

"Oh, I'm moving in two weeks," I tell her. "West just left."

I feel her attention move from the empty apartment to the side of my face, and when I smile over at her, her blue eyes are round with worry. "Holy shit, Anna, I had no idea. Are you okay?"

"I'm fine," I tell her, looking down the street as the moving truck makes a turn and disappears from view entirely.

"Okay," she says with a frown in her voice. "I'm glad." She sets a hand on my arm. "But if you need to talk, you know I'm here, okay?"

I realize with a gust of happiness that the cover story doesn't matter anymore. I've finished my bachelor's and have a life of unknown adventure ahead; West has finished his doctorate and is on his way to his brilliant future as something impressive and serious. We both got what we wanted.

"Oh no, I'm fine!" I assure her. "I barely know him."

Candi stares at me. "What?"

I point at the apartment behind me. "Family housing. He was just a random dude I married so I could live here. Thank you, though."

With one last smile, I squeeze her hand where it rests on my arm and turn to go inside. I have zombies to kill.

One

ANNA

Three years later

If you'd told me back in college that my primary source of income at twenty-five would be working as the night cashier at the corner convenience store, I . . . well, I might have believed you. Having done a one-eighty junior year when I acknowledged that my brain does not "science" and pivoted from premed to art, I remained realistic about what life as an artist might entail. Every fine arts major at UCLA has dreams of becoming the next big set designer, costume mastermind, or art scene It kid, but those of us whose ambitions are simply "afford rent and health insurance" are aware we will most likely be waitresses by day and hobby painters by night. So the fact that it's 12:44 a.m. and I am womaning the register at the Pico Pick-It-Up and not at some fancy party rubbing elbows with the creative elite shouldn't surprise anyone, least of all myself.

But with my dad's medical bills slowly climbing, my ambitions might have to climb, too.

I carefully turn the page of the *US Weekly* I borrowed from the magazine rack. There are lots of lucrative jobs on display here. Do I have what it takes to be the next big art influencer, someday featured in the Celebrities . . . They're Just Like Us! page? I'm young and know how to wear a T-shirt without a bra. That's at least half of what's required, right?

I imagine it:

Instagram sensation Anna Green caught with a perfectly messy topknot outside of Sprouts!

TikTok star Anna Green and her sexy actor boyfriend caught canoodling in front of Soho House!

I wonder how much an influencer makes these days and whether it's worth the humiliation of monologuing into a selfie stick in front of Picasso's *Woman with a Book* at the Norton Simon, or the patience it would take to get a ring light positioned just right to draw tiny tigers on my eyelids using only vegan skin care products.

This thought exercise has clarified something for me: I'm too lazy for an influencer life.

But it's fine. Between five nights a week here, three lunch shifts at Amir's Café, the occasional dog-walking hustle, and plasma donation when things get really tight, I'm paying my rent. I'm covering most of Dad's health insurance and medical expenses. That's what matters. Deep breath. I flip the page, moving onto the Red Flag Exes! section.

"Anna."

I lean across the checkout counter and look both ways. My boss, Ricky, stands in the doorway to his small, cramped office, his wispy blond hair falling over his boyish eyes, tight fists planted on his narrow hips. He's wearing a *Naruto* T-shirt and sweatpants bearing the logo of his recent alma mater, Hamilton High School.

"Yeah?"

"Could I speak to you for a moment?"

"Sure." I hook a thumb over my shoulder toward the store's entrance. "Want me to close up for a few?"

He shakes his head. "It's one in the morning. We average half a customer from one to two."

"Fair." I hop off my stool and gently place the magazine back on the rack before dancing my way down the aisle. Ricky graduated last June but had no interest in college, prompting his parents to offer him the challenge of managing their Pick-It-Up location at Pico and Manning sandwiched quite literally between a Subway and a Jimmy John's. Barb and Paul are two of my favorite people in the world, but Ricky has been using this Stern Boss voice with me ever since he asked me to dinner on his eighteenth birthday and I said no. Be serious.

I lean against the doorway and brush my too-long, barely-pink-anymore bangs from my face. I'm in desperate need of a cut and color, but such things fall very far down on the priority list these days. "What's up?"

He straightens a string-bean arm and tries to look authoritative as he motions to the chair across from him. It looks like one of those old elementary school chairs, with the contoured plastic seat and tubular steel frame, but the closest school is over half a mile away. It showed up in the alley one day and it's been in the office ever since. "Could you come sit down, please?"

I take a seat but glance over my shoulder at the front of the store. Even if Ricky has called me back here, it's still my till in the register. The last thing I need is someone bolting in and doing a quick grab of all the cash in there. The Verizon store three doors down was robbed just last week. "Are you sure we can't chat out there? It makes me uneasy leaving the store unattended."

"Well, that's ironic."

I turn back to look at him. From my little chair I see that he has a distinct height advantage, which I realize now is probably intentional. "Pardon?"

He flips a pencil between his fingers. His nails are all chewed up, there's a faded blue stamp on the back of his right hand from Randy's Arcade, and he's wearing his high school class ring. Ricky straightens his spine and tries to look taller. He's five seven standing on a box. It's not my most mature coping strategy, but sometimes when Ricky is particularly condescending, I'll draw little caricatures of him dwarfed in his dad's broad-shouldered suit, his feet swimming in his dad's giant shoes. "It's ironic when you pretend to be concerned about the store being robbed."

"Ironic?" I ask. "How so?"

"I saw footage of you taking a pack of gum yesterday. You never paid for it."

I squint, thinking back. I did take a pack of gum. Probably thirty minutes into my eight-hour shift. "How do you know I didn't pay for it?"

He points to the security camera in the corner of the office, reminding me, I suppose, that there are cameras everywhere. But if he knows I never paid for it, then . . .

"You watched eight hours of footage of me?" I ask.

Ricky shifts in his chair and the faux-leather squeaks under him like a fart. He tries to do it again and fails. With his face red, he clarifies, "On fast-forward."

I know how old those security cameras are. Fast-forward is, at best, double speed. "So, you're saying you only watched four hours of footage of me at work?"

Flushing, he waves this off. "The time I spent isn't the point."

I swallow down the response I know won't get me anywhere: *Four hours of your wasted time seems like a bigger theft of resources than a single two-dollar pack of gum in three years' employment, as does you being here working the graveyard shift with me when we average zero-point-five customers every hour.*

Instead, I say, "I just forgot. I didn't have any cash and I didn't want to pay a five-dollar debit fee for a transaction under ten dollars."

"You should have put an IOU in the cash drawer yesterday."

"An IOU? Like . . . on paper?"

He nods. "Feed out the receipt paper and use that."

"How would Kelly have accounted for that when she came in at seven?"

"She could have told me you took a pack of gum and would pay for it later."

"But you *knew* I took a pack of gum. You watched the entire video."

His nostrils flare. "The point is we can't trust you."

"Ricky, I'll pay for the gum now. God, I've worked here for three years, and this is the first time you've ever had an issue with me."

The face he makes tells me that I don't have this quite right.

I sit back in my little chair. "Oh. I see. This is about the date."

Ricky leans forward on his forearms, clasping his hands the way his dad does when he's in Mentor Paul mode. But Paul could give me a two-hour sermon about how to be successful in business and I'd eat it all up because he's charismatic and caring and worked his ass off to get a chain of four stores in downtown Los Angeles. Ricky got an Audi for his sixteenth birthday, a store for his eighteenth, and apparently spends his managerial time watching security footage of me on the days I wear skirts to work. So, I don't believe a word he's saying when he says, "It isn't about the date."

"Really?"

"It *isn't about that*," he insists.

"This is so dumb, Ricky!"

"It's Derrick."

"This is so dumb, *Derrick*."

He flushes. "This is a business owner handling an employee issue. I'm sorry, Anna. We have to let you go."

My ears ring. A panicky flush blankets my skin. "You're firing me today over a pack of gum?"

"Yes."

"Do Barb and Paul know?"

"My parents are aware, yes." This lands like a punch to the gut. Barb and Paul know that Ricky is firing me over a pack of watermelon Trident? And they're okay with that? Ouch.

Ricky leans in to catch my attention. "Anna? Did you hear what I said? You can turn in your set of keys, and I'll mail out your final paycheck."

I blink back into focus, pushing to stand. "Make sure to deduct the cost of the gum."

"I already have."

THE MOMENT I STEP out onto Manning and don't see my beat-up Jetta where I usually park it, I realize that I am at the beginning of a domino train of terrible shit. My memory reels back to six hours ago when Manning was temporarily closed off to clean up a fender-bender. I'd had to park on Pico, where I'd made a mental note to move to Manning when it opened or feed the meter by eight . . . and I hadn't done either.

That stupid two-dollar pack of gum has turned into a forty-five-dollar parking ticket.

But not only is there the expected white envelope under my windshield wiper, there's also a giant black scrape down the driver's-side door where someone apparently sideswiped me and kept going on their merry way. The dent has bent the frame, and now when I climb in, the door won't shut all the way.

Fuck.

It never rains in April in LA, but it begins the second I get on the freeway. Big fat raindrops falling in a bratty, torrential downpour that leaves the streets slick with oil and the left side of my body soaking wet. When I pull into my apartment complex, my roommate's boyfriend is parked in my spot, and I can't even be mad, since they didn't expect me home for another three hours. I block him in, turning off the ignition and resting my head against the steering wheel for a few deep breaths.

One thing at a time, Dad's voice says in my head, deep and low. *Get the car sorted, then talk to Vivi tomorrow about picking up more shifts at the café.*

"It's going to be okay," I say to a sky that has miraculously cleared of any evidence of rain. I repeat these words to myself as I climb out of the car, as I stare at the door that won't close and then lean back in, digging out anything that's of any value inside, as I realize that the AirPods Dad gave me for Christmas and which I'd left in the center console have already been taken. As has the emergency ten dollars I leave there for late-night fast-food emergencies.

Why the fuck didn't I use that ten-dollar bill to pay for the gum?

But—no! Why the fuck did *Derrick* fire me over something so meaningless? It's so petty!

One thing at a time, Mental Dad reminds me.

I jog up the steps to the apartment, sliding my key into the lock, and the "Oh shit!" on the other side translates only once I swing the door open to see my roommate, Lindy, and her boyfriend Jack in a deeply compromising position on my beloved divorce couch. He's stark naked, incredibly sweaty, and—oh God—still hard. I whip around the second what I'm seeing crystallizes. Her hands are tied to her ankles so she can't even make a quick getaway, and he frantically works to free her while the two of them shout mortified apologies. My own apology for coming home early disappears into their chaos, and I press my forehead to the wall, wishing I could melt into it and live in the building's foundation for the rest of my days. I would make such a good ghost.

At the sound of her bedroom door closing with a slam, I turn, leaning back against the wall, trying to decide whether the pricking behind my eyes is oncoming hysterical sobs or laughter.

When I open the fridge, I see that Bondage Lindy and Sweaty Jack have eaten the leftover lamb tagine I'd been saving for when I got home from my shift at the store. All I find inside is a half block of cheddar cheese, an old pint of half-and-half, and a couple of ancient, floppy carrots.

In my room, I fall back onto my bed and stare at the ceiling, too bummed out to even revenge-draw a cartoon Ricky. The walls around me are stacked three deep with my paintings, nearly all of them giant canvases of flowers: nature's real masterpiece. No brush could perfectly replicate the intricacies of the shadows deep in a petal's core, the gentle variations of color along delicate filaments, or the complex patterns of light climbing up a naked stem, but I have to try, can't stop trying, in fact. I finished my new favorite piece yesterday morning—an enormous red poppy with a hidden galaxy of pollen in the deep black center. It's currently leaning against the wall, partially hiding the one behind it—a tight fist of tissue-thin ranunculus petals, heavy with raindrops.

Sadly, these paintings don't pay the bills. I have no idea what to do now, but I know I don't want to find another job like the one at the Pick-It-Up. I don't want to work at a 7-Eleven or a Starbucks. I don't want to be someone's overworked assistant, an influencer, an Uber driver, or a career waitress. I want to paint. But I am drowning in completed canvases and unable to sell a single one. The canned dream I keep kicking down the alley—supporting myself with my art—is nothing but a distant echo. I sold a few pieces after I graduated from college, even signed a manager after a buzzy art show in Venice Beach, but I haven't had a single painting at a show in eighteen months and my manager hasn't called in nearly a year. Whether or not I want to, I'll have to apply at every coffee shop and convenience store I can find tomorrow.

My phone pings on the bed beside me and I immediately reach for it, hoping it's an email from Barb and Paul at 2:14 a.m. apologizing for their dipshit son—but it isn't. It's a bill from the hospital for Dad's latest chemo co-pays.

I grab a fistful of my comforter and drag it with me as I roll over, burying my face in the pillow.

Two

LIAM

There is a Safeway two blocks from my house in Palo Alto, which is great because of the convenience factor, of course, but it's also terrible because every time I shop here, I fear I'm going to be caught on camera in the Weston Foods security room four hundred miles south in Irvine.

It doesn't matter how much distance—geographic or emotional—I've put between myself and my family's corporation, this is my one remaining childhood fear: that when the automatic doors part at any other supermarket, and I set foot inside, my perfectly groomed mother with her custom suit and not a hair out of place will receive an alert. Standing in front of a wall of screens in a security room, she'll lean in, touching the tip of her manicured index finger to a tiny figure in the corner.

"There. Right there," she'll say into a walkie-talkie that feeds into my father's earpiece. "I see Liam in the Safeway on Middlefield and San Carlos."

It's an absurd fear. Never mind that my mother never bothers herself with security footage, or that there are a million reasons I might venture into a non-Weston's supermarket, including something as loyal as scoping out the competition. But this is the kind of paranoia a man lives with when his family business is the US's sixth-largest grocery chain and has a decades-long beef with the fifth largest. It's also the kind of paranoia a man lives with when he shuts his powerful father out of his personal life for years. (Never mind, too, that if my father really wanted to know what I do every day, he could easily find out. Raymond Weston is simply too narcissistic to imagine that the distance between us might not be his idea.)

But my instincts don't care about logic. So when Mom calls while I'm at the register paying for a post-run coconut water, I abruptly tap my watch, declining the call, and look around me for cameras in view.

Calm your shit, Weston. I take a deep breath and smile at the woman at the register, pulling my phone from my armband to pay. It lights up with another call.

I press Decline once more and hold the phone to the payment screen in front of me. It doesn't register, and I try again. The cashier is reaching over to see if she can get it from another angle when a text lights up my screen: William Albert Weston, answer my call or so help me I will fly to your house right now.

Well, shit, we can't have that.

"Yikes," the cashier says, reading the text with a sympathetic wince. "You'd better answer, William."

Just then, my phone rings again.

With a resigned laugh, I answer the call on my watch as I try desperately to pay for my water with my iPhone. We may be in Silicon Valley, where everyone has fifteen devices on their person at any given moment, but I can still feel everyone behind me in the express checkout line glaring. I am absolutely that tech asshole right now.

"Hello?"

Her voice carries through my single earbud. "Liam? Finally."

"Sorry, Mom," I whisper. "Where are you?"

She pauses, confused. "I'm . . . at home? Where are you?"

"Just grabbing water at the Weston's on Alma and University." The cashier looks at me in confusion and I smile, waving her off. The lie was needlessly specific and likely won't work anyway: the problem with AirPods is they pick up every noise in a room. I glare up at the high ceiling, wondering how much ambient noise is bleeding through the line. My parents began dating their freshman year in high school, waited until they'd graduated college before getting married, and then waited an additional five years before having my older brother, Alex. All this to say, Janet Weston has been in the family business since she was fourteen; the woman has spent so much time in supermarkets that she could differentiate the sound of a Safeway from a Weston's even while standing at the 101 and 80 freeway interchange at rush hour. I have to get out of here.

Finally, my payment goes through. I snatch the water, wave off the receipt, throw an apologetic smile to the annoyed line behind me, and jog out of the store, ducking into an alley between buildings.

"What's up?" I ask, like we both don't know exactly why she's calling.

I'm grateful for the time she gives me to brace myself; I hear the tidy click of her shoes and imagine her strolling out through the living room onto the terra-cotta tiles of the sunroom looking out over the Newport Coast. "I'm calling about Charlie's wedding, sweetheart."

I wince, pinching the bridge of my nose. "Of course. Can't wait."

"We all leave for the island next week, and your RSVP arrived yesterday. I'd really hoped you'd be RSVP'ing for two. We've reserved one of the five private bungalows for you."

"You know how busy she is, Mom."

"Which is exactly why she needs this vacation, darling." She sighs. "Liam, honey, it looks bad if the entire family isn't there. *Vogue* is coming to do a profile on Charlie and Kellan. *Forbes* is sending someone to interview your father. People will talk." Mom pauses. "I hate to say it, sweetheart, but your father is getting strange about it, too."

My stomach drops. "Strange how?"

"You know." And I do, though I wish for once we could all just speak plainly with one another. This is as close as my mother will come to saying, *Your father is beginning to think maybe she shouldn't be in this family if she's never around.*

"Mom, come on."

She sighs. "We barely know her," she says. "Just bring her and everything will be fine."

Everything will be fine.

I *need* everything to be fine. I'm so close to finishing this long game, I can feel the silvery promise of it on my fingertips. The last thing I want is my father turning his attention to my personal life. But he might. And the fiction of this life I've built for my family—the life upon which every plan I've made relies—is a precariously balanced house of cards.

I take a deep breath, squeezing my eyes shut. I have no idea how I'm going to make this work, but I'm backed into a corner, and I know it. So, I let the words burst free: "Okay, Mom. We'll both be there." The tremble in her relieved exhale is amplified through my AirPod, and the confirmation of how stressed she's been sends a wash of renewed resolve through me. "We'll figure it out."

"That is *wonderful* news, sweetheart! Oh, I'm so thrilled! Why don't you fly down to John Wayne the night before, stay at the house, and we'll all take the plane over together? The flight to Singapore is a bear."

"We'll get ourselves there." I say it more sharply than I'd intended, and my words are met with a nervous pause. I wince, and my eyes land on a discarded crate with a word stamped in red across the bottom. Desperate to alleviate her worry that this is about the continued friction between me and my father, I add a bewildering lie: "She'll be coming from Cambodia."

Oh God. God. Why did I say that? No one handed me this shovel, but I'm digging my own grave anyway.

"Cambodia! How *exotic*!"

"Right." I squeeze my forehead. Panic is setting in. "So we'll meet you there."

She leaves another pause, and I realize I can't escape it after all. "Liam, darling," Mom says quietly. "Even if you travel separately, perhaps you could call your father beforehand? I'd like you two to iron out your wrinkles before we arrive on the island with everyone else. I don't want any tension to be visible from the outside."

I take a deep breath, trying to not react to her use of the word *wrinkles* to refer to my father's enormous betrayal. "Mom," I say, wincing when a delivery guy on a bike darts through the alley, almost clipping me with his handlebars. "I think these are more than wrinkles. I need an apology."

"Well . . ." She sighs again. "I'm sure he regrets what he did."

"Has he told you that?"

"We haven't discussed it, but I apologize on his behalf. Does that work?"

I stare at the wall across from me. My parents haven't discussed the absolute shit show that resulted in my father and me not speaking for nearly five years? What a perfect example of the Weston family dysfunction. "Not really."

She ignores this. "We'll both be on our best behavior," she assures me. "I won't say a word about her clothing. Or her hair."

I tighten the grip on my forehead.

"You need to leave by Wednesday afternoon," she continues. "May first. The private transport will meet you at the airport, so please send along your commercial flight information and I'll arrange it." She says "commercial flight" like she's expecting a rotten banana in her inbox. "We'll arrive in Pulau Jingga the day before you and have activities and a wonderful ten days planned for everyone."

Ten days. Ten days on a private island with my family. Ten days on a private island with a virtual stranger.

If I'm lucky.

For a fevered second, I consider telling my mom everything, untangling myself from this web of lies. But I know she'll tell my father, who will only use the information as leverage. Renewed fury climbs its way up my throat like a predatory vine. I swallow the impulse to come clean.

"Liam? You heard me, honey? Arrive in Singapore by the third."

I close my eyes and rub at my temple where one hell of a headache is starting. "Got it. We'll be there."

"Let me know if there's anything I can help with. I'll email over the wedding itinerary. Love you, sweetie."

"Love you, too."

Mom hangs up and I stare down at the screen. Not to be melodramatic, but it feels like my life has just been sawed into two halves: before and after.

Sure, *before* was a pile of lies, a complicated cover story that started with an innocent scam and slowly turned into full-on deception. *Before* was a boulder, precariously balanced on the edge of a cliff. But *before* had also reached a sort of uneasy stasis, a tentative calm.

After is the wake of chaos and destruction when the boulder gets a sudden, hard shove.

The way I see it, I have three options:

1. Fake my own death.
2. Finally admit to my parents that I've lied to them for five years.
3. Fly to Los Angeles and bargain with my wife.

*T*hree

ANNA

I'm about two hours into an edible, watching *Conan the Barbarian* with a mixing bowl of Froot Loops on my lap, when the doorbell rings.

"What time is it?" I ask the television. "Who's at the door?"

Conan doesn't answer either question, but he does begin what is one of the best lines in cinematic history.

"Run from me . . . and I will tear apart the mountains to find you!"

I raise a fist into the air and shout along with him, "I will follow you to hell!"

The bell rings again, and I haul myself up from the couch, wrestling one of my feet into a Big Bird slipper. The doorbell rings a third time and I give up on locating the second slipper, swing the door open, and come face-to-face with a beautiful stranger on the other side of the threshold. Thick golden-brown hair and warm honey eyes lined with absurdly thick lashes. Tall, serious, sober. A sharp contrast to the passing glance of my reflection I got this morning: faded pink hair, bloodshot eyes, yesterday's smudged eyeliner. Unkempt, unemployed, baked.

He gives me a wary smile before his shocked gaze sinks to my legs. Which is when I remember I'm not wearing any pants.

The thought quickly dissolves, preventing any true embarrassment, because I'm dedicating every molecule of mental energy to figuring out who this man is. I know I know him. He's hot, but not in the shaggy way of any of the recent guys I've slept with. (Though the last one played Legolas in a *Lord of the Rings*–inspired band, and I must admit he took elvish hair care very seriously.) I also don't think this guy is the landlord, but it's only now that I realize I have no idea what our landlord actually looks like.

Finally, I give up.

"Hi." I wave awkwardly. "Can I help you?"

"Anna?" he says, like he's not entirely sure, and then does a full top-to-bottom sweep of my body, which recalls the lack of pants. When he digs his hand into his luscious head of hair, I forget to be embarrassed again, because it all comes back to me.

"Hey," I say, pointing. "You were my husband. West, right?"

The expression he makes is like the meme of that one kid who smiles and then immediately bursts into tears. West is staring at me like he's doomed but must pretend to be happy about it. "Anna. You look . . . great?"

That question mark in his voice is entirely justified. I put my hand on my hair. A few strands are still loosely captured in the ponytail from last night. "Thanks." I grin. "I woke up like this."

West huffs out a laugh and lifts his chin, indicating the apartment behind me. "Mind if I come in?"

Stepping aside, I let him pass, and he pulls up short at what's on the television screen. Conan is enthusiastically fucking a witch in a cave. We both clear our throats and look up at the ceiling instead.

He cups the back of his neck. "Looks like you have the day off."

"In fact, I have all the days off." Seeing his frown, I add, "I got fired yesterday for forgetting to pay for a pack of gum."

He looks around the room. I won't deny it could use a little tidying. "Did you truly forget?"

"Sort of? But doesn't termination seem like overkill?"

West's frown deepens, and I shuffle to the couch and settle back into my seat. "Did my eighteen-year-old former boss and sexual harasser Derrick send you over to have a conversation with me about this? Because I have a lot to say."

"No, no, of course not." He studies me for a beat and then blinks away to the surrounding apartment again. "So, I'll admit I'm a little confused. Are you not in school anymore?"

"I graduated right around the time you moved out, remember?"

"Right, but I mean," he begins, tilting his head, "did you not go to medical school?"

I stare at him for a long beat until understanding lands. "Oh, man." I press my fingers to my lips. "You didn't finish the book, did you?"

His expression flattens. "What?"

"I switched majors."

"When?"

"Like, four months after we moved in together?"

West pales. "To what?"

"Fine art." I grin, pointing at a vibrant dahlia on the wall, its thousands of intricate petals a series of violent, orange spikes. "I paint now. And work odd jobs to pay for this sweet lily pad you're standing in."

"I thought painting was just a hobby," he says, voice tight.

"It was, until I realized I hated biology and loved paint. What's the big deal?" I stare up at him expectantly but get distracted by his hotness. He looks great. I mean, three years have passed—three? I think three. And he looks like a real man. I realize he was a man then, but this is, like, a *manly* man. A professional man. A man who does not get high at ten a.m. and eat cereal out of a mixing bowl.

It might be the current state of my brain, but he seems to weave in place a little. "Hey. Are you okay?" I ask.

He passes a hand down his face. "Yeah, I'm just . . ." He exhales, and I swear he finishes his sentence with a whispered "fucked."

"Can you tell me why you're here?" I ask. "I'm high as shit and can't tell if I'm imagining you."

West frowns and glances down at his watch. "High?" he asks. "On . . . ?"

"A gummy."

His expression relaxes. "Oh." He looks around the apartment and then back to me. "Is that the same sofa?"

"It has the same bones. I don't think either it or I will be the same after what my roommate and her boyfriend were doing on it last night."

"Condolences."

"Thanks."

"So, listen, I find myself in a strange situation, and I'm wondering if you can help." He pauses, and the misery seems to overtake his expression again. "Though I seem to have made a much bigger mess for myself."

It takes a beat for this to sink in. "You need *my* help?"

"Yes."

I press an index finger to my breastbone. "Specifically, me?"

West sighs mournfully. "Yes."

"Should I put pants on for this? It feels like we're leading up to a pants-on conversation."

"That's entirely up to you."

I stand, limping in one slipper to the bedroom. When I emerge in a pair of shorts, West is still standing exactly where I'd left him.

"You can sit, you know." I gesture to the splendor of my living room: the half-empty Big Gulp cup on the coffee table that Jack left a few days ago; the dog toy on the floor that Lindy bought even though we don't have a dog; the laundry basket overflowing with clean clothes neither of us feels like folding. "I know the place feels like an interior design showroom, but we aren't fussy."

With vague trepidation, West sits on the couch. I climb back on, leaving a little distance between us, but reach out to poke his knee. "Okay. You're real."

He squints at me. "How high are you?"

"I'm like a five right now. I can't ever get to a ten. I only sort of like edibles, but I didn't know what else to do today."

"A job search felt ill-advised?"

"I thought I deserved a day to wallow."

He looks around again like he's not sure I can afford to wallow. He's right.

"What have you been up to?" I ask.

"I'm a professor with a joint appointment in economics and cultural anthropology at Stanford."

My brain screeches to a halt. "Wait, are you fucking serious? Like Indiana Jones?"

He exhales patiently, and even stoned me realizes he must get that a lot. He runs a long finger along an attractively dark eyebrow. "This is anthropology. You're thinking archaeolo—"

"Do you go in caves? Swing from vines?" I lean forward. "Yes or no: Have you ever been chased through a jungle?"

West blinks at me and says flatly, "Routinely."

I reach forward, slapping his arm. "Shut the fuck up!"

He stares at me, trying to hide how distressed he is over everything happening right now. The *I'm doomed* look is back. I sit up, trying to compose myself. Truthfully, the man before me does not fit my mental image of a modern-day Indiana Jones. I expected more of a Patagonia half-zip, cargo pants, and well-loved hiking boots look than the expensively tailored white dress shirt and navy pants he's wearing. His shoes are so polished I could probably lean forward and see my reflection and realize how grubby I look in contrast: A ratty old Tom Petty concert shirt of my dad's that falls off one shoulder. Terry shorts barely covering my ass. Still just the one slipper.

"Didn't your family live in the area?" I ask. "I haven't seen Jake in like two years."

"They're down in Orange County, yeah. Jake is in Newport Beach working for the family business."

"Cool." Other than the sound of Conan grunting on the TV, silence falls, and I've lost the thread of why West is here.

He adjusts his posture on the sofa, turning slightly to face me. Oh, right. He came here to ask me for help. I sit up, too, tucking a loose strand of hair behind my ear. *Focus, Anna.*

"Okay, so here's the situation," he says. "You remember, I'm sure, the circumstances of how we came to be roommates?"

Indeed I do. At the end of my sophomore year, my two roommates graduated, and I couldn't afford the rent for our one-bedroom apartment near campus alone. In fact, I couldn't afford any rent on any apartment within biking or walking distance. Jake already had a roommate; Vivi lived at home with her parents and commuted a half hour to school every day from Playa del Rey. Even though the Amirs offered me a room, I didn't have a car and LA public transportation is so deeply shitty that if Vivi and I didn't carpool, it would take me nearly two hours to get to school from their house every day. Given my penchant for oversleeping, I knew it wouldn't work.

But Jake's older brother was working on his doctorate and needed graduate housing; unfortunately, he'd been offered only family housing, which required him to be married. So Jake had the idea to connect the two of us for a little harmless rule-breaking. A legal lockdown on my vagina was well worth the pennies in rent I'd have to pay. I met West for the first time at the courthouse, where we had a brief ceremony. I signed some papers when he moved in and some papers when he moved out, and that was that. Easy.

For two blissful years, I had cheap housing and an apartment all to myself most daylight hours. West had been one of the best roommates I'd ever had—certainly I had never caught him with his ankles tied to his wrists on the couch.

"I do remember," I say. But then something occurs to me and panic washes me out for a second. "Wait. Are we in trouble for fraud or something?"

"No, no, nothing like that."

I deflate back into the couch. Adrenaline plus gummy is a heady combination. "Thank fucking God. Believe me, that is the last thing I need."

"No, this situation is entirely of my own making, unfortunately."

"And you think I can help you? I can barely feed myself a balanced diet."

West eyes my soggy bowl of Froot Loops. "I think only you can help me, in fact."

"Is this my Chosen One moment?" I flatten a palm to my chest. "I thought it would come sooner than my twenty-fifth year." Pausing, I add, "I also thought there'd be a sword. Maybe dragons."

"Maybe we should wait to have this conversation."

"No, no." I reach for my mixing bowl. "This is perfect timing."

He seems unconvinced, but continues anyway. "As you likely remember, my family owns a large company."

Swiping a drip of milk from my chin, I admit through a bite of Froot Loops, "I honestly have no idea what your family does."

He looks surprised. "Even being friends with Jake?"

"I knew what Jake ordered for lunch and what kinds of stupid movies would make him laugh, and I could predict all his pickup lines at parties, but we didn't ever, like, sit down and do backstory. He didn't even mention he had a brother until he suggested I marry you."

West coughs out a dry laugh. "Okay, well, in that case, my grandfather Albert Weston founded a grocery stand back in Harrisburg, Pennsylvania, in 1952, and—"

"We're starting in 1952! Oh my God, I am so high." I take another bite.

"And that grocery stand eventually became a storefront, and that storefront eventually became a grocery store chain, which—"

"Wait." I set the bowl back on the table. Understanding is setting in. "A grocery store chain? Are you talking about Weston's? Like the giant supermarket two blocks from here that has the good cheese I can't afford?"

"I am."

"Are you shitting my dick right now?"

West squints at me. "I—no? My father is Raymond Weston, son of Albert, and current owner and CEO of Weston Foods."

West is the grandson of the Weston Foods empire? "You guys are like one of the biggest grocery chains in the country."

"The sixth, in fact."

"Holy shit. Holy shit! Wait—your first name is West." I press my hand over my mouth and speak behind it. "Are you West Weston?"

"Anna. What?" West stares at me. "Are you being serious right now?"

"Is that a yes?"

"My first name is William. I go by Liam." He stutters out a few sounds. "Sor— Di-did you really not know that?"

"Liam," I say, and squint at him. Thick auburn-blond hair, those matching whiskey eyes. It seems like a Scottish name. I can picture him in a kilt, fists planted on his hips as he stares out at the Highlands before him. "Okay. I can see it."

"Anna, are you telling me you didn't know what my first name was the entire time you lived with me?"

"Everyone just called you West."

His mouth opens and closes again. "You never read the legal documents I gave you? The ones I told you to take to an attorney and sign?"

"I was fake-marrying you because I couldn't afford rent off campus. What made you think I could afford an attorney? It was a simple divorce, right?"

"Had I known you couldn't afford an attorney, I would have—"

I cut in, laughing. "What college undergraduate who is so desperate for housing that she marries a stranger *can* afford an attorney?"

He gapes at me for a beat longer and then bends, resting his head in his hands. "Oh shit."

"*Oh shit* what?"

"*Oh shit* as in, if you didn't read any of our contracts, this is a mess. I think I need to go back to the beginning with you."

"I definitely need to go back to the beginning," I say, wiping my eyes. I mime an explosion at my temples. "Like—my mind is blown right now. You dressed like a middle schooler around the house. All basketball shorts, all the time. You drove a Honda! West, you're incognito rich! No wonder Jake never told me anything about his family! I would have made him pay for Jersey Mike's every fucking time! Wait. Why did you need to live on campus? If you're the grandson of the founder of Weston's, you could probably buy an entire apartment building on Sunset."

"In theory, yes," he says, shifting uncomfortably, "but just before we got married, I found myself suddenly having to pay for housing, tuition, and living expenses without a job."

"What? Why?"

"My father supports his kids financially, provided we do what he wants. His plan had always been that I would finish my MBA, join Weston's corporate office, and eventually take over his role at the company. But by the time I finished business school, I already knew I didn't want to do that. I'd interned there for a year after college, and it was miserable, due to reasons that aren't worth detailing now. I told my parents that I would be continuing school to get my PhD. My father and I had a huge fight where a lot of these old issues came up. He cut me off completely until I agreed to come work for him."

"Well, he sounds fun."

"Initially, our marriage was just so I could cheaply live on campus and finish my degree. But once we were officially married, I realized what I'd inadvertently done."

"Granted, I'm super high—"

"You've mentioned."

"—but is it weird that I'm not sure I've ever heard someone use the word *inadvertently*?" West takes another deep, patient breath. "Sorry," I mumble. "What had you inadvertently done?"

"My grandfather left money to each of his four grandchildren—my three siblings, and me. A condition of the trust was that our inheritance would become accessible to each of us only when we got married."

It's my turn to gape. "What in the smelling salts waistcoat gentleman shit is *that*?"

"Agreed."

I attempt a British accent: "The lord must find a wife!"

"Well, as far as the family attorneys knew, I did."

That lands in a puddle of silence, and it hits me after a couple of seconds filled only with the sound of Conan kicking someone's ass on TV that West expects me to catch his meaning.

And then I do. "You mean, marrying *me* triggered your inheritance?"

"Correct." He looks down to his lap. "Only Jake knew the real situation. The rest of my family was disappointed that I didn't let them throw me a big wedding, but I guess they weren't all that surprised. I've always been private."

"So you married me for housing but ended up getting a ton of cash, too?"

He nods. "With the inheritance, I could pay my tuition and living expenses and avoid having to ever work with my father."

"Okay," I say, dragging the word out. "I'm happy for you, but you started stressing out about the legal documents, and now I'm stressing out about them. What exactly did I sign? I thought the first was a standard prenup."

He nods at this. "It was a document saying you are not entitled to any of my income or property."

I frown. That's a bummer. "I get nothing?" I grimace, realizing I sound greedy. "I guess I already got this couch and the old TV."

"You also get ten thousand dollars once our divorce is final."

Sitting up, I feel my lips stretch into a smile. "Seriously?"

West gives a tiny flicker of a smile. "Seriously."

"Ten thousand dollars." I pass a hand down my face, trying to keep it together, but that amount of money is life-changing. I could pay down over half of Dad's remaining hospital bills. And then his words penetrate my fog. "Wait. What do you mean, 'once our divorce is final'? Are you saying we aren't divorced?"

He nods slowly. "I'm saying we are not divorced."

I have to reach out and touch his leg again to make sure my brain isn't making up this entire conversation. The firmness of his thigh under my fingers, the sheer strength of muscle there, tells me I'm not. "I thought the second set of papers I signed when you moved out were, like, standard divorce papers."

He purses his lips, swallows. "They were not."

I lean back against the couch. "Whoa. This is heavy."

West nods. "The trust stipulates a five-year marriage. It does this to prevent one of the grandchildren from marrying someone and immediately divorcing them simply to get access to their money. The trust pays out a stipend every year for five years, and then the entirety of the remaining balance is mine. If we divorce before the five years passes, I forfeit the remaining balance of my trust."

"What is your grandpa's *deal* with being married? Like, can't a dude just . . . date? Sow some wild oats?"

"He and my granny Lottie have both passed away, but they were very happily married for nearly sixty years. He created the business to be a family business, and this marriage stipulation was a way, he thought, of ensuring that it *stayed* a family business." There's something in his eyes, some tension that I am too high to translate. "He wanted that happiness for his grandkids."

"Well . . . you do seem blissful, West. Really just a portrait of laid-back joy."

I am rewarded with a smirk. "The contract you signed before I moved out states that we would remain married until September first of this year."

I count out the remaining months on my fingers. May, June, July, August. Four more to go. "Okay, that's not too bad."

"After September first," he says, "I can tell my family that things didn't work out for us."

"What if someone had wanted to marry me in the meantime?" He hesitates just a little too long. "It could happen!"

"You do realize we talked about all of this before I had the second contract drawn up?"

I wince, drawing my shoulders up to my ears. "It's possible it felt like a lot of irrelevant details?" At his expression, I deflate. "I had a lot going on! I was graduating and finding a new place to live and dealing with stuff with my dad."

We stare at each other.

"West? Hello, I still have no idea what the fuck is going on. How am I supposed to help you right now?"

"My family still thinks we're married, but . . . there's tension there with my father. He wants me to return to the family company."

"Just tell him you're very sorry, but you're too busy being Indiana Jones now."

"It isn't that simple," West says gently. "If my father suspects that our marriage is fraudulent, he will use my inheritance as leverage to get me to come back. I can avoid the conversation if I don't see him, but seeing him is about to be unavoidable. Unless you help me, I'm concerned that he'll begin to wonder whether I married you only to trigger my inheritance."

"Because you did."

"Not intentionally."

"Dude, you have a job. Why not just let go of this inheritance and live your happy life without it?"

West nods, understanding. "I do have a job. And so far, the trust has paid out a million dollars over five years." I whistle long and low. I mean, holy *shit*. Two hundred grand a year would change my life in ways I can't even wrap my head around. "But," he continues, "the remaining balance I stand to inherit is nearly one hundred million dollars. It's hard to walk away from that."

I choke on air. "Oh. I guess that does change things."

"It does. And I've recently discovered a loophole I didn't know about before. A very big loophole."

I lift my chin, grinning smugly. "Well, look who else missed some fine print on a contract."

West swallows audibly. "It's complicated and boring, but the point is this: I don't think anyone in my family knows about this loophole, and I really need it to stay that way. No one else can find out that you and I are married in name only."

"So, do you need me to, like, write an email? Take a picture where we're kissing?" I wince, at a loss. "Forge some love letters?"

He looks me over again, top to bottom, and the defeat in his eyes makes me realize the true extent of my unshowered, feral chaos. "Actually, Anna," he says, "I need you to come with me to my sister's wedding in Indonesia and convincingly play the part of my very loving wife."

$\mathcal{F}$our

LIAM

My invitation sends Anna's expression into a frozen mask of consternation, and she blinks past me, eyes trained on the wall. I would have thought the real bombshell here would be the realization that we are not, in fact, divorced, but she appears to have weathered that one with relative calm. It seems to be the suggestion that I need her to act like my wife that's sent her into a mental spiral.

Of course, that could be the gummy.

Regardless of what's going on in that brain of hers, I don't blame her for being upset. Yes, it was her responsibility to read through any legal documents before signing, and it would have been incredibly bad for both of us had she become seriously involved with someone, but we seem to have dodged that bullet. Now we just have the cannonball of Ray Weston to contend with, and I feel like a dick already knowing I won't warn her about how bad it might be. I need her to say yes too desperately.

And so I wait, letting her think this through.

It's surreal to be here with her after all this time. I was so close to being done with this, so near to the finish line, yet here I am, having to improvise an intricate plan B at the eleventh hour with a Muppet in human form as my co-conspirator. Don't get me wrong, beneath the baked, unshowered disarray, Anna is still a beautiful woman, with enormous brown eyes, creamy skin, and long, willowy limbs. I'd always been fascinated with the perfect beauty mark just above her lip. Unfortunately, right now she looks like she's fallen out of a tree and crawled through a field of tangly briers to get back to her apartment. This is probably the closest I've ever seen to her natural hair color because the pink has grown out a good inch, leaving a stripe of brown at her roots. Her makeup is, I presume, from yesterday; shadows of mascara carve dark circles beneath her eyes. Despite the old makeup and frazzled appearance, there's still something striking about her. Her eyes are enormous and bright, framed with dark lashes, her steady gaze entirely without artifice.

Though I am nearly certain her mind has wandered to something other than the topic at hand, I let her stare at the wall a little longer so I can stare at *her* and reconcile this version of Anna with the one I lived with for two years.

Let's start with the biggest surprise and, more importantly, a huge wrinkle in my already flimsy plan: Anna is not a medical student.

As roommates, we didn't know each other well—that much is probably obvious—but there is an intimacy to sharing a space with someone, a certain kind of kinship that comes with daily proximity. Anna was reasonably tidy and paid her half of the rent when it was due, but she'd never struck me as the organized, driven, premed type. The one time we talked about it, she said something about medicine being the most palatable of the "real job" options, but she seemed overwhelmed a lot, studying late into the night and painting to decompress in what little free time she had. That she ultimately switched her major to fine art makes a certain amount of sense, but I want to punch myself for not realizing she wasn't studying medicine at all anymore.

Especially after everything I've told my family to keep them out of my business. I haven't quite wrapped my head around how this will work—how this messy, stoned, unemployed wreck of a woman will fit into the glossy stories I've carefully manicured over the past several years, but here I am. I'm committed. And I suppose the sooner she agrees to this, the sooner we can get started on all the work we have ahead of us.

"Anna?" I prompt.

Slowly, she turns her face back to me, blinking into focus. "Sorry. This was a lot to absorb."

"I'm sure."

"Indonesia?"

I nod. "The wedding will be on a small island called Pulau Jingga."

Anna squints at me. "You said 'small,' but I think you meant 'private.' Your sister is getting married on a private island, isn't she?"

"Yes." I work to not let my gaze do another sweep of her apartment. I've never been to Pulau Jingga, but my mom has been sending me info that I've mostly ignored for months. I know the basic idea—a luxury resort and conservation area set in the Indonesian archipelago—and it's about as far from this dark, cramped living room as I can imagine. Right now, I need Anna to believe she can do this. Yes, she may be at rock bottom, but I need her to think she is just one fairy godmother moment away from sliding gracefully into the world she's imagining.

"Who will be there?" she asks, her voice a little wobbly.

"My family. You know Jake, of course. Family friends. Some of my sister Charlotte's friends. Her fiancé's family. Some business partners of my father's. Some press."

"Press?"

"Yes."

"To cover . . . ?"

"The wedding. And to write a profile on my father, I think. Just the standard Weston bullshit."

She lifts her hands, making air quotes. "'The Standard Weston Bullshit.'"

"Right."

"So, lots of fancy people."

I don't sugarcoat it: "Very fancy people."

Anna looks down at herself and I follow her attention to the front of her shirt, where a Froot Loop adheres to the cotton over her left breast. She plucks it off and pops it into her mouth. "Why not just find someone who can pretend to be me and who knows how to behave around *societay*?"

"Because my mother knows what you look like."

She squints at me. "How? I've never even met her."

I hesitate. "I've shared a few photos."

Anna cocks her head. "Photos from when we were roommates? Did we ever take any together?"

"I have the one of you and Jake hiking the Hills in a frame in my living room. It looks enough like me from the back." I pause, scratching my jaw. "And . . . I've had a few others digitally photoshopped."

"That's . . ." She whistles. "That's weird, my dude."

I blow out a breath. "It's very weird. I concede that."

"But I guess I'd do weird shit for a hundred mil, too." She looks to the side, thinking. "Why can't you hire a look-alike?"

"Five ten, pink hair, beauty mark, and oddball fashion sense? I seem to remember my mother saying something about your nose."

Her hand moves to her face. "My nose?"

"That it's small, upturned. She described it as 'the nose Jenny Nelson wanted and didn't get.' She'd notice if it was someone else's nose."

"This sounds . . . I mean, that sounds crazy, West."

"I know." This isn't only her rock bottom; it's mine, too.

"In what universe am I your type?"

"You were present and willing. At the time, that's all I required."

She twirls a pretend mustache. "Ah, *amour.*"

"This isn't about romance, Anna. I'm asking for a business arrangement."

"A business arrangement where we'll also have to canoodle to be convincing. This feels very *Indecent Proposal.*"

"I'm sure my family doesn't expect me to be overly affectionate in public. It's not really my style."

She guffaws. "Really."

"We'll have to share a bungalow," I say, ignoring her, "but I expect it will be large enough that we'll have our own spaces when we're alone."

"When is all of this happening?"

"We'd have to leave on the first."

A pause. "*May* first?" She slowly counts on her fingers. "That's four days from now."

"You're unemployed and high before lunch," I say carefully, fighting a laugh. "Can you squeeze this in?"

"Excuse me, Mr. Weston, not everyone gets to live off their grandparents' money for the rest of their lives. Working for a living is hard. Sometimes we sullied masses will make mistakes and take a pack of gum!"

I don't love the implication that I don't work, that I'm trying to breeze through life on my inheritance, but I understand why she sees it that way. The truth behind everything isn't important right now, and if this goes the way I hope it will, this will be an easy twelve days together and then we'll never have to see each other again. "Anna, are you available to do this? Please. I will pay all your expenses. I will even give you some money if you need to buy clothes."

She sits up, self-consciously straightening her ancient T-shirt with its frayed hem. "I *have* clothes."

I'm skeptical that we mean the same thing. She's removed the Froot Loop from her breast, but the ketchup stain on the collar remains.

Anna points at me again. "Okay, I see that look, and so let me ask: what manner of clothes are required on this trip?"

I sigh. "My mother keeps a pair of Gucci slides by the back door to wear to take the recycling out."

"I'm proud of her for not making the butler do it."

"He gets off work at six."

Her expression deflates. "Oh."

"So, an all-expenses-paid trip and a clothing allowance. Do we have a deal?"

Anna opens her mouth to respond and then closes it again, eyes narrowing shrewdly. "No way. That isn't enough."

It isn't . . . enough? I look around her apartment like, *Are you fucking kidding me?*

"Ten thousand dollars after our divorce is fine," she says, "but I think you should also pay me for my time. This is separate and I'm sure you didn't think to put this in the contract. I won't be able to search for a job while we're on the private island."

I consider this. "That's fair. What's your hourly wage? I'll double it and pay you for two weeks of work."

"No, no, no." Anna sits up and runs her fingers under her eyes, clearing away much of the mascara there. She pulls her ponytail free and reties it. Both actions do wonders for how chaotic she looks. "This is much more de-manding. I'll have to act. I'll have to learn about everyone I'll be meeting. I'll have to manage your complete lack of humor. I'll have to *hobnob*. This is an entirely new skill set."

"Name your price, then."

She takes a deep breath through her nose, studying me. "Another ten thousand dollars."

I gust out an involuntary laugh. "Done."

Her eyes go wide. "That fast? Just"—she snaps—"like that?"

"Yes."

"Then I want more."

"Anna. You named a price, and I accepted it. This isn't how negotia-tions work."

"Says who? I could be perfectly happy spending those twelve days eat-ing gummies and watching *Conan the Barbarian*. I have nothing to lose. Can you say the same?"

"What do you want, then?"

"What number would make you sweat a little?"

"I'm not— I don't understand."

"Sure you do," she says, leaning forward. "Tell me an amount that would be just on the border of you saying no, but you'd still say yes. Is it twenty thousand?"

I try to sound very stressed-out by this. "Yes, that's a lot of money."

"You're a fucking liar. Fifty."

My jaw twitches. "I'd pay fifty."

"Then pay me one hundred thousand dollars, West. *Plus*, a fancy cloth-ing budget." She holds out her hand for me to shake. "If you can agree to that, then we have a deal."

$\mathcal{F}$ive

ANNA

It's been five hours since West shook my shaking hand and left my apartment, and I'm not entirely sure what happens now. I still feel like I might vomit. He put his number into my phone—after reminding me that I should already have it—but the way he left things had a very "don't call me, I'll call you" vibe, and as my gummy wears off, the sense of *oh shit what have I done* starts to take hold.

Google tells me that West is the son of a billionaire, and a glance at my banking app tells me I am a thirty-dollaraire. We don't exist in the same galaxy, let alone metaverse.

I haven't been to a salon in months, haven't shaved my legs in weeks, and haven't carefully looked in a mirror in a few days, unless you count this morning's passing glance in the toaster. (I do not recommend: Its curves turned my forehead into a sevenhead and stretched my day-old makeup halfway down my face.) Yet somehow, I'm supposed to convince a bunch of one percenters that I'm now one of them—have, in fact, been married to one of them for five years now? Guffaw!

To distract myself from this nebulous waiting game, I take a long shower, put on a hydrating mask I got at the dollar store, and consider painting my toenails before realizing it's going to take a lot more than some Essie polish to clean me up. I'm going to need someone to come at these feet with pliers and sandpaper.

Panic is starting to really set in, and I reach for my phone, which is down to two percent—absolutely something a billionaire's wife would never let happen!

Or maybe she would? Maybe the billionaire's wife version of me is so busy and important I never remember to charge my phone? But more likely I have someone whose entire job it is to make sure my devices stay fully charged? With a groan, I hit Vivi's profile photo in my contacts.

"Sorry, sorry," she says as soon as the call connects. "I was going to call you in a few. I talked to Mom about getting you some more shifts and—"

"Viv, no, this isn't about that."

"Oh." I can hear in the resulting silence the way her concern intensifies. Unless something is on fire or I think I've just spotted Zac Efron at Target—for the record, it's never him—I don't *call* her. Texts are perfectly fine for civilized people these days. "Oh shit. Is it David?"

I press a shaking hand to my forehead. Of course that's where her mind went—it's where mine would go, too. "My bad, no, no. Dad is fine. It's not that. I agreed to do something and it's sort of huge and unhinged and I think I need you to talk me out of it. Or into it. I'm undecided."

"Anything," she says immediately.

"Can you come over? I need you here."

An only child raised by a single father, I am stubbornly independent. Vivi has never heard these words from me before.

"I'll be there in thirty." Vivi's love language: coming to the rescue. She hangs up without further discussion, and instead of plugging in my phone like a normal person, I toss it to the mattress beside me. *Vivi's coming*, I tell myself. *Just breathe.*

But I can't. I don't know how to do this. I don't know if I should. And if I do, I absolutely don't know how to prepare. Why the hell did I say yes? And how can I ensure that I don't end up being completely fucked over by a man who has spent his academic life so far learning how money works?

IT TAKES ALL OF fifteen minutes for me to explain the situation to Vivi, but another forty-five for her to stop screaming about how crazy and amazing this all is long enough for her to register that I'm in a blind panic.

"Babe, babe," she says, cupping my cheeks. "There is no downside here. Are you kidding? This is *life-altering* good."

"You don't see a downside because you love chaos."

"I do not!" she protests.

This liar. I've read that people who grew up in an unstable environment often seek out that unpredictability. This couldn't be further from the truth with Vivi. Her childhood was idyllic; her parents are actual angels. Personally, I think she loves chaos because she's a Scorpio.

We both scream when the doorbell rings and stare at each other in shock.

"Is it *him?*" she whispers.

"I don't know!" I whisper back.

"Do you think he's bringing you a briefcase of money?"

My eyes go wide. "Is that really how they do it?"

With glee, I fling the door open. It isn't West with a suitcase of money. It's a courier in a blue and yellow uniform.

"Oh," I say, deflating. "Hello."

"Name?" he asks, looking down at a clipboard.

"Anna Green."

Vivi leans over. "I thought it was supposed to be Weston."

"Right!" I say. "Anna Weston. Wait." I speak to her out of the side of my mouth. "Would I go Weston? Wouldn't I firmly stay Green?"

The guy clears his throat and looks at me, flat boredom in his gaze. "Either is fine. I have both here." He passes over an envelope thickly stuffed with papers. "This is for you. Liam Weston asked that you review and sign. In fact, he said, 'Tell her to *actually* review this, and then sign.'"

"Wow, drag me, West," I whisper.

"Once you're done," the dude says, "come back out. I'll be over by my van and can bring the rest up."

I take it with a mumbled thanks and close the door again.

"Holy shit does West Weston love a contract." I pull out a chair at the kitchen table and sit. "You bet your ass this time I'm going to read every single word of this." I open the envelope and the thick stack of documents slides heavily onto the tabletop. Staring down at it, I amend, "I'm going to read some of this."

"What did he mean, 'bring the rest up'?" Vivi asks, parting the curtains at the front window and peeking out at the parking lot. "Maybe you sign that first and *then* get the briefcase of money."

I have no idea what "the rest of it" could possibly be, but there's no time to think about that now. The top sheet is a nondisclosure agreement stating that I'm not to share the terms of this arrangement or the conditions of our marriage with anyone for all of eternity, otherwise West can sue my face off. Whatever, easy. I just won't tell him about Vivi, whom I presume is grandfathered in anyway: I haven't signed anything yet.

But beneath the NDA is a contract detailing what I've agreed to do: I've agreed to remain married to William Albert Weston until September first of this year or a mutually agreed upon date of our choice, whichever is later. I've agreed to come to the wedding of his sister, Charlotte Weston, to a man improbably named Kellan McKellan—I bark out a laugh—on the private island of Pulau Jingga from May first through twelfth. I've agreed to play the role of a happily married woman, to engage with all wedding guests appropriately and as needed. The contract states that West will fill me in on the details of what he's told his family about our life together "no later than May first" which, frankly, makes me very nervous. If there's so much backstory that he didn't have time to put it all in the contract, is it really possible for me to remember everything I'm supposed to have been doing for the past five years? I couldn't even remember to put two dollars in the Pick-It-Up till.

There are a lot of zeros under the "Payment Terms" section, which is pretty exciting, but there are even more stipulations about what actions on my part would forfeit said payment. Some are obvious: Of course, West won't pay me if I accidentally or intentionally mention that I recently got canned from my convenience store job, or that I reside in a shithole apartment in Northridge, or if I reveal anything that doesn't align with the details he'll share with me "no later than May first."

But other things are in here, too. Requirements about my hair, my makeup, my clothes, my foul language (okay, fair), my use of recreational or illegal drugs (also fair). Each of these clauses is a rubber mallet to my feminist knee-jerk reflex, but simply put, if he doesn't get his money, neither do I. Scrounging around the kitchen, I find a nearly dry ballpoint pen and sign the contract, reminding myself what a hundred thousand dollars can do.

It can pay off my student loans.

It can allow me to support myself for a little while, so I can paint.

And, most importantly, it can pay for my father's medical care.

When it comes down to it, there's absolutely no question. I'll dress like a Kardashian and act like a fembot in a heartbeat if it means I can take care of my dad.

When I wave to the courier out in the parking lot, he nods and strolls to the back of his van, hauling out a large parcel onto a dolly and wheeling it directly into my living room. It's even bigger up close.

"Several briefcases could fit in that," I whisper.

"A *body* could fit inside that," Vivi whispers back.

I stare at it. "I'm really hoping there's not a body in there."

"Me, too," our courier says dryly.

I hand him the sealed envelope with the signed NDA and contract and, after a pause, he leaves.

"Shit." I stare at the closed door, finally translating his hesitation. "Was I supposed to tip him?"

"Let West tip him."

"But it's this kind of stuff I don't even know," I say. "Like, who gets tipped? That guy? And how much? Is couch change insulting?"

"I think it depends if there's a dead body in there. We'll add tipping etiquette to the research you have to do later."

"Research?"

"Designers, real estate, restaurants, travel."

"How do you know all of this?" I ask.

Vivi shrugs. *"Real Housewives."*

We get to work on the box, coaxing it open with a steak knife and spatula. Inside there is neither a stack of briefcases nor a dead body but another box, this one with an envelope taped to the outside.

The envelope contains a set of papers stapled together and folded into neat thirds, a check for $10,000 ("Initial deposit" it says in the memo section and hello, this feels very *Pretty Woman*), an American Express black card (holy shit it's *heavy*), and a first-class plane ticket on Singapore Airlines.

I need to sit down again.

Vivi takes the metallic credit card from my hand and whistles, tapping it against her manicured nail. "I've never even seen one of these. You could buy a house with this card."

"I know." I take it back, looking at it. It has my name on it. Goose bumps break out along my arms. "How does he know I won't use this to buy a giraffe?" Is West this trusting, or this desperate?

We work together to pry open the interior box, which holds a beautiful set of bright blue RIMOWA luggage, complete with personalized luggage tags.

" 'AGW,' " I read. "I guess I went with 'Weston' after all."

Vivi runs her hands over the suitcases. "These are the sexiest bags I've ever seen."

"But overboard, maybe?" I stare down at them. They're gorgeous but come on. "I *have* luggage."

"Anna, I've seen your luggage. The only thing sadder would be a handkerchief tied to the end of a stick."

"Okay, but this?" I point to the gleaming hard-sided cubes. "These look like Transformers."

Vivi ignores this, unfolding the crisp set of papers. "He sent an itinerary." She whistles. "Girl. There's a party almost every day."

My stomach drops. "What? More than just the wedding?"

Vivi openly laughs at me. "Rich people love a party. Oh," she says, perking up, "there's a list of the clothing items you'll need." Distractedly, while

I try to figure out how to set the lock combination on my new robot bags, I listen as she reads the list aloud: "Travel attire, four cocktail dresses, three day-party dresses, a rehearsal dinner gown, wedding guest gown, casual outfits for ten to twelve days, three to four bathing suits, shoes, undergarments, blah blah, upscale loungewear—"

I look up. "What's 'upscale loungewear'? Like, yoga pants?"

Vivi stares at me in concern. "No, sweetie. Like, cashmere robes and silk pajamas."

"Cashmere on an island?"

"I'm pretty sure when you're this rich you pay somebody else to sweat for you. Besides, I'm just describing the category. He probably means you should have a set of pajamas that perfectly complements your diamond necklace."

"I don't have a diamond necklace."

She holds up an iconic turquoise box. "You do now."

"Holy shit. Do I open it?"

"Seems the only way you'll find out what's inside. I could open it if you wa—"

"Give it to me." I tug at the white satin ribbon and take off the lid. Inside is another turquoise box, this one velvet and hinged. Inside sits a diamond solitaire pendant on what I assume is a platinum chain. I can barely breathe. "Vivi. This cost him *Baby Driver* money."

"I hate you so much right now," she says. "Are you sure you never banged this guy?"

"I can't wear that! What if I lose it? What if I'm robbed, or held for ransom?"

"Insurance," she says. "These people insure everything." While I continue to stare at the rock, she returns to the list and laughs. "Get this: 'Anna, please feel free to schedule any hair, nails, spa, or grooming appointments and use the card to pay for those.'"

It takes a beat for one very specific word to land. "*Grooming?* Why is that separate from hair, nails, and spa?"

Vivi whistles and motions to my bikini area. "Rich ladies lack wrinkles, self-awareness, and body hair."

"Oh God."

Vivi already has her phone out. "I gotta google this guy now." Three seconds later she's scrolling wide-eyed through a browser full of Dr. William Westons. "I hope this is him because he is *delicious*." She turns the screen to show me a faculty profile. It's him. In the photo, he's wearing a suit and tie and has all that luscious hair combed off his forehead. To my shock and delight, there's something vaguely naughty in his gaze.

"Is West the hot professor?" I ask, taking her phone to look more closely. "Imagine his poor, slobbering students."

"He's got the Theo James down-to-fuck look but with those wild butterscotch eyes and a better hairline." Vivi blows out a breath. "Jesus, Anna. Maybe you *should* bang him. Make the most of this trip."

"Despite the vibe of these photos, I'm convinced the man himself only performs perfunctory missionary with his eyes closed." I'm devastated that I can't even banter about banging West. I'm starting to get overwhelmed again. I fall back on the couch. "There's not enough time to prepare for this. I have three and a half days."

Vivi sits down beside me and opens her Notes app. "Let's make a plan. We need to shop for all these clothes. You need to get your hair colored, nails done, a pedicure, waxing above and below the hood, and a facial."

"In three days?"

"Three days is plenty. It's not like you have a job."

I press the heels of my hands to my eyes. "I also have to go to Dad's and let him know that I'll be gone, pay the balance on his bills, and find someone to check in with him while I'm gone."

"Me," Vivi says. "I'll do that. I also know that you suck at shopping, so I'll take the list and do that in the next couple days. You just focus on your transformation into a billionaire's wife." She leans forward and hugs me. "This is going to be a disaster. I'm so excited!"

$\mathcal{S}$ix

LIAM

There are two kinds of airport people: those who like to get to the airport three hours before departure to sit within eyesight of the gate, and Anna Green.

Even though I sent a car to pick her up, even though I texted her a QR code to enter the Singapore Airlines lounge to relax before our flight, even though I warned her when I sent her boarding pass that the Bradley terminal at LAX is unpredictably chaotic, with only twenty minutes remaining until we board, I remain alone in the plush leather chair, nursing a strong Manhattan. I'm waffling between anxiety that she's going to accidentally miss our flight, and anxiety that she is going to intentionally miss our flight. Fuck.

I know she's been preparing for this trip, at least. The check I sent her was deposited on Saturday. And she's been steadily using the credit card, too: at a salon, a spa, and at a whole range of stores on Rodeo Drive. *She signed the contract,* I tell myself. *She won't miss the flight.*

Trying to relax, I sip my drink, sending warmth across my tongue and down my throat. A pair of shapely legs enters my line of sight, and I direct my attention to this much preferable fixation, lifting my gaze from pink-tipped toes, across the straps of gold high-heeled sandals, up smooth, toned legs to crisp white shorts, a soft short-sleeved blue shirt, the gentle curve of breasts, a long neck, full red lips, soft pink hair—

Pink hair.

Oh my fuck.

My eyes go wide, meeting Anna's just as she stumbles, ankle twisting awkwardly on the skinny, murder-sharp heel of her shoe.

"Motherfucker," she cries, collapsing into the seat beside me, seemingly unaware of the attention she's garnered from both her incredible hotness and loud swearing. "Vivi said these would be easy to walk in. She's a fucking liar. I almost flagged down one of those little airport cars." She claps a hand over her mouth. "No swearing. My bad."

I can't find words. Now that she's here, I realize I hadn't even tried to imagine who might show up today. But this person in front of me is unlike any version of Anna Green I've ever seen. During the tenure of our roommateship, she never wore much makeup, and of course a few days ago in her apartment, she looked—I'm so sorry to say it—like a demented Care Bear. Today she looks like she stepped out of a *Vogue* spread. I half expected she'd change her hair, but now I'm glad that she didn't. It's bubblegum pink and falls around her shoulders in shiny waves. Her skin is glowing, eyes bright, nails . . .

"Wow, Green." I stare at her hands and the sharp, shell-pink talons tipping each finger. "Those are—"

"Terrible," she admits glumly. "I feel like a cat with tape on its paws."

I bite back a laugh. "Why did you get them, then?"

"Vivi's always look so fun and glamorous. Besides, I needed claws. I should be a lioness if I'm heading into the den."

I can't entirely refute this idea. I've been out of my parents' circle long enough to understand how disorienting it will be for Anna to step into it. She bends her fingers, turning her hand and looking at them from another angle. Frankly, they're so pointy I'm worried she'll scratch her own cornea. "But I asked the woman at the spa what the really rich ladies get, and she said it's this fancy hard gel. I think I get the urge to have fake nails. I feel like a badass." Twisting in her seat, she deposits her purse in my lap. "Watch this for a sec?"

"Where are you going? We'll need to head to the gate soon."

"Bathroom."

"Take your phone at least?" I call after her. She turns, opens the bag, and delicately plucks an ancient iPhone from inside.

I make a mental note to buy her a new one as soon as we return from the island, and watch until she disappears down a narrow hall, glancing away only after realizing I'd been staring directly at her ass.

The designer bag sits open in my lap. It feels lighter than it looks, holding its shape even though, without the phone, it appears to be relatively empty. Curious and unable to resist, I tilt my head to peek inside, and my heart does an unexpected twist behind my breastbone at the sight of the shaggy coin purse she must use as a wallet, the simple Burt's Bees lip balm, her passport, and her scuffed house keys on the same UCLA key chain she's had ever since we lived together years ago.

Anna truly has nothing.

And she is absolutely right: I'm taking a lamb directly into the lion's den.

My phone buzzes on the small table near my knee, and I bend to retrieve it. There's a text from her.

I need you for a sec

I stare down at the words. Did I not hear her correctly that she was going to the bathroom?

Where are you?

In the ladies' room

I don't understand

My phone rings, and I swipe the screen. Before I can say anything, she speaks, her voice a low whisper: "Can you please just come in here?"

"For what?"

"For . . . something. Just—come here."

Oh God. I press my hands over my eyes and lower my voice, too. "This really isn't necessary, Green."

"What isn—"

"You don't have to do *that.*"

The line goes dead silent before she bursts out, no longer whispering, *"Oh my God, this is not for sex! Are you kidding me?"*

"I just wanted you to know that I'm not expec—"

"Jesus Christ, West! Just please come in here!"

"Okay, okay. I'm on my way." Slinging her purse over my shoulder and collecting our carry-ons, I make my way to the ladies' room, where Anna peeks out into the hallway. As soon as she sees me, she reaches forward, grabbing the front of my shirt and jerking me inside.

Apologizing over her shoulder to a woman washing her hands at the sink—"I swear we aren't going to have sex in here!"—Anna pulls me into a stall and flips the lock.

I break eye contact to look around us. Nothing seems to be broken. She doesn't appear to be injured. I am just as confused as I was a minute ago. "I cannot imagine what you need me for."

With a grimace, she moves her hand, revealing to me that her shorts are completely unfastened. The white lace of her underwear is visible, as is a soft stretch of her navel, and a fever climbs up my neck.

"Tell me what's happening here," I say, averting my eyes. "I'm not risking a guess again."

Her shoulders slump. "I can't button my pants."

At this, my gaze jerks back to hers, and she holds up her hands, wiggling her pink-tipped fingers. As if to demonstrate, she reaches for the zipper but with her long nails can't grasp the pull with her fingertips. A laugh rips out of me.

"It's not funny," she growls.

"Are you sure?"

"What am I going to do the entire time? Have you button up my pants for me?"

"How did you get dressed this morning?" I ask.

"I had to use a paperclip and a hanger."

"It didn't occur to you that you wouldn't be able to use your hands the way you're used to?"

"Vivi uses her nails as tools. Honestly, I thought I'd be able to put Ikea furniture together with these things." She pauses. "Not that anyone in your family would ever require help with Ikea furniture."

"You didn't have to change your entire personality to do this."

She looks up at me, eyes narrowing. "Say that again. I wasn't watching and I want to see if you can do it with a straight face."

"I need you there," I clarify. "And I need you to look like you're comfortable with me, comfortable being married to me. But I don't need you to pretend to not be Anna Green, Muppet-human hybrid."

Her smile breaks across her face like a sunrise. "Okay. That was pretty good. But you're paying me a lot of money. I want to look the part."

That's fair enough. It sounds sleazy, though, and I don't love this situation for about a million reasons, but there are a hundred million more reasons why I'll shut up and deal with it. With a short, fortifying breath, I reach for the front of her shorts, surprised by how steady my hands are as I pull the zipper up. My pulse turns to machine gun fire when the knuckle of my index finger accidentally brushes against her stomach. I fasten the button and then step away, clearing my head.

She runs her hands over the front of her shorts, exhaling a relieved sigh. "Thank you."

"No problem."

We stare at each other in silence. She smells like sugared oranges and my mouth waters. I need to get my shit together. "You should know," I tell her, "that my family thinks you're meeting me in Singapore."

Anna frowns. "Why's that?"

"Because I told them you're flying in from Cambodia."

She waits for me to say more and when I don't, she laughs. "Why's *that?*"

"I needed a reason why we couldn't fly with my parents on the family plane."

Her eyes go round. "The fam—" Anna shakes her head. "You know what? Never mind. Of course you have a plane." Straightening, she asks, "So, why was I in Cambodia? Photography? Fabric design?"

I roll my lips between my teeth, inhaling a deep breath. This probably won't go over well. "You were there as part of a medical school course."

Her mouth shapes out a few sounds before she manages to speak. "This is why you were freaking out about me changing my major! Oh my God, West, they think I'm in medical school?"

"In my defense, it wasn't a lie when we knew each other. I just embellished a little."

"A *little?* You have me studying in Cambodia."

I hesitate but know I should just get it over with. "They think you've just finished your third year."

"West, there's a reason I switched to fine arts. I was a solid C-minus student in every premed class. I barely know what temperature is considered a fever."

I can only hope she's being dramatic, but either way, this is going to be a shit show, and I can only blame myself. I reach for the handle on the bathroom stall, telling her quietly, "Fortunately, you have thirty hours to learn."

$\mathcal{S}$even

LIAM

Once, when we were roommates, Anna flew to Seattle with a friend. It had been her first time on an airplane, and she struggled so much navigating the travel website that she brought me her laptop at midnight and asked for help. I finished the transaction for her, prebooked the car to the airport, and then quietly tracked the ride the day she left to make sure she got there okay. When she got home, she made a point of thanking me for the help. Apparently, the trip itself was fine, but the highlight for her had been flying on an airplane.

Even if it was a spectacular flight to Seattle, I'm betting that experience is nothing like this one, where we each get a small pod with a fully reclining seat and a TV screen that extends on a long, automated arm, controlled by a remote. I watch her push every button on her seat and giddily open every gift bag to reveal a sleeping mask, slippers, pajamas, and all manner of toiletries.

"Can we live here now?" she asks, tugging the sleeping mask on and letting it sit over her forehead. She pulls out a bottle of hand lotion and squirts a thin line down her forearm, happily rubbing it in. "This seat is better stocked than my bedroom and bathroom combined."

"Trust me, you'll be more than ready to get out of that seat when we land in Singapore."

A female flight attendant comes around with a tray of bubbly wine. "Would you like some prosecco before takeoff?"

"How much is it?" Anna asks, and the woman laughs sweetly like Anna is joking.

"It's free, Green," I murmur, my stomach sinking with the realization that we should have been practicing for this charade for a lot longer than the thirty hours we have until we reach Pulau Jingga. Of course she wouldn't be accustomed to any of this.

Anna's face lights up. "Free? Oh, hell yes then!" She takes the flute and holds the bubbles to the light. "West, this is so fancy." She sits back in her seat and looks around. "You've flown a lot, right?"

I decline a glass of prosecco and look back over at Anna. "A fair amount."

"What's the weirdest thing you've ever seen someone do on the plane?"

"I sat next to someone who was giving themselves a pedicure."

"That person deserves jail time." She brings the glass to her lips, taking a tiny sip. "Mmmmm." Anna turns to meet my eyes. "And by the way, it's anything over ninety-nine."

"What's that?"

"A fever," she says, taking another sip.

"Okay. Well. The island has a physician in residence so you should be fine. I'm sure your skills won't be needed."

"That's good because I don't really have any unless someone breaks a leg and wants me to paint them a new one."

It's quiet for a moment and I close my eyes, leaning my head back against my seat.

Her voice comes out echoing, as if she's speaking the words directly into her prosecco: "I've never been a girl for hire before."

I sit up again, feeling the need to address this misunderstanding. "Okay, I realize that's not what you were asking for help with in the restroom, but you do know that I don't . . . I'm not thinking we're going to . . . you know."

Anna smirks at me. "Are you trying to say the word *sex* aloud, Dr. Weston? You're saying you're not expecting sex?"

I feel the shifting of a few passengers around us as they turn our way. "Of course not," I whisper.

"I appreciate that. And I'm not for sale in that way." She pauses and then grins at me. "But for *two* hundred thousand—"

"Anna."

"I'm kidding! God, lighten up." Careful of her nails, she gingerly pulls out a pencil and a thick sketchbook. As she flips through it, I catch flashes of drawings, and a handful of vivid watercolors. Coming to a stop, she smooths a hand over the blank page and looks up at me expectantly. "I have thirty hours to learn everything I need to know about being a med student married to a bajillionaire. Let's start with your family. Tell me about your mom."

"Her name is Janet Weston. She's been working for the company since she was fourteen. That's how she met my father, Ray—they worked together at the flagship store in Harrisburg, where she started as a cashier. She comes from a middle-class family, but you would never know it now. She doesn't have an official role at the company anymore, or if she does it's, like, president of customer experience or something."

Anna's smiling at me like I amuse her. "I meant more as in, is she *nice*? Does she have hobbies or a favorite band?"

I close my eyes, thinking. I love my mother. I see her vulnerabilities, her strength. I see what she has to put up with every day. But I'm not sure I'd ever describe her as *nice*. "I suppose it depends who you are. She may be nice to you because you have something she wants."

"I do? What's that?"

"Access to me."

"Oh. Power. I like it. I'm not sure how to wield it, but I like it. And you have three siblings, including Jake?"

"That's right."

"You're the second oldest?"

"Correct. Alex is the oldest. He's married to Blaire. They have four children—Reagan, Lincoln, Nixon, and GW."

Anna smacks my shoulder. "Look at you! Did you just make your first joke?"

"I wish."

I give her a second to absorb this. "How old are these kids?" she asks.

"Reagan is twelve, Linc is eight, Nix is five, and GW is two. They're cool kids."

"And Alex does what?"

"He's the chief financial officer for Weston Foods," I say. "Blaire is the former head of HR but quit when she got pregnant. They were married soon after."

"The CFO was banging the head of HR? *Escandaloso!*"

I sigh. "Yes."

"Okay, what are they like?"

Shrugging, I tell her, "Alex is weak and insecure."

"Wow, straight into the deep end."

"There's no point sugarcoating it. His only goal in life is pleasing our father."

"I would never have guessed any of you have daddy issues."

I choose to ignore this. In fact, Anna couldn't guess the half of it. "Blaire had it mostly together until she had three kids under the age of ten and another on the way. Now I think all she wants in life is a girls' trip where she has accidental sex with a waiter. Or several waiters. Don't be surprised if she asks us for a threesome."

Anna leans in. "Okay, and how should I answer?"

I ignore this, too. "You already know Jake."

"Jake Weston. Youngest son. Happy drunk. Charms everyone. Slept with my friend Isabelle in college. Reviews were mixed."

"He's CMO, head of marketing for Weston Foods now."

"*Jake?* C-suite? Man, there's a bell curve for everything."

This makes me laugh. "Just remember, he's the only one who knows the truth about us."

"Can I be honest? That feels dangerous. He's got a streak of Satan in him."

"I know. I made sure to compensate him for his cooperation on this trip."

"He's as rich as you. What on earth did you give him?"

"My Warriors season tickets. Courtside."

Anna whistles. "Let's hope that's enough to keep him silent."

"If it's not, I'll kill him."

I feel her looking at me for a quiet beat. "I think you're joking. I'm not sure." Anna downs the rest of her prosecco. "A hint of danger. I like it."

"And Charlotte," I say, thinking. "Charlie is the baby of the family and absolutely a daddy's girl. She went through a rebellious phase in high school, but she met Kellan—"

"Is now a good time to discuss how you looked at me like I was lobotomized when I thought your name was West Weston and yet a man named Kellan McKellan actually exists and will soon be your relative?"

"I wouldn't even know where to begin with that. He's a great kid. His parents are unbearable."

"I would imagine."

"Kellan and Charlie met at USC. They're great together. He works for his parents' industrial glassware company and she's a VP in the Weston Foods commercial group."

"Sorry—how old is she?"

"Twenty-three."

"And a VP?"

"Raymond Weston never met a nepo baby he didn't like."

"You're—what? Thirty? Thirty-one? You'd be the head of something, too, then, right?"

"Thirty-one. And yes." I drag a hand down my face. "As I said, my father eventually wanted me to take over the CEO role, but had I joined the company, I would have currently been the chief operations officer."

"What's that?"

"A COO is second in command. The role implements strategies into daily operations." Off her blank look, I say, "I would have overseen store logistics and managed all of our tech advances."

"Tech? But you're an anthropologist. That seems . . . like not the right fit."

I take a beat to steady my pulse and figure out how to answer this. "I grew up obsessed with computers," I say, "and even developed some software for the family when I was younger."

"But you aren't doing that now?"

"I still like tinkering with programming, but my interests moved away from computers after . . ." I pause, amending, "In college. Now I have a joint appointment in economics and anthropology." I've told her this before, but at least this time, she's mostly sober. "My research is on sociological anthropology, specifically the ethics and behavior of people working within a corporation, but also how a good business does not encourage a one-size-fits-all approach. How microcultures within corporations can be a positive thing and contribute to the broader company culture, how they make employees feel more valued and seen."

"So you're definitely not being chased through the jungle, then, you little liar."

"It's all boring family dynasty shit," I tell her.

"Nothing boring involves the word *dynasty*."

"Here's what my wife would know," I say, redirecting. "She would know that I don't like my father's way of doing things. She would know that my grandfather was a little eccentric."

"*Eccentric*. Another word only rich people use. For the rest of us, I believe the word is *nutty*."

"That fits, too. But I adored him," I continue. "My wife would know that if he were still alive and running things, I might have stayed with the family business. She would know that I don't like to talk about what happened between my father and me. So much so that I haven't seen my parents since around the time we got married."

"So, something specifically happened that sent you as far away from your family as possible?"

"Yes, but she would also know to leave it alone."

"And my husband would know that I wouldn't marry someone who keeps enormous secrets," she counters.

I turn, meeting her eyes. "My parents have never once talked about it, so trust me, they'll have no problem believing that we don't talk about it, either." I blink away, fixing my gaze on the back of the seat in front of me.

I can feel her staring a beat longer before she turns away to hand her empty flute to the flight attendant. Anna returns her focus to me. "Okay, what else?"

"What else what?"

At this, she laughs. "What else do I need to know about you, West?"

"Just . . . make up whatever you want."

"No way. If you don't get paid, I don't get paid. Tell me something. Some *things*. Hobbies? Favorite foods? Ticklish spots? Secret kinks? I should know you better than anyone if we're married, right?" She jerks away, as if she's just remembered something. "Oh, shit."

"What?"

"Wouldn't I have a ring? I didn't even think to buy one!"

"Oh, right." I reach into my pocket and pull a ring box out, setting it onto the console between us. "There you go."

Anna stares down at it. "This is so surreal."

"What's that?

"This just—even as a little girl," she says breathily. "This is exactly how I dreamed it would happen."

"Are you ever serious?"

Her smile straightens and she gapes at me. "You've told me I'm supposed to be a married medical student on the way back from Cambodia. I'm wearing actual Chanel and two days ago had my labia waxed by a woman with hands bigger than yours. My fake husband just dropped a ring box onto the console between us and said, 'There you go.' And you want *me* to be serious?"

I have no idea what to say to this. My brain is still stuck on the word *labia*.

"If you're wishing you chose someone else," she says, picking up the box, "I know the feeling. I made the same wish two days ago while having my upper lip threaded."

"It'll be fine," I say. "The point is, we're getting divorced in a few months anyway, so we don't have to seem very close. The more distant we seem, the better." I look at the velvet box between us. "Are you going to put the ring on?"

She creaks the box open and then immediately snaps it shut, dropping it on the console between us as if it burned her.

"I can't wear that," she says, voice shaking.

"Why not?"

"That diamond is like . . . the size of my nipple."

I find myself fighting a laugh. "Jesus Christ."

"I thought the necklace was bad, but this is obscene. Like, if we crashed into the ocean that thing would drag me straight to the bottom."

"What if I told you it's fake?"

She looks at me. "Is it?"

"Yes."

She narrows her eyes, and I hear it, too, the way I paused a beat too long. "Are you lying?"

"Just put it on, Green." I lift my chin to the box. "We're taking off soon and it could slide into the interior of your seat. They'll have to disassemble the entire thing to get the ring out."

"Why would they bother if it's a fake diamond?"

I exhale a laugh, sending a hand down my face. It's going to be a long flight.

&ight

ANNA

think, across my lifetime, I've now spent less time in school than I have on this plane. And yet the flight from LA to Singapore isn't even the longest part of this journey. In fact, when we land in Singapore, we are met with a private escort who drives us from the airport to the ferry port, where we take a boat to Batam, Indonesia. *Unbearable* is a relative term, but I think it's safe to say that it is unbearably hot and humid in Indonesia. I'm used to living by an ocean, but this is like nothing I've ever felt, and by the time we've boarded yet another flight there, which is on an amphibious plane that takes off from land but descends onto water, both I and my adorable Chanel shorts set are showing prominent wrinkles of defeat. I'd love to change but I have no idea where my robot luggage is. I assume it's followed us of its own volition somehow.

I was worried that we'd have to scrounge for food during rushed layovers and random bus trips, so for all the dummies like me out there, know this: the rich don't travel like the rest of us do. West and I were fed and liquored up every moment of the flight we weren't sleeping in our fully flat, first-class beds. The car to the ferry was stocked with water, wine, beer, sandwiches, and an enormous platter of fresh fruit upon which I descended like a vampire on a pulsing, nubile throat. The amphibious plane looks like a rubber duck from the outside, but inside it's all smooth cream leather couches; low, polished wood tables; and yet more booze to lock us firmly into vacation mode.

However, for as much as I would say he could use a stiff drink, West barely had anything. He barely smiled, either, but that's how he's always been. And as much as I wanted to be sauced the entire time, I took it easy, too, because the closer we come to the gleaming white sand, the more aware I am that I'm on the job. Everything I've seen so far tells me that the money Vivi spent on the clothing in my luggage is a drop in the ocean for this family. The ten-thousand-dollar check that was life-changing for me is nothing to the Westons.

That realization is both intimidating and nauseating. The odds are very high of me spilling wine on an article of clothing that is worth more than my life. I can absolutely imagine I will, at some point, crack an inappropriate joke to someone who turns out to be the leader of a NATO country. I'm probably not going to like anyone there, but I must make them like me anyway. I simply don't know if I possess that level of moxie inside my underfed, lower-middle-class body.

I feel the warmth before I hear his velvety voice. "Gorgeous, isn't it?"

I turn to see West so close, only a few inches away as he's looking out the window beside my shoulder. Up close, his skin is amazing. Smooth and clean, with just the right amount of shadow darkening his jaw after our long day of travel. We both took a few minutes to freshen up in the lounge in Singapore, and he smells like soap and that crisp, astringent bite of dude deodorant. He doesn't look the slightest bit rumpled, and I wonder, for what I'm sure will not be the last time, whether the rich ever get swampy like the rest of us.

"What?" I ask, lost in the realization that he has a perfect nose. Straight and even. His bone structure is unreal. I swear there isn't a pore anywhere. I'd like to paint him.

To be clear, I mean paint *on* him.

"This water," he says, lifting his chin so that I follow his attention outside. "It doesn't look real."

He's right. And to an artist, the view is overwhelming. The crystalline azure water undulates below us, so clear that the coral reefs are visible from the air. It's like looking at a mirage; one main island orbited by five smaller moons, the surface of each ringed in white sugar and capped in emerald green. As we approach, the island topography rises from a flat canvas.

There are rugged bluffs and rocky interiors, a smattering of blue pools nestled inland and sheltered by overhanging foliage.

"It's beautiful," I agree quietly. "It's the kind of view I can't entirely wrap my head around."

For some reason, this moment recalls the first time I saw a ranunculus. I didn't think I'd ever come close to re-creating their delicate wrinkles on canvas, to accurately capturing the soft, tight bunching of the layered petals, the delicate baby-soft hairs down the stem. But I tried over and over until I got close. Being an artist is sometimes about not being afraid to do it badly first.

Is that why, in the end, I chose art? Because it's forgiving? My brain wasn't wired for medicine, fine, but was I drawn to art because the bounds are loose and subjective? Because this . . . this trip . . . it isn't something I can do badly at first. There are no loose boundaries. I don't even know what the boundaries are. I don't know the rules of this game.

I distract myself, thinking how I'd paint this view if I could, trying to locate my first brushstroke in the sparkling surface of water. It's overwhelming to imagine trying to paint something so vast, so unending, but the familiarity of the exercise is still better than thinking about everything waiting for me out on that island. I'd mix French Ultramarine Light Extra with Cobalt Green. I'd add small bits of Titanium White and mix until it was exactly the color that remains when I close my eyes.

I visualize painting until, with a tiny jolt and the sound of water rushing all around us, we land on the surface of the ocean. I grip West's forearm as turquoise waves crest over the yellow rudders; the island is a green and white gem only half a mile away. Okay. It's really happening.

Think like a millionaire, I tell myself. *Cristal. Hamptons. Chanel. Hedge funds. Racehorses.*

The flight attendant approaches. "Are you ready to deplane? The hosts are waiting on the beach to welcome you. Your belongings will be brought directly to your bungalow."

West and I stand, stretching in unison, and I do a few uppercuts into the air. "Let's do this!"

"The island is wonderful on bare feet," she says, and it takes me a moment to realize she's speaking specifically to me; at some point in the flight, West took off his expensive sneakers and put on flip-flops. "Guests are encouraged to enjoy their visit here in sandals, or without any shoes at all." Although her expression is only warm, when she glances at my strappy shoes, I get what she's saying: *Not even the filthy rich can walk on sand in four-inch spike heels, dollface.*

"What a relief," I say, laughing as I attempt to unbuckle them. My nails are a real hindrance here, and adding to the comedy is the giant diamond on my finger that slides around, weighing an entire pound. When West sees me struggling with my talons, I feel his firm hands slide down my calves and cup my ankles, his fingers making quick work of the straps. I like it a lot more than I should. "My hubby loves me in tall, sexy shoes but the little wifey in me loves the feeling of being barefoot!"

She laughs politely at this and turns to lead us to the exit.

"Tone it down a little," West says, straightening to hand me my shoes.

"I'm just being playful."

"Play a little less."

I turn to face him, whispering, "I know you think it's fine if we don't get along, but didn't you say your dad wants you to come back to the family company to be the chief something officer?"

"Operations."

"Right. And you think he might suspect our marriage isn't real and use your inheritance as leverage to pressure you? Why not be a little lovey? We can't get him off your back if we're cold and robotic."

"There's a wide gulf between getting him off my back and you calling yourself a 'little wifey.'"

"I'm just playing the part, dude. I'm just going with the tiny scraps of information I have here."

West stops me before I reach the stairs to exit the plane, his big hand wrapped around my forearm. "Have I grossly miscalculated this?"

"Uh, undoubtedly?"

Panic washes him out, makes his eyes a little wild. "*Can* you play the part? Don't call me 'dude.' Don't rave about your favorite bongs and Takis and flavors of White Claw. These people aren't kidding around, Anna. My father spends millions—I mean *millions*—destroying people who fuck with him. You think he won't do the same to me if he knows I've been lying about our marriage? You think he won't destroy *you*?"

I make a little *meep* sound because that hadn't occurred to me. I also want to yell at both of us for how I ended up here, but his anxiety is already palpable. One of us has to keep our shit together.

"You told me it was fine to be a Muppet-human hybrid, remember?" I hiss back at him. "And listen, I get it. This is stressful for you. I'll cut you some slack and I won't call you 'dude' anymore, okay? But you're his *kid*. He's not going to destroy you." At least, I think. The most I know about rich families I learned from *Succession*, and I concede there's some brutal shit there. "Besides, it's not like he's a weapons dealer. He's a *grocer*. What, is he gonna ban me from every Weston's in the greater Los Angeles area? I've got news for him, I can't afford it anyway."

West looks at me with unmasked concern. "Please, Anna," he says gently like I'm very, very naive. "Just follow my lead."

I MOVE TO TAKE my first step onto the dock and stop, seeing West's outstretched hand, his expression expectant and the tiniest bit pleading. I reach forward and his fingers wrap firmly around mine. Yes, it's part of the show, but it's also a physical reminder that we're in this together. If he sinks, so do I.

We follow the pilot down the pier and it's somehow even more beautiful up close. I spy brightly colored fish in the water beneath us, and the corner of a guest bungalow on tall stilts in the distance where the shore begins to curve. What I don't see—or hear—are the things one usually associates with a resort. Aside from a pair of kayaks cutting silently through the water, there's no marina traffic, no noisy tourists, no cheeky steel drum serenade. There are no flower beds, pots of foliage, or anything remotely manicured. It feels a little wild; truly isolated but not deserted. A utopia.

At the end of the narrow boardwalk, our feet sink into the sand. It's so soft and fine it sifts like warm water between my toes. Waiting a few yards up the beach is a group of four employees. The vibe is very *White Lotus*—all of them stand shoulder to shoulder, smiling in welcome, wearing matching khaki shorts and white polo shirts, and holding something for us: small bunches of local flowers, a bowl with cool, wet cloths, a tray with cups of ice water, a plate with sliced fruit. The four hosts introduce themselves as Maria, John, Eko, and Gede before handing us their items. While we wipe our hands, drink the water, and eat the fruit, Gede steps forward.

"Welcome to Pulau Jingga," he says. "I am your private butler for the duration of your stay. May I tell you a little about the reserve?"

"Holy shit," I mutter under my breath. A freaking butler. This is amazing. But I remember I'm rich: "That would be lovely, thank you."

His face breaks open in the most delightful smile I've ever seen. "In 1993, dynamite fishing was declared illegal within the hundred-mile radius surrounding Pulau Jingga. Now the island you stand on as well as the five neighboring isles are a certified conservation area." With a sweep of his arms, he gestures around us. "The entire resort was constructed using traditional Indonesian methods and built to protect the shoreline from erosion as well as from destruction of the undersea ecosystem and the local flora. There are thirty-five guest villas: fifteen tent cabins along the beach, fifteen cottages in the gardens, and five luxury overwater bungalows, which is where you will be staying."

"Luxury overwater bungalow," I whisper to West. "The best three-word combination ever uttered."

He smiles stiffly, and Gede continues. "Hot water and electricity are generated by solar and wind power; waste is recycled and reused. Meals are all locally sourced, and our restaurants are Michelin-starred. Everything is

inclusive, including meals, spa treatments, and activities. We offer kayaking, paddleboarding, and snorkeling. You may also take a paddleboat to any
of the nearby islands to fish. Snorkeling equipment is available in the boathouse just there," he says, pointing, "and there are two shipwrecks nearby to
explore. The interior of the island is thickly forested, and there are marked
trails to follow if the mood strikes. Or, you may do absolutely nothing while
you are here."

"Ah-ha-ha," I laugh fancily, setting my left hand on my chest to display
my ring. "That sounds *amazing*."

"I can be of as much or as little assistance as you want," Gede says. "Just
let me know." He holds out his hand, gesturing down the beach to the bungalows. "You'll find more information in your bungalow, but we can answer
any questions that come up along the way. We rarely keep to a schedule
here, but according to the itinerary provided by your party, you have a few
hours before the cocktail reception at our flagship restaurant, Jules Verne.
Perhaps you'd like to retreat to your bungalow to rest and refresh?"

Frankly, what I really want to do is drop my fancy purse and run like a
maniac down the beach, splashing in the surf before taking a nap in one
of the hammocks stretched between the skyscraping palms. But West still
carries visible tightness in his shoulders, and we both could use a shower
and a change of clothes.

"That sounds divine," I drawl, sliding my arm through West's. "Don't
you think, sweetheart?"

He gazes down at me, quickly tucking away a flash of amusement. "Yes.
Very divine."

Waving goodbye to our four new friends, we begin the surprisingly
long trek toward the overwater bungalows. I do my best not to skip along
the sand, because I don't think a Weston Wife would do that, but the plane
hostess was right: the island feels amazing on my bare feet. Meanwhile,
West walks beside me, quietly miserable. At least he *looks* great: his linen
pants rolled up just above his ankles, his white button-down flattened by
the breeze into his chest, revealing to me that he's got some great muscles.

His flip-flops dangle loosely from his fingers. What must his life be if he can be walking in literal paradise and look like he's being led to the gallows?

But then I look up to see two figures walking toward us. The man is small-framed and rigid, with salt-and-pepper hair and a boardroom stride that looks wildly out of place in this tropical oasis. The woman is thin and graceful with platinum blond hair. Her glamorous maxi dress billows in the island breeze.

I know without even asking who they are.

$\mathcal{N}$ine

ANNA

Seeing West's father walking toward us on this tiny island, in linen shorts and an open-collared floral shirt, is a little like seeing a wildcat at the mall: mortal danger completely out of context.

However . . . he is also oddly compact, standing a good six inches shorter than his barefoot wife. Listen, I try not to play into stereotypes, but as Ray Weston crosses the beach—wiry, unsmiling, irritation hovering like a cloud around him—the aforementioned wildcat looks a little less intimidating.

"Didn't believe you'd show up," Ray calls from about twenty feet away.

Not *Hello*, not *Welcome to the island*. Just snark from the top of the page. Didn't West say he hasn't seen his father in nearly five years?

"Liam, darling!" the woman cries, opening her arms as she jogs the last twenty feet to us. Liam picks up his pace a little, folding her into his arms as they meet. There's something heart-achingly lovely about it, how real the embrace is, and it catches me off guard. My mind whispers, *Celebrities, they're just like us!*

I reach them just in time to see the painfully awkward moment when West looks over at his father and the two men seem to struggle with how to greet each other. They settle on a quick, hard handshake. Now, I read a lot while working at the Pick-It-Up; whatever I could find near the registers. Lots of magazines, journals, comics, travel brochures, newspapers, almanacs—I'm not picky. It means I've accrued a lot of random knowledge in my many years spent selling Red Bull and Snickers. I know a little about a lot of things, and I've learned about people, too. Ray offered his hand palm down: a classic dominant move.

I try to imagine shaking my father's hand in greeting and, honestly, I cannot.

I meet Ray Weston's eyes, and they're the same color as West's, but whereas on West I'd describe them as butterscotch, honey, whiskey, on Ray the color lacks all warmth. They are brownish, khaki, muddy beige. His are the amber eyes of a predator.

And even though West greeted his mother first, and warmly, he presses his hand to my lower back and angles me to face his dad. "Anna, this is my father, Ray Weston."

"Yes, hi," I say, and extend my hand to him. "Nice to finally meet you."

Ostensibly, this is the first time he's meeting his daughter-in-law but he doesn't even look at me when he briefly shakes my hand with a powerful squeeze that has me fighting a wince. "It's been so long," he says to his son. His smile is a sneer. "I'd forgotten what you look like. This wife of yours keeps you locked up."

Houston, we have a problem(atic man).

"Chained, too," I say, and wink. "But only when he asks for it."

Abruptly, loudly, West rolls past this. "And my mother, Janet."

Janet steps close, her hair in a perfect white-blond chignon, her collarbones so defined they're like hangers holding up her delicate yellow sundress. I have to assume she has an extremely deft plastic surgeon, because she somehow looks like a twenty-five-year-old sixty-year-old.

"Anna, darling!" The woman I need to remember is my actual mother-in-law air-kisses both of my cheeks. "My goodness, in person your hair is so *pink*!"

As far as first-ever greetings go, it's weird, but I don't have time to ruminate on it because she leans into West's other side, speaking in a low voice as if I can't hear her from only a foot away: "Did I tell you a group of employees got together and wrote a letter to headquarters asking us to revise our corporate policy on piercings, hair color, and visible tattoos? It failed, of course. Too trashy for the stores. Unappetizing, you know?"

I feel my jaw slowly drop, imagine my mouth opening wider and wider until I become a pink-haired travel-grimed version of *The Scream*. This woman is *savage*.

Straightening, she adds, "But on you, Anna?" Her eyes do a sweep of my head. "Lovely."

I smile. "Thank you, I think." I'd briefly debated going back to a more respectable dark brown before I left, but ultimately decided against it. I barely feel like myself in this costume; the last thing I need is to have that feeling confirmed each time I look in the mirror.

She rolls on: "Have you two seen your bungalow yet?"

"We were just heading there to freshen up," West says.

"We put you in number three. Right in the middle between Alex and Blaire's two and ours. They're adorable." Her eyes wander to the top of my head again. "Though the sheets are white . . . I'll ask Gede to switch them out for something dark in case the pink bleeds."

West presses closer to my side and my throat goes tight when his hand slides down my forearm and wraps around mine. "I'm sure the resort can manage, Mom."

"Had to book a trip to paradise to lure you out of that dusty office," Ray says with a derisive lean to the words.

West's reply is smooth and calm: "We wouldn't miss Charlie's wedding for anything in the world."

"Missed my sixtieth birthday party, though, didn't you?" Ray says.

If there was a camera nearby I'd be looking straight into it. I am flabbergasted.

Janet's nervous laugh cuts the tension like a shard of glass through flesh. "Oh, it's so nice to all be back together!" She reaches for West's free hand. "Just wonderful!"

The two men are doing some sort of eye-contact wrestling match, and I realize we need to break this up before it escalates into something physical. I lean into West's arm, pressing my cheek to his shoulder. "It's great to see you both. I think I'm going to take my husband to the bungalow for a bit, if you know what I mean."

"She means for showers," he says quickly.

"Yes. Showers together," I say, grinning. "After all these years, I still can't get enough of him."

"Okay. Well. That's nice." Janet pats his hand in hers. "Don't forget about the cocktail party at six." She leans in, kissing her son's cheek again. "Can't wait to get some time with you all to myself."

She gives me a meaningful glance, and Ray doesn't bother looking at either of us again as the two continue down the beach.

ONCE I'M SURE THEY'RE out of earshot, I exhale forty metric tons of held breath. "Jesus. That was intense."

West drops my hand, and I don't miss the way he wipes his palm on his pants. "That was nothing."

"Awesome." I jog to keep up with his power-walk pace.

A tall white bird watches us from a nearby tree. It has a slender, reddish beak, with a bright yellow top and its head tilts curiously as we pass, as if it's wondering, *What the hell is the hurry?* Frankly, I agree.

"What's up with your mother and pillowcases?"

"She'll look for anything to hold over you."

"Well, that was a dumb one," I say, "given that every woman on this island likely colors their hair."

"Yep."

"Any other potential pitfalls to anticipate with her?"

He glances at me over his shoulder. "You'll hate my answer," he says.

"Let's hear it anyway."

"When it comes to me, defer to her. She thinks I will always love her the most. She'll drink like a fish, but you should never have more than two drinks per evening. Smile a lot. Don't ever finish what's on your plate, even if I do."

"Exactly how far back in history would you like me to go? Will I still be able to vote?"

He lets out a weary sigh. "Green. I warned you you'd hate my answer."

"Fine. Fifties housewife it is."

"Anna," he says finally, very gently. "The truth is, you could just smile on my arm and be okay. I promise I'm not trying to leave you unprepared. The sad reality is that my parents are unlikely to pay you much attention regardless."

I picture David Green meeting someone I was literally married to and not taking a very keen interest. I try to imagine him only now meeting someone I'd been married to for five years, and I just can't. It would never happen. If I as much as mention a third date, Dad wants me to bring the guy over for dinner at home. We'd never set foot on a beach like this—would never in our lives be able to afford even the coach-class plane fare—but we have something much more valuable.

I glance up at West and feel a pang of sadness for him.

We continue in silence. At the edge of the beach, the soft sand gives way to craggy rocks, and a smooth wood-slat path has been built into the side of the cliff, making it easy to walk along the wide curve of the island. We come around a bend and now that we're right in front of it, I gasp at the view: the wooden path branches off into five long, narrow bridges over the water, leading to the overwater bungalows. Each is about a city-block distance apart, making them incredibly private.

It's this moment right here when it sinks in that we won't just be sharing a room for ten days; we'll be sharing a bed. "Ope," I mutter, pulling up short at the bridge that we've been told is ours, the third down the path. "I should have anticipated this."

"Anticipated what?"

"Unless that tiny, romantic hut has two doubles inside it, we'll be sharing a bed."

West shakes his head. "I'll sleep on the couch."

But when we reach the end of our long, curved bridge and step onto the deck of the beautiful bungalow, we see the seating options: two round papasan chairs facing the ocean. Inside the long, narrow bungalow is a single enormous bed and along one wall a carved wooden bench that's barely wide enough for West's left thigh.

"I think that's just meant to be decorative," I whisper. "I'm not sure you'll fit. Unless you sleep in a coffin perched on top."

West frowns at the bench. "I'll make it work," he mumbles.

"The bigger problem is that." I point down the length of the bungalow, which is essentially a long rectangle, with the bedroom portion taking up roughly two-thirds, a small half wall behind the headboard, and a bathroom occupying the very back third of the space. While the sinks and closet are hidden by the partial wall, the shower is gloriously open and visible even from the entrance. The only space that closes with an actual door seems to be the tiny room with a toilet inside. Help. I cannot imagine pooping in there when West is anywhere in this bungalow with me.

"I can shower in the spa," West says.

"That won't look suspicious."

"We'll just have to time it all strategically."

"Or we'll just have to decide to deal with it," I say. "After meeting your parents, I can't imagine seeing me naked will be the hardest part of this trip."

"Point taken."

I do have a point, but I can't help the warm crawl of awareness that he is a man, and I am a woman, and we are going to be cohabitating in this very small, very romantic place. "Okay, let's just put on our big-kid pants—or take them off, I guess—and deal with it."

He stares. I stare back. West blinks a few times, rapidly. "What? *Now?*"

"West, we've been traveling for seven hundred hours. I need a shower. Don't you?"

"Yes." He sighs. "You go ahead. I'll be outside."

He walks out to the bi-level balcony, one level in the shade, and one in the sun accessible by a set of stairs on the side of the bungalow, and rests his arms over the railing of the lower level, looking out at the ocean. I follow him out and stand next to him for a moment, taking in the view. The horizon stretches forever and I'm not sure I could come close to capturing the feel of the undulating clear turquoise water. The tide rolls toward us, breaking against the wooden deck piles and stilts supporting the bungalow. We're several feet above the surface, but it's hard to wrap my head around the fact that the sea is directly under our feet.

"What if there's a tsunami?" I ask. There are so many great potential answers: *Then we make this bungalow into a ship and sail to Singapore! Then we surf our way back to the California coastline! Then we grow gills!*

But no. West says, without hesitation: "Then I suppose we get swept out to sea."

He's gonna be fun.

I walk back inside, realizing I'd been so focused on the sleeping situation, I haven't properly flailed over the sheer bliss that is our bungalow. In fact, I'm pretty sure the only thing in here I could afford is the roll of eco-friendly toilet paper I can clearly see from where I stand. And even that looks pretty fancy. There's a real Isle Esme feel to the decor (if you know, you know), with carved bamboo, recycled teak, jellyfish light fixtures, and a massive canopy bed. Wide windows and the open entrance bring the outside in and allow me to glance over at West, who seems to be mid–mental spiral, managing to look even more morose than he did thirty seconds ago. Isle Esme vibes or not, there will be no headboard breaking here. Near one wall is a chest with our names stamped into the top, a pair of towels folded to look like stingrays, and a jar of chocolate chip cookies that are probably made with the world's most expensive chocolate but hey, Gede did say it was all-inclusive. I help myself.

For the record: they are fucking delicious.

Our bags have already been brought in and unpacked for us; our clothes hang in the closet or are neatly folded on the shelves nearby. I haven't seen most of what Vivi bought for me, but I'm praying that somewhere in the dozens of outfits there is a pair of shorts and a T-shirt I can pull on before curling up with my sketchbook in a papasan chair, because this Chanel doesn't breathe in ninety-five percent humidity.

Suddenly, I can't wait to get out of my clothes. They feel Velcroed to my skin, itchy and definitely unfresh. Looking to make sure West is still staring morosely out at sea—he is—I toss all my clothes in the woven hamper and climb into the shower, turning on all three showerheads.

If I had to choose between this shower and a lifetime supply of Takis, I would choose this shower. If I had to choose between this shower and seeing Pick-It-Up Ricky-Derrick walk face-first into a sliding glass door at a party, I'd choose this shower. If I had to choose between this shower and a date with Harry Styles . . . I would choose Harry Styles, but I'd hesitate. This is the best shower of my entire life.

Unfortunately, if West is feeling what I felt ten minutes ago, then he's itching to get out of his clothes, too, so I turn off the water and wrap myself in a giant, fluffy towel. "I'm done!" I call, grabbing a hairbrush and padding barefoot into the bedroom area. West passes me as I sit on the end of the bed facing the water.

When his clothes land with a whoosh-scratch in the hamper, I ignore the way the sound makes the tiny hairs on my arms stand on end. I ignore, too, the gentle slap of his bare feet stepping into the shower and the way his low groan of pleasure rattles down my spine. Did I make those noises when I was in there? Oh God, I think I did. I think I spent the entire shower talking dirty to the hot water and organic bodywash.

Now he's totally naked behind me. Why do I care! He'd been naked on the other side of a wall from me hundreds of times when we lived together, and it barely registered. But it all feels different now, because we are pretending to be in love, pretending to be familiar in a way that I honestly cannot imagine being with anyone, but maybe especially him. I have no idea how often married people have sex, but I happen to like sex, and I like to think if I was married, I'd have it a few times a week, at least? Five years times fifty-two weeks times four times a week is, like . . . I have no idea, but it sounds like a thousand. A thousand times we would've had sex—at least! A thousand times his naked body is supposed to have touched mine! I should at least know what that looks like before I try to pretend to know it, right? For realism's sake?

Wrong, my conscience whispers. *You should be ashamed of yourself, Anna.*

My awareness of his nakedness is like a mallet tapping at the inside of my forehead. I draw the brush through my hair, trying to think about unappealing things. Bug bites. Flat pillows. Gas pain. Yeast infections. But nothing entirely distracts me from those low groans he lets out every now and then.

He peeked. He had to have. Right? He definitely peeked. Just a tiny twist of his head, chin tucked to shoulder, eyes lifting for only a beat to catch a glimpse of me in the shower.

Under the guise of brushing the hair at the nape of my neck, I turn my head, drawing the pink strands forward. I lift my eyes for the tiniest beat, but it's long enough to completely destroy any illusion I have that West is some stuffed-shirt, uptight loser and I'll be able to share a room with him without peeking again. His head is tilted back into the water spray, eyes closed, hands sluicing suds down his very fit torso. He looks like he's in a bodywash commercial. My fingers ache for my sketchbook, wanting to capture every line and ridge so I can gorge myself on it later. His body is like carved stone, his legs thick and muscled. The rest of him? Goddamn.

I have a lot of faults. I drink milk from the carton, I never make my bed, I am slothful, and sometimes I'll just set the new roll of toilet paper on top of the empty roll instead of changing it. A monster. I am also gluttonous: I don't want a few peanut M&M's; I want the entire bag. Why have one margarita when three is such a nice, satisfying number? Everyone knows why! And that's why I go back for seconds right now. But karma is Team West: his eyes open just as I glance again. They widen and he reaches down to cup his Goddamn before he turns, facing away. "Anna," he says, his voice spluttering in the water's spray. "Are you peeking?"

"No! Sorry!" But frankly, (1) I'm not very sorry, and (2) him facing away isn't any better, because I am a sucker for a great ass, and his is probably ranked between the Grand Canyon and the Great Barrier Reef on a list of things everyone should see at least once in their lifetime.

"I couldn't help it!"

I roll over on the bed, clutching the towel to my chest so I don't wind up totally naked, and press my face into the soft comforter. The water turns off, the sound of a towel being pulled from the rack reaches me, and then West's feet pad over to the bed. I know he's standing there, staring down at me with that increasingly familiar look of dismay on his face. I brace myself for a lecture about how I must do better than be a trash-can horn-goblin about his nakedness, about how I have to behave like a grown-up for the next ten days.

"Don't yell at me," I mumble into the pillow. "I'm sleep-deprived and generally incorrigible."

The mattress dips and I crack one eye open. West has planted a knee on the bed and stares down at me, one hand clutching the towel wrapped around his narrow, muscular waist. "Calm down," he says, smirking. "I peeked, too."

$\mathcal{T}$en

LIAM

From the ages of six to twelve, I played Little League. I quit once I started middle school and girls or computers took over my every waking thought, and by that point I was also desperate to avoid my father's competitive intensity whenever possible. But for those seven years, I was one of the best kids on the team.

At least when it came to fielding.

At bat, I was a distracted mess, unable to follow the golden rule: Keep your eye on the ball. No matter how often my dad ordered our nanny to pack a lunch and take me to the batting cages to practice, no matter how much he berated, threatened, or taunted me after games, I was never confident in the batter's box. If I made contact, I'd slug it, sure. But at least half the time, I'd strike out.

"You're pulling your head," Dad would yell at me after every game. "Watch the ball hit the bat! For fuck's sake, Liam, *focus!*"

He was right. Focus was always a challenge, and apparently it didn't end with baseball. I came here with the knowledge that all I need to do is limp this lie to September, and I can finally exhale, but we're less than an hour into this farce and I'm already off track: I peeked, and it was a huge mistake. It's not that I didn't know Anna was attractive all those years ago; it's that we barely saw each other, and I was so driven to finish my degree and never have to work for my father again that Anna—attractive or not—was easy to overlook.

In reality, this trip should be very simple. Anna and I need to be in attendance, passably social, and not discuss our inane cover story anywhere in earshot of anyone but Jake. I realize she's nervous about how well she'll pull off her role, but what I told her was true: Anna could just smile on my arm and it would be fine. The fact that she's here should be enough to get my self-obsessed father off my trail.

So the last thing I need to do is add more fuel to the emotional fire. The last thing I need to do is *notice* her.

But when she steps out onto the deck of our bungalow, dressed for the night's cocktail party, there's no escaping it. The dress is black silk, landing high on her upper thigh, and with only a delicate silver chain holding it up over one shoulder. Another crosses her chest, connecting to the opposite strap and, when she turns around and goes inside to grab her small purse, I see the view from behind is even worse: low-cut, with two of those same tiny sparkling chains draped together diagonally across the width of her back.

I hear the creaking, choked sound of my own surprised inhale. The only thing I see is skin.

So much skin, and legs. Legs for days.

"Okay," she says, returning to the deck and running her hands down her sides, unaware of the way my eyes rake over her. "If this isn't the right vibe, tell me. Vivi put about twenty dresses in that trunk, and this feels . . . like, weird to wear barefoot? But I think they'd all be weird to wear barefoot? Honestly, I don't know why the dress code for everything wasn't 'beachy' but here we are. In silk."

Finally, she looks up at me, brows raised as she waits for the verdict. I have no idea what my face is doing, but I work to get my voice to come out steady. "That dress is fine."

"You sure?"

"Yeah," I say, clearing my throat. "It's a cocktail party." I point a finger attached to a very sweaty palm. "That's a cocktail dress."

"Okay. I just—" She pauses, fussing with the hem, which, no matter how much she tugs at it, is never getting longer. "Do you have a recurring dream? Mine is that I wake up and plan to wear a new, cute dress that I like but which I haven't worn yet. But by the time I leave the house, it feels shorter than I remember. Then I get to school—high school, because nightmares are always about high school—and the dress barely covers my ass, and I start to feel really self-conscious. By the time I walk into my class-room, I realize what everyone around me already knew, which is that I'm wearing a shirt and only *thought* it was a dress, and I'm basically walking around with no pants on."

"That's not your nightmare, Anna, that's you just lounging around your apartment."

She grins. "Touché." Another hem tug. "Okay, and also? I didn't take the tag off this, so you can return it after the trip."

"That's not necessary."

She cups a hand to the side of her mouth. "*West*. This dress is *Givenchy*. It was like twenty-five *hundred* dollars."

I smile at her and cup a hand to the side of my mouth, whispering, "It's okay." Truthfully, I love that she thinks about this. I love that she's horrified by that price. I'm horrified, too. It's a good thing Anna isn't my real wife; I would constantly worry that my proximity to this world would destroy her.

We head back inside so I can cut the tag off for her—it looked like a flat rectangle on her ass, she wouldn't have fooled anyone—and make our way along the softly lit private bridge to the wooden path, and then to the beach where we can begin to make out sounds of the party in the distance.

From my perusal of the map left in our bungalow, there are a handful of large guest structures on the main island: Two restaurants, two bars, an enormous infinity pool and pool house, a reception hall, the gym, a spa, a learning pavilion for classes and activities, a retail shop, and a green-house where guests can help plant, tend, and harvest some of the plants and herbs used on Pulau Jingga. According to the information in our room, the restaurant where tonight's party is held is known not only for the amaz-ing menu but also for its custom as well as classic drinks, a long list of zero-proof cocktails, and a heavily curated list of top-shelf and very expensive wines and spirits. The itinerary said that dinner will be a mix of drinks and various small dishes prepared exclusively for our party. So, a quick meal and enough alcohol to plow through the night. *I can do this*, I think. *We can do this.*

But as we near, the sound of my father's braying laugh makes a chill crawl up my spine. As if she senses the tension rising in me, Anna slides her arm through mine and squeezes. "We've got this."

"We just have to get through it."

"Get through—?" Beside me, she stops abruptly. "Look around you. Look where we are! We can do more than just get through this! This is literally paradise."

I look past her, out at the crashing surf, the swaying palms. Just moments from dusk, the lip of the sun still clings to the horizon, melting like spilled paint into the sea. *She's right*, I think, looking over as the last rays of sunlight wash her in gold. Even being this tense means that my father wins, again. "Okay."

"Is your whole family here?" she asks.

"They should be."

"You gave me advice about how to handle your mother," she says, turning to adjust my collar, tucking it under the lapel of my sport coat. "I'm going to give you some advice, too: Put your hand on my lower back when we're together. It makes you look physically comfortable and a little possessive, which is hot. Kiss my shoulder when you think someone is watching." She runs her hand down my chest and then lifts her gaze to mine. "Gaze into my eyes when I'm speaking to you, like I'm the only person in the room. Try to remember what it felt like the first time you were truly, madly, insatiably in love. Look at me like that."

Unconsciously, my eyes flicker briefly to her lips. They're full and soft, shiny with a tiny bit of gloss. Legs and lips. My weaknesses.

"Perfect," she says quietly.

"And what will you do?"

The hand on my chest slips down to my belt where her fingers rest on top of the buckle. "Look at you like I adore you. Like I want to consume you. Like I want you to take me back to the bungalow to rip this dress off and ruin me."

I swallow, my throat dry.

"Is this William Albert?" a voice booms, and I turn to see Jake approaching with three small glasses in his hands. "And Anna motherfucking Green?"

Her hand falls away. "That's Anna motherfucking Green-hyphen-Weston to you." She lets out a happy squeal, jogging over to hug him as well as she can without spilling the shots on either of them. "You look amazing!"

"Me?" He steps back so he can get a good look at her. "You look like a goddamn goddess, Anna."

"Thank you." She seems to resist the urge to tug her hem again.

The two of them walk back to me, and Jake looks over his shoulder to make sure we're alone. "How are my favorite liars doing?"

"I'm nervous!" Anna whispers.

"You're gonna be great." He lifts his chin to the party going on behind him. "They're all assholes." My little brother hands me a drink. "She looks fucking gorgeous. You should stay married to her."

I ignore this. "Shots, Jake, really?"

"Trust me, you'll need it to get started in there. There's a *Time* reporter inside who thinks Dad used to work for the CIA."

"Good God, why does he think that?" Anna asks, waving off the shot when he offers.

Jake shrugs and does hers right after his own. "Because Dad told him that he did."

"Wait," Anna says, lowering her voice. "*Did* Ray work for the CIA?"

I laugh. "Of course not." Lifting the shot glass to my lips, I toss the ice-cold vodka back and stifle a wince. How does one explain Ray Weston to a person like Anna, who lives fully in the real world? "Dad just talks shit.

It's his favorite entertainment. Having smart people believe his nonsense makes him feel like the smartest person in the room."

She looks into the tent over my shoulder. "Well, that's weird." Her eyes go wide. "Oh. There's a woman who just did a double take when she saw you two—she's walking over here."

"Describe her," Jake says, leaning in, his hair falling over his forehead in thick waves. There are moments where I see the man he could someday be: playful but grounded, flirtatious but loyal, clever but humble. I want to know that version of him and worry he will forever be frozen in this caricature of the irresponsible youngest son as long as he works for Weston's.

"Blond," Anna says out of the side of her mouth, drawing my attention back to her. "Curvy and beautiful. Lots of gold jewelry. Wearing a very, I mean *very* low-cut dress. Lotta boob happening."

Jake and I look at each other and grin. "Blaire," we say in unison.

"Alex's wife?" she asks.

I turn and look. "Yes." My sister-in-law waves excitedly and I lift a hand, smiling. I like Blaire, even if she's a little batty, handsy, and boozy. But in a world full of people who wear many masks all the time, Blaire is the one woman who says exactly what's on her mind. It's hard not to respect that, even when the kinds of things she says are—

"Well, hello, you little fuckboys!" she calls, and pulls me into a hug, pressing her boobs hard into my chest, her hands moving uncomfortably close to my ass. The first time she did this in front of Alex, I was so rattled I had to excuse myself to go get some fresh air. I'm not sure she'd actually have sex with me or Jake if given the opportunity, but I'm also not sure she wouldn't.

Over her shoulder, I see Anna clocking this odd greeting with a bemused frown, and when I manage to extricate myself, Jake has leaned over and is whispering something in her ear. Anna gives a quiet "ohhh," and then nods. "Right, okay, I remember."

Hopefully she remembers, too, that if the question is whether we're down for a threesome with Blaire, the answer is unequivocally no.

"Anna," I say, "I'd love to introduce you to my sister-in-law, Blaire. Blaire, this is my wife, Anna."

My voice breaks on the word *wife*. The sound of it seems to ping-pong around the small circle we make, but thankfully Jake doesn't say anything, and Anna follows Blaire's lead, accepting her air-kisses with a smile. "It's really nice to finally meet you."

"You, too, honey," Blaire says in her Dallas twang. "Liam's been keeping you all to himself for so long!" She cups Anna's face, and for a second, I worry she might lean in and kiss my wife on the mouth, but instead she just looks at her for a few beats longer. Finally, Anna's eyes slide to me, like *help*.

I sidle up to Anna, putting my arm around her shoulder, and Blaire steps back. "She's a pretty one."

"That she is." I look down at Anna and we share a brief "look at us rolling with it" smile. And it's possible I like how her shoulder feels in my cupped palm. "Where's Alex?" I ask, though I don't really care where Alex is.

Blaire shrugs, not bothering to look behind her. Blaire doesn't care where Alex is, either. "Somewhere in there talking about work, drinking whiskey, or measuring dicks."

Anna barks out a bawdy laugh before covering her mouth with her hand. "Sorry," she says from behind it. The diamond on her ring flashes in the flickering light. "That surprised me."

Blaire looks at her with new eyes. "Oh, I think I like this one." She takes Anna's hand, tugging. "You're coming with me."

I resist, keeping my grip on Anna's shoulders. "Where are you taking her?"

"Inside for a drink."

"I don't trust you, Blaire."

My sister-in-law winks at me and does a little shimmy. "You shouldn't."

Anna smiles at me, and in her eyes, I see it. *I can handle this kind of crazy*, she's saying.

"You want me to come along?" I ask.

"I'll see you in a few," she tells me, and then disappears with Blaire into the tent.

I groan as Blaire leads Anna through a mass of bodies. "This could be bad. If memory serves, Anna is a very chatty drunk."

"It'll be fine," Jake says. "She's less likely to get cornered by Mom or Dad if she's with Blaire." That much is true. At social events, Mom and Dad avoid Blaire's brand of unpolished bluntness at all costs.

The restaurant, Jules Verne, lives up to its name. With installations of fishing nets and vintage sailing paraphernalia, it's a nod to *Twenty Thousand Leagues Under the Sea*. The floors are sand; the roof is reclaimed lumber and bamboo. There are long uninterrupted stretches of glass windows, but they are all thrown open, letting the outside in. A beautiful canvas tent has been raised just beside the bar to provide more space, and inside, the nautical theme continues. Lanterns made of green sea glass and rope swing overhead, sending ripples of light that look like water pooling across the floor. The bar is lined with highball glasses, and a bartender in a white shirt and vest agitates a cocktail shaker near his ear. A set of long tables are filled with what looks like tiny cups of prawn and papaya salad alongside platters of brightly colored fruit and roasted vegetables. My eyes snag on trays of fried brown rice on prawn crackers and chili, stir-fried noodles, grilled fish and octopus on sprays of fresh herbs, poke bowls, and a variety of local dishes I can only guess at. Across the room, I see Blaire introducing Anna to Reagan, Lincoln, and Nixon. She kneels down to shake Nixon's hand and a tiny, fond twist behind my ribs makes me hold my breath, for just a beat.

"Did you prep her for the names?" Jakes asks me.

"I did."

"Good. Anna has no poker face. How's she taking everything?" he asks, and I know what he's referring to: the planes, the island, the money. The family.

"As well as one can hope, I guess."

He makes a sound of agreement as we watch the party around us. "The good ones usually run away."

"Luckily I'm paying her," I say quietly. "She can flee with her money when it's over."

"Alex asked earlier how much time I've spent with the two of you." He looks over at me, grinning. "If it comes up, we've been to Santa Barbara and Cabo, where you and Anna bought a house." Off my annoyed look, he adds, "I had to add some details to make it feel believable."

"You think it made the story more believable that I, a man who has driven the same Honda Accord for ten years, bought a house in Cabo? If anything, that's going to make him more suspicious."

With a laugh, Jake rids himself of our shot glasses and snags two tumblers of whiskey off a passing tray. He hands me one before lifting his own. "Well, whatever. To the final few months: if you pull this off, you're free."

My stomach dips. If he only knew how critical this farce was . . . for all of us. We clink glasses and take a sip. "How's work?"

My brother shrugs. "Fine. The usual."

He looks past me at the party, and I take stock of how he seems from the outside. He's got Dad's dark wavy hair and light brown eyes, but like me, he got his height from our mother, who is almost six feet tall without the benefit of heels. Jake is good-looking, charismatic, and always up for some (mostly) good-hearted shit-stirring. My stomach sours with guilt for what I'm keeping from him. What I could potentially fuck up.

Jake's happiness is my lifelong, constant vigilance: making sure Dad isn't turning any of his brand of tough-love parenting on my younger brother. For the most part, Jake has managed to escape it. It's almost like our father gave the largest dose to Alex, the second largest to me, and by the time he got to Jake, he was too bored to pay much attention. He skipped right to Charlie, where the adoration is lavished. Frankly, I'm fine with it. It's better this way, and from a very young age, Jake realized it, too.

Our father's dream was to have his three sons beside him in the C-suite. Alex was trained in accounting from the time he could read, and Jake is social and magnetic—a perfect fit for marketing. I took a natural liking to computers, but I suppose my temperament and the strategic invention of a computer program when I was in my teens that simplified a huge waste and inventory issue had my father's laser sights on me as CEO.

But I'm where this plan broke down, and Dad has no one to blame but himself, though it would never occur to him to do so. I was the first to join the family business, if inadvertently: At fifteen, for a summer programming class, I created an inventory system to be used across all of the stores. It was a game changer at the time, and Dad became obsessed with all the ways new technology could put Weston's above every other chain out there. He pulled me from school, hired private tutors so that I could spend more time programming new systems, tinkering with employee portals, forums, and retail pages, and less time in the classroom. I did everything he asked of me, and yet, years later, when his feet were held to the fire, he fucked me over.

But like Jake said, I'm nearly free. If Anna and I pull this off, we're *all* nearly free. And standing here with my little brother . . . I'm relieved that even working for Dad, he seems good, too. Maybe we'll both survive our father with minimal damage after all.

"Anna really does look amazing," Jake says, pulling my thoughts in a new direction.

"You've mentioned." I search the room for her, finding her still talking to Blaire. "And I agree, she does."

"I mention it because . . . have you two . . . ?"

"No," I say, too quickly, blinking down into my glass. "It's not like that."

"It *could* be like that. I saw you looking at her in that dress."

"Everyone's looking at her in that dress." I turn to him, suddenly curious. "Did you two ever . . . ?"

"Hook up?" he asks and takes another sip. "No. But I did sleep with her friend Isabelle." Jake leans in. "The best sex of my life, no lie."

I stifle a smile. At least I know now which way those "mixed reviews" went. Poor Jake. "Ah. That's good."

"But you—"

I hear a squeal, and then am attacked from behind by a set of familiar arms thrown around my torso, two hands weaving together against my chest. My sister presses her face to my back and squeezes. "Liammmmm!"

Turning, I pull her in for a long hug. "Hey, little miss," I say, kissing the top of her hair. I've known a lot of people who grew up with complicated feelings about discrepancies in the way they versus their siblings were treated by their parents. Jake and I have been to therapy to work through ours, Alex would *never*, and Charlie simply won't have to. I don't begrudge her this; I wouldn't have it any other way. You know those *Best of* and *Most likely to* lists they put in the back of yearbooks? Charlie would be voted Best All Around, every time. Her face is welcoming, always with a smile that makes her nose scrunch and a dimple hollow out each of her cheeks. She has the best of our mother's features: golden hair, wide eyes, skin that benefits from genetics as much as money—all in a pint-sized Ray Weston package. It's been at least six months since I've seen her, and a tight, clawing sensation invades my chest. I miss her. I miss Jake. I don't want to lose these two, no matter what Dad does to fuck it all up.

Lifting Charlie's hand, I pretend to be blinded by her engagement ring. "Good God, how do you walk?"

She laughs, angling her wrist so the diamond catches the lights overhead. "I know, right? For six months I just walked around taking photos where I had to casually point at something with my left hand." She scans the crowd. "Where's Anna?"

I look up, too, searching the room again. She's over by the dance floor, jumping around with little Nixon's hands in hers. The band is playing covers of pop hits, and Anna is entirely in her element: laughing, dancing, blissfully forgetting where she is.

I'm relieved she hasn't been cornered by some asshole hedge fund bro or senator's son. As she and Nixon turn and dance, she looks up and her eyes meet mine. Her smile could light up the sky outside.

"Come here," I mouth, lifting my chin to her.

She nods, bending to say something to Nixon, who turns and holds tight to her hand, unwilling to let her go. But halfway across the room, as she skips over with Nix, Anna's smile falters. Blinking away, I look to the side, and I see why: my parents are approaching with Alex in tow. And there's no way for Anna to turn around. She's headed right into the belly of the beast, about to be the center of attention with all of the Westons together.

$\mathcal{E}$leven

ANNA

Well, shit.

There's no way out of this. I know West sees it roll through me—the instinct I have to do an immediate one-eighty and go back to dancing with a five-year-old as far across the room as I can get. But his eyes widen, and he does a quick, warning shake of his head. "It's okay," his lips say.

And I can do nothing but trust him.

Little Nixon is smarter than I expected, peeling off and running back to Lincoln just as we approach the circle of his family: Ray, Janet, Jake, and West. And with them, the two people I assume from family resemblance are Alex and Charlotte.

Like his father, Alex is shorter, with Janet's thin, birdlike frame. Honestly, he looks almost exactly like I imagined he would. Hawkish and intense. But Charlie got the best of all of them: the thick, honey hair, full mouth, and graceful posture. Each child has inherited their father's eyes, but like West's, Charlie's are warm. They're also playful like Jake's, and she immediately turns to me, pulling me into her arms.

"Finally!" she sings. "There is no excuse! None! I am never letting you go! Another sister!" Laughing, she pulls back and hello? I am immediately in love.

"It's so good to meet you," I say, taking her hands in mine. "It's crazy that it's been this long."

"It must be so amazing, though! To be in medical school and go to Cambodia for a class? Your life is unreal!"

I glance at West, and he avoids my eyes, lifting his glass to his lips. "It is *actually* unreal, I agree!"

"I was in Thailand a couple weeks ago, and I could have come to visit you in Battambang if I'd known sooner!"

This cover story has made my palms so sweaty I'm tempted to reach up and drag them down West's chest in retaliation. "No, no. No apologies needed."

"I hope after the wedding we'll see each other more?"

"We absolutely will."

Hoping to head off any questions from Charlie about Cambodia, a place I sadly have only experienced through the LA food scene, I turn to Alex. "Hi," I say, extending my hand. "You must be Alex. I'm Anna. It's lovely to finally meet you."

"Yes." He loosely clasps my hand in his and then lets go. If Ray Weston gives a grizzly-bear handshake, Alex Weston's is a jellyfish. He says nothing else and aims a pained smile somewhere over my shoulder.

A brick wall, interesting. I knew West and Alex didn't get along swimmingly, but this is bigger than I imagined.

West still isn't looking at me—he appears to be listening to a conversation between Jake and Ray, but I can feel his passive attention anyway. And there are one hundred thousand reasons why I need to up my charming game. Alex seems like a dead end, so I brave the odds that Charlie might ask me about Cambodian geography and turn back to her. "How are you? Ready for everything that's going to happen this week?"

"I am!" She launches into a happy spiel, describing the events of the week ("The itinerary is amazing!" I agree), how excited she is to see everyone ("I'm sure!"), how I must meet her best friend coming in from New York who just finished her residency in otolaryngology (*fuuuuuck me*), how she can't wait for the Old Hollywood party night and she hopes I will make it ("Of course, are you kidding?" I enthuse, because honestly what else would I be doing that night?) before she does an adorable little overwhelmed gesture and hugs me again. I catch West's eyes over her shoulder and see it on his face, how much he loves her.

"Your hair is so pretty!" Charlie cries when she steps back. My God, this is like conversing with a flower.

Janet, who had been talking to Jake and Ray, turns to us. "Charlotte wanted to color her hair in high school. I said absolutely not."

"Actually, Mom, you said if I got straight A's, I could do it."

Janet smiles tightly. "Exactly." Welp, there it is. She turns her laser focus to me. "How do your professors react to your hair?"

I feel West's hand settle on my lower back. "I mean," I say self-consciously as all other conversation halts and every eye is on me now. "I'm sure they like it but are probably more impressed with my amazing doctor skills."

West's fingers flex against my back in response to this, and *yes*, Mr. Perfect, I realize that sounded idiotic. I want to stomp hard on his big, stupid foot. If he's going to judge how I fake-doctor this, then maybe he should have given me a different job.

"How *was* Cambodia?" Charlie asks in a low, reverent voice. Every member of the Weston family waits for my answer.

"So humid." I pause, and in the silence realize that this isn't exactly what Charlie meant. "Oh, but there were also, like, a *lot* of broken bones?"

Oh God.

Alex frowns, decides to speak. "Bones, specifically?"

West's hand does the flexing thing again.

"Right," I say. "Well, I was helping in a clinic near a bridge. Without rails. A lot of people fell off."

Janet gasps. "Dear God, that's horrible!"

I shrug, smiling. "But good for business, I guess!"

The circle falls deathly silent. West drowns himself in his whiskey.

"Medical humor." God, this is a train wreck. "Wrong crowd. Hey, did you hear that West—Liam—is training for a triathlon?"

At least, he looks like he is, and his physique is the first thing that popped into my head. That shower really destroyed me.

"Is that right?" Ray asks, turning his focus to his son. "We gonna race?"

Hand flex. Heavy sigh near my ear. "We—" Another sigh, and I feel a pang of victory even though I've clearly said something wrong. *How does it feel to have to play along, Dr. Weston!* "Dad, we could just run. It doesn't have to be a—"

"Meet me at sunrise tomorrow." Ray says, eyes like laser beams. "We can race to the black beach and back."

West drops his hand from my back. He's given up. "We'll see."

Ray laughs. "Come on. Play with the big kids this week, Liam."

"It's vacation, Dad, I'm not setting an alarm."

"Look at this fucking academic!" Ray crows. "What kind of man needs to set an alarm?"

"I've never needed an alarm," Alex cuts in. "Up with the sun even after a late night at the office. Nothing to be embarrassed about, Liam. You probably just need more sleep than the average man."

West doesn't rise to the bait, but a muscle in his jaw clenches repeatedly. I, however, am not here for the recreational dragging.

"It's unlikely," I say, and every head turns my way. "Everyone needs seven to nine hours of sleep a night. You can try to convince yourself you don't need more, but over time you'll build up a sleep debt. It probably affects your mental and physical health more than you realize, Alex."

Thank you, *Psychology Today.* On newsstands six times a year.

Ray laughs, delighted, but Alex's gaze intensifies. "Yeah, no, I think I'm good with four hours."

I smile up at West. "Being well rested is good for your mind and body, isn't that right?" I wiggle my eyebrows and he stares down at me, fighting a smile.

Jake snorts into his empty glass but at least Charlie is with me. "I'm going to start going to bed earlier," she says with sweet worship. "I agree we all spend too much time talking about how busy we are and not enough time taking care of ourselves!"

"Do less, but better," I say, raising my drink to her.

Her jaw drops and she stares at me with worship. "Less, but better! Oh my God, that's so inspirational!"

"Jesus Christ, this generation," Ray mumbles, and puts a hand on West's shoulder, turning him. Ray tilts his head, indicating the rest of the room. "Has the *Forbes* guy found you yet?"

West frowns, and it's clear he would rather be at the top of an active volcano than right here. "Not yet, no."

"Make some time for him this week," Ray says. "His name's Ellis. Good guy. I told him I'd give him a little time every day, but let's be real: that's top-tier access. Some of that time you all can take for me."

"On it," Alex chirps.

But Ray keeps his eyes steadily on West. "Tell him about the company. The growth I created after Pops died. You know."

West lifts his drink to his lips. He hasn't agreed to do anything, but I don't think Ray's noticed.

"I could have breakfast with him tomorrow," Alex says, wedging his shoulder between Ray's and West's and frowning in a way that looks like his brand of excitement. He consults the calendar on his phone like we aren't on a private island with all the time in the world. "Around nine?"

"Am I your secretary?" Ray laughs a get-a-load-of-this-guy laugh and hooks a thumb at Alex. "Just take care of it."

"On it," Alex says again, furiously typing something into his phone.

Jake pulls his attention away from this and pretends to see someone across the room, wandering off. Charlie and Janet start bickering about some details of the wedding. The family dynamic is so loud, it's thunderous.

With Alex vying for Ray's attention, West takes the excuse to pull me aside. "Let's get out of here."

"It's barely been an hour," I say. "Are you sure that's okay?"

He nods. "It's perfect. You met Charlie. You met Alex. My family saw us here. Let's go."

We walk to the bar, grabbing cocktails to take back to our bungalow, and then duck out a side exit.

The stone path is smooth under my bare feet as we walk in silence. A look at the water shows the tide coming in, the waves frothy in the moonlight. *Phthalo Blue, Cadmium Yellow Light, and a touch of Titanium White,* I think, still pondering over the right mix of colors. A little Burnt Umber to capture the way the water moves in the moonlight.

"Charlie is a delight," I say, and do a quick hopscotch once we hit the sand. "I feel like I've had a personality shower."

"She's great. A little sheltered . . ." A pause, and he amends, "A *lot* sheltered, in fact, but she has a good heart. Charlie is a pure soul living in a very plush bubble."

West's tone is flat and detached, incongruous with the gentle words. I glance up at him. His jaw is tight, eyes narrow and focused on the steps ahead of him. "On the other end of the spectrum," I say, hoping I'm reading him right, "your dad sure is something."

"Mm-hmm." The jaw clenches tighter.

I know it's not fair to compare our fathers. They come from completely different worlds, have led starkly different lives, but all I can think as we walk is *David Green would NEVER.* "A dad like that casts quite a shadow, I imagine."

It's a good five-second pause, but then we both burst out laughing. "I wasn't making a short joke," I say, still laughing, "but now that I said it, I mean, it's odd! I expected him to be tall, too!"

"The height is from my mom's side. You'll notice she never wears a heeled shoe."

"I would say we love a short king, but in your dad's case, I'm not sure we do."

West laughs again. "We do not."

"And what's the deal with Alex? Based on the way you talked about him on the plane, I expected you two to jovially poke at each other, but that was like dragging a proverbial sword through each other with your eyeballs."

"It's always been like that between us."

"But why?"

"Well, mostly because he's an asshole. But also, kids growing up in a normal family get to be themselves, whoever that may be. But in families like ours, one where everything basically revolves around keeping a single person happy—my dad—everybody has a role. My therapist used to refer to Alex as a flying monkey."

I laugh, sure I've heard this wrong. "A what?"

"Like in *The Wizard of Oz?* Alex was my dad's willing henchman, doing everything he said, kissing his ass, stirring up shit just to turn us all in, then sit back and look like the good guy. He's never grown out of it."

"That sounds healthy."

"And for all of Alex's ass-kissing, Dad is probably the hardest on him."

"So if Alex was the ass-kisser growing up, what were you?"

"If you asked Alex, he'd say I was the golden boy."

"And if I asked you?"

"I'd say I worked hard so I didn't embarrass my father."

This sends a tiny spear of pain through my side. "And Jake?"

"As soon as Jake could, he just stayed away from home. I mean, like when he was ten, eleven. Jake was the invisible son. He does whatever he needs to do to fly under the radar. Work for Dad? Sure. Crack a well-timed joke to defuse tension? Sure. Avoid Dad at all social functions so he's never in the spotlight but also doesn't risk doing something wrong? That's Jake. It's one of the reasons Alex thinks Jake doesn't deserve his current title. He thinks Jake didn't put in the time learning from Dad and walking in his shadow, and he's probably right. But in my opinion Alex spent too much time doing that. Dad wants us to listen to him and do what he says, but the irony is he doesn't respect a yes-man. To Dad, Alex's drive looks like desperation instead of ambition." West runs a hand through his hair, blowing out a breath. "I tell you what, Alex is not going to be happy if he thinks I'm back in the picture."

"So you're saying Alex wouldn't mind if you lost your inheritance."

He hesitates long enough for me to notice. "I think as long as I don't get in his way, he'll leave me alone. The issue is that even if I try to stay out of his way, Dad might drag me back into it."

"Is Alex smart enough to take you down?"

This question seems to throw him for a beat. "I don't know. If he was truly smart, he would already know enough to not try."

"What does that mean?" I ask. If Alex knew enough, he wouldn't try to take West down? Is this about the mysterious loophole in the trust?

West doesn't answer for a few long seconds. And I realize he's not going to. Whatever. Money is so messy.

"This is some serious K-drama shit," I mumble.

"You'll get no argument from me. Everything is so much better when we're not all together, but . . ." He gestures around us, and I must assume he means he couldn't exactly miss his sister's wedding.

"This is so icky. I always saw the Weston commercials and thought it was, like, this sweet family company."

"I'll pass your compliments on to Jake's marketing team," he says with a laugh.

I like his voice. I like his laugh, too. And my filter is fried after all the hard work tonight; the words tumble out of me: "You have a nice laugh."

He sobers, glancing at me and then quickly away. "Thanks."

What a sudden change in his demeanor. I can't help but call him out on it. "Such a flirt, too."

"We don't have to flirt when we're alone."

Something flies overhead and I remember the conservation material saying we might see fox bats at night, and to simply leave them alone if we do. I blink up at the sky, hoping to see one. "Maybe if we did, it would feel more convincing that we're married."

Frowning, West concedes, "True."

We reach the entrance to our bungalow, and I follow him inside as he sheds his sport coat. I don't know how he managed to keep it on. I'm practically naked in this dress and sweating in the humidity.

A glance around the room shows that housekeeping has been here. The bed is turned down, the gauzy curtains drawn. More importantly, the cookie jar has been refilled.

West sits on the bench and pulls a shoe off. I set my clutch down on a shelf in the open closet. "I'm thinking Alex will take a keen interest in exactly how happy we seem." I narrow my eyes, staring into the distance. "West . . . this assignment is no longer just 'show up and wear a wedding ring.'"

West is still holding the shoe he took off, and he stares down at it in his hand. "I think you're right. I was hoping it would be enough to show up, but it's going to take more than that."

"This is actually kind of fun!" I walk over to him, taking the shoe and then his other one, and setting them near the wall. "I realize incomprehensible sums of money are at stake here, but for me, it's like a murder mystery party."

Finally, he blinks out of his trance, looking up at me in silent question.

"You know," I say, waving my hand forward. "Being suspicious of everyone. Wearing costumes. Getting progressively drunker as the party goes on." I walk to the bathroom area. "Don't peek." I sip my drink. "Or do peek. What do I care?" I peel off the itchy cocktail dress and reach for one of the fluffy bathrobes, muttering, "These robes are the shit."

"They are really soft," he agrees.

Bending to wash my face, I say, "You going to be okay sharing a bed?"

"Yeah. Are you?"

I scrub the soap into a lather. "Sure. I basically fall asleep and don't move an inch all night, so it doesn't matter to me where you are."

Patting my face dry, I walk behind the half wall to where our clothes have so helpfully been put away, pull out a pair of very silky, very skimpy pajamas Vivi packed for me, and hold them up. "Fuck me."

"What?" he asks from the other side.

"I let Vivi shop for this trip and she got me slutty pj's."

"You'll be under the covers," he says.

"With *you*," I say with false misery, and he laughs that low, seductive sound.

"You just assured me you'll stay on your side of the bed."

"True. Will you?"

His laugh is confident. "Yes."

I slip out of the robe and pull on the tiny shorts and tiny tank, and then brush my teeth. It's only ten, but I'm wiped.

I don't meet his eyes as I walk to the bed and climb in, and I'm not sure whether I love or hate that he doesn't seem to look at me at all as he gets up to go get ready for bed. A handful of minutes later, West shuts off the lights, climbing in beside me.

My brain screams: WHAT IS *HE* WEARING?

Clearing my throat, I say, "No hands or feet or boners on my side, sir."

Another laugh. I really like that sound. "If my boner could reach that side, I think you'd be intrigued."

I ponder this. "I would be. You're right."

The thing is . . . half of his family sucks, but this, right here, isn't all bad. I like hanging out with West Weston.

The ocean stretches outside, the waves falling back before rushing forward again. The calming reflection of water dances along the ceiling. I listen to him breathe along with the waves. *A person could get used to this,* I think, my eyes growing heavy.

"Good night, Anna."

"Night, West."

He sighs. "Liam."

I roll over, laughing. "Night, Liam."

$\mathcal{T}$welve

LIAM

Arms, *legs, lips, heat.*
My feet pound against the sand, each step sounding out the rhythm like a song looping in my mind. I can't get the four words out of my head.

Arms, legs, lips, heat.

". . . and of course, Gary Petersson gets hard the second we start talking about merging, but I string him along because . . ."

Not even my father's voice breaks cleanly through; it's just a vague drone in the background.

I woke up around two this morning to find Anna wrapped around me. Despite what she'd told me about sleeping in one place all night, at some point she'd migrated across the massive bed to throw a leg over my hip, send an arm over my torso, and press her face to my neck. It took monumental focus to not go hard against her inner thigh, and because of it, I'd slept like absolute shit.

Our running route has circled the beaches of the main island before switching to marked trails that cut through the lush forest. At various points, a spotted lizard darted across the path, a nest of baby birds squawked from a nearby tree, a sea turtle sunned itself on a rock in the foamy sea spray, but I barely lingered on the magic of any of it. With every blink I see the curve of Anna's hip where the sheet fell away, feel her firm breasts pressed against my ribs, hear her warm, sleeping breaths so close to my ear.

Arms, legs, lips, heat.

Arms, legs, lips, heat.

". . . some hot piece on the back nine, and I said, 'Steve, I'll let you take a shot at . . .'"

We reach the end of the main beach again and I bend, cupping my knees, trying to catch my breath as my father finishes whatever one-sided conversation he was having.

". . . Doug Krantz all over my jock, and that's where I need him, because he's got that connection to the dairy lobby."

Should I bring it up with her? One night in and I already feel like Anna and I need to set clearer boundaries.

Or should I let it go? It's not like she intentionally did anything wrong. Some people are just sleep-cuddlers, I guess.

But if I let it go, it's unlikely to be a onetime thing. If she found her way to me on our first night together, she's only going to do that more as we grow more comfortable with each other.

"What do you think?"

My father's question penetrates my fog, finally, and I straighten, pushing my salt-water-and-sweat damp hair off my forehead. The sun has only just come up and it's already sweltering. I bet Anna has already kicked off the blankets, letting the air cool her overheated skin.

Her legs—

"Liam."

I snap over to where he's watching me expectantly, annoyance etched in every line on his face. There's some real dark magic at work here, because he's sixty-one years old and barely breaking a sweat. "About what?" I ask.

"About Krantz."

I squint to the distance, piecing together the words from the past few minutes. It infuriates me that he thinks he can ask me for my thoughts on business issues after everything, but I know Anna is right and showing up isn't enough. The only way to placate him this week is to play along. "I think if he can't even come up on share price, then he doesn't get a meeting. Eighty is a nonstarter. Call Marty Chu over at Liberty and see if he's willing to play now that Doug is hungry for it. Marty always lets others do the legwork for him. I bet he bites now." I hook a thumb over my shoulder. "We good? I'm gonna go shower."

Without waiting for an answer, I turn and jog back to the bungalow and the woman who, after a single day here, is hijacking my every waking thought.

"JESUS CHRIST," I BLURT, the second I turn at the corner of our bridge and step onto the deck of our bungalow. Anna is curled up in a papasan, with a sketch pad in her seemingly bare lap. Honestly, from the first glimpse I get, I think she might be naked. "What are you doing?"

I've got a hand over my eyes, but I hear the creaking sound of her standing, the soft padding of her bare feet on the deck. "I'm sketching. What the heck do you think I'm doing, you weirdo?"

I can smell sunblock and her shampoo, and carefully lower my hand to find her only a foot away from me. I'm relieved to see she isn't actually naked, but she might as well be. Her . . . bathing suit? Is essentially a few palm-sized scraps of tropical-print fabric. "Oh. I thought you were sitting naked in the chair just now."

"Right?" she says forcefully, gesturing to her, wow, incredibly lithe body. "Vivi bought me four suits, and this is the one with the most coverage. How am I supposed to swim in it? It's dental floss. Also, the tag was still attached, and I pulled out my phone to do the math: the price per square inch is criminal. I might have to wear it to the wedding to help justify the cost."

My tongue feels too big for my mouth. Thank God she managed to get it on with those nails, because I never would have survived having to tie those flimsy straps around her back. "I need to shower."

"I see that, Mr. Shirtless." I frown, and she laughs, amending, "Sorry. Of course, I meant Professor Shirtless."

I turn to walk inside, but she stops me with a hand on my arm. The muscles of my stomach jump with the contact. "Just be quick, okay, because we have kayaking in an hour, and I want to grab something to eat first."

"Kayaking?" I shake my head and walk toward the bathroom. "Pass."

Anna follows me. She's loosely made the bed, but it still looks rumpled. Slept in. By both of us. I squeeze my eyes shut against the reminder.

"You can't pass," she says. "It's on the official itinerary."

"It's not like they'll fine us if we don't show up to everything."

"Sounds good. I'll send a message to your mom that we're too busy having kinky sex to see anyone today. I'm sure she'll understand."

My brain shorts out before I can formulate a response.

She glowers at me. "It's your sister's wedding, you cyborg. You're a groomsman."

I sigh. I know she's right but I'm already sleep-deprived and functioning on less than full brain power today. I'm not sure I'm capable of dealing with both my family *and* Anna in this suit after last night. "Fine."

But she doesn't move. I raise my eyebrows. "Hello?"

"What?"

Her eyes are focused on my bare chest, and I feel a current of satisfaction at seeing her derailed, too. Perhaps she doesn't remember what showering in this tropical goldfish bowl means. It means I'll be standing in a very beautiful but very open tiled corner at the back of the room.

Fuck it.

I reach up, tucking my thumbs into my waistband and dropping my shorts to the bathroom floor.

"Oh!" Anna jerks a hand over her eyes. "Your Goddamn! Right there!" She turns away. "Sorry! I just—spaced out—on your—*God*. And you're not even *harrrrrrr*— Fuck me." She coughs. "Okay. I'll just meet you down at the restaurant."

I see her shadow pass by the window near the bedroom, hear her footsteps grow distant as she jogs down our bridge. I hold my breath, waiting a few seconds longer until I'm sure she's gone before I turn on the water and step beneath the spray. With the memory of the heat of her leg over my hips, the view of her in that tiny bikini, and the echo of her soft breath in my ear, now I *am* hard.

And I take my aching length in my hand imagining—just one time, only this one time—that it's her bringing me relief.

BY THE TIME I make it to the beach, the wedding party is gathering around Eko, the activity host, who is passing out double-ended paddles. Anna stands with Blaire, Reagan, and Alex, who, I note, is definitely checking out Anna's ass behind his wife's back.

Approaching, I step directly into his view and give him a pointed look as he jerks his eyes away. I send my arm around her waist and realize immediately that it's a mistake. My hand rests on her nearly bare hip.

Arms, legs, lips, heat.

And she leans into me, pressing the side of her bare arm against my chest. With her free hand, she passes me something warm wrapped in paper.

I lift to smell.

"It's a biscuit with scrambled egg, cheese, and some roasted tomatoes," she says quietly. "I asked them to make you a little breakfast sandwich. I was worried you'd be starving after the run."

"Thank you."

She smiles brightly up at me. "You're welcome."

Breaking eye contact seems suddenly impossible, and I look away only when Alex speaks up.

"Heard you went running with Dad this morning."

"Yep" is all I say, pulling my arm free to tuck into the sandwich.

"Guess you fold as fast as everyone else when you're with him. Early morning probably left you pretty tired, huh, little bro? Don't worry, I'll take it easy on you."

I can feel Anna's eyes on the side of my face. This is how it always starts with Alex, and whatever suspicion he has about my marriage will only make it worse. I know it's irrational and a remnant of how we used to one-up each other for our dad's approval when we were kids, but I want to beat him. At everything.

It's an instinct that's hard to shake.

Anna slams the brakes on this line of thinking by putting an arm around my back, resting the other hand on my stomach and gently scratching, just like she unconsciously did last night. I work to suppress a shiver. Turning, she looks at him over her shoulder.

"He probably is tired," she tells him with a brazen smile. "My bad."

Jake catcalls. My mother tells him not to encourage us, but I appreciate this save. I lean a little closer to her, breaking her gaze only when Eko calls our attention so she can go through the plan.

"We'll be paddling about half a mile out to the reefs just past that small island you can see on the right side of the horizon." She points to a little speck of green in the distance. "The only tricky part is getting past the waves right here, and you can see that they're pretty calm now, so it's a great time to get started. Once we're out there, we can tie the kayaks together and everyone is welcome to hop in and do some snorkeling." She looks around at those of us gathered and splits us into pairs: me and Anna; Alex and Blaire; Jake and Reagan; Mom and Dad; Charlie and Kellan; Kellan's parents; and two of Charlie's bridesmaids who I think arrived last night.

Eko goes through the basics of paddling, giving us tips about what areas of the reef to avoid as we approach. "Is everyone comfortable with the basics of kayaking?" she asks.

Alex squints out at the water. "Got a couple Nash Sea Hawks back home. Blaire and I take them out on the Back Bay most mornings."

"Here we go." Blaire rolls her eyes. "It's not a race, babe."

Alex and I exchange a look. We were raised by Ray Weston. Everything is a race.

I reach back, pulling my T-shirt up and off, tossing it to the side. Alex hesitates and then does the same, his expression turning homicidal when I smirk down at his soft little paunch.

Beside me, Anna claps obliviously, bouncing on the balls of her feet. "I'm excited for kayaking!"

Alex snorts, looking at her derisively, like she's an idiot. In a hot flush, my hackles are up, and every rational thought goes out the window.

"Course you are, sweetheart," I say, steadying my voice and looking down at Anna. "I went running without you this morning and you really let me have it."

She looks up at me, confused. "I did?"

I hum, letting my eyes drop to her lips.

"Does that mean what I think it means?" Blaire whispers to Anna.

"I . . . think so?" Anna says vaguely, still frowning up at me.

"We work out together every morning." I'm speaking to Alex but holding Anna's gaze. Maybe it's the pent-up frustration from last night, or maybe my brother just brings out the worst in me and the best way to drag him is through his wife's dissatisfaction, but I keep going. "Gets the blood flowing, doesn't it?"

Blaire exhales a shaky breath. "Jesus Christ."

Anna's eyes go wide, and she nods enthusiastically. "Sure does."

I kiss the top of her head. "This'll be fun."

"Regardless, Blaire and I can't be beat on the water," Alex says, more aggressively now. "We go out nearly every morning. We exercise together *all the time.*"

I nod, smiling in the condescending way he hates. "You said. Not sure we're talking about the same thing, though."

"I'm talking about kicking your ass," he says.

My mother steps between us, hostess smile firmly tacked to her face. "I hope everyone has a lovely, relaxing time this morning. This vacation is chock-full of things to do!" Then lower, Mom Tone activated: "Let's *enjoy* each other."

"Eh, let them battle it out," Dad says. "Alex has got his panties up his ass."

Eko has clearly dealt with family bullshit before and rolls on as if she hasn't heard any of this. "Everyone ready?"

Without further permission, I take Anna's hand, leading her immediately to the best-looking kayak in the group.

"What the hell are you doing?" she mumbles when we're out of earshot, stumbling after me.

"Nothing," I tell her. "Alex just gets competitive."

"*Alex* does? Really?"

"Just . . . let me do the paddling."

"I can help once I figure it out," she says, laughing. "I've been in a kayak once, when I was, like, seven."

And that much is immediately apparent. She trips as she tries to climb in. I hold the boat steady for her, but she still ends up getting in backward and then having to awkwardly turn around in the tiny space. I pretend to scratch my shoulder with my chin, glancing behind us. Fuck. Alex noticed.

I climb into the back, pushing us off the shore with the oar, and paddling hard, propelling us forward in a blur. Alex and Blaire are still climbing into their boat. I grin, turning to face forward. "Hell yes," I hiss with satisfaction.

But then Anna digs an oar in, and we veer hard right, our momentum slowing immediately.

"Just leave it to me," I tell her. "I'll get us out there."

"But I *want* to paddle," she says, trying again. With the force of my strokes, her inept paddling just sends us into a wide circle.

"Anna, come on."

"No, West, it isn't a competition! We're here to have fun!"

I look behind us again; Alex is working furiously, close to catching up. In the front seat, Blaire half-ass paddles, yelling something over her shoulder at her husband.

"Please, Anna, I know this is dumb, but I'm in it now."

She sighs, resting her paddle across her legs. "Fine."

I get us going, sweating and exhausted from the erotic nonsleep and the run earlier, growing too warm under the sun's insistent heat. My arms burn, my lower back grows tight, and as the distance between us and Alex's boat grows, I wonder what the fuck I'm doing.

This isn't who I want to be.

Just then, Anna looks over and lets out a high-pitched shriek. "West! A sea turtle!" She leans to the side, and her oar slides off her lap and into the clear water.

"Shit—Anna—your oar!" I point to where it starts to float away. "Grab it!"

The kayak wobbles precariously as she leans to get it, and already it's out of her reach. With a tiny yelp, she dives in, but no sooner has she dog-paddled a few feet from the boat than she screams, scrambling for the side of the kayak. "Oh my God, something touched my leg!"

"It's just the water moving," I tell her. "Grab the paddle!"

"It wasn't the water! It was a shark! Or a ray! Oh my God, West, pull me in!"

I reach for her, but she's panicking and slippery with sunscreen, and in the chaos, my paddle falls in, too, and I dive in to fetch it. I can't even see hers anymore; it's already been carried away by the current back toward the shore.

"Please," she sob-laughs, seemingly aware how crazy she's being but unable to help it. "Help me in, West, I'm terrified of deep water and had no idea until right now."

I set my oar on a stable point in the boat, and then help her climb up and flop onto her seat before hoisting myself in.

"I'm so sorry," she says, twisting around to look at me. The sky is a perfect stretch of clear blue behind her. A flock of black-headed gulls fly overhead. "I won't fall in again. And look, I can't even paddle, so it's all you now! We can still beat them there!"

I look to the side and realize how far we've drifted from the group, our kayak bobbing gently in the current. The other boats are small, colorful dots just passing the small island about a half mile out from shore. It really is beautiful out here. I wish I could pull my head out of my ass long enough to enjoy it.

"It's fine," I say. "Leave it."

She gestures helplessly to the water. "Don't you want to go snorkeling with the group?"

I shake my head, feeling immense relief the second I decide to let this stupid race go. "It's nice just to be out here. We can snorkel here if we want."

"I tell you what: I am not getting back in that water. The ocean is monster soup, and I don't want to die today." She lies back against the stretch of kayak between us, and I stare down at her nearly naked body, wondering precisely how fucked I am.

With her eyes closed, Anna says, "Tell me more about your relationship with your brother."

"It's not therapy hour, Green."

"Okay, then I want to go snorkeling with the group."

"He and I have never been close," I say quickly, suddenly and deeply uninterested in spending the morning anywhere but right here with Anna. "I think from the moment he was born, the only thing he cared about was impressing our father."

"What's the age difference?" she asks.

"He's three years older," I say. "Then Jake came four years after me, and Charlotte four years after that."

"Your mom was pregnant and raising kids for over a decade?" Anna whistles, dropping a hand over the side of the boat to skim her fingertips through the water. Her limbs are so long, so graceful. With her eyes closed I can just look, admiring the shape of her collarbones, the small valley of her breasts beneath her swimsuit, and down the smooth skin of her stomach. "Actually, so was Blaire, now that I think about it. No wonder they always have drinks in their hands."

"Oh, don't worry," I say, forcing my gaze away. "They have help."

Anna laughs. "Help being pregnant and birthing children?"

"No, I mean nannies."

"Look how quickly you dismiss all that work." Anna lifts her hand, flicking water back at me. "Your mom birthed four babies and helped your dad manage an empire. Blaire birthed four and is married to Alex. Of course they have nannies."

We bob in the water while I sit with this. She's right. So why am I diminishing what she's done, just like my father does? When I poke at it, resentment builds.

"I have a complicated relationship with my mother," I admit.

"I get it," she says easily. "Is it like, your dad is a dick, and your mom enables it?"

I stare at her, wondering how she so concisely summed up the pathos I spent the better part of my twenties working through. "Something like that."

"But back to Alex . . ." Anna says, her voice somehow soothing even when she's pressing at all of my bruises. "Maybe you two are so competitive because it serves your father for you to be at odds with each other."

This makes me laugh a little. Nail on the head. "You think?"

"You drive Alex crazy because he can't ever beat you even though he's the older brother. He's probably jealous because you're tall and hot and smart and he's short and—"

"Annoying. You can say it."

"You two don't seem to bring out the best in each other," she says instead.

I laugh wryly. "No."

"Why not try being nice to him?"

It takes a second for me to know I've heard her right. "Nice to Alex? Why?"

"Uh, because it doesn't seem like anyone else is? Because you're his family?"

"Spoken like someone who has no family."

The second the words are out of my mouth, we both go silent. Fuck. What a terrible thing to say. "Sorry. That wasn't great. Let's strike it from the record."

"All good."

"Do you . . ." I reach up, cupping my forehead. "Please tell me you have family. Otherwise, I'm going to dive into the monster soup."

Anna laughs. "My dad, yeah."

"No siblings?"

"No."

"You're—"

"Don't say lucky."

"I wasn't," I say. "I was going to say, are you close to your dad?"

"Yes." She smiles. "Very."

I pause over this next question. "And your mom?"

"Well," she says, drawing out the word, "you have daddy issues, I have mommy issues. We're evenly matched."

She doesn't elaborate, so after a few quiet moments, I change course. "I realize I never asked why you switched your major."

She smiles up at me, squinting against the sun. "You mean telling you I was shitty at all the coursework wasn't a sufficient explanation?"

I laugh. "Fair enough. But now that I've spent some more time with you, I guess I'm surprised you ever chose it to begin with. You lack the typical med student—"

"Intensity?" she finishes for me.

"I guess so," I say, quickly adding, "That's not an insult, or at least I don't mean it as one."

"Oh, trust me, I know this about myself. Whenever someone asks me what my Enneagram is, I'm like, 'Whichever is the lazy, affectionate, cheese-loving one.'" She shields her face from the intense sunlight. "And, I don't know. In hindsight I went premed for all the wrong reasons, related to the aforementioned mommy issues. She left when I was five, though she'd pop in and out without pattern or warning, which made it hard to ever move on from her leaving in the first place. My mom was an attorney, my dad is a mechanic, and I think when they first met, she was attracted to the hot blue-collar guy, the kid from the other side of the proverbial tracks. But as an aspiring adult, now I see how those kinds of surface attractions wear off. She didn't hide her feelings about his coworkers or things like how his hands are never fully clean, even after scrubbing. Even as a kid I absorbed the sense that his was a job, not a career, and that there was a value difference there, in her mind." Her rib cage expands and relaxes with a deep breath. "It sucks, honestly, but when I was starting college, I chose what I thought would be a career. We hadn't spoken in a few years by that point, but I was still trying to make myself lovable to her."

"You were just a kid. You weren't doing it to reject your dad."

Anna smiles. "I know. Dad knows, too. Once I figured out that I chose premed for the wrong reasons, it was easy to choose to do what I loved, rather than what might make someone love me. The bottom line is that my mom was never really interested in being a mom. But David Green more than made up for it."

She says this like any other fact: it's hot today, the sky is so clear, my mother wasn't ready to be a mother. For a breath I'm so envious of her easy vulnerability. My siblings and I were raised with our shields up, swords drawn. It's taken me years of therapy to be able to talk about what's going on inside me, and I'm still not very good at it.

"Remind me where you grew up?" I ask.

Anna pulls her hand from the water and sends it absently down her stomach, leaving a trail of water that quickly pulls into droplets and evaporates in the heat. "Is it weird that we lived together for two years and you don't remember this?"

"You didn't even know my first name," I remind her, laughing.

She grins. "Yes, but no one's money is ever on me to be the keeper of details, Golden Boy." She reaches up, throwing her arm over her eyes, and I look at the long line of her body soaking up the sun. "I grew up in Fontana. I can hear that face you're making, you coastal snob."

I rearrange my grimace. "I wasn't making a face."

"You were. And before you ask, no one calls it Fontucky anymore."

I'm not so sure, but manage an unconvincing, "Fontana is . . . nice."

"See? That's how you do it! Say things like that to Alex."

"I'll try."

"Practice with me. I'll be Alex, you be you."

"No."

"Why?"

"Because that's stupid," I say, but my smile softens my words. "Tell me more about your dad."

She takes a deep breath, causing the bikini to press into her breasts, and I might dive into the monster soup just to cool my rapidly heating . . . Goddamn. My sanity certainly isn't in this boat with me anymore. "He's a Taurus," she says, "loves fishing, and always has a baseball game on in the background. He's worked on cars since he was a kid. He specializes in Volvos but can fix anything. And not just cars, actually: TVs, plumbing, refrigerators. He rebuilt the frame on your old couch when I hired some high schoolers to help me move and they dropped it. They wanted me to pay them in weed, so I'm not all that surprised they sucked at the job."

I don't know what face I'm making, but whatever silent emotion it's communicating is enough to make her bark out a laugh. "I said they *wanted* me to; I didn't say I did it! Who do you think I am, giving weed to America's youth! Anyway, back to my dad. He's amazing."

The current is returning us to the island, but I steer the kayak with a gentle dip of the paddle into water. The closer we get, the more I can see beneath us. The jagged reef, schools of brightly colored fish, some kind of crustacean making its way along the sandy bottom. "What did he think about you coming here?"

"I didn't tell him the specifics of our arrangement. I told him I was coming here to paint wedding portraits."

"Good cover story."

"Even if I told him everything, though, I think he'd understand. It's good that I'll be able to—" She cuts off, frowning below her arm. "It's just a good thing I'm here, that's all. I really appreciate the opportunity to make some money."

My paddle stills in the water. "What were you going to say?"

"No, it's really nothing." She moves her arm, cupping her hands over her eyes to block the sun. "You may have noticed I have a tendency to overshare."

"You were digging about my relationship with Alex. Isn't this therapy hour? What's said in the kayak stays in the kayak."

She laughs but doesn't elaborate further. It bothers me for reasons I can't entirely dissect—and which certainly don't feel fair—that she's suddenly sealing up with me.

"Are we moving?" she asks, pushing up onto an elbow to watch.

"The tide is taking us back, but we can stay out here as long as you want."

I squint, though, realizing a number of the boats are already returning to shore. Even from out here I can hear shouting.

"What is that?" Anna asks, pointing.

Paddling in earnest now, I tell her, "I don't know. Something's going on; let me see what it is."

The second the kayak pushes up on the beach, I'm out and jogging over to where Jake is sitting on the sand, his leg covered in ice. "What the hell happened?"

Our father paces on the sand, on the phone with someone, voice raised. I get the impression the island doctor isn't in-house today. Mom bends beside Jake, rubbing his back. It's only now that I realize her cover-up has the word *Gucci* printed all over it, and she's wearing bulky gold jewelry on her neck, wrists, ears, fingers.

"I got stung by something," Jake says, and Anna's head whips to me, her eyes wide like *See? Death brew!*

Eko winces. "We think it was a jelly, but they're not often in these waters."

Mom waves Anna closer, her bracelets clinking together along her thin wrist. "Dear, can you take a look at it?"

Anna recoils. "Why?"

I set my hand on her lower back. "Because you're the closest thing we have to a doctor here, sweetheart."

She snaps to attention with a muttered "Oh, right," and, with obvious trepidation, approaches Jake's rapidly swelling leg.

He gazes up at her, smirking. "What's the prognosis, doc?"

Gingerly, Anna lifts the ice, gasping at the small wound there. She sets the ice back down, flushed, and nods decisively. "You'll live."

"You sure?" he pokes. "What's the best thing for the swelling?"

"Ice," I tell him flatly.

My brother grins at me. "I asked the doctor-in-training."

"Ice," Anna says robotically.

"That's it? You're not going to touch it? Inspect it? Drain it?"

Anna scowls at him, and with the circle of people watching, crouches down, setting two fingers on his leg. She immediately jerks her arm back. "Wow, it's hot."

"Is that normal?" Jake asks, feigning worry. "Are you sure I'm not going to lose it? It's my favorite leg."

"It's normal," Anna says, cheeks turning pink from embarrassment. "It's the . . . blood, and oxygen . . . interacting . . ."

"With the inflammatory cells," I break in, frustrated with Jake, and frustrated with myself for putting her in this position in the first place. "If I've heard her talking about inflammation once, I've heard it a million times. Luckily, Jake, it looks like you're going to live."

He frowns up at me. "I wonder if Anna should start an IV, just to be safe."

"I could pee on it if you want."

Reagan gags. "Gross."

"I'm good." Jake waves me off.

I take Anna's hand and tug it. "Let's go get a nap."

To the side, Blaire sighs. "He means 'Let me throw you around the bed until the party tonight.'" I look over right as she stares meaningfully at Alex.

We turn to leave, and my older brother calls after me, "Hey, remind me, Liam. When's your wedding anniversary? Isn't five years coming up?"

The group goes still. Anna and I look at each other. Fuck.

She says, "August fifth," just as I say, "August twelfth."

Anna laughs. "Well, technically the twelfth, but the fifth was when he wrote me a song and got on his knees to sing it to me, so that's the night I see as our actual marriage." She looks up at me, eyes soft. "He cried."

I frown down at her. "I didn't cry."

"You mean you didn't *just* cry. Sobbed is more like it." She lifts my hand and gently kisses my knuckles. "It was beautiful, babe."

My dad, having just ended his call, walks over to us. "The fuck did she just say?"

Anna smiles up at me. "Sing a little of it for me?"

"No."

"Oh, please?" Blaire asks. "That's so romantic. My husband's idea of romance is three pumps and a high five."

"I'll sing it to you in the bungalow, Anna. Let's go."

Thirteen

ANNA

West follows me into the bungalow, and I look at him expectantly.

"What?" he asks.

"You know what."

He scowls. "I'm not going to sing."

Housekeeping has come and gone, and I fall back onto our fresh and very neatly made bed. "You made me a medical student and an avid co-exerciser who punishes you with great sex. What's next? Did I save a bunch of orphans from a fire? Climb Mount Everest?" He walks around the small partition to turn on the shower, and I roll to my side, calling to him, "I toyed with the idea of saying you dressed up in a Breton shirt and beret and mimed a dramatic proposal but that seemed a little too far, even for me."

He emerges while the water warms, scrubbing his face in frustration. "I think Alex is definitely suspicious."

"What gave it away?" I ask dryly. "Him specifically asking about our five-year anniversary?"

"I don't want to be back in this family any more than he wants me here. Can't he just mind his business for once in his life?"

"Maybe he would if you didn't antagonize him." I shake my head at him in wonder. "It seems even less credible having me here if you're going to act like such a basket case."

West sighs miserably. "My family brings out the worst in me."

I make a fist of solidarity. "Keep your eyes on the prize: your inheritance."

His face does a weird little wince, like I've made a dig. Have I?

I must have, because he pauses before turning back to the shower. "It's not just about my money."

Rolling off the bed, I walk over to him. "West, dearest! I'm not judging you! We all have things that motivate us. I'd sacrifice a virgin to get my art placed in a big show." I pause. "Hell, even a small art show. I just want my work out there. A hundred million dollars would motivate the hell out of me. I might even kill *two* virgins."

West looks like he wants to say more but doesn't. "I'm gonna shower."

He stares and this time, I read the translation: *Linger at your own risk.*

I walk out to the deck and curl up in a papasan chair, facing the ocean. The sky has grown dark to the north, and I wonder if we'll get a storm later. I pick up my notebook and pencil, starting to sketch out the horizon when I hear that maddening shower groan. I imagine his perfect Goddamn and have to close my eyes, focusing on the sound of the waves and not on what sexy things might also elicit more sexy noises.

I look down at my paper and begin sketching, not thinking, just drawing whatever runs through my mind. I'm not particularly good at figure drawing, but as the minutes pass, my hands move on instinct. A rough sketch of a chest, the geometric slash of collarbones. My pencil scratches across the page as I shape out bulky shoulders, long, defined arms. A torso narrowing at the muscular hips, with a dark line of hair leading beneath a waistband. I definitely do not think about running my fingertips there, biting his thighs, or wrapping my hand around his long, thick Godda—

"Anna."

I startle, jolting upright and slamming the sketchbook shut. West is standing in front of me in shorts and what looks like an incredibly soft T-shirt.

"Sorry, were you working on something?" he asks with a smirk.

"It's nothing." I sit up, tucking the book behind me. "That was a fast shower." Though I guess it was long enough to almost sketch a naked version of the man in front of me. "I'm going to take a nap," I say standing to stretch. "I don't think I slept very well."

When I look up, West is gaping at me.

"What?" I point. "What is that face?" Gasping, I ask, "Oh my God, did I snore last night?"

His shock melts into an amused smile. "No, you did not snore. You were . . . a little cuddly."

"Cuddly?" I ask, horrified. "Meaning what?"

"Don't worry about it. Listen." He sits in the chair beside mine and reaches for my forearm, guiding me back down. "I was thinking in the shower, and—"

"Oh, yes." I lean forward. "Wait, wait. No." I settle back and close my eyes. "Start from the beginning. You're in the shower, the water pouring over your rock-hard abs . . ."

"Stop it," he says, laughing. When I open my eyes, he's gazing at me through long, dark lashes. "You were right last night. We—I mean I, really—need to take this more seriously."

I shift in my chair, noticing the way West's honeyed eyes track the movement. I look down and who can blame the man—there's just so much boob visible in this Band-Aid of a bikini. Vivi and I are going to have a long conversation when I get home about what constitutes a swimsuit so the next time a billionaire asks me to pose as his wife, I'm better equipped for water sports.

"I'm all ears," I say, but he doesn't seem to believe me. His eyes linger on my chest.

"I . . ." He begins, and then rakes his hand through that glorious head of hair, blinking hard and turning his face away. "Tonight is the main welcome party. Most of the wedding guests should be arriving throughout the day and will be in attendance. There will be business contacts of my father's everywhere. Reporters, photographers, you know."

"I do not know, but I believe you."

He smiles, but it vanishes quickly. "I think we need to be . . . affectionate."

I've said as much myself, but hearing it from him now makes my confidence wobble. In what universe can I be closer to this man and not end up slobbering all over his chest? I barely kept it together this morning at his insinuation that he betrayed our routine by going for a run without me, and I punished him with some good old-fashioned anger fuckin'. I imagine him looking at me tonight with feigned love in his eyes at the party and my hands gravitating to his crotch like twin magnets.

I hold up my fists and give a silent cheer. "You know I'm down for whatever the job requires."

West's gaze dips to my boobs again and he squeezes his eyes closed. "Great."

"So, the Operation Inheritance plan for tonight is to be more affectionate," I say. "More of a team vibe and less of a 'throw each other under the bus' vibe."

"Right."

"How affectionate are we talking? Like we just had crazy sex, or like we'll have crazy sex later? Or both?"

He rubs his hand through his hair, this time with a groan. "Do you really have to keep saying the word *sex*?"

I open my mouth to say it again just for kicks, but the sound is drowned out as an amphibious plane comes in for a water landing.

"I think you better give me a rundown of who'll be there that you want me to charm," I yell above the noise.

"Right," he says again, his voice rising as the plane lands smoothly on the water only a couple hundred feet from our bungalow. "Well, the best ones to read up on a little are Danny Shoe, Patrick Lemon, and Nicola Ricci."

I see movement behind him and stand up in shock, because a toddler—who must be two-year-old GW—has somehow walked along our narrow bridge all the way out to our bungalow?

"Sweetie, what are you doing?" I run over to him, picking him up, and immediately West is there, too, taking him from me, holding him tight in a panic. This tiny human just walked out ALONE along a bridge with NO RAILS built directly OVER THE OCEAN.

It hits me like a slap: what the fuck kind of place builds a long-ass bridge to a bungalow and has nothing but a flimsy rope for a handrail? Does no one ever bring children or disabled or elderly people here? Are the guests who come here so obsessed with capturing the perfect *vibes* in their Instagram post that they don't want fucking guardrails ruining their shot?

West walks in a few circles, hugging his nephew and talking quietly to him and I'm temporarily distracted from my disgust. My ovaries stand up and exit my body with a forlorn salute, launching themselves into the monster soup.

"Is he okay?" I ask, coming up and resting my hands on GW's shoulders. "You okay, buddy?"

"He seems fine," West says, and meets my eyes. "I'm sure he has no idea how dangerous that was, do you, kiddo?"

"This bridge is so treacherous," I whisper to West. "What are they thinking, putting the kids in a bungalow?"

"It's fine," West mumbles back, and I'm sure he's seen a million private islands with all kinds of inaccessible features. I'm sure this is nothing. "They just have to keep a closer eye on him."

GW snuggles into West's neck and says, "I went for walk."

"Yeah, you did." He looks at me over his nephew's shoulder. "I'm going to take him back over to Alex and Blaire's. I'm sure they're freaking out wondering where he is."

I EXPECT WEST TO be back and hanging out on the deck when I come out of the shower, but the bungalow is still empty. I do think he's right, though; if the most important thing in our plan is to be convincingly married so his family has no reason to start digging into our lives, then we need to step it up a bit.

I'm not sure, but I think women in rich circles are good about knowing things about the people they'll meet at parties. At least that's the way it goes on *Real Housewives*. The Wi-Fi on the island is, perhaps not surprisingly, incredibly slow but it works, and I pull a page from my sketchbook, writing down information on the names I remember West saying: Danny Shoe, Patrick Lemon, and Nicola Ricci.

But I don't just go to their LinkedIns or Wiki's; I dive deeper. If there's one common skill every adult woman possesses, it's how to scope out a friend's prospective or cheating love interest on the Internet. This knowledge is half of why I have zero Internet presence. (The other half is laziness.)

And thank God I dive deeper, because after some Instagram cross-referencing between West, Jake, and Charlie, I realize that Danny Shoe is in fact *Danielle Xiu*. She posted an airport selfie yesterday with the caption IAD > SIN, along with several airplane and bridal emojis. She is also quite the Barbie aficionado, and I send a silent thank-you to the universe that nobody keeps anything private anymore.

Just as I wrap up my glacially paced but successful googling, an email pops up from my manager, Melissa.

Dear Anna,

Amazing news! I have placed three of your paintings at a gallery showing in Laguna Beach! They will need to be picked up tomorrow; I'll send a courier. What is a good time to meet at your apartment?

The price will be set at $200 each—how does that sound to you?

Call me if you have any questions.

Best,
Mel

I stand up, do a few circles in place, not sure what to do with my hands, my feet, my face. Excitement is helium in my bloodstream; I feel jittery, high, floating outside my own body.

Where is West? Did he go and sacrifice a virgin on my behalf? If so, it was not necessary but so appreciated. This is not the kind of email one wants to receive alone! This requires celebration, shouting, maybe some hot making out—*no, Anna, stop that.* At the very least, I need a high five.

I high-five myself, and then type out a quick reply.

I'm out of town but will make sure my roommate is there to meet the courier. This is so exciting! The price sounds perfect. Thank you, Mel!

xo
Anna

I text Lindy and ask what time she can be home tomorrow and whether she can bring the three paintings to the living room. She replies immediately, and I forgive her for eating my tagine. Ladies and gents, things are looking good for Anna Green!

With West still MIA, I have nothing to do but venture out to the beach to potentially get accosted by a member of the Weston family or get dressed for the cocktail welcome party tonight. Everyone will be excited for their first day here, so I decide to go all out.

By the time West's footsteps sound along the bridge, I'm finishing the final curl in my hair. My initial primping enthusiasm has worn off and now I fear my vibe is less "beachy hot" and more "desperate D-lister on red carpet."

He rounds the corner, already speaking. "Sorry! Sorry. I got caught by Blaire—she slapped my ass three times when I—" West stops abruptly when I step out from behind the half wall behind the bed. "Holy fuck."

"It's overboard," I agree immediately. "I went overboard, right? With the curls? And the winged liner? And who needs lips this pink? Definitely not me." I turn to go grab some toilet paper to wipe it all off. "This is not a beach vibe."

"Don't you fucking touch the lips," he says, voice hoarse. "You look amazing."

"Oh." Suddenly, I am hot all over. "Thank you. You're good at this game."

He drags his attention from my toes, up my legs, over my breasts, along my neck, to my eyes. My dress reminds me of something a flapper from the 1920s would wear: square neckline, thin black straps, falling straight to midthigh and covered in long, rectangular silver sequins that shake like fringe when I boogie. "Yeah. This is a good look for you."

"You have horny eyes," I tell him.

"Yeah? Well." He squeezes them shut.

"I will need you to zip me up, though." I turn around, pulling my hair forward and looking back at him over my shoulder. "Please?"

He takes a deep breath. "Sure."

Am I imagining that the air warms when he steps up behind me? I feel the slightest touch at the base of my spine as he reaches for the zipper, and then the slowest, softest, graze of his thumb as he pulls it all the way up.

"There." Another deep breath, and when I face him, he turns toward the closet. He looks winded. "I can change really quick."

"Don't go changing," I sing, "to try and please me."

"Well done." West rifles through his clothing options. "You've doused the horny fire by singing my mother's favorite song."

"I just want you to know that unlike *some* roommates of this bungalow, I'm here to serenade whenever you feel the need."

"Noted."

"Okay. I'll step outside while you change."

"It's fine," he says, and looks back at me. "You were right. At some point, we just have to say fuck it, I think. Besides, there's no mystery left after that bikini."

He's right. But I still want to pretend to be respectful. I spend the next ten minutes studying my notes on Dani, Patrick, and Nicola. I am ready for these bigwigs.

A hand comes over my shoulder, and I turn to see West in a crisp white shirt and heathered gray pants he's rolled at the hem. I didn't think a man could dress up for a beach party without looking like a knob, but West has done it.

Also, those pants do amazing things for his . . .

Goddamn.

I clear my throat, but it doesn't matter. My voice comes out like the mewl of a cat in heat anyway: "You look very nice."

He laughs, pulling on a sport coat. "Thank you. Eyes up here, Green."

I drag my gaze away from his crotch. "Right."

"Ready?" He holds out his arm for me.

"Ready."

$\mathcal{F}$ourteen

ANNA

Let me tell you something about rich people. They can be on a tropical island, smack-dab in literal paradise, where nothing more is needed but a few tables and some chairs, and they will still find a way to spend gobs of money.

Case in point, according to the itinerary, tonight's party is being held at the island's other restaurant, the Boathouse. On any ordinary night, I imagine it's magnificent exactly how it is. To the naked eye it looks like a large driftwood structure, with no real walls to detract from the stunning beach just yards away. Intricately carved ceiling fans oscillate from wooden beams stretched overhead, and beautiful iridescent shell-covered chandeliers glow above long tables set in pristine white sand. See? Gorgeous. Perfect. Expensive.

But because this is a Weston Party™, it doesn't end there. Clustered down the center of each table are vases bursting with white orchids and sprays of spiky green palms. The plates are bone china, and they look old, *rich* old, vintage, with about seventeen matching smaller plates and crystal champagne flutes at each place setting. I wonder idly if Janet had these brought over from her own collection, and then I realize she'd be more likely to just buy an entirely new set of priceless china.

Candles flicker in mercury glass votives. Each chair is topped with a creamy linen pillow. More flowers are arranged in boughs over the bar, and fresh tropical greenery encircles every wooden beam and column. It's like being in a terrarium on the beach. The air is warm and smells like sea salt and sugar, and I feel slightly drunk before we've even stepped inside.

"Why does this still surprise me?" I say, looking at the splendor in front of us. There are so many people here, swarming the bar while ignoring the buffet. You won't see me making that mistake. Thanks to Vivi's crash course in being fancy, I spot Valentino and Chanel, Dior and Bottega Veneta. Hermès bags and red-soled Christian Louboutin sandals. Brands I can barely pronounce, let alone spell. It's a safe bet Janet isn't the only one in attendance who takes her trash out in a pair of Gucci slides.

"I know what you mean," he says, and there's a hint of sadness there. Disappointment? He's also hesitating, his feet planted in the sand like he's being led to an audit.

With a hand on his elbow, I coax him to turn toward me. "Hey."

He smiles and I wonder for the hundredth time why he doesn't do it more often. "Hey."

"I forgot to tell you something awesome."

He tilts his head, the stars reflecting in his eyes. "I love awesome."

"My manager emailed while you were being accosted by your sister-in-law, and three of my pieces will be at a showing in Laguna!"

His smile grows and I screech as he wraps his arms around my waist and lifts me from the ground. "That's amazing," he says, peering up at me. "Congratulations, Green."

"Thank you."

After an awkward amount of *what now?* eye contact, West sets me down and I'm glad to see that his expression is lighter, his shoulders looser. Mission accomplished. "See? No virgin sacrifice required," he says.

"Oh, good to know," I say, grinning. "You were gone so long, I wanted to ask if thanks were due, but it felt like that sort of gift is best left unmentioned."

"Just your talent, absolutely zero blood spill."

Music drifts from the restaurant as a band begins to play. "Okay," I say. "So we are madly in love, are the types to have sex before *and* after this party, and these suckers can only dream of being this happy." I reach up, smoothing the front of his shirt. "You ready, Dr. Weston?"

"No, but let's do it anyway." He winks. "Champagne's on me."

As we enter, we are greeted by a beautiful young woman wearing a Weston's name tag. "Welcome to the Weston-McKellan welcome reception." She hands me a heavy white bag.

"What's this?" I say, peeking inside.

West leans in. "Probably a swag bag."

I blink up at him. "Like at the Oscars?"

He laughs. "Something like that. Stuff from my parents but probably things from other guests, too."

"They got sponsors? For a wedding?" I push the tissue paper aside. "West," I say, and pull out the iconic white box. "There's an iPad in here." Next to it is an envelope with a crisply folded sheet of stationery. "Oh my God. Ten shares of Samsung stock . . . a week at a luxury Canadian resort . . ." It goes on and on: a canister of hand-harvested gourmet dates, Belgian chocolates, a year's supply of vitamin supplements, luxury bath salts, several vouchers for skin-care products and . . . my excitement deflates. "A gift card for liposuction?"

West lifts one weary shoulder, leading me farther inside.

Across the room, Charlie and Kellan greet guests as they arrive, and she looks so genuinely happy that my heart grows four sizes. I want that for West so much. I want him to take what he loves in his family and leave the rest, to build a perfect combination of chosen family and given and finally find some relief from whatever the history is with his father.

He leaves me to grab us drinks, and I scan the seating, knowing Janet will not have left something like a seating chart to chance. I set my gift bag next to the place card with *Dr. and Mrs. William Weston* embossed across it. Married to a doctor, well done, Past Me.

Mother would be so proud.

I look around, hoping to find Jake, but he doesn't seem to have arrived yet. Nearby is a banquet table heavy with desserts, each accompanied by a tiny silver label. Saffron poached pears with gold leaf and spun sugar cages. Sheep's milk mousse, pandan curd, and caramelized puff rice. White chocolate mousse with cardamom espuma and clementine sorbet. Papaya curd with black currant jelly, oatmeal, and mint glass.

I think of the last wedding I went to, of a friend from high school who was married at the Los Angeles County courthouse and had the reception at Level Up Dance Studio in Signal Hill. She ordered Domino's, and afterward we all shared a chocolate sheet cake she got for free because the bakery accidentally piped *Congratulations on Your Weeding*. Best cake I've ever had.

I reach for a plate, filling it with everything I can carry, and turn to see West on his way back. But he doesn't just have drinks. He has an older redhaired man with him. "Anna, this is Patrick Lemon. Pat, this is my wife, Anna."

I set down my plate and shake his hand enthusiastically. "Pat is the chairman of the American Dairy Farmer Coalition," West adds.

"Mr. Lemon, it's such a thrill to meet you. I am a huge fan of your work."

He smiles at me, unsure. "Thank you."

"I personally think a mixing bowl is the correct serving size for breakfast cereal," I say, winking at West. "And my best friend, Vivi, is lactose intolerant but will happily polish off an entire pint of ice cream as if she won't be in my bathroom for the next three hours."

West looks like I've just pushed him off a cliff, but Mr. Lemon tilts his head back and laughs. "There's nobody more fearless than people who can't have dairy," he says. "My wife can't tolerate cheese but she's always the first to suggest pizza."

I lean in conspiratorially. "Make it good enough that they're willing to pay the price, am I right?"

"That's the idea," Pat says with a nod.

The two men chat for a few minutes before Pat wanders off and Liam turns to me, an amused smirk tugging the corner of his mouth. "I wouldn't think a conversation about lactose intolerance could be charming, but I stand corrected."

My cheeks are still warm from his praise when he introduces me to Danielle Xiu, the congressional aide and avid Barbie collector. As luck would have it, my former boss Barb kept old issues of *Fashion Doll Quarterly* in the back office of the Pick-It-Up, which I, of course, devoured. Dani and I talk vintage gown re-creations, the brilliance of the *Barbie* movie, and BarbieCon.

I note the wedding ring on her finger. "Where is your Ken? Or your Barbie?"

She laughs. "My Ken is back home with our kids. He's a litigator, so he's thrilled to get some downtime playing Dad this week."

I wrap my arms around West's torso. "My Ken's job this week is Beach."

"And Drinks," he says, taking our empty glasses with a charming smile and leaving to get us refills.

The night goes on like this, easy and surprisingly fun, and it's only after West and I say good night to Nicola Ricci, a vitamin corporation CEO *and* new emu farmer (thank you to the r/Emu subreddit for all of the amazing intel) that I realize how chatty I've been, while West played the part of bemused bystander.

When we're finally alone again, West puts his hand on my lower back and leads me to the edge of the party. "Okay," I start, "before you say it, I know I've been talking too much." It doesn't seem fair that I should get the giant, warm, sexy hand on my back when my entire job here was to smile and be polite, not chitchat and stand out.

West frowns. "Are you kidding? Everyone was completely charmed. Where did you learn all that anyway? Like emus having double eyelids and all that shit about Barbie legs?"

I shrug. "I read a lot. My old job at the Pick-It-Up stocked every magazine ever. And Reddit is both a trash fire and an invaluable resource."

"I'm impressed, Green. You're doing amazing."

These words make my ocean-dwelling ovaries incinerate, but then a shadow looms over the sunshine: this *is* easy for me. *Too* easy. The realization makes me feel icky inside, because I suddenly can't imagine my dad at all, let alone him laughing easily with these people, some of whom have never personally delivered their vehicle to a mechanic. Maybe I'm more like my mother than I thought.

But I don't have more time to spiral, because the sound of clinking glasses rises in the room all around us. Over near the bar, Charlie and Kellan lean in, coming together in a kiss that is so perfect I wonder if she learned it in finishing school.

When they pull away, they do an adorable "gazing into each other's eyes" move before Charlie gasps, clapping. In her tiny micro minidress, she attempts to jog-shuffle in her spiked heels—so much for no stilettos on the beach—over to the microphone. "Alex reminded me earlier today that our sweet Liam has been married to Anna for *five* years this August!"

A knowing smile pulls at Alex's lips, and he lifts his glass. Fucking Alex.

Bouncing excitedly, Charlie waves to where we stand in the back, and the entire room turns to face us, seventy-five bleached white grins forming a spotlight. I am sure even without the benefit of a mirror in front of us that both West and I look like we have just emerged from a cave to bright sun. "We are so happy to have them with us!" Charlie cries. "Congratulations, you two!"

The clinking starts up again, but this time, I realize we're the ones who are meant to be kissing.

"What do we do?" I say through my clenched-teeth smile.

"I think," he says back through his own tight grin, "that we kiss."

My jaw is cramping. I'm fake-smiling so hard. "Okay, great!"

"Yeah?" he asks, and his own smile is now straightening, his expression turning to determined focus. A big hand comes up, cupping my jaw, and I manage to get out a breathy "yeah" as my knees turn to jelly. His eyes drop to my mouth, and I hold my breath as he leans in.

I realize, just before we touch, that he's about to erase everything I know about the act of kissing.

The first contact is just a brush of his lips over mine, the briefest sweep. I'm going to be devastated if that's all I get, but then I hear the quietest moan escape his throat as he leans in again, pressing his soft, strong mouth to mine and taking my top lip between his, sucking gently before he turns his attention to my bottom one. With a smile forming against my kiss, West tilts his head and takes me with a heat I could not have predicted but which makes me feel like I'm falling backward into clouds.

Or maybe that's the way he's cupping the back of my head in one hand, holding me around my waist in the other, and dipping me so low I'm nearly on the floor.

The room is quiet and then erupts in cheers as West smoothly brings me back up in what has to be the sexiest move any man has ever pulled off. I feel the ground shake beneath me, but it isn't the noise in the room. It's the realization that whatever I thought kissing was before was a poor, diluted impostor to *that*.

"West Weston," I say, resting my hands on his chest. "Who knew you had it in you?"

He smiles knowingly down at me. "I'm pretty sure you did."

Fifteen

LIAM

The end of the kiss isn't a passive closing off, an easy pulling away. It's forced, it's purposeful, and with the warmth of her lips on mine, it's nearly impossible. But with all eyes still on us, I lift Anna up, making sure she's steady on her feet, and resist the urge to go back for more.

The attendees murmur their approval, quiet calls of "adorable" and "romantic" and "dazzling" floating around us—as well as one shouted "That was hot as shit!," thank you Blaire—but Anna and I just stare at each other in mute shock. I realize I need to appear to have done this a million times, not just this once, so I try to pull my features together even though the sensation of her full, pillow-soft lips against mine still feels like an earthquake rolling through me.

Blinking away, I focus on her shoulder, and on the strap that has slipped an inch to the side, revealing a tan line from her bikini today. I reach up, stroking the line with my thumb. I want to suck her there, bite it. I want to leave a mark.

She reaches up, touching her lips, speaking behind them. "You're good at that."

"At what?" I ask, distracted.

"Fake-kissing."

I hum. Nothing about that felt fake.

"Wonder how you kiss when it's real," she whispers.

I'm about to open my mouth and suggest she follow me outside to find out, when a man approaches.

"Anna?"

She pauses, searching his face. After a couple seconds, recognition lights her features. "Holy sh— *Jamie?*"

"Yes, my God, it's so crazy to see you here!" They hug easily and pull away, both smiling.

"No kidding! I'm—" She cuts off, looking around, and her startled eyes meet mine. "West, this is my—well, okay, a little awkward—" They both laugh, sharing some inside joke I don't follow until she says, "My ex."

My body temperature plummets. "Ex. Wow."

"Jamie, please meet my husband, Liam Weston."

We shake hands, smiling, but it's tense. With the way she looks tonight and even if he saw that kiss just now, I'm sure he's thinking about all the times he made love to her. And now I'm thinking of all the times I haven't.

I manage an even "Nice to meet you." He's tall, but I'm taller, and God I know it's childish, but I straighten my spine, emphasizing it. He's also extremely good-looking, with the same kind of easygoing smile that makes it possible to imagine them together.

"You, too," Jamie says, and turns back to her. "Married? And to a Weston! Anna, I swear I never would have called this."

"I'm not sure I'd have called it either back then," she says, laughing. "That and running into you on a private island." To me, she adds, "Jamie and I met in a pottery class."

"She was a virtuoso with her hands," he says, and I know he means it playfully, but the innuendo lingers like a sneering echo. I imagine landing an uppercut that sends him through the ceiling.

"Meanwhile, Jamie finished his project. Pretty much all I can say about that," Anna teases.

"Hey," he protests, laughing. "My grandmother still uses that coffee mug."

"She would have to," Anna says. "That thing was so huge, I'm sure it's still full from the first time she poured coffee into it."

I am not here for this flirting. I step closer, sending my hand around her waist, pulling her into my side. Redirecting, I ask, "Jamie, what brings you to the island for the wedding?"

"My father is the US head of operations for Bimbo, but he's under the weather, so I'm here in his place."

Beside me, Anna startles, delighted. "Did you say 'Bimbo'?"

He nods, laughing, but I cut in. Jamie has had enough screen time. "Grupo Bimbo," I explain. "It's a global food company. They have some American brands now, like Oroweat, Thomas' English muffins, Entenmann's . . . a few others."

Leave it to my father to invite business contacts to his daughter's tropical wedding and use it as a tax write-off.

"I had no idea you'd even gotten married," he says to Anna. "And five years ago, too, wow. I must have been living in a cave."

Some unspoken communication passes between them, some disappointment on his end that he's run into her too late, and I can't read in her silence whether she's sharing his regret. I look down at her, drawing her attention to my gaze.

Fuck, I hope she wasn't dating him when we were roommates.

"When did the two of you . . . ?" I begin.

"Sophomore year," she says quickly, understanding, I guess, the tension in my eyes. "For about six months from, what was it? October to March? Something like that." Anna puts her hand on my stomach in that way I'm starting to like too much, stretching to kiss my cheek. Warmth spreads down my neck. "You and I met that summer and had our whirlwind romance."

I'm relieved that she wasn't dating this guy at any point since she and I got married, but for the first time the broader idea feels sour: of course Anna has been with other men while she's been legally mine.

I can't look away, even when the wake of this thought leaves me feeling both ashamed and increasingly possessive. I want to take her away from this party and find a dark place to kiss her until she's gasping for more.

I realize we've been staring at each other too long only when Jamie leans in, chastely air-kissing her opposite cheek. "Good to see you, Anna. Nice to meet you, Liam. I'm sure I'll see you more this week."

We shake hands and he walks away, but I don't take my arm from where it circles her waist. Instead, I pull her closer.

"You had a little bit of a vibe there," she says, grinning up at me.

"A vibe? I did?"

"A little . . ." She curls her fingers into claws, pretending to growl at me, but my eyes are drawn to the tan line again. "Like you were on the verge of kicking his ass. That was some good acting."

"Well." I look around the room, grateful that Jamie has fully disappeared into the crowd. "He didn't need to comment on your skill with your hands."

"Maybe he just meant I made good coffee mugs in pottery class."

"Do you *think* that's what he meant?"

She laughs, lifting her drink to her lips. Her voice echoes a little when she says, "No, probably not. I do make a great clay mug, though."

"Liam!" my mother crows, approaching with two glasses of champagne. "I have been trying to make my way across the room for *ages*!" She hands me a flute and I expect her to hand the other to Anna, but instead she lifts it to toast only me. "To your anniversary!"

Pointedly, I hand the flute to Anna, who I realize is unfortunately now double-fisting it with her mostly full vodka tonic. With an annoyed glance at me, Mom passes me her flute, and snags one off the tray of a passing caterer.

"I'd forgotten the date, since we never see you together," Mom says, "and when Charlie reminded us tonight, I just thought, 'Oh, we must have a party!'"

"We have a trip planned," I lie. "Anna and I will make a big deal out of it together, but we don't need anything else, truly."

"It would mean a lot to your father and me. He insisted we add something to the wedding itinerary."

I laugh. "Mom, it's already packed."

"We can squeeze in another party."

"There's no—"

Anna cuts me off. "Janet, that would be amazing. Thank you. There are never enough celebrations in life, isn't that right?"

My mom turns her eyes on Anna as if she'd forgotten she was here. "Especially on someone else's dime, I suppose!"

Ice-cold mortification washes me out. "*Mom.*"

She lightly smacks my arm. "I'm just teasing her. I mean, truly, why not fold it into the wedding festivities? It's a great idea, and Charlie wouldn't mind sharing the spotlight."

Anna is flushed red, visibly humiliated.

"Mom," I say, "*you* suggested it. She's just agre—"

"Liam," my dad cuts in, suddenly appearing at my side. "Son, I need you for a minute. I've got the senior editor of *Forbes* over there—"

"Ray, honey," Mom says quietly. "Do we have to do this tonight? It's a party."

"I'm holding a glass of champagne," my father says irritably. "What the hell else do you need me to do?"

"That's my husband, always working. Even at his only daughter's wedding . . ."

I smile with false warmth at my father, but my pulse is still thundering over what my mother did. "We were just talking about the anniversary party you want to throw us."

Dad squints. "The fuck are you talking about?"

Mom threads her arm through his. "*Raymond.* Didn't you hear Charlie just now? Liam and Anna are coming up on five years married."

My dad snorts into his champagne glass. "Call me at twenty. If you're still sharing a bed, then we'll throw you a party."

"Oh God," Anna exhales. Against me, she's shaking from the tension.

Mom does a double take when a catering cart passes, full of some non–Weston brand soft drinks. "*Mystic Cooler?* Not on my fucking watch," she growls, stalking off after it.

"Liam." Dad claps a hand on my back. "Follow me."

He turns without waiting and I look down at Anna and her thousand-yard stare.

I reach for her chin, tilting her face to mine. "Hey. You okay?"

Our eyes meet and when she nods, I see how this must be for her. Raised alone by her father, who, I can tell from the way she talks about him, wouldn't dream of answering even the stupidest of her questions with "The fuck are you talking about?" Would never in his life gaslight her the way my mother just did.

But then, her eyes clear, she straightens, and puts on a brave smile. "I'll be fine. I'll go find Blaire or Jake." She sends her hand down my arm, squeezing my fingers. "Go."

Without thinking about it, I bend, giving her a soft, brief kiss on the lips. Before she can react, I speak into her ear: "You're pretty good at this, too."

Her breath shakes on my neck. "At what?"

"All of it."

$ixteen

LIAM

T here he is," Dad says by way of greeting. "My middle son, Liam, the future CEO of Weston Foods."

My heart comes to a sudden, lurching stop, and I'm unsure how to respond in front of the senior editor of *Forbes*, Ellis Sikora. Throughout my life, Dad has said this to me a hundred times, but given that we haven't spoken in five years—after the fight about my return to school rather than my return to the family company—any rational person would have assumed he'd have given up on me succeeding him at the top. It's one thing to hope I'll come back to Weston Foods; it's another thing entirely to think I'd ever step into his corrupt shoes.

But of course, most people don't know my father the way I do.

In the handful of seconds that follow, my brain cycles through a dozen different responses, trying to estimate the public fallout as well as my dad's reaction to each one. A yes would be binding; a no would make the family gossip fodder and send the stock tanking, not to mention sending my father into a rage in private later. He's daring me to choose which way I want to drag the razor blade across my throat.

What I'm not sure of is why he's chosen to do it now.

So I play his game, sinking a hand into my pocket, adopting an easy posture. "I think it's better for you to keep me on the outside," I say, all corporate chitchat, cagey evasion. "I advise you whenever you ask me to, but you don't have to put me on the payroll."

Both men laugh, but Dad's is forced, his eyes tight.

"He's a professor at Stanford, no?" Ellis asks, and then sips his drink.

"Specializing in corporate culture and ethics. Would be an interesting transition back to C-suite for the family business."

"It's been a great way to get diverse leadership experience," my father agrees, as if the way I broke ties with the company and decided to pursue academia was his idea from the start. "He gets to dabble in his models of corporate harmony shit and learn the ropes of administration constipation, then come settle down in the family business and put it to good use when he's ready."

"I guess he's always had a hand in the family business, though," Ellis says slyly, eyes hawkishly on me. "Even as far back as when you were a teenager, I mean. Liam, the technology you built was objectively extraordinary. I know you've never commented on the PISA scandal, but—"

"And I'm definitely not going to at my sister's wedding," I say, cutting him off and forcing my voice to remain steady. Even the sound of the acronym still sends a chill down my spine, makes me want to sink a fist into my father's jaw. "It's great to meet you, Ellis, and I'm sure there will be plenty of time to talk business after this vacation, right?"

"Right." Ellis lifts his glass to me.

I lift my gaze, searching for Anna. I find her standing near the bar, talking to Jamie. Her dress sparkles in the low light, rendering her a glowing goddess in a room full of mannequins.

Beside me, my father says my name in a way that makes me think Ellis has had to ask me something more than once.

I blink back to him, leaning in. "Sorry. What was that?"

"I said," Ellis says with a smile, "I realize we aren't going to touch on PISA tonight—"

"Or any night," I correct, as much to Ellis as to my father. "Just so we're clear. Even if we were at an event where it felt appropriate to speak on the matter, I wouldn't."

"Okay," he says, not working to mask his disappointment. "I wish you felt differently, but I understand. I'd still love to hear any comments you might have about taking over the CEO role when your father retires."

How about not a chance in fucking hell? I think, but Anna's bright laugh rises out of the din, teasing at my attention. "A statement? Right now?" I look around us, gesturing. "Is this a board meeting? Dad, do we have a quorum?"

Dad laughs heartily at this, but his eyes are still ice. I know for a fact that we don't. Only three of eleven members have arrived, in fact. I've been counting.

"I think any statement would need to be cleared by the board," I tell Ellis. "I know *Forbes* is excited to get some buzz out there, but let's do this the right way, what do you say?" There. Evasive enough, but not a flat-out denial. I hold out my hand, and Ellis takes it with an amused smile. "Have a great time on the island, okay?"

Without acknowledging my father, I turn to leave, intending to walk directly to Anna, but she's no longer at the bar. As calmly as possible, I wander around the party, shaking hands when I'm stopped, saying hello, returning hugs, but everything gets only half of my attention. My mind spirals beyond this moment, beyond this room, wondering what my dad is up to, wondering where Anna has gone. It's then that I notice I don't see Jamie, either.

With tension ratcheting in my gut, I walk out of the restaurant, heading down the trail toward the beach and the bungalows, searching every shadow for her and dreading what I might find: two figures entwined in the shadows, one long and willowy, wearing a dress like a million tiny stars glimmering in the moonlight.

I hear her voice, low and reassuring, her quiet, husky words reaching me in a shapeless murmur, as if she's having a private conversation. My pulse rockets, jealousy raging inside me.

But then I pull up short at the view of her from behind, sitting on a long branch that dives down from the tree and runs parallel to the sand for several feet, forming a perfect natural bench. She's not alone; she has her arm around someone, but it's nothing like I thought.

Beside her is Reagan.

I approach but stop when I hear the telltale sound of a jagged sob.

"There's nothing harder than seeing your friends having fun when you're gone," Anna says soothingly. "Yes, you're on a private island. Yes, you're in paradise. But our hearts don't care. Parents forget what it's like sometimes."

Reagan's voice is thick with tears. "I know I'm lucky to be here! He didn't have to yell at me!" I swear to God, if my brother repeats our father's habits with his kids, I'll beat his ass myself.

"Weddings are stressful for families, you know?" Anna turns to face Reagan, straddling the big branch, so focused on the girl in front of her that she doesn't care if her tiny dress rides up. "A big, expensive event that everyone puts their busy lives on hold for and has to be excited about and engaged in the whole time? I think sometimes parents forget that you had to put your life on hold, too. And it always sucks to see your friends out doing things when you can't be there."

"Julia and I got the outfits together," Reagan says. "We were going to go when I got home. Does she think I won't see her posts? I'm on an island, not Mars."

I have no idea what the hell all of this is about, but obviously Anna seems to. "Maybe Eileen invited Julia?" she asks.

Reagan sucks in an angry breath. "Whatever! They're barely even friends. Julia knows I hate Eileen. She pantsed me in PE last year!"

"She didn't," Anna says with the appropriate level of dismay.

"They suspended her, and she blamed me! She's been so mean ever since." Reagan sends a hand across her tear-streaked cheeks. "She's always trying to start drama with *everyone*. Julia should have said no. She's been *my* best friend since first grade!"

"How about this: when we get back to California, you and I will go to Disneyland in matching outfits, and Eileen and Julia can suck it."

Reagan nods. "Okay."

"Dang it. If I had some paper, I'd show you something I do to make myself feel better."

Reagan reaches into her little sparkly evening bag. "I have one of the welcome programs. Will that work?"

Reagan hands it to Anna, who takes it and pulls something out of her own bag. "Perfect. We wouldn't normally do this with a Chanel lip pencil, but desperate times and all that." Anna turns the program over and lays it flat on her leg. "Before we start, if any adults ask," she says, and I bite back a laugh at the dramatic clearing of her throat, "I am not encouraging you to make fun of someone. That's not what this is about. Even if they maybe, possibly deserve it a little. Got it?"

"Got it."

"Good. How often do you draw?"

"Almost never," Reagan admits with a laugh.

"That's fine," Anna says, smiling over at her. "The nice thing about art is that it can be terrible, and people will still call it art." She bends, beginning a sketch I can't see. "But this here? This is also self-care."

Reagan giggles.

"I had this boss, this guy named Ricky," Anna says, turning the page to come at her drawing from a new angle. "I'd worked for his parents for a few years, but then he took over the store. He was a lot younger than me. Like seven years."

"But you're only like twenty-five."

"Right? With an eighteen-year-old for a boss. And one day, he asked me out on a date."

"He what!"

Anna nods. "I said no, of course, and he fired me not long after."

In the shadows, I suck in a breath to keep from reacting audibly to this. Is this why she was fired the night before I came to her apartment?

"That isn't fair!" Reagan protests.

"It isn't fair, you're right. It's terrible. And there isn't much I can do about it because lawyers are expensive. But you know what? Drawing terrible pictures of him made me feel incrementally better." She turns the paper to face Reagan, who bursts out laughing. "I don't know what Eileen looks like, but you can make it accurate."

She hands Reagan the lip pencil. Reagan works for a bit, before Anna quietly says, "Give her a pimple."

With another giggle, Reagan bends, drawing on the paper.

"Oh, a mustache, love it," Anna says, leaning in. "I'll have to give poor Eileen my waxing lady's number."

Reagan pulls back, admiring their handiwork, and Anna puts her arms around my niece.

"I'm sorry, honey. This is hard, but we'll have as much fun here as humanly possible."

Reagan's next "okay" is muffled by Anna's shoulder, but I hear it anyway, watching her thin, pale arms come around my wife's waist. "Thank you, Auntie Anna." Anna stills for a moment, and I think it hits us both at the same time; she's not just my wife, she's Reagan, Lincoln, Nixon, and GW's aunt, my siblings' sister-in-law, and my parents' daughter-in-law. As an only child, she's never had those things before, and this suddenly feels so much bigger than just the two of us. I knew what I was asking her to give while we were here, but had no idea what I was asking her to give up at the end of this.

Just then, over Reagan's shoulder, Anna's eyes go wide as she spots me, watching her give my niece something I'm sure she rarely gets anymore—the pure, undivided attention of an adult. Anna lifts her fingers in a subtle wave.

What an asshole I was for thinking she snuck out with Jamie. What an archaic, bullshit reaction. I can't help the smile, can't help the thought as it rises like the dark tide only a handful of yards away: it's complicated, but I'm so grateful that Anna's here.

Seventeen

ANNA

Well, West Weston isn't a liar, I can say that much.

A little cuddly? The next two mornings I wake up plastered to him, with one leg thrown lustily over his hips and one arm around his rib cage. And today is the worst. If mornings one through three were cuddling, morning four is a full-body dry hump.

I'm not just plastered to him, I'm on top of him. My legs are on either side of his hips, my face is in his neck, my fancy tank top has ridden up, and my boob is just right there! Pressed to his! Every morning so far we've been super "cool" and very "chill" and not awkward at all as we get out of bed, pretending like I haven't migrated over to his side of the bed. But this morning it takes me exactly seven seconds of drowsy, cozy bliss to realize why I'm so warm, why the bed is so soft, but somehow also really . . . *really* . . . hard?

I peel myself away and carefully—oh my God, so carefully—slide from the bed. I'm sure I leave a boob imprint on his chest. But to be fair, his enormous boner probably leaves a matching imprint on my thigh. I'm doing everything I can to not think too much about that, but Goddamn.

I'm also trying not to think too much about how he gets up ten minutes after me, pulling on running shorts and leaving to go for a jog on the beach barefoot and gloriously shirtless. *Or* about the way he doesn't even make a millisecond of eye contact. Odds are good he's aware that I spent most of the night sleep-humping him, and now I must live the rest of my life with that humiliation.

To distract myself, I reach for the small watercolor palette I packed, my brushes, paper, and a cup of water, and walk out to the balcony to paint the sunrise. The view is just . . . unreal, a horizontal rainbow that touches everything with rose-colored light. Even if I woke up to this every morning for a hundred years, I would never get sick of it. The sight of it changes by the second and, flat brush in hand, I wet the paper and start with a section of cobalt blue near the top, letting the color diffuse at the bottom. I drop in gauzy streaks of raw sienna, rose, and violet. I'm still learning how to paint with these nails, but manage to add my horizon and mirror the sky in the water, laying down a touch of vermilion where the rising sun is most intense.

Despite the ever-present toxicity that is the Weston clan, the trip has been amazing. Yesterday, West and I attempted to escape the oppressively rich crowd and take a boat to one of the smaller islands, but Reagan and Lincoln spotted us on the dock and asked to join us. I've never spent much time with kids before, but it ended up being way more fun than I expected.

West is a great uncle. He's patient and funny, and Linc looks at him with stars in his eyes. While West and Linc attempted to fish yesterday, Reagan and I talked about school and boys, music and life and friends. She showed me the sketch we'd done together and how she'd added train tracks for Eileen's braces, and a conversation bubble over her head that said, "I'm a buttface." I should have done the adult thing and reminded her not to call people names, but that kid pulled Reagan's pants down in front of a gymnasium full of sixth graders; Reagan deserves to be a little salty.

When my phone pings in my backpack, I dig it out, my pulse taking off when I see a text from Vivi.

> Hey favorite.

>> Hey. Is my dad okay?

> He's perfect.

> We just watched the
> Lakers cream the Suns.

> He ate an entire burrito.

> > Oh, that's amazing!

> I was just checking in
> to see if you've banged
> the husband yet.

Well, this is a track change. I stare down at the screen, wondering whether Vivi installed a camera in the robot suitcase and watched me sleep-hump the poor man last night.

> > Absolutely not.

> It's just a matter of time, Anna.

> > No.

I hit Send, and then send another, just to be clear:

> > No.

> There's a story behind
> your need to repeat that.

> > I don't need these
> > ideas in my head!

We kissed the other night.

Oh and we went to a party that was very fancy.

You would have loved it.

Are you trying to distract me from asking about the kissing?

Yes.

How was it?

The kissing, not the party.

His mouth is really great.

Like, REALLY great

But that's not why I'm here!

Isn't it a little bit why you're there?

To fake-kiss him?

I'm being paid to be the perfect wife and so far I'd give me a C-

I think a perfect wife bangs.

Which is why banging could and should happen.

It would definitely knock you up to an A

Vivienne Amir. pls.

Also never say "knock you up" in a fake-wife situation

You wouldn't say that if you weren't already thinking about sex. . . .

Hush

Your last sex was Micah, right?

Micah. A waiter at her parents' café. Very hot. Very unskilled.

Yes. Two stars. Would not return.

Which is honestly such a bummer

He looked like he knew how to read a map but i guess not

> Narrator: Like most men, Micah didn't stop to ask for directions

And now every shift we work together I'm like

Sir I know she left your bed as soon as she could

Like the body wasn't even cold

And he knows I know

And it is all very awkward

> Ok but real talk: Dad is ok?

David is great.

He said he might be up to coming to dinner at the cafe this week.

I almost can't believe the words I'm seeing. Dad eating? Dad getting out of the house for a meal? I'm not always good at managing the white-knuckling fear of losing him, and hearing this makes hope expand inside me until it seems to push every other feeling aside.

But then I look up and see West jogging back down the beach toward me and another feeling shoves its way back in: predatory lady hunger.

> West is jogging on the beach near me.

Vivi replies with a gif of Whoopi Goldberg saying *You in danger girl*, and she could not be more correct.

> OK gotta go actively resist this.

> Love you.

> LYB

Footsteps pad along the bridge, and then West is there, turning the corner onto the balcony. "Hey," he says, wiping a forearm down his sweaty face, and I have the intrusive thought that I wouldn't even need to be dared to lick his chest right now. His nipples are . . . well, I enjoy them. I would like to touch them. Maybe with my boob again.

"Hi."

He walks over, pulling a towel from where it's drying on the railing, and uses it to wipe down his torso.

I'm momentarily devastated but soldier on. "How was the run?"

"Pretty good." He motions to my abandoned paints. "What's this?"

"I was painting the sunrise but got distracted."

"Ah." He rubs the towel over his sweaty hair. "By the way, I wanted to thank you for that."

"For what?" I ask.

"What you've been doing for Regs. I think she often gets lost in the shuffle. I just wanted to tell you, I really appreciate you spending that time with her."

"Are you kidding? She's so much fun. I remember how much it sucks being a preteen. How universal is the experience of life sucking when you can feel like you're missing out even when you're on a private island."

"Yeah."

"So how's it going with your dad?" I say, standing and stretching. West was pretty shaken up after Ray blindsided him in front of the *Forbes* editor. I can't imagine what it's like wanting to avoid your own father.

West hops up onto the railing, sitting with the ocean behind him. It's a glorious view. "He's trying to back me into a corner."

"What I don't understand is why he has such a boner for you being CEO when you clearly don't want the job. Let him give it to Alex. He clearly wants it."

"This has been his plan for as long as I can remember. It's all about his legacy, and what Ray wants. He doesn't want Alex. He obviously thinks my being here at all means I've had a change of heart."

"Oh, sure." I grin up at him. "I mean, why would you be at your own sister's wedding unless it had something to do with him?"

The side of his mouth twitches up. "Sounds like you're now fluent in Weston." His expression straightens. "Speaking of . . . sorry about what my mom did the other night. I guess we haven't talked about it yet."

"You mean about the anniversary party I inadvertently asked for?"

He nods, grimacing. "Yeah."

"I just remind myself I'm here doing a job. I don't ever have to see her again after this."

West swallows and then nods. "Good."

"What about you?" I ask. "If everything goes the way you want this week, will you ever see them again?"

"Occasionally," he says. "But not regularly."

"Not even Jake and Charlie?"

He shrugs a muscly shoulder. "I'll see them, sure. My parents and Alex . . . no."

I study him, trying to piece out what sent West running for the hills after his internship.

"Trying to read my mind?" he asks after a few moments of silence, lifting one side of his mouth in a smile. "Just ask."

Just ask. The two sexiest words ever spoken by an unreadable man.

"You said your dad did something shitty about ten years ago." West nods, his expression turning guarded. "And then you had an internship that cemented that you did not want to come work for the company." He nods again. "Will you tell me more about what happened between you two?"

His brows flicker down as he turns to look out at the water, and I take the opportunity to memorize his profile again. This damaged, hot man. Maybe Vivi is right and sex is the answer for everything.

But when he turns back, his eyes seem so troubled that all sexy thoughts evaporate. "He was a really shitty dad. That much is probably obvious. There are a million stories, of course. Him kicking Lego sets we'd pains-takingly built because we did it in the hallway in front of his office. Alex wet the bed until he was maybe thirteen or fourteen, and Dad would make him hang his wet sheets outside in front of the house because he thought the shame would fix it. Jake broke his ankle during a soccer match and Dad made him walk through the gravel parking lot to the car because he'd let a goal pass and they'd lost the match."

"Jesus," I whisper, finally adding, "And you?"

He shakes his head. "I have plenty of personal grievances, and those alone justify staying far away. But the reason I'm not coming back to work for him isn't one of them. I don't like the way my father runs the business. It isn't one thing; it's a million things every day. But here's an example: One of my responsibilities during my internship was to manage the facilities at headquarters in Irvine. Shift schedules for the hourly workers, mainte-nance, deliveries, et cetera." Absently, he reaches forward, toying with the tie of my bikini that hangs over one shoulder. And I'm trying to pay atten-tion, but his hands are so warm and the fact that he's grounding himself with his fingers on me? That feels . . . incredible.

"There was a manager at the loading dock," he continues, "a guy named César, who'd been with the company for thirty-five years. He was great. Funny, kind, sort of like everyone's grandpa, and he knew the delivery system inside and out. He needed a schedule change in order to take the bus to work." West's thumb strokes down my shoulder and he watches the movement, lost in thought. "His car had broken down, and he had to walk his grandkids to school and asked for a different shift so he could catch the bus. It was one of those simple requests that turned complicated for reasons that aren't interesting, but Dad overheard me discussing the schedule options with my assistant and blew his lid because I was wasting my time on something so menial. His solution was to tell César to get his car fixed and figure it out or find another job."

A breath escapes my lips, and I put my hand over his on my shoulder. "Wow."

"This man was one of his first hires, and he's telling him to find another job because we aren't paying him enough to get his car fixed? Because we can't move a few things around? Dad wouldn't ever bother himself with something like that if he hadn't walked in on me talking it out."

"Right," I say quietly.

"It was such a crystallizing moment," West continues, "because it's so clear to me that it's the people who make the company great, but Dad thinks everything that matters is at the top. Without César, that entire department wouldn't be what it is, the loading dock would be a disorganized mess, and shipments to stores would be disrupted. Moving his shift would prevent all of that." West shakes his head. "Everything about a good business starts at the bottom. Anyway, that divergence in our philosophies combined with everything Dad and I had been through when I was in college . . . I didn't want to stay at Weston's anymore. But I was inspired to find out whether and how corporate culture can be changed. It's why I decided to pursue my PhD and what ultimately sent me and my dad into estrangement."

"It takes a lot of bravery to walk away from the security of an executive position when you're only, what? Twenty-six?"

He exhales a sharp laugh through his nose. "Nothing about interacting with my dad ever makes me feel brave. It makes me feel placating and restrained and disgusted with myself."

"I don't see it that way," I tell him. "Whatever this loophole is, it's important enough to you to come here and do what you have to do."

West meets my eyes, and his gaze clears and then softens. "Yeah." His attention dips to my lips. "Thank you for reminding me."

I take a step closer, moving into his space, and I realize the moment he registers he'd been touching me. His eyes go a little wide, and he gently moves his hand from under mine. "The only answer here is to avoid him for the rest of the trip."

His lips curl in a surprised smile. "Oh yeah? How should I manage that?"

I think it's because he's shirtless and sweaty, or maybe it's because I left my dignity along with my boob prints all over him this morning, but the words bubble right up and out of me: "We could make out the whole time."

Coughing, West squints out to the side, farther down the row of bungalows. "You might be onto something. Jake confirmed that Alex thinks we're full of shit."

"That's probably because we *are* full of shit."

"Well, if he gets wind of what my dad told *Forbes*, he'll figure out a way to prove it."

I angle my eyes over his shoulder and speak of the devil. There, down the beach, is Alex. He's too far to hear anything we're saying, but he's just standing there, looking up at us, watching us interact like tentative strangers having one of their first vulnerable conversations.

There's something in Alex's posture, some *gotcha!* that makes me deeply uneasy.

Without letting it show on my face that I've seen him, I step closer to West, hand high on his bare thigh, just below the hem of his shorts.

West's brows disappear beneath his messy, glorious hair. "Hello."

"Don't look, but Alex is watching us from the beach."

West drags his attention from my hand on his leg to my face. "Oh yeah?"

"Yeah. So I'm just trying to look wifey and horny for you."

"I could go inside and shower," he says quietly. "He'd just walk away."

"You could." I lick my lips, stepping between his legs, shamelessly wanting another of his libido-electrifying kisses. For as much as I dislike Alex in theory, I'm not mad about this moment. West looks like he could use a little distraction. And after we kissed the other night, I thought there'd be more opportunities. I was wrong. "Or you could just pretend to be horny for me, too."

He stares at me, unmoving.

"Or not," I say, smiling while inside I'm dissolving, atom by atom, in mortification.

When I try to step away, he clamps his thighs around my ribs. "Where are you going?"

"To die of shame under a rotting log somewhere."

West laughs, low and frankly dangerous. "No, see, my only hesitation is"—he leans in, running his thumb along my lower lip—"acting was never my strong suit."

"I was a counselor at drama camp." I speak against the pad of his thumb. "I'll give honest feedback."

He laughs, his lips so close. "Thank you."

West's mouth brushes over mine, giving me one of those feather-soft kisses again.

"Well," I say as we share a breath, "that wasn't bad."

He kisses the corner of my mouth. "Anything that could make it more convincing?"

"Maybe another? Longer this time?"

West lifts both hands now, cupping my face and leaning in, pressing a soft kiss to my mouth before he parts his lips and gently nips at my bottom one. "Longer, huh?"

And with just this playful start, he has poured gasoline into my blood-stream. Does he know how fragile my restraint is right now? I am a sex demon in disguise. I am a fembot with only one program. I am only sec-onds away from licking the residue of sweat from his chest. I'm discovering things about myself, such as: I like sweat.

I set both hands on his thighs, stretching onto my toes for more, for longer and deeper, his surprised huffed breath coming out warm against my mouth as he lets me suck that beautiful lower lip, dragging my teeth along it in a way that makes him let go of a tight, helpless sound and which sends one hand into my hair. I fear I'm going to send him toppling back-ward into the ocean, but he leans in just as steadily, squeezing me close with those powerful thighs.

West's mouth is unreal, commanding and firm, but with full, soft lips that beg to be bitten. He likes it when I do, too, releasing rough, rumbling sounds that seem to come from a cave filled with long, unsated need. My hands have a mind of their own, rising up over his hips to come to a stop on the warm solidity of his waist as our kissing ruse turns into an all-out groping session. He keeps one hand firmly fisted in my hair and sends the other down my back to my ass, pulling me close until I feel the hard press of him just beneath my breasts. He lets out a gasping laugh as I drag my teeth along his jaw, down his neck.

"To the contrary, your acting is pretty good," I say, licking the salt of his throat.

He jerks at the contact, tightening his grip in my hair, holding my head close. "Yeah?"

"The erection is a great touch. I mean, *very* convincing."

His laugh turns into a groan when I suck his neck, baring my teeth and pressing down. "Fuck yes."

Well, well. Dr. Weston likes it a little rough.

I get high on his soft, dirty noises, and suck harder, scratching my nails around his back and up past his shoulders where I finally get my hands in that ridiculous head of hair. With his own grip on me, he yanks my head away and, eyes wild, comes for my mouth again, deeper now, setting a pace that is both slower and hotter, languid drags of his tongue over my lower lip, kisses that can only be described as *claiming*.

"God, your mouth is fucking amazing," he says, dragging his teeth to my jaw, biting, sucking at my pulse point.

I have no idea how long we've been at it but my lips are tingly, there's a very insistent boner pressed to my chest (hello again), and my legs are starting to shake from standing on my tiptoes. When I lift my gaze over West's shoulder, Alex is gone. The beach is completely empty. Future me will kick myself for the rest of the day for saying it, but the words slip out: "He's gone."

West exhales shakily near my ear and then rests his forehead to mine. "Well . . . good. I guess we can stop."

"I guess we can." Leaning back and taking stock of him—rumpled hair, swollen lips, scratch marks on his sides, I realize I've also left a small purple bruise on his neck. "Oops."

He frowns at me. "Did you give me a hickey, Green?"

"I might have." I don't miss the way his pupils dilate, inky black in the golden pools of his irises. "Well, the good news is now everyone will know for sure who you belong to."

He laughs. "Unfortunately, Blaire will still grab my ass."

"It's a pretty great ass." I step back, telling my body and brain to calm the hell down.

"Sorry, you're . . ." West gently runs his thumb over my lips one last time. "You're all red from my stubble."

Maybe so, but I'm not the only one who looks like they just went at it pretty hard-core. His neck and chest are flushed, his eyes still burning as he hops from the railing.

I absolutely do *not* look down at his shorts; what kind of a trash goblin do you take me for?

But if I *did* look down, I would see quite a tent happening.

"Careful where you swing that thing."

He laughs wryly. "I'm going to go take a cold shower."

I nod, swallowing down the lusty scratch in my throat. "I'll give you a few minutes of privacy."

He retreats and I pull my phone out of my backpack, texting Vivi:

> SOS. I am so fucked.

*E*ighteen

LIAM

Contrary to whatever Anna thinks I'm doing in the shower, I'm actually lecturing myself: *You fuckwit. You imbecile. You are stronger than this. This absolutely cannot go any further.*

I'll say it as many times as I need to, because it's the truth. Anna and I are two strangers in paradise, experiencing an attraction that absolutely would not persist back home. We are too different—temperaments, lifestyles, ambition, location—and we have one very simple task: fake a marriage. The goal here is to make it through the wedding, return to life as we know it, and quietly divorce in September. The goal here is the clean removal of my father from my life.

But my body continues to deprioritize all that. Last night, I climbed into bed to find Anna curled up on her side, already asleep. She'd been wearing one of those absurd excuses for pajamas that her friend Vivi packed for her—tiny satin straps on her camisole, shorts barely covering her ass—but as I'd pulled back the sheets, I hadn't been transfixed by her body, but by that stupid tan line. I wanted to slide in behind her, press my hips against the soft curve of her ass, draw that strap off her shoulder, and suck at the skin there. That tan line that feels, strangely, like it belongs to me.

And somehow, I ended up with my fingers all over it today without even realizing.

This is the exact brand of thought that I cannot have, but with it back at the forefront, my mind wanders to the feel of her lips gasping open just now when she felt my cock pressed against her chest, of her small, soft tongue licking at mine, so paradoxically gentle while her sharp nails dug a path of fire around my rib cage and up my back. The bite of her teeth on my neck, the bright sting of those nails . . . I wanted more, and harder. It shook me how she could pay such close attention to learn, so quickly, what I like.

I reach forward, shutting off the water, squeezing my eyes closed as the cool droplets run from my hair and down my face. I've hired Anna for a job. Like she said: *I just remind myself I'm here doing a job.* For all intents and purposes, she is my employee, and it's enough that she's having to deal with my family. It's enough that she's forming emotional connections to my niece. I cannot let this turn sexual and risk her getting hurt in other ways.

Unfortunately, the sight of the hickey on my neck in the mirror sends renewed heat across my skin. I carefully lather the shaving cream, drawing the razor slowly over my jaw, remembering the shock of her bite, the slow, searing burn of her mouth sucking at my throat. I give myself to the count of ten to imagine the way I would take her, languid and teasing at first, kissing and licking all of her sweet, aching places, and then hard and fast, pinning her beneath me, ruthless, leaving her eagerly, feverishly clawing at my skin.

That's it, I tell my reflection as I pat my face dry. *That will live only in your imagination. You can kiss when you need to, for show. Not like that. Never like that again.*

I have bigger things to focus on.

Out on the balcony, I expect to find Anna back at work on her sketches, but instead there's a note:

Going snorkeling with Reagan! See you later.

I blow out a breath, saying, "Thank fuck," aloud even though a betraying twinge of disappointment snakes through me. And the feeling darkens when I glance at my watch and realize that in five minutes,

I have to meet the groomsmen—including both fathers—for the suit fittings.

CHARLIE HAS CHOSEN CREAM linen for the groomsmen, and I trust that she knows what she's doing, because in this heat and humidity, I suspect it will be only a half hour before the wedding party looks like a collection of wadded-up newspaper.

But there's food and drinks and a mostly great group of guys. We're in the groom's prep room, a wide, bright space where a few tailors have set up for the day. My father and Alex aside, Kellan and his best friend, Nate, are hilarious together. Add in Jake, and the room gets loud with overlapping accent impressions, stories of Kellan's pre-Charlie mistakes in romance, marital predictions that I probably don't want to hear, and laughter.

"How are the toasts coming?" Kellan asks. The Weston brothers have each been tasked with a short speech at the wedding. Alex will probably use his time to kiss Dad's ass. My speech will be thoughtful, sentimental, and most importantly, short.

Jake is the wild card. Given the way he was expected to be either charming or invisible as a child, my baby brother never misses an opportunity to be the center of attention in a crowd, and standing on a wooden pedestal at the front of the room is his time to shine.

"Oh, I have mine ready," he says, grinning at his reflection. The tailor continues to move around him, pinning and measuring, but Jake will not be deterred. "I thought I'd start with something like, 'When I was four years old, our mom said we were getting a present. The best, most exciting present ever. When it turned out Mom didn't mean we were getting a dog, I took Charlie to the neighbor's house and offered to trade.'"

Laughter fills the room.

"Or I could talk about the time when I was twelve and we were watching *Forrest Gump*. After the movie, Charlie looked at me and asked what

I thought the most important lesson from the movie was. Wanting to be a good big brother, I told her I thought it was about never underestimating yourself. Now, I should have prefaced this story with a few things," he says, adjusting his tie. "First, I had blood sugar issues as a kid, and couldn't eat a lot of sweets. Second, I had two older brothers who gave me copious amounts of shit, so I spent a fair amount of time giving it to Charlie. So, this adorable little eight-year-old looks up at me with her big, innocent eyes and says, 'No, the most important lesson is that life is like a box of chocolates. Do you know what that means, Jakey? It means that you're fucked.'"

The room erupts. Finished with his fitting, and like the great performer that he is, Jake grins widely and steps off the podium to head my way. Unfortunately, this is also the moment he zeroes in on my neck.

"Wait a minute, wait a minute," he says, quieting the room as he leans in to get a better look. "Hold the phone. Does my big brother have a hickey?"

Catcalls surround us and I shove him away, feeling my skin heat under my collar.

"Not surprised," Alex calls from his side of the room. "They were putting on quite a show earlier." He lowers his voice: "You'd never catch me behaving like that."

"Yeah, your wife has mentioned this once or twice," Jake says, and the laughter starts up again.

Oblivious to the jovial atmosphere in the room, Dad steps up beside me at the long mirror and doesn't waste any time. "What kind of bullshit was that last night with Ellis?"

"It wasn't the time or place, Dad." The tailor approaches, crouching to adjust the unfinished hem of my dress pants. "It's not the time now, either."

The last thing I want is for Alex to hear any of this and mistake whatever it is for me gunning for the CEO role.

But my father doesn't pick up on the cue. "Are you fucking kidding, Liam? More business happens at a wedding than at a weeklong conference at a Hilton. Why do you think I have half of these people here?"

"To celebrate the beginning of your only daughter's life with Kellan McKellan?" I unbutton the collar of the shirt and then tug my cuffs down in the linen sport coat, looking at the tailor. "Could we lengthen the sleeve on the coat a bit?"

Nodding, the tailor helps me out of it and pins a note with measurements to the sleeve. I'm done with my fitting, and despite all the laughter and how much I needed a little time to think about nothing, I am suddenly, keenly ready to get out of here.

My father stops me from leaving with a hand on my arm. "This has to be settled."

"It is settled, Dad." I glance across the room to make sure Alex hasn't heard. "And regarding last night, it is absolutely *not* going to go over with the board if you soft launch me in front of the editor of *Forbes* as your successor without their input."

When I look back, my eyes meet Dad's in the mirror. "Are you saying yes, then?" he asks.

"How—I mean, how on earth does that translate to yes?" I run my thumbnail along my eyebrow, trying to keep my cool in this crowded room. "Dad. I'm not coming on board. I have no idea why you would think that."

"You're the only person in this family who has what it takes to do this job."

I stare at my father in shock. There are about a million things I want to say in response, but what comes out is the one I would want to say the very least: the most vulnerable. "Then why did you throw me to the wolves?"

There's a shocked pause, and then my father tosses his head back and laughs. "Oh, it's going to be this sob story again."

I can't do this.

Mute with rage, I change back into my shorts and T-shirt, forfeiting the rest of the time together with the other men for the sake of my sanity. I hug Kellan, shake Mr. McKellan's hand, and pat Jake's shoulder as I pass.

He starts to ask why I'm leaving, but one look at my face and he knows. He glances to Dad and I see my younger brother in action, the way his mind wildly searches for an anecdote, a joke, some story to divert the path from potential explosion and back to good times as I make a quiet exit.

It's a ten-minute walk back to the bungalows, but I get only five of them in peace.

"When are you going to grow up?" my father calls from only a few feet behind me.

I keep walking.

"I'm not going to have expanded my father's business into what it is today only to see it crumble in the hands of my three sons!"

"That's the point, Dad," I say over my shoulder. "You have two other sons already working with you."

"Alex is a fucking head case!" my father booms, and the words echo down the path.

He didn't even bother to consider Jake, and I laugh humorlessly. "Maybe if you did more than humiliate him once in a while, he wouldn't be."

He snorts. "Like you're one to talk."

"I'm not his father."

We walk in tense silence, emerging onto the beach, walking toward the wooden footpath leading to the bungalows.

"If this is about PISA—" he starts, but I immediately cut him off with a low, growled, "I'm not fucking talking about PISA with you, Dad."

"What do you want from me? A hug and an apology?" He laughs incredulously. "You know why we handled it that way. You were a kid. A fucking child when you made that software. You would rather I shoulder the blame and watch the entire company fall apart because of what happened with a thing *you* created?"

I wheel on him, white-hot with fury. "You and I both know it was never created for that. So, *yes*. I expected you to shoulder the blame because what ended up happening was *your fault*."

"So that's why you skulked away?" he sneers. "Took the limp-dick route through life instead? Went to school to prove to the world what a nice guy you are, that you couldn't possibly have been behind all that ugliness because deep down you're a jacket-with-elbow-patches good guy who teaches a bunch of rich virgins about how to be a nice executive when they get their first seven-figure salary?"

"I had to redeem myself!" I yell. "I had to run as far away from that world as possible just so I could—could—could imagine a time when everyone we knew wasn't talking about me and what they thought I'd done. I had to find a way to get myself out of the business section of every newspaper in the world. At twenty, Dad. *Twenty.* None of the blowback ever touched you, and you never even fucking acknowledged it."

Dad's expression morphs. His teeth pull back into a grotesque sneer. "You want a thank-you? Fuck you. You want an apology? *Fuck you.* The only reason you exist is because of what I gave you. The only reason you can live is because of my money." He steps closer, getting in my face, his spit hitting my chin as he huffs out a derisive laugh. "Do you forget? Everything I gave you, I can take away just as fast. I own you. Every single one of you."

He shoves past me down the path toward his bungalow and I feel the planks beneath my feet vibrate with the force of his footsteps.

He has no way of knowing how direct a hit that was. That he's got me in the soft underbelly, my biggest fear, that it won't just be my life I'll ruin, it will be all of ours. I haven't felt this close to crying since I was twenty years old and my entire world shattered around me. I never wanted to go back to this feeling, and yet here we are. I can't avoid it if he's nearby. I just can't.

Shaking, I turn down the bridge toward our bungalow.

But the sight of Anna staring down from the upper balcony pulls me up short. The look in her eyes, the devastation gleaming there . . . she heard all of that. Or at least enough to know it was messy and painful. Enough to question what the fuck PISA is, what the fuck I did, what my father did, what on earth could have happened between us eleven years ago that has angry, ashamed tears burning the surface of my eyes.

I don't want to talk about it. I don't ever want to go back to that time in my life. But when she comes down the stairs, hurrying, like she's in a rush to get to me, I let go of all the rational hesitations, the reality of our circumstances, and walk faster, too, desperate to get to her. We crash together with her two steps above me on the stairs, pulling me into her arms. Wordlessly, she presses my face to her ribs and holds me, whispering a soothing "Shhh, it's okay" against the top of my head. I send my arms around her hips, curling into her as I shake. I don't know what she can possibly be thinking, and for the moment, I don't care. I have never needed anything more than I need this, from her, right now.

$\mathcal{N}$ineteen

ANNA

I have always been an oversharer. Whether I slept badly, am experiencing some minor tummy upset, or have strong emotions about the ending of a long-running TV series, chances are, if you ask, I'm going to tell you how I feel. If someone doesn't really care how I am, then why not just say hello and go about it? I prefer honesty, I prefer openness, I prefer *real*. I know I'm lucky to have been raised by a dad who impressed upon me the importance of sharing my emotions, but I don't think I realized just how lucky until I was surrounded by a half dozen dysfunctional Westons.

It's not that family breakfast the next morning is awkward, exactly, but the elephant in the room—that Ray Weston is a controlling, narcissistic asshat and his entire family has to make excuses for his behavior and accommodate his moods—is impossible to ignore. Everyone is walking on eggshells. People cut their food delicately, with intense focus, asking about the weather, remarking upon the size of the waves down on the beach, laughing loudly at his jokes that aren't particularly funny. Charlie is getting married in a matter of days; she is about to embark on the emotional journey of her lifetime with a man who gazes at her like she's made of stardust, and somehow Ray is the center of attention. No one is asking Charlie and Kellan anything about their nerves, their hopes, their shared dreams.

Just watching ten seconds of this family at a meal, even if Liam had told me nothing at all about them, I'd know Jake Weston was the charming underachiever who evaded his father's attention, Alex Weston was the intense pleaser who chased his father's attention, and Liam Weston was the golden child who naturally exuded the kind of capability and virtue that a narcissist gloms onto and takes credit for. I'm sure West rarely rocked the boat, and I'd bet all the money he's paying me that his decision to pursue a doctorate and the almost five-year estrangement that followed was his first real bird flip to his shitty dad. Which, good for him.

And yet, here we are.

Next to me, West stares out at the water, chewing a bite of egg-white omelet so thoroughly I think it ceases to exist as matter. When he senses my attention, he blinks over to me, gaze unfocused, and returns my smile with a distracted, flickering one of his own. But even if he's mentally aloof, physically, he's close: his shoulder is pressed against mine; he eats with his left hand and has his right hand planted firmly on my upper thigh. It's supposedly all for show, but news flash, Dr. Weston: nobody can see your hand under the table.

It didn't surprise me that he put himself back together almost immediately after our hug yesterday. He's clearly been taught that feelings are bullshit and the only action that's acceptable is one that benefits his father. "I'm gonna grab more coffee and then we can go," he says. "Want anything?"

"I'm good."

West stands from the bench and his spot is immediately filled by Blaire.

She nods to West's retreating form. "Somebody seems a little tense this morning." My eyes immediately drop to her boobs, and my goodness that's a lot of cleavage for brunch. "Bad sex earlier?"

I choke down a sip of my ice water. "Um . . . no."

"Yeah. I'd guess not." She takes a long drink from her mug. Something tells me there's more than just coffee in there.

"Blaire, can I ask you a question? Weston wife to Weston wife."

She slides closer, a devious glint in her eye. "Kinky."

"No," I say with a laugh. "About the family."

She picks up a fork and takes a bite of West's abandoned omelet. "That's less exciting, but let's hear it."

"Is it always like this between Ray and the guys?"

"You mean like a lion ready to devour its young at any moment?"

"Yeah," I say.

"Unfortunately." She sets down West's fork. "But you learn how to navigate it, you know?" She takes another long drink, draining whatever's in her cup. "The first time I visited House Lannister," she says with a smirk, "Alex was a nervous wreck. I'm sure you've seen how he gets with his dad, and I know I can be a handful. I'd already met Janet and Ray, of course—I'd worked for the company for three years by that point—but I was officially being introduced as The Girlfriend." She lowers her voice. "I was also fifteen weeks pregnant at the time, so you can imagine that didn't help. Janet was so catty, my lord. Just scathing. I've always lightened my hair and she asked if I'd considered dyeing it brown, because the blond wasn't doing my intelligence any favors. I was also pregnant, like I mentioned, and already starting to show, though nobody knew it was anything but a few extra pounds. That first night at dinner, Janet called me voluptuous and talked about how lucky I was because she'd never been able to put on weight."

"Yikes."

"She tried to clarify that she merely meant curvy, darling," she says with an affected accent. "She said it was admirable that I could eat whatever I wanted without feeling guilty, and she was *so glad* I wasn't one of those girls who stressed constantly about their weight, because why would I care about being skinny anyway? It's so boring!"

I whistle through my teeth.

"It's not all terrible, though," Blaire says, and then winces. "I mean, okay it *is*, but there were funny moments, and I know you'd never believe this, but when he's not with his parents, Alex is so much more relaxed. They really do bring out the worst in each other."

"I can see that," I say, even though honestly, I can't imagine a funny, relaxed Alex.

"But, you know, the money certainly helps, and the good news with a messy family is that there's never a dull moment." She picks up West's fork again and then pauses with it hovering in the air as she remembers something. "Oh my God, there was this one night Ray was just going on and on at Sunday dinner about some beef with an executive, and everyone was on edge. Charlie was away at school and Liam hadn't been around for a while, but Jake was there and he'd brought a girl with him—which *never* happens."

"I wonder why."

"Lincoln was only a few months old, and I couldn't drink because I was breastfeeding. I was about to murder everyone, so I excused myself to the downstairs powder room. I wasn't the only one with that idea because I open the door and there's Jake and his date and he's got his hand completely up her skirt. I'm telling you he was wearing that girl like a mood ring."

I have to cover my mouth to contain the laugh.

A waiter materializes at Blaire's side and places a mimosa in front of her. She smiles up at him with gratitude and turns her attention back to me. "Listen, if I could have disappeared into that bathroom with them, I would have. But like I said, you get used to the weirdness. And you're doing great. Everyone loves you."

"But is this healthy?" I say quietly. "It's not my place to say, but Ray is pretty terrible with the guys."

"He is. You didn't hear it from me, but I think they're all waiting him out. I know Alex is. Ray will announce his retirement soon and Alex will step in."

Acidic guilt crawls up my throat and I have to swallow it down. So everyone in the family except West is expecting Ray to pick Alex as his successor? Blaire lifts her champagne flute and takes a sip of her drink before leaning in and lowering her voice. "Ray can golf all day or whatever he does and be someone else's problem. But between us, I'd prepare yourself for Ray to start turning the screws on Liam."

"You mean pressuring him to come back to the company?"

She hums. "As COO. Ray's dad, Albert, was a real stickler about family and wanted them all working together. Family is everything to the Westons.

Now that Liam is back, I can't see Ray letting him go again. Frankly, I'm surprised he let him stay away as long as he did."

BACK IN THE BUNGALOW, West and I are quiet for a little while, each doing our own thing, and it's nice. It's easy. He's even-tempered, resilient, and deeply capable—a combination that is so rare it's no wonder the Ray Westons of the world try to drain him of every good thing he creates and gobble it down into their rotten, fiendish mouths. I never want to be like that with him. I see his goodness and only want to protect it. I think of what Blaire said and I'm ready to challenge Ray Weston to a duel.

"So," West says, startling me and setting his phone on the table. "What do we have going on this afternoon?"

"How could you forget?" I ask, spreading my arms wide and singing, "Spa day!"

West groans. "No."

"I'm not saying, but maybe I'm sort of saying, that there is one person in this bungalow who could absolutely use a massage and his name isn't Anna Green."

West scrubs his face with his hands. "This island is shrinking down to the size of a shoebox."

"Well . . ." I have nothing useful to say to that, so I just pat his shoulder amiably as I walk by and climb onto the bed. "You should know I've been going over the treatment menu like I'm studying for a test."

"What do you mean?"

"I feel like this crowd is very spa-literate. I don't want to stumble over the words when I ask for the color vibration therapy or red pepper lipolysis."

West works on untangling a mess of cords he's pulled out of his backpack. "They can't possibly be that intense about these things."

"*Qué?* Are you joking? Not intense? This spa has a whole menu of things you can put in your *nose.* Is that normal?"

"I'm sorry, what?"

"Yes," I say, reading from the pamphlet. "'An ancient Ayurvedic practice called Nasya is the nasal administration of medicinal herbs and oils to clear sinus congestion and expel toxins from the head and neck.'" I read farther down. "Oh, this is good: 'Because the nose is the gateway to the brain, you'll relax knowing you're treating your mind and your body together.'"

"This . . ." His frown deepens. "I don't know if you should choose to ingest any oils this way, Anna."

"Hello, I'm pretty sure I'm the medical doctor in the family." I grin at him. "I will, of course, be putting nothing in my nose." I look back down at the menu pamphlet. "I know I'm probably overthinking this, but I've never been to a fancy spa before. Unless you count the one Vivi took me to before I came here." I cup my hand next to my mouth, adding in a loud whisper, "The waxing one."

His brows flicker up as he goes back to untangling the cords. "Ah."

"I swear I blacked out after one particularly delicate part of the Brazilian. At one point they had me get on my hands and knees and—"

"I'm going to stop you there," he says gruffly, but when I look at him, he's fighting a smile. I bite my lip to force the laughter down, but it fails, and the sound bubbles up and out of me, a rolling belly laugh. West breaks, covering his eyes with a hand. "Jesus Christ, Green, the shit you say."

"I just wanted to hear that sound," I confess. "I didn't really have to get on my hands and knees to be waxed. But I did have to hold on to my ankles like—"

He holds up his other hand, laughing hard. "Stop."

I want to hug him again. The urge feels like a breath held in, the tension ratcheting up with every passing second. But there's an invisible force field there now. I don't know how I know, but I do.

Finally, he gets his smile wrangled and looks over at where I've composed myself. "What are you worried about? The rules? The price? It's all-inclusive. You can get anything you want."

"It's just the intimidation factor. That's all. All the fancy ladies."

West runs a finger below his lip. "You'll be okay, you know. You come across as incredibly sure of yourself." Now, this I can't believe, and I make a dorky face. "And right now?" he adds. "You look very fancy. Don't let them intimidate you."

I look down at my beautiful blue-and-white floral sundress. "That's just clothes. Not me. Stop trying to distract me with your flirting. Are you going?"

"I think all the groomsmen are scheduled for something."

"Are they splitting up the guys and girls?"

"I assume so."

I push out my lower lip in a pout, but stand, checking the time on my phone. Strange that the Westons chose an island that specifically prides itself on its lack of schedules and then created a packed itinerary. "I guess I'll see you later? At dinner? We have that Old Hollywood party tonight, right?"

He trains his gaze over my shoulder, staring at the wall, deflating. "Yeah."

I don't know why I do it; I probably shouldn't. Everything about his posture since yesterday screams, *Leave it.* But I'm terrible at leaving it. So, on my way out the door, I bend down, pressing my lips to his warm, smooth cheek. "I know this trip is draining, but I'm here with you. Try to relax and enjoy today—you deserve it. I'll see you tonight."

I'm sure I went too far. I am being too intimate, feeling too protective of a man who doesn't need protection. Besides, no matter how good the kissing is, we aren't *really* married. I mean, we are legally, but not, like, emotionally or—even sadder—biblically. With a smile plastered to my face, I leave before I can make it weirder, walking straight out of the bungalow and onto the beach.

$\mathcal{T}$wenty

ANNA

The paradox of a fancy spa on a private island, of course, is that you are meant to immediately feel relaxed and calm, but I'm not sure I've ever been more stressed in my entire life.

Not to be dramatic, of course. It's just that on my walk over, I can't stop mentally tabulating all the ways I might completely fuck things up. Blaire was delightful and surprisingly down-to-earth, but she was an outsider. Today I have to breach the inner circle. I have to be in an intimate and chitchatty setting with West's mother and sister. They could ask me something as simple as his shoe size and the only answer I'd be able to muster would be a wink and a "way above average."

Much like the other buildings on the island, the spa prides itself on being eco-conscious and powered by solar and wind. The interiors are bamboo, reclaimed wood, and polished stone. It's clear that the primary inspiration is water, which is creatively used, as a small stream cuts through the floor and meanders down the center of each room. Hydroponic plants cling to the surface of a large water feature that covers most of the main lobby wall, and you can see the roots stretching into the trickling fountains.

When I walk in, an employee greets me warmly and escorts me to the plush lounge where a cluster of women already sit in fluffy robes and slippers, sipping champagne. Conversation halts at my entrance, and even though I'm wearing a Tom Ford sundress and Givenchy sunglasses that cost more than my rent, I still feel like I don't belong here. No one in this room has their natural hair color, I'm sure of it, but none of these women would *dare* go bubblegum pink. Every head looks perfectly coiffed and natural: sun-kissed gold, inky black, warm mahogany.

I'm sure, too, that no one in this room has ever had to choose between filling up their gas tank and buying groceries. I'm sure no one in this room has ever been afraid to open their mail or cried under their kitchen table over the stress of unpaid bills. I'm sure no one here has ever walked into a room and wondered whether they belong.

I suddenly want West in here with me so acutely that it feels like a fist pressed against my breastbone.

But then Charlie sees me, hurrying over to throw an arm around my neck and pull me close. "Anna! You're here!" She pulls back and looks at me, smiling with genuine warmth. "I have been so excited for sister time! Everyone!" She turns, keeping her arm around my shoulders. "This is my sister-in-law Anna!"

The word *sister* presses on something else in my chest. As an adult, I have never, not for a day, wished I had a different childhood. There wasn't much money, sure, but there was always laughter, love, and fun. My dad was the only child of a single mother who passed away too young, so what I didn't have was siblings, grandparents, cousins. Hearing Reagan call me *Auntie* plucked at that hidden thing, a secret wish I had to expand my own circle, to be connected the way only real family can. And it's not his fault, of course, but it's not lost on me that the very thing West has tried to distance himself from—his family—is the one thing that I always wanted. Just . . . not all of them.

I have to remind myself that this non-thing between us is temporary anyway, because with Charlie's arm wrapped tightly around my waist and her joy like a living creature in the room, it's easy to forget.

As a result of Charlie's obvious approval, faces that were pinched or distant begin to relax into smiles. Murmurs of "Oh, this must be Liam's wife" reverberate around us. Some women even look at me with grudging envy. I know it can't be true, but it feels like the air itself warms a few degrees.

Janet unfolds herself from her chair, floating like a vampire across to me, where she delivers a kiss to the air on either side of my face. "Hello, darling. Nice of you to come."

"Thank you for including me."

Stepping back, she takes in my outfit. "I love that you will just wear *anything*. Good for you, dear. Really," she says, patting my cheek. "So brave."

"Um . . ." I tuck my hair behind my ear. "Thank you."

With a wan smile, she drifts off as the spa manager peeks in to coordinate who is doing which treatments with whom. Charlie gives me one more squeeze before returning to a couch full of adorable twentysomethings who are almost exactly my age but somehow feel a decade younger.

And I am once again standing alone, feeling like a complete impostor.

A group of deep voices rises up as the groom's party passes the women's lounge, and I catch Jake's eye. With a little smile, he makes a detour, peeking his head into our lair. "Is everyone decent?" he calls flirtatiously.

A few giggles erupt from the couch, and I meet him in the doorway, grinning at him. "I think you have a few fans in here," I say quietly.

"It's the Leighs," he explains.

"I'm sorry, the who?"

He lifts his chin to indicate where the bulk of Charlie's bridal party sits, their size-zero bodies all smooshed together on the sofa. "Ashley, Haylie, Kayleigh, and Just Leigh," he says.

"Surely you jest."

"I jest not."

"How many have you bedded?" I ask in a whisper. Jake squints at me, and I gasp. "No."

His squint turns into a wince. "Yes?"

"All four?"

"Only three," he corrects.

"'Only'?"

"How are things going with Liam?"

"Nice redirection, you slut," I say, laughing.

"Who's the slut, you hickey demon?"

"Oh, you saw that, did you?"

Jake laughs. "We all saw it."

"He's . . . surprisingly adorable."

Jake's expression flattens. "Adorable? He's a cyborg."

"Well, whoever managed the installation of his emotional programming did a great job."

"I think that's called 'therapy.'"

A shadow appears behind Jake, approaching with determination through the spa's small lobby. Jake startles as West appears at his side, breathless, looking down at me. The room behind me quiets.

"Hello, Liam," Jake says dryly.

"Hi," West says, putting a hand over his brother's face and unceremoniously moving him aside. He gazes down at me, saying more gently now, "Hi."

"Hello." I smile. "Did I forget the lunch you packed me for school?"

A tiny smile is there and gone. "I wanted to tell you to enjoy yourself at the spa today."

"We already did the 'Have a good times,'" I whisper.

But I can't help it, I press my hand to his stomach, wrapping my fist around the soft fabric of his T-shirt. This is all very cute and unexpected. I look briefly at Jake like, *See? Adorable.*

With a smirk, Jake wanders off. But West touches a finger to my chin, redirecting my attention to his face. And before I can say anything, he bends, setting his lips softly on mine. One soft kiss, and then another. My blood turns to smoke, and I lean in, chasing his lips when he slowly straightens.

"You left before I could do that," he says.

Is this all for show? Or is this real? It's so wild that I can't tell at all. He's said it quietly—it can't have been for anyone else to hear—but then again, he's found me in a crowded room. I pull on the reins of my emotions, reminding myself to not sprint ahead. Kisses aren't feelings.

But . . . what if they are?

"I . . ." I clear my throat. "Thank you for fixing my mistake."

Those honeyed eyes crinkle at the corners in a tiny smile. "You're welcome."

The intensity of West's expression is like an aphrodisiac. If he doesn't get out of here soon, I might end up slobbering all over his neck again, but this time in front of his mother and sister.

"Now go get pampered," I tell him, lifting my chin in the direction Jake wandered off. "And relax. Get those hobbit feet scrubbed."

Liam looks like he'd rather eat a large rock, but he does, stepping back and finally turning to walk toward the men's lounge. I'm sorry to see him leave but allow myself the pleasure of watching him go. Whew, dat ass.

I turn around to find a roomful of women pretending to not have watched that entire interaction, but after that kiss, I honestly don't care.

Twenty-One

ANNA

I am pleased to say that I don't stumble over my spa menu selections. I have the manicurist shorten my nails just a little, and then enjoy a total body scrub and a divine hot oil Swedish massage from a man named Bern whose hands are so strong I think he could crumple me like a piece of paper in his fist. The pampering lasts about three hours, and at the end of it, I smell amazing and am slippery enough to fit through a boba straw.

The spa hostess leads me to the relaxation area, handing me a glass of ice-cold cucumber water. "Please, enjoy all of our amenities for the rest of the day. The steam room and sauna are down that hall. The mineral pools are this way." She gestures down a second hall. "We recommend starting with warm and working your way to the ice-cold plunge."

"Plunge," I repeat numbly.

"We've put your belongings in a locker." Gently, she fits the elastic key ring around my wrist, predicting, accurately, that I'm unable to coordinate motor functions beyond holding my arm out for her.

For a few seconds after she leaves, I'm overwhelmed with options. Mineral pools? Ice plunge? A sauna? In this main room, a hot tub gurgles invitingly. I want to live in this boneless, jelly feeling a little longer but am worried if I slip into that warm water, I'll pass out and drown.

Steam room it is.

Inside, I find something unexpected: Janet Weston, completely naked. And, on the other side of the long, narrow room is Blaire Weston, also completely naked but perhaps less of a surprise. They're sitting on their towels on the teak benches, eyes closed and heads resting against the wall, but when I enter, their eyes drowsily open.

"Hello, Anna," Janet murmurs sleepily.

"Hi. Okay if I join you?" I ask, because it feels like nakedness requires an invitation, and it's not like I can just turn around and leave without making it weird. But do I get naked, too? Wouldn't that also be weird? Or would it be weirder to sit down in this thick, fluffy robe and slowly sweat to death in it?

"Come on in, hon," Blaire says, patting the bench right beside her, even though there is a long, unoccupied bench between them.

With my breath tight in my chest, I loosen the tie at my waist and quickly slip the robe off, hanging it on the wall peg beside Janet's and Blaire's. Working to not crouch over with an arm over my boobs and a hand over my privates, I ignore the press of their eyes on me as I quickly walk to the empty bench, laying a towel down, and sitting. I'm positive they saw my butt crack and am so thankful eighteen-year-old Anna never got the Elmo ass tattoo she'd fallen in love with while high on mushrooms. My heart is a squirrel in my chest, scrambling madly.

How does one sit naked in a steam room, postmassage? Not with their legs crossed, as I very quickly learn. My legs slide apart the moment I try, my left one making an audible slap as I return it to the bench. I glance at Janet and mimic her posture but am convinced I look like I'm sitting miserably in the principal's office.

"Mmmm," Blaire moans, a little too sexually to not be awkward. "This is heaven."

"It sure is," I agree brightly, like we're sipping lemonade on the veranda. I wipe a drop of sweat when it rolls down my forehead and onto my eyelid.

"About your anniversary dinner," Janet cuts in, her voice rising out of the quiet. "Unfortunately, I don't think there will be time for a big to-do. We'd like to keep the focus on Charlie."

I stammer out a few sounds before settling on "Of course you would. It's her wedding."

She opens one eye, studies me coolly, and then closes it again. "I hope you're not too disappointed."

Blood rushes hot to my cheeks, making me feel lightheaded. Is this gaslighting? I think this is textbook gaslighting. "Oh, to be clear, West and I didn't expect you to do anything."

"No?" She adjusts her hands on her lap. "I must've misunderstood you the other night."

I don't even know what to do with my face right now. I glance at Blaire, who is looking right at me. When our eyes meet, she mouths a sympathetic "Don't worry about it," and I feel better, but still stunned.

"I did order a case of Liam's favorite wine," she says and seems to wait for me to provide the name, though the only wine I can think of is Boone's Farm and I'm pretty sure that's not it. "Mount Brave cab," she supplies, finally.

"That's the one." I snap, but my fingers just slip across each other soundlessly and I really fucking hope neither of them watched me do that. "That's very nice of you."

"Any thoughts on grandchildren?" she asks, a hard-thrown curveball, and this time I know there's no use schooling my expression. I look over at Blaire, who is just laughing quietly to herself.

"We, uh," I say, before coughing. "It's been busy. With the doctor things I have on my calendar. But we're definitely trying. Very hard."

"I bet y'all are," Blaire says, and winks at me. "You've got that newlywed glow, even after all this time." She adjusts her posture. "The quiet ones are the wildest, aren't they? I've seen Liam's arms. I bet that man hoists you up and—"

"Blaire." Janet reaches up, delicately wiping her brow. "Honestly."

Blaire winks at me, and I'm glad we're in a steam room and that I'm already red. The idea of West hoisting me up in his arms during sex is . . . *whew*. It's a lot.

"What was he like when he was younger?" I ask Janet.

"Liam?" she asks. "Oh, he was a good boy." She pauses, smiling to herself. "The best boy, in fact. Protective, loyal, devoted." Her expression straightens, and after a moment of silence, she stands, sauntering in her impressive nudity to the wall. "He would do anything to protect the people he loves. Remember that."

Janet slips on her robe and then looks at me levelly, saying, "Be good to him, Anna," before ducking out of the room.

I don't know why this hits me so hard, in such a tender place. I remind myself once again that West isn't my husband in the ways that matter. I shouldn't let myself get wrapped up in this complicated, fucked-up family, especially since I have so much of my own complicated, fucked-up nonsense to figure out the second I land on US soil. But my heart doesn't care that this isn't my business; the odd combination of sadness and brittle love in Janet's voice still makes me want to cry.

BLAIRE CHEERS ME UP with more anecdotes about what Janet was like when Blaire and Alex first went public with their romance. There were holidays that felt like final exams, miscommunicated dates and times meant to make Blaire look disorganized and irresponsible, and cutting insults murmured under her breath. I can imagine myself pledging my undying devotion to Blaire, but then she loses all credibility when she reassures me that, despite how prickly she can be, Janet is one of her best friends now. Which is a nice enough lie but frankly does me no good, since I don't plan on being around long enough to get us out of the Mother-in-Law Hazing phase anyway.

When I start feeling a little lightheaded from the steam, I slip back into the security of my robe and duck out, finding my way back to the relaxation room.

The dim retreat smells like eucalyptus and mint, has candles flickering on every flat surface, and includes a large assortment of inviting couches, chaises, and plush chairs. It also has only one occupant now, one Dr. West Weston in the back corner, wearing a fluffy robe and resting with his eyes closed, head settled against the back of the broad chair. I don't want to wake him, but the bamboo-wind-chime-vibe music playing in here doesn't cover much sound, and my fresh glass of cucumber water and ice tinkles in my hand when I lift it for a sip. West opens one eye, and then two, and his face breaks into a smile that looks so genuine it makes my heart hiccup.

"Hey," he says, all warm honey and sex.

"Hey." I shuffle over to him and set down my glass. "Don't you look cozy."

"You look like you've been sleeping in the forest for a month." He bites his lip. "Your hair is a pink bird's nest."

I reach up, touching it. "It is, in fact, a newly protected Indonesian wildlife habitat."

He laughs, reaching for my hips and angling me down onto the chair with him.

"Hello, what're you doing?" I ask, grinning slyly as he coaxes my legs over his thighs so I'm sitting sideways on his lap.

West sets a hand on my hip and shrugs. "It'll be easier to talk quietly in here if you're closer," he whispers, nodding to the sign nearest us that reads, THIS IS A ROOM FOR RELAXATION. PLEASE REFRAIN FROM CONVERSATION.

"That's some good thinking." I reach up, brushing his hair off his forehead.

He looks so yummy, especially with the robe spread open down to his sternum. I get a hint of those gropable pectorals and want to dive in there and fall asleep like a cat against his torso.

"Did you get the treatment names right?" he teases quietly.

"I did. But then again, I just had a body scrub and a massage."

"Nothing up your nose?"

"Correct." I pull in a deep breath as if to demonstrate and feel him shift beneath me to pull me deeper onto his lap. "I feel like I've been transferred into new skin. Plus," I say, brandishing my shorter nails. "I had the claws trimmed."

I can't be sure, but I think he looks a little disappointed. "Ah. What will I do with all the free time I have not helping you get dressed?"

"I don't know," I say. "Maybe spend the time in front of the mirror practicing new ways to be clever?"

"Good call."

"Did you get your feet scrubbed?" I ask.

"I think I got everything scrubbed." I quirk an eyebrow at this, and he laughs. "Yep. Even my ass."

"Your mom's boobs are really great," I say. "No wonder you breastfed until you were four."

West's bursting laugh is definitely too loud for the relaxation room. "I'm not sure my mother even fed me a bottle."

He runs his hand up my shin. Goose bumps break out on my thighs.

"Well, with both her and Blaire naked in the steam room with me," I begin in a whisper, "Blaire speculated that you often hoist me in your thick, muscled arms during coitus."

This time, West laughs deep in his throat. "Wonderful."

"To be fair, Janet started it." I send a hand up around the back of his neck. "She asked when you were going to knock me up."

"Oh God. She didn't."

"She did. So I basically said we were doing our best and hit it daily."

His eyes drop to my lips. "We would."

"Oh, we totally would."

I would have expected the pause that follows to be awkward, but it isn't. West slowly strokes his big hand up and down my shin before sliding it around to cup my calf.

"My dad showed up," he says then, quietly.

My stomach grows twisty and protective again. "Oh. And?"

A small shrug. "We had to keep it civil because we had gentlemen's facials and massages scheduled."

"Does that mean you had them *together*?"

West nods. "Charlie booked them for us. Charlie is the one person Dad would never say no to. But he mentioned every two minutes how weird it was to be in a room with his sons while he was getting massaged."

I grimace. "Like he's usually getting a different kind of massage?"

"I don't really want to think about it too deeply. I'm not sure I'll ever forget the sound of oil being slathered on my father's chest."

I cup his cheek. "Well, your skin *is* very soft."

"It felt good."

"It does feel good."

Silence stretches again. My attention is dragged down to the tiny, glorious hickey, and I'm unable to stop stroking his freshly faciated cheek. West looks at my lips, and his fingers move to cup the back of my knee, just beneath where my robe has drifted open. Heat engulfs my skin.

"I was thinking earlier that we shouldn't do this again," he says, his thumb running in soothing circles just beneath my kneecap.

"You mean the way you're casually fondling my knee?"

He nods, laughing quietly, his eyes still fixed on my mouth. But I notice he doesn't stop stroking my leg.

"I'm finding it hard, however," he says. I grin saucily and he closes his eyes, his head falling back with a quiet groan. "You know what I mean."

"I do."

"Someone could come in," he says.

"Which wouldn't be an entirely bad thing. The ruse, and whatnot."

West frowns and seems to work through a few words before getting any out. "That's one reason maybe we shouldn't do this."

"Isn't that the point?"

"Kissing for show is one thing," he says. "We—earlier—" He tries again. "It was more than kissing."

"It sure was." I wink dramatically and whisper, *"Boner."*

He laughs. "It's just that . . . I don't want you to feel obligated."

"What?" I gape at him, playing with the hair at the nape of his neck. "I don't."

"Okay." His forehead relaxes. "That's good."

"I mean, I *do*, in the sense that I'm being paid to pretend to be your wife. But you were very clear that the physical side wasn't part of that. And, West?"

"Yeah?"

"It isn't a hardship, you know. Kissing you isn't a chore."

He nods, fingertips gliding seductively down my calf and back up again. "Yeah. But the money makes it—"

"Makes it complicated," I finish for him. "I get it. But allow me to be completely honest: Now that I've spent some time with you? And now that I've seen your crazy family? I want to be here on your team."

His eyes search mine.

"Even if you told me the offer was all fake, and you don't actually have two nickels to rub together," I tell him, "I'd still stay and help you pull this off. I'm your ride-or-die, West Weston."

West's expression crashes, features going slack, and I quickly amend with a laugh, "Oh my God, I'm not saying you're lying about being loaded! It is very obvious to me that you are superrich, West. What I mean—"

"Anna." His voice is low and emotionless.

"—is that I'm here for you," I babble, even as he's shifting me off his lap. "I'm saying I like you. Kissing or no kissing." Why am I still talking? He's standing up and tightening his robe around his hips. He's moving toward the door.

He's leaving?

"West?"

Stopping, he turns and looks in my direction, his gaze landing somewhere just past my shoulder.

I open my mouth, but at first nothing comes out. Finally: "Are you mad that I implied you don't have money?"

He gusts out a disbelieving laugh. "No, Green."

"Then what?" I ask. "What did I do wrong?"

He swallows thickly. "Nothing."

But he turns anyway and disappears down the hall.

Twenty-Two

LIAM

My longest relationship, with a woman named Chiara, was in college. She was raised in Italy by her two psychologist parents and moved to the states to attend UC Berkeley, where we met. She was perceptive but bossy and in hindsight the relationship was fairly miserable, but something she said, near the end, always stuck with me: "Liam!" she'd yelled in exasperation. "Why don't you ever know how you *feel?*"

In truth, Chiara got me at my worst—from ages eighteen to twenty-one, privileged beyond belief and totally unaware, several years pre-therapy. Tragically, our relationship spanned the years where I was utterly destroyed by my father—so she was right, I hardly ever knew what I was feeling. It's not that I was apathetic, but I hadn't yet learned how to give names to the tension inside me.

I have now. A decade after my breakup with Chiara, I know when I'm happy, when I'm angry, when I'm frustrated, anxious, lonely, hurt, embarrassed, elated. I let myself feel things; I don't shy away from big, consuming emotions.

So it's bewildering now to be unable to identify this churning, rioting feeling in my gut.

Given what just happened between me and Anna, and the way all my previous hesitations about physical intimacy seemed to simply evaporate the minute she was on my lap, I would expect to be on a high from her proximity and the way she so frankly confessed that I have someone in my corner. I have never, not once in my life, had someone show up for me so deliberately and unreservedly without wanting anything in return.

But instead of feeling awash with gratitude, I feel the vague and disconcerting tendrils of anger.

So I bolt. I shower quickly, get dressed, and then leave before she can find me. I walk until I run out of beach, and then I sit on the sand and stare out at the unending ocean, trying to understand why my heart is pounding like something's wrong with it, why the last thing I can make my body do is go back to the bungalow.

I prod at the feeling, trying to determine whether it's related to the fight with my father, the awareness that I'm stuck on an island with him for another long stretch of days. But when I look at it, really inspect it, I realize that this simmering panic isn't currently linked to Ray Weston. That I hate him is a fact unchanging.

And it isn't linked to the loophole in the family trust, that terrifying pitfall I'm avoiding every step of this trip.

It's the idea of seeing Anna again tonight that makes my stomach feel hot and uneasy. It's the echo of her words that turn my gut into a bubbling cauldron of anxiety.

I want to be on your team.

I'm here for you.

I'm your ride-or-die, West Weston.

This feels like anger. Or dread. Or fear.

And that's when I force myself to stop, because what I'm truly afraid of is giving this fear a name.

I SIT SO LONG that the sun begins its slow descent into the horizon. Some time alone to just breathe is restorative; my thoughts settle, my pulse eventually eases. But as much as I am soothed by the idea of sleeping on this beach or—better yet—climbing into a boat and drifting to the next island over, I know I can't stay away forever. At some point, I'll have to throw myself back into the fray.

The packed agenda keeps us busy and all the socializing really does turn the island into a shoebox; every night there's a gathering, a party, some way for my parents and the McKellans to display their enormous wealth. Tonight is no different.

I heard Jake and Kellan talking about the spectacle of it at our grooms-men fitting—something about an Old Hollywood soiree. Kellan confirmed that his mother applied for a waiver from the Indonesian government to adjust the number of allowable items visitors can bring to Pulau Jingga simply so she could ship two crates full of costumes here for the party. It's just like everything else so far this week: excessive to the point of distasteful.

I wonder if Anna knows this; I can't imagine how she'd react.

And as soon as I have the thought—of Anna back at the bungalow, alone, waiting for me, wondering what the fuck happened—that tightness is back, the feeling of something wrong inside me.

ANNA MUST HEAR MY footsteps because she jogs around the lower deck to the wood slats of the bridge, throwing her arms up, hands resting on top of her head. She blows out a huge breath, turning in a half circle when she sees me. And the way it looks like she might cry makes me feel another strange wave of paradoxical anger.

I don't get it. I have no fucking idea what's going on with me.

"There you are," she says, voice shaking. "*Jesus Christ*, West. I was about to go looking for you."

I frown. "I was fine."

"Where did you go?"

I know there's no way around this, but the urgency to turn around and walk back along the bridge and down the beach to the quiet tip of the is-land feels like a second heartbeat in my torso. "I just went for a walk."

"A walk?" she repeats. "You've been gone for like three *hours*."

"I had to get some air."

I feel her staring at me as I look out at the water. I can see this from the outside, how terrible this is, how fucked up I'm being after how things have been between us, after opening up to her, and after what she said.

I'm your ride-or-die, West Weston.

I know it's not fair to sound so clipped, but I simply do not have the mental fortitude to walk it back. I don't know how to explain what's going on inside me. I feel like an uneasy, outdated version of myself, and I hate it. I know it's not possible that seeing my dad has wiped out the years I spent working through this exact kind of thing, but I'm twenty years old again and staring down the barrel of emotions that are too big to wrap my head around.

"You're being weird," she says quietly.

Finally, I meet her eyes. "How so?"

Anna stares at me. "Seriously?"

"What do you want me to say?" I swallow as a shiver runs down my spine. "I just went for a walk. Don't make it into something it isn't."

"Someth—?" She cuts off, jaw tight as she looks out at the water. I listen to her taking three deep breaths before she says a quiet "Sure. Okay. I say nice things and you bail. Nothing at all to read into there."

"We barely know each other," I say. "Just remember that."

At the wounded look in her eyes, I immediately want to pull the words back into my mouth.

Anna huffs out a laugh. "Oh, I will." After another beat of silence between us, she takes a final, deep breath and then turns fully to me, smiling in a way that feels both familiar and devastating. Everything in her expression looks the same as it always does, but her eyes are completely blank. "I took the liberty of choosing a couple options for you for tonight." She lifts her chin to the inside of the bungalow. "I laid them out on the bed."

"Thank you." I thought that going for a walk, getting some distance from her, would make this feeling go away, but if anything, it's worse.

It isn't anger. It's *anguish.*

"You didn't have to do that," I say.

"Actually, I did," she says. "Everyone was going through the trunks, pulling what they wanted, and I didn't know where you were. I was worried all that would be left for you was the dress Jack Lemmon wore in *Some Like It Hot*."

I laugh dryly. "Thank you."

She doesn't smile back and of course she doesn't. I'm being a dick. "You're welcome." She turns to go inside and then stops. "Will it make you weirder if I get ready in here tonight? I can go over to the spa and get dressed there if you'd prefer."

"Anna," I say, "it's fine."

"Cool," she says, and disappears inside.

It TAKES ME ABOUT five minutes to get my tux on, and the remaining time before the party I spend on the deck, answering emails on my phone, responding to faculty texts and questions, and generally avoiding thinking about anything within a twenty-foot radius. Which is a strategy that is handily obliterated the second Anna walks out onto the deck in a cream satin dress that perfectly hugs her curves, and when she turns to blow out a citronella candle on the deck, I see that the dress dips so low in the back it reveals the twin shadows of her tailbone. The smooth expanse of her back is interrupted only by the tan line, which sends a fresh wave of frustration through me, and I look away, sucking in a deep breath.

Anna goes quiet, and then I feel her coming closer. "We have to be friends again," she says quietly. "We have a show to put on."

"We never stopped being friends."

She laughs a little at this, exhaling a puff of air that fans warm and minty across my neck.

"You look nice." She reaches forward to adjust my lapel and our eyes meet. Her smile has a tiny bit of the real Anna in it. A tiny bit of *knowing*. Does she see straight through me? Does she know that every time I look at her, I want to run? My nostrils flare and the urge to bail on this party and tell her to go ahead without me sends a chill across my skin. But Anna just stares up at me and then laughs. "You're such a weirdo."

She tucks her arm through mine, and we make our way across the bridge in silence. On the beach, she finally breaks. "Am I correct in believing that someone had these costumes sent here from the United States?"

I nod. "I think the McKellans organized it all."

"Imagine shipping trunks of old glam outfits here just for a party!" She pauses and snickers. "What if they sent the wrong ones? Like, imagine Janet opening it to find a bunch of furry outfits." She laughs. "Or, like, *Lord of the Rings* cosplay."

"Random."

"I'd have made you go as Gollum tonight."

I fight a smile. My unidentified frustration is momentarily silenced by a rush of satisfaction that I knew she would make a joke out of this party.

"I dated a guy in a *Lord of the Rings* tribute band," she says, and then amends, "or slept with him, I guess."

Heat returns, spreading like wildfire under my skin, and I clamp my mouth shut.

"Aren't you curious which character he was?" she asks.

I slide my gaze to her. "Gimli?"

She laughs. "Legolas. It was the saddest thing you've ever seen. Trust me, Legolas would *never* be the drummer. Way too sweaty in that wig."

"What would he play?"

She shrugs. "I dunno. Keytar?"

"I can see that."

Anna looks up at me, bumping my shoulder. "Careful. You might use up your word quota, and you're committed to being monosyllabic tonight."

At this, my mouth seals shut again.

The party comes into view in the distance, a huge white tent set up on the beach, strung lights glimmering in delicate, parallel strands that stretch down the length of the interior. Bright, jazzy trumpet notes drift across the air.

"I mean, come on," she says, gesturing to what's in front of us. "We could all just drink Pacificos and lime on the beach and be completely happy. Is all of this necessary?"

"It's probably the McKellans showing off to my parents."

"Who knew grocers were so powerful?" she asks, and I try to resist the urge to explain it to her, but the words rise up out of me anyway.

"Dad's power isn't just about Weston Foods," I tell her.

"What does that mean?"

"His hands are in everything," I explain. "Every huge industry, he's there. Here's an example: He gave seed money to a few friends of Alex's when they wanted to start a little website called Twitter—I refuse to call it X." Anna snickers. "He invested early in Apple, Uber, even Amazon. He serves on the board of five different Fortune 500s. He knows everyone. Has dirt on everyone, too." That one hits close to home, and I kick a stray branch out of her path so she doesn't trip on it. "At some big dinner recognizing charitable CEOs, this one guy, a college friend of Dad's from Penn, joked that he saw my father with his arm around a woman at a hotel bar. Maybe it was true—I suspect it was—but I think my dad would have destroyed him for starting a baseless rumor, too. He was an executive at a hedge fund and Dad leaked his personal financials to the board; this guy had to empty his retirement savings to pay off his wife's credit card debt and the board found him unfit to advise clients. He couldn't get another job and they had to leave New York and move back in with her parents. Last I heard, they'd divorced, and he was working as a bank manager in Tulsa."

Anna lets out a shocked breath. "Can I ask you something?"

"Yes."

"Do you honestly care that much about the money?"

I open my mouth and then close it again. I may not have the words yet for what's going on between the two of us, but talking about the family trust opens up the trapdoor to feelings I *can* identify, feelings like guilt and obligation, panic and loyalty and dread. "I can't just walk away. It's not that simple," I say, hoping she'll leave it.

But this is Anna. She never leaves anything. "Then explain it like I'm a toddler."

"It's—" I cut off, shaking my head. "I'm not only here because of my inheritance. It's much bigger than that."

Her eyes go wide in disbelief. "Bigger than *a hundred million dollars?*"

I look over at her and nod, but that's all I can do for now because we're here, out in front of the party tent.

Anna threads her arm through mine and we step in together, taking it all in. It's not technically a costume party, but I spot an attempt at Audrey Hepburn in the crowd, Lucille Ball and Desi Arnaz look-alikes, a Sammy Davis Jr., and a handful of Marilyns. A band plays in the corner, a backdrop behind them built to look like the Southern California skyline, complete with towering palm trees, art deco buildings, twinkling windows, and of course, the HOLLYWOOD sign. Long tables are dressed in glittering fabric and topped with vases of arching white ostrich plumes.

Gold dominates everything, from the towering croquembouche wrapped in golden spun sugar to yards of gossamer fabric and shimmering beads draped along the tent's outer walls. It strikes me that there aren't any flowers anywhere; instead, the real showstopper is a gilded tree in the center of the room, its branches heavy with pearls and teardrops of sparkling gems. I can only hope it's all fake, because while what they've managed to pull off on a tiny island in the middle of the ocean is impressive, I agree with Anna: some beers and beach chairs would be preferable to this every time. If they wanted something this lavish, this elaborate, why not just host the wedding in California, where everything is right there?

But I know why. Everything—literally everything—is for show.

Even this woman on my arm.

Next to me, Anna looks out over the extravagance and whistles. "Just another simple family get-together. I hope I never get used to this."

I drag my free hand through my hair. "Yeah."

Anna turns to me, arms outstretched dramatically like she's ready for me to waltz her across the dance floor. She speaks out of her mouth, playfully old-timey: "What do you say, old chum? Ready for some hotsy-totsy?"

I give her an apologetic smile. "I was thinking I might check in on my sister. I haven't seen much of her since we've been here. I'll find you when I'm done?"

Her face falls but in true Anna fashion, it bounces right back again. "Okay, yeah."

With a little smirk, she stretches, kissing my cheek and whispering, "See ya later, weirdo," in my ear before she walks across the room to the bar, where Jake and Jamie are talking. Feelings I thought I'd banished return, hot and insistent. Is she doing this on purpose? Walking to Jamie to make me jealous?

With a groan, I take a glass of wine off the tray of a passing waiter and pull in a deep breath. Anna's right: I'm being a basket case. If my urge is to run from her, to disentangle myself from whatever it is we started and which tripped this strange, impatient feeling in my gut, then the best thing for it is to imagine her moving on, to remind myself that, in only a handful of days, we will *both* move on, and in a matter of months, we will never have to see each other ever again.

And yet here I stand, decidedly *not* finding my sister, instead watching heads turn as Anna crosses the room. This place is full of beautiful gowns, but nobody looks like her. Even if her dress is simple, it fits her like a glove—hugging the narrow dip of her waist, the flare of her hips, the decadent curve of her ass. Wherever fabric exposes flesh, her skin seems to glow under the strung lights.

Jake greets her with a kiss to the cheek, saying something that makes her burst out laughing bawdily. She does a little dance and Jake immediately joins in, sending the three of them into hysterics.

"What has you smiling like this?"

I look over at my mother, who has materialized at my side. I . . . hadn't realized I'd been smiling. She's dressed like Grace Kelly, in a fitted black top and full white skirt, her usual updo smoothed back into loose blond curls. My mother idolized Grace Kelly when we were growing up and has dressed as her character from *Rear Window* to at least half a dozen fancy Halloween parties. Now she tracks my attention to Anna standing with Jake. "Ah. I see." My mother brings her glass to her mouth, taking a long sip of her dirty martini. "She looks lovely in that gown."

"She does."

"She seems like a sweet girl, darling."

"She is." I sip my wine. "Maybe you could ease up on her?"

Mom laughs. "Oh, I will. Eventually. That's part of the deal, you know? Grandma Lottie scared the living hell out of me, now I get to do it."

"Granny Lottie didn't have a mean bone in her body."

"To you," she intones. "It's possible to have varying experiences with people. Your sister would probably tell a very different story of your father than would you or your brothers."

She'll get no argument from me. Four siblings and we've all handled the fallout in our own ways. Alex turned into a desperate yes-man. Jake is the sunshine clown who looks for a joke to get out of every tense moment. And I'm the chronic overthinker who internalizes everything. No wonder I can't make sense of my feelings today. We watch Jake as he animatedly tells a story. Anna says something that seems to refute whatever he's saying and the two play-argue, pointing at each other. With a smile, Jamie sets his hand on her back, leaning in—

I'm moving before I fully register it, shouldering my way through the crowd, passing family and acquaintances and business associates of my father's without engaging before coming up behind Anna so close that Jamie immediately withdraws his hand from her skin.

Skin that I hadn't yet touched in that dress.

Anna startles when she feels me behind her. She turns, finding me standing barely inches away from her back. "West."

Wrapping a hand around her hip, I nod to my brother, then to Anna's ex. "Jake. Jamie." I bend, kissing her shoulder. "Wife."

My little brother smirks. "Liam."

But when I look down at her, her brown eyes blaze up at me. And it's only when she excuses herself and walks away, marching straight out of the tent that I finally register the unnamed cocktail of anguish that's been churning in me all day.

It is the comfort of having an ally. It is the powerlessness of infatuation. It is the terrifying beginning of more.

Twenty-Three

ANNA

*U*ghhhhhh.

What a gross, gross feeling. I have become West's emotional rag doll.

Let me be clear: I am incredibly proud of myself. In the past week I've spent with this mess of a man, I've learned that I am capable of more than I ever imagined. I can mostly hide my horror when people around me discuss buying giant swaths of land for tax write-offs. I can make a single vodka soda last three hours. I can have my butt massaged without giggling, and I can wear a satin gown like a motherfucking boss.

But one thing I cannot do, even if I'm being paid handsomely, is allow myself to be emotionally manipulated.

My mom left when I was five—ostensibly just to "take a break" and "find herself"—and the games she played over the next nine years really fucked us up. She would call every few months and tell Dad she missed him and wanted to come home to us, and then remember that she was above it all and leave again. She would send postcards out of the blue with nothing but the words *Thinking of you*, but never remember our birthdays. She refused to sign divorce papers until I was fourteen and my father finally filed for abandonment. I saw the way she manipulated him, and as an adult, I can spot a mind-fuck a mile away.

See, West? You aren't the only one with fucked-up family dynamics.

But his family, whew, it is fucked up. And if he thinks he's going to find a gently placating and toxically enabling woman in me like he has in his mother, he is mistaken.

I will not be the toy to West's anxious cat, even if he is paying me. I will

fake-kiss him and smile at parties and wear every hideously expensive gown
Vivi picked out for me, but I will not let my emotions become part of the
game. And seeing the way he freaked out this afternoon, the cool distance
he forced between us—fine. I can handle that. I fully support him deciding
he needs to focus on the Weston detritus and on cooling whatever lusty,
real, or vulnerable thing we have brewing. But what I am unwilling to do is
be jerked back to his side the minute I talk to someone else.

Outside the tent, the night air is humid and thick; it feels like a storm is
rolling in and man, if I didn't think they'd make the people who work here
clean it up, I'd hope for it to settle right over us. This party is gorgeous, but
we're on a perfect island in the middle of the ocean, a lush, protected jewel
of land, and these fuckers have carted more junk here than I could fit in
my entire apartment. I'd love to see how their props hold up in a downpour.

"You, too, huh?" a voice says from the shadows, and I squint into the
darkness to see Reagan. She's sitting on a low tree branch in a blue-and-
white-checked dress and glittering ruby slippers. An adorable Dorothy.

"Did I just say that out loud?" I ask.

She looks up at me with the trademark Weston eyes. "Say what?"

"About how I hope the storm lands directly over us?"

She laughs. "No. I just meant you ditched the party, too?"

"Oh. Yeah."

"What's your reason?" she asks, looking back down to where she's drawing with a stick in the sand.

I squint at her in the darkness. "What's yours?" I bounce back.

"Grown-ups being annoying."

"Hey, bestie, same." I walk closer, offering a high five and sitting down
beside her. "Didn't you go snorkeling with Eko today?"

Blaire mentioned Reagan having zero interest in spa day, and frankly,
after West's weirdness made an appearance, I wonder if I should have made
the same call.

"Yeah, she took us to the reef off the north side of the island. It was
amazing. I asked her to please not bring us back here."

I laugh. "Bet she didn't pack enough food for the boat trip back to Singapore, eh?"

"Sadly, no."

"Ugh. Planning fail."

Reagan laughs down at her sand drawing. "Five more days," she says. "I'm having fun but I miss my dog and my friends."

"Bet it feels like an eternity."

"It does."

I remember this feeling, the sense that everything was boring when I was home but that being away for even an hour meant that I was missing something intensely fun and irreplaceable, that everything, always, was completely out of my control. Being an adolescent fucking sucks.

But I know that in all the times Dad sat with me on the swings in the backyard while I cried over friends or boys or school or my mom, never once did he tell me to cheer up, to try to see the bright side, to have a posi-tive attitude. He knew I was an upbeat kid, and when I wanted to feel bad, he let me feel bad. The only thing he ever said was "It'll get better." And he was never wrong.

"It'll get better," I say to Reagan now.

"I hope so."

"It will," I assure her. "In a few years you'll have more independence. More autonomy. Do you know what that means?"

She shakes her head.

"It's like having control over your own decisions," I say. The tide is coming in about twenty yards away, and I wiggle my toes in the cool sand. "Soon you'll be old enough to say no to things you don't want to do. Right now is the time in life that teaches you you'll get through it even if you hate it."

At least I get a small smile out of her. "I'll take your word for it."

"Boredom never killed anyone." I bump her shoulder with mine. "It just made them wish it would."

She laughs and we both turn as a twig snaps behind us.

West steps into view, one hand in his pants pocket, the other drawing back a branch so he can see us. "Hey."

"Hey," Reagan says, and it's for both of us because I don't bother.

"What're you two doing out here?" he asks in that low, soothing voice. I straighten my back, reminding myself I'm mad.

"Planning the downfall of the patriarchy," I tell him.

He laughs. "Cool."

"What are you doing out here?" Reagan asks him. "Looking for Anna, probably."

"Yeah . . . I was wondering if my wife would like to dance with me."

I tilt my head to the convenient excuse of the kid at my side. "I'm Reagan's ride-or-die tonight."

The way West's smile falls hits me like a shove. The confirmation that he got my meaning isn't as satisfying as I'd expected it to be.

He blinks away, aiming a wry laugh down at the sand before he looks back up again. "Shots fired, okay." He looks over at Reagan. "Then would my niece like to dance with me?"

Reagan recoils. "Absolutely not."

"You sure?" He huffs out a surprised breath. "You sound a little conflicted."

"No offense, Uncle Liam, but I wouldn't even know how to dance to this old-timey shit."

I pull back, looking at her in feigned surprise. "She swears!"

"Sorry," she mumbles.

"I could teach you," I tell her.

West's honeyed voice slides between us. "Or *we* could teach her."

He holds out a hand to Reagan and I can't blame her for the way she seems to enter a trance and take it, following him inside. I can't resist following, either, and I was actively trying.

Just as West sets his wineglass down on an empty table, the band breaks into a song I remember from high school band—Benny Goodman's laid-back "In the Mood"—and West leads Reagan to the floor, where she absolutely refuses to move her feet. Laughing, he steps back and shows her the basic choreography of a dance I've definitely seen on *Dancing with the Stars*.

The pair practice together a few times, and when Reagan starts to get the hang of it, West picks up the tempo, slowly drawing her into his arms and setting off around the floor, much to the delight of the growing audience. With a wicked grin, he deftly leads her in a simple dance around the room while I watch from the sidelines, stunned. Reagan's expression goes from reluctant and mortified to amused as he turns them to face the same way, kicking up their heels, then pulls her back to him, lifting her up to twirl her in a smooth circle. Her smile grows the more he sweeps her around the dance floor, and she breaks into delighted hysterics when he flips her over his arm. The captive audience watches as they come to a laughing, gasping stop at the end when West dips her and she throws her head back, laughing.

With a sweet kiss to the top of her head, he mouths, "Thank you, sweetheart," and she runs over to Lincoln in the periphery, covering her face but beaming beneath her hands.

A hefty number of ladies observe West appreciatively as he makes his way over to me, the viper. His gaze is tentative, and he accepts a glass of water from a waitress with a small mumbled "Thanks."

"Well, Satan, that was fucking adorable."

West laughs. "She swears."

"She sure as shit does." I lift my chin to the dance floor. "Where'd you learn all that?"

"Granny had us all in dance classes when we were young. Charlie did cotillion. Alex, Jake, and I did young men's. We basically learned how to be gentlemen. To my granny, dancing was a big part of that."

"I suspect it makes me a bad feminist to think that's hot."

"I suspect you're right."

And of course, a slow song begins to play.

His expression straightens, eyes turn earnest. "Would you dance with me?"

I wrap my arms around my stomach. "No, thank you."

"I know you're mad at me. And I know why."

"Good."

He gazes down at me. "Want to dance anyway?"

I chew my lip, thinking it over. He doesn't look away, doesn't shrink from the direct way I'm studying him.

"How do I know you won't do a one-eighty and freeze me out again?"

"I've been spending the past hour or so thinking about that exact question."

"And?"

"And let's talk while we dance."

Finally, with a deep breath, I let him lead me to the floor, where I resist his attempt to pull me close to his chest.

"This song is called 'Cheek to Cheek,'" he says, smiling cutely. "We can't do the jitterbug to this one. You should come a little closer."

This is all in-bounds, I think. *Dancing in front of his family. Fake-kissing at a party. I will build a wall of pillows between us tonight to keep my body firmly on my side of the bed.*

I let him draw me close. His big palm feels like fire on my lower back, and a rough groan rumbles deep in his throat at the contact. West tucks my hand against his chest and bends, pressing his face to mine as he begins to move us around the floor.

Frankly, he's an amazing dancer. I saw it when he was with Reagan, but I feel it now, the way my feet barely touch the floor. Which is good, honestly, because I have no real idea how to dance to this kind of stuff. I was basically going to show Reagan that there's no wrong way to dance, but I suspect in this crowd, that isn't true.

"Anna," he says, his lips brushing my ear. I ignore this subtle call for my attention, and I definitely ignore how much I like it when he calls me Anna. "I'm sorry."

"What do you think you're apologizing for?" I say quietly into his neck.

"For disappearing after what you said at the spa. For coming back and being a weirdo."

"You know, I don't mind that you disappeared. After the initial sting of it, I didn't mind that you got weird, either. I'm sure all of this acting is draining. I'm sure keeping your shit together with your family here is exhausting. This is an objectively weird situation. And I'm weird all the time. But I'm not *cold* weird. I'm not *hurtful* weird."

"You are, in fact, one of the most level-headed people I've ever met. And have more class than me, or anyone here." He spins us a few times, fancy moves. Hot moves.

I will not be swayed.

"I know this is one big game," I say, "but at least keep the rules consistent. You keep changing them on me. You came to find me at the spa and kissed me so sweetly, and then ran away when I said something nice."

"Understood. I really am sorry."

"It's probably easiest if we continue to be fake-happily-married in front of everyone and keep it simple. Just for show."

He nods against me, turning us, and we dance our way along the long side of the floor.

"You're right." He says after a few quiet moments. "That's probably easiest. But if it's okay with you, I'd like to explain why I went for a walk today."

"I think I understand. I mean, anyone with a father like yours—"

"It wasn't my father. Well—let me amend that. I'm sure anytime I'm weird, he's part of the why. But I think the real issue was that today, in the spa with you . . . I've never had someone be firmly on my side before. At least, someone who wasn't asking for more from me. I know I'm paying you, but when you said that you didn't care about the money, when you were touching me and looking like you wanted to kiss me . . . it felt real."

I swallow around a tight ball of emotion in my throat. "Well . . . yeah. That's why it was hurtful for you to shove me away and then act jealous the second I simply spoke to another man."

"I haven't felt real things with a woman in a long time, though. It's disorienting to get blindsided by that here. Especially when it went against everything I had planned. I think the idea of opening myself up to another kind of hurt sent me to a strange place."

I pull back, looking into his eyes, impressed with how open he's being. "I get that."

"Are we okay?" he asks.

I squeeze my eyes closed, feeling the tight, clenching sensation mirrored in my chest. I don't love how attracted I am to him. It feels precarious, like walking a tightrope and the fall would be so easy and so deadly. But I also know myself: there's no cork inside me to bottle it back up. Besides, this talk was good, his transparency is good. I do feel so much better. "Yeah. We're okay."

He pulls back, looking at my mouth. "My instinct is to kiss you now."

"That certainly is what a married couple would do."

"I'm not really sure what the rules are anymore," he admits. "I agree we need them, but I don't think I can make them alone."

I study his face, wondering if I can give in to this. I think I can, especially if I stop taking it so seriously. "I mean, truthfully, a kiss doesn't have to mean everything," I remind him. "I read the contract this time, and there's nothing in there about physical intimacy. Kissing doesn't change the terms of our agreement."

"Correct."

"And whatever we do," I reason, "we can agree it's only for this island."

"That's true."

"So we're in agreement?" I ask. "Collaborators with benefits? Vacation ride-or-die? No strings attached beyond this?"

He nods, a small smile curling his lips. "Collaborators with benefits."

West sends one hand up my side, over my shoulder and higher, where he cups the side of my neck with his big, warm palm. His eyes fall closed, and he leans in, pressing his mouth to mine.

I've kissed guys. A lot of guys. Sometimes it's good, sometimes it's great. But mostly it's fine. Mostly it feels good but doesn't hit me like a spear to the chest and a slap to the lady parts. But this kiss? It's chaste but has me melting. It's soft, no tongue, just the lingering press of his mouth to mine followed by the easy parting, a pull of my bottom lip between his. Slow, deliberate kisses. Chaste, because we're in front of everyone, but still so intentional, so claiming, so thorough I feel the sweet exploration in my fingertips and my spine, I feel it in my chest and my belly and between my legs. But most of all, I feel it in my brain, a firework flash, a dopamine flood, the sealing of a happy memory firmly into place.

We pull apart and stare at each other.

"That was nice," I say.

"Nice?" he repeats, feigning offense. "Looks like I have my work cut out for me."

"I may invade your side of the bed tonight."

He gusts out a laugh. "For once?"

"Listen, wise guy, tonight I'm warning you."

"I'll brace myself." His grin widens, and we stop moving as the song comes to an end. West leads me off the dance floor to an empty cocktail table. "Want a drink?"

"Would Janet Weston frown at a dirty martini?"

"Please," he says. "Janet Weston drinks dirty martinis for breakfast." He kisses me one more time. "Be right back."

I watch him go and wish the jacket of his tux didn't cover his ass, because watching West Weston walk away from me is my new favorite art installation.

"Hey, little sis."

I turn, startled, to find Alex standing, swirling his cocktail, right next to me.

"Hey . . . big bro."

"Enjoying the party?"

"It's amazing." I struggle to find something more to say, coming in with the brilliant follow-up, "It's all been amazing."

He shrugs, lifting his highball glass to gesture to the splendor around us. "Yeah, but come on. I'm sure you're used to this kind of thing."

"Yes, totally. Very used to fancy parties."

"You were the same year as Jake in school, right?" He lifts his glass to his lips, eyes fixed somewhere in the distance.

"That's right. That's how I met West."

"Funny—I've only heard his guy friends call him West. Girlfriends called him Liam."

My smile drips with sugar. "I guess the wife gets to call him both."

"True, true. So, you're—what? Twenty-five?"

"That's right."

"And medical school at . . . ?"

I scrape my brain for what West told me in a rush of information on the plane. Alex turns to look at me and the pressure to answer rises. Oh, duh. Of course. "Stanford" bursts suspiciously out of me.

He snaps with his free hand. "That's right," he says. "Aquarius?"

I turn to look at him. That's random. "Yeah. January 28. How did you know?"

He shrugs, laughing. "Blaire went through an astrology phase. I thought it was bullshit but sometimes it seems spot-on. I absorbed more than I thought."

"What's your sign?"

"Scorpio."

I wince, and Alex laughs easily. His smile warms his face and I remember what Blaire said, about how he can be fun when he's not around his dad. Is that what this is? Is he not the actual worst human?

"Did you keep your maiden name?" he asks.

But at this, uneasiness returns. What an odd question.

With relief, I watch West return, our drinks in hand. His expression darkens when he sees Alex at my side. He approaches, handing me a glass and bending in to kiss my jaw.

"You okay?" he asks quietly.

I nod, smiling a smile that means *Everything feels weird, let's skedaddle.* West reads it, setting his hand on my bare lower back.

"We're going to grab some fresh air."

Alex wordlessly raises his drink to us.

We leave the tent, walking a few minutes down the path, and he stops me at a stand of mangrove trees. "What was that about?"

"He was asking me about what year I graduated UCLA, where I'm doing medical school. At first, I thought maybe he was just making conversation and is generally socially awkward, but then it got kind of weird."

West takes a sip of his drink, and I want to lick the taste off his mouth. "I don't like it. Alex doesn't really do conversation for the sake of conversation."

The tension ripples through him.

"There's nothing for you to do about it tonight," I tell him, taking his hand.

West looks down at our interlocked fingers and then up at me. "You're right." Slowly, he backs me into a tree, bending to speak into my neck. "What do you think I should do instead?"

Twenty-Four

LIAM

I've traveled to every continent, but I don't think I've ever been somewhere as beautiful as this tiny island in the middle of the vast ocean.

The moon reflects a million overlapping crescents across the rippling surface of the water; the ocean projects deep, cerulean blue up to a night sky so heavily blanketed with stars it's hard to believe it's the same sky overhead back home. The beach is sugar-soft, silver in the moonlight, and completely empty, with everyone on the island back at the party.

The path from the tent led us here, and this stretch of beach leads to the wooden path, and the wooden path leads to our bridge, which leads to the bungalow, the bed, and all the possibilities of what comes next flashing like wildfire in my overheated brain. Finally, I can translate everything aflame in my thoughts and it's all just the complex sequence of wanting someone in a hundred different ways.

But this view pulls us both up short and we stop, hand in hand, to take it all in.

"Do you ever feel completely insignificant?" Anna asks, staring out at the water.

"All the time."

"But," she adds, a smile in her voice, "in a good way."

"I knew what you meant." I tug a little on her hand, urging her to sit down, right here on the beach.

But she resists. "West . . . this isn't a costume from a trunk. Vivi bought this with your card."

"I don't care."

"Okay, but I do. If you don't want me to return it, all of this is coming home with me, and I'm selling it on Poshmark or the RealReal."

Pain splits my next breath. "Of course. You can do whatever you want with it. But that dress specifically?" I shake my head. "It would be a tragedy if you didn't keep it and put it on every now and then. It's made for your body."

"Yeah?" She sends her hands down her sides and smiles down at me. "I've never owned anything like it in my entire life."

"Then please don't sell that one. Enjoy it. We can't take any of it with us when we die." I give her a pleading look. "But however you want to do it, please sit with me."

She considers the sand and then jogs behind me, disappearing for a minute, and returning with a wide, flat palm frond. Setting it down, she carefully lowers herself.

"You don't think the leaf is dirtier than the sand?"

"Isn't sand literally dirt?"

I shake my head, laughing, and look out at the water. Anna threads her arm through mine, leaning her head on my shoulder. "Is there *anything* you own that you cherish? Or does the ability to buy anything make everything lose its value?"

Taking a deep breath, I think about the question. "I know this might surprise you, but I don't live like this at home. I own a house, but it's not marble floors and chandeliers. It's pretty basic."

"No helicopter pad? No butler?"

"Sorry to disappoint. I was never that into *stuff*," I admit, and then catch the sound of it, a dickish, superior side of myself I dislike. "I traveled with my grandparents more than Alex did; he didn't like the change in his routine and he was an incredibly difficult child if his schedule was disrupted, so every summer until I was about fifteen, when my grandfather died, I would go on all these amazing adventures with Granny and Grandpa. On safari in Tanzania, on a boat in the Greek islands. Japan, New Zealand, Tonga, Peru."

"Wow," she says on an awed exhale.

"I always assumed I was so grounded—like rooted in reality or had a perspective on the world my siblings didn't have because I'd seen so much of it and didn't ever really want *things*. Looking back, I was insufferable. I'm sure I made Alex feel like a materialistic idiot. Because, of course, the punch line is that I had more privileges than any of them. I didn't only have money—I had love, I had access, I had our father's esteem. I had the knowledge that I could walk into any room in the world and get exactly what I wanted." I look down at the sand between my feet, realizing I've rambled off topic. "The things I own that mean the most to me are my grandfather's watch and my grandmother's wedding ring. But I think the better answer to your question is that the second part is true: when you can afford anything, nothing is interesting anymore, and there's something really depressing about that."

She takes a deep breath, and I hear the question she doesn't ask: *And yet you want* more *money?*

"What about you?" I ask before she can take us down another road. "What's your most cherished possession?"

"Probably my kitchen drawer that's full of packets of red pepper flakes and Parmesan cheese."

I laugh. "Jesus Christ, okay, never mind."

She bumps my shoulder with hers. "Why not that drawer, though? I mean, it makes me so happy that I know I can always find a pack of cheese for whatever I'm eating. I guess I could say one of my paintings, but in an ideal world, I'd sell them all off. My AirPods? I loved those. But they were stolen out of my car the night before you came to my door, and look, I'm still breathing."

"Exactly. It's just stuff."

"So then what loss *would* devastate you?" she asks.

This one here on the island, I think immediately. *Losing the battle that loses the war.*

But I can't say that aloud, even if she already suspects it's true. And when I try to think of a better answer . . . I can't. I am suddenly, devastatingly aware that I have made this battle with my father the most important personal event in my life.

After I've been quiet a long time, Anna leans forward into my field of vision. "I'm sorry. I went way too serious. Should we talk about red pepper flakes and Parmesan again?"

I laugh, leaning forward to kiss her. "Yeah, maybe. Although I'm not sure what more needs to be said about packets of shitty pizza parlor cheese."

"Well, in fact I do have a Parmesan cheese story," she says. "And it relates to you."

"I can say with confidence that no one has ever said that to me before."

"The night after you moved out of our apartment, Vivi came over. We ordered some Enzo's and camped out in the living room. A giant veggie pie, real sloppy. But they forgot the cheese packets—a tragedy—so Vivi went digging into our fridge, where luckily, I had that enormous Kraft Parmesan can."

I laugh, remembering. "That can was unreal. You wouldn't be able to get through that much cheese in three lifetimes."

"Oh, but I'd try." She rests her head on my shoulder again. "Anyway, when we cleaned up later—"

"Wait, *you* cleaned up?"

"Har," she says, lifting her head and smacking my arm. "Viv was in the living room and called out to me, like, 'Hey Anna, I'm going to throw the can of Parmesan to you to put away.'"

"I feel dread."

"So she launches it across the living room and her throw is really great. I mean, professional quarterback great. It sails perfectly over the countertop and into the kitchen—"

"I still feel dread."

"—but she didn't close the can first. So, Parmesan cheese is just, like, spraying in these wide arcs over and over out of this canister and throughout the entire apartment. It was like a traveling pinwheel of cheese dust."

She lifts her arm that isn't hooked through mine and gestures all around. "Cheap cheese, *everywhere*."

"Horrible. This is the worst story I've ever heard."

"We had to go to her parents' house to get a vacuum because I didn't have one after you left, and it didn't matter how much we went over the rug, it still smelled so bad."

"I bet it still smells like dirty socks in there even three years later."

She laughs. "I bet you're right." Anna sighs, resting her head on my shoulder once more.

We sit in silence for a while, just listening to the gentle lapping of waves on the shore.

"You know what sounds amazing right now?" Anna whispers.

"Pizza," I say.

"Pizza," she agrees.

ANNA AND I TIPTOE like bandits from the southwest tip of the island near the bungalows, past Jules Verne, and past the pool complex using the flashlight of my phone to see our path. No mammals live on the island, but the trees are full of waning birdcalls and the odd flapping of wings. Droplets fall from leaf to leaf before landing with a plink on the damp earth. Branches creak and insects click, chirp, and trill; the siren-like call of cicadas pierces the humid air.

The sea greets us as we emerge from the thick foliage of the trail to the northeastern point of the island, where swimming is ill-advised but the most raw, breathtaking views can be found. There's a small black sand beach in a cove, protected by craggy obsidian cliffs. The tide comes in sideways, breaking foamy and violent and bringing the powerful undertow to a deceptively gentle finish on the shore. Green vines drip from the rock faces, hiding small grottoes and waterfalls. Even in dim light, the vegetation is so lush that it seems to glow.

"How did you even know this was here?" Anna asks, looking at the only structure on this side of the island, a circular teak pavilion, its pitched roof rising out of the darkness. Attached to the back side of it is a small industrial kitchen.

"Dad and I were running over here the other morning. He pointed it out and said this is the beach where they'll have the ceremony, and the building here is where they'll have the wedding reception if it rains."

The door, like every other one on the island, is unlocked, and we slip inside. Darkness swallows us up and I pull my phone from my pocket, turning on the flashlight again. Even through the walls we can hear the ever-present sound of the ocean.

The small banquet room is empty; tables and chairs are stacked neatly against the walls. On the opposite side from where we entered is a span of glass doors that slide open to reveal the views that, right now, just look like blackness outside. But I know from seeing it in daylight that there's a wide covered patio and, beyond that, the startling black sand beach of the northern tip of Pulau Jingga.

I reach back for Anna's hand, guiding her after me. "This way."

"Are we going to get in trouble?" she whispers.

"My mother's been given free rein of this building. It's where all the wedding supplies and decor and gifts are being held."

"Then shouldn't we turn on the big lights?"

"Where's the fun in that?"

The kitchen is spotless and stark; our footsteps echo on the tile floor. To the left, there's a long wall of gas ranges, and in front of us is a stretch of stainless-steel prep counters with a sink at the end of each. At the back of the room are two large walk-in refrigerators and a walk-in freezer. We could certainly order room service and have anything we wanted delivered to our bungalow, but if I'm starting to feel claustrophobic among all the excess, I'm guessing Anna has to be feeling it, too.

"Imagine we get locked in one of those," Anna says, "and they find us days later, wearing salami and cheese to stay warm."

"Someone should study your brain," I say, tugging the freezer door open. A light goes on automatically, illuminating the organized shelves lining three walls.

We take stock of our options, scanning the shelves before striking gold: a tall stack of frozen pizzas. Carefully, we slide a large pepperoni pie from the pile.

Back in the kitchen, Anna hops up on a counter while I crouch to turn an oven on to preheat.

"How did you know how to do that?" she asks.

I stand, brushing off my hands. "How did I know how to turn on an oven?"

She laughs. "A fancy oven. A big-kitchen oven."

"I was a line cook for a while," I tell her. "In a hotel restaurant."

"West Weston, you what!"

"In college," I tell her, nodding. "I told you I had no money. My girlfriend at the time got me a job at the Claremont Hotel. I would help make the little canapés for wedding receptions, and she was one of the waitstaff who would walk around and offer them on a tray."

"Romantique," she says, grinning. She's pulled her silky gown up past her knees and her legs kick forward and back.

I walk over to her, stepping between her tanned thighs. "We used to take the leftovers home, and to this day I can't look at a stuffed mushroom or bacon-wrapped shrimp without feeling queasy."

She laughs, reaching forward to push my tux jacket open and set her hands on my waist. "Tell me more about what you were like in college."

I lean forward, kissing her once. "You did know me in my youth."

"Yes, but graduate school." She kisses me. "And I mostly saw your backside as you left the apartment. Not a bad view, even then."

I kiss her again. "Hmm, let's see. College Liam was pretty shy, still into computers," I say, and then catch myself, "until he wasn't. He didn't really party, loved hiking and sailing on the bay. . . ."

"And did you have this girlfriend for all of undergrad?"

"The first three years."

"Wow, that's a long time."

"It was."

"Where is she now?"

I shrug, kissing Anna's jaw, her throat. She smells like sugared oranges. I want to sink my teeth into her neck. Being this close to her, smelling her, feeling her . . . I'm suddenly so hard, I feel lightheaded. "Probably back in Italy."

"Is she—?"

"Hey, Green?" I murmur, dragging my lips over her collarbone. "I don't really feel like talking about Chiara right now."

"Chiara is a pretty na—" She halts at my glare and covers her mouth with both hands, mumbling, "Sorry," from behind them.

I slide my hands under the hem of her dress, coaxing it higher up her thighs. The satin is heavy and lush and moves over her skin like water. Her legs are strong, skin warm as if she was just in the sun. But when I reach her hips, there's nothing else there.

Straightening, I look up at her face. Fire licks down my spine. "You're not wearing underwear."

"Everything gave me a panty line and I hate thongs."

There's a quiet beep behind me, the oven alerting us that it's preheated, and I pull my hands from her dress and turn to quickly slide the pizza onto the rack. When I return to her, I immediately get back to where I was, spreading her legs to step between them.

She sends her arms around my neck, pulling me close. "Hug me," she says, pressing her mouth to my neck. "I didn't like being mad at you earlier."

I wrap my arms around her waist, holding her close. "I didn't like it, either."

When she shifts, she presses herself against my cock. With a quiet moan, Anna drags her teeth up my neck to my earlobe and I slide my hands over her back, bare in the plunging dress.

"This dress makes me crazy," I say, kissing along her shoulder. "It's what sent me across the room earlier. Seeing Jamie touch your back set me off."

"I know." She tilts her head, giving me better access to her neck as I kiss my way up to her jaw, to her mouth, where I suck at that full, perfect bottom lip. When I release her, she whispers, "I'm not saying I didn't sort of like it."

"Yeah?" I trail my fingers up her spine, reaching the strap of the dress and drawing it off one shoulder, kissing the skin there. "What did you like about it?"

"Well, Dr. Weston, I think that version of you would fuck me into the floor."

At these words, heat flashes beneath my skin, my hand curls into a fist around the strap of her dress, and I sink my teeth into the sweetness where her shoulder meets her neck. "Is that what you want?"

"Sometimes."

"Sometimes . . ." I flick my tongue over her collarbone, and she moans quietly. "What about now?"

"Right now, I really want to get to know your body," she says, running her hands up my sides, over my chest, up my neck, where she cups my face, bringing it to hers. She kisses me, slow and lush and sweet. "I want you to learn mine, too."

I pull back to look at her. What she said is so simple, so obvious really for two people who are careening headlong into being intimate, but it feels so rare to hear it. I bend, half groaning, half laughing, into her shoulder. But I'm distracted by the warm bare curve, her sharp inhale when I kiss her skin, and the way she pulls me closer, pressing her chest to mine. A rogue thought takes hold: What kind of bra could she possibly have on? "Are you wearing any undergarments at all?"

"Yeah," she says, and my soul leaves my body when she pulls the dress down over one breast. It's covered in a skin-toned silicone cup. "These." She reaches up, carefully peeling it off, and, with a delighted laugh, slaps it to my tuxedo jacket, cackling when it adheres.

And this, right here, is where I don't know what to do. I don't know whether I'm supposed to laugh at Anna Green, ravage her, or marry her all over again—but this time for real.

Twenty-Five

ANNA

'm not sure I've ever loved a laugh as much as I love his. Even when I'm being particularly hilarious, West's laugh is usually quiet and reluctant—a huffed exhale, a single amused cough—but there is nothing better than when a surprised burst rips from his throat. I'd say a laugh like that comes from the belly because the sound is so round and joyful, but in West's case I think it comes from his chest, from that secret room in his heart that he keeps so carefully locked. When I manage to blow that door wide open, I feel like a goddess.

When he drags his eyes from my bare breast, he looks down at the silicone adhesive bra cup and tries to peel it off his tux jacket.

"Wow," I say, grinning at my little soldier. "She's really on there."

"How did you take this off without removing skin?" he asks, flummoxed.

"I guess now is when I tell you the truth," I say with quiet solemnity. "You may have noticed that I sparkle in the sunlight. That my skin is like marble." I pause. "This is the skin of a killer."

He laughs—sadly, we're back to just a little gust of air—before giving up and taking off the jacket. This is preferable anyway, because the shirt for this Old Hollywood tux is a smidge too tight on his shoulders and biceps. Yum. I send my hands up his arms, around his back, pulling him into my arms.

"Come here."

West hums in my favorite way, the sound like a hungry purr, kissing my neck, moving to my other shoulder to pull that strap down, too. I shrug my arm out of it, and the satin falls heavily to my waist. He stops, staring at the other silicone cup, still holding my boob in place. I watch the battle unfold behind his eyes.

"You do it," he says, lifting his chin. "I'm suddenly afraid of them."

With a laugh, I carefully peel it away, and the playful trepidation in his eyes turns to fascination. My skin heats from his focus and West reaches forward, tracing a line from my throat and down, and then slides his hand to my hip and higher, cupping a breast in his palm as he bends to kiss my lips, soft and hungry, the pad of his thumb circling my nipple with perfect, tormenting focus.

Digging my hands between us, I work on his shirt from the bottom up. He angles his torso helpfully away when I reach his neck, laughing into a kiss at my struggle because too late I realize I should have started with his tie. Together, we work to loosen the knot, to get that tiny button at his neck free. Tie finally undone and with his shirt open, his chest bare and perfect, he comes against me, pulling me tight to him, his kisses different after skin hits skin, urgent and impatient. His hands bunch my dress up my thighs and he jerks my hips closer, right to the edge of the counter.

"Tell me what you want," he says, grazing his teeth on my jaw.

"Yes," I say mindlessly, and we laugh, but I guide his hand between my legs, my fingers shadowing his exploring touch, and wow, I'm wet. My body is obsessed with him.

He's wild, one hand in my hair, the other between my legs, fingers all over me, easing inside me and then moving, rough in a way that makes me feel like frantic is okay but messy is better. I undo his belt and it clangs against the metal counter, echoing around the kitchen. His zipper is the loudest thing in the room when I draw it down, and then I'm sliding my hand beneath the elastic band, finally getting my hand on him, squeezing him as he groans helplessly, feeling the weight, that generous length I've been thinking about for days. Impatient, I shove his pants down his hips and guide him forward, replacing his fingers, stroking myself with him.

West presses his forehead to mine, rocking his hips, teasing, barely easing the head into me and back out. "Just like this, okay?" he whispers. "That's all until we get back to the bungalow. I just need to feel you."

"What if I want all of it now?"

His quiet laugh is a warm puff of air against my lips. "You're trouble."

I nod against him, watching between us as he reaches down, angling himself up against the most sensitive part of me, sliding over my clit as he rocks. Pleasure sends waves licking along my skin, makes me want to claw at his back, jerk him closer, gobble this moment down in one all-consuming bite.

His hands grip my ass, pulling me slightly off the edge of the counter, and he chokes off a groan at the way he's just given me a nice slice of my wish and pushed partway into me. I can hear my own rhythmic panting as I breathe through accommodating the size of him.

He grits out the words: "We should stop."

"No."

"I'm not— I don't have—"

"You don't have condoms hidden somewhere in this kitchen?" I joke, my voice tight and broken at the feel of him jerking inside me.

His answering laugh is distracted and soundless, a gasp in reverse as he pulls all the way out. "No."

"I'm not feeling responsible," I admit.

"Me, either, but we can—"

I pull his mouth to mine, kissing him messily, hungrily, whispering the truth against his lips, that I'm on birth control and also? I wouldn't fuck a single person in LA without a condom, now or ever. "I want you." I suck his lip into my mouth, roughly dragging my teeth over it. "I want this."

He closes his eyes, kissing me before speaking the next words against my mouth. "If you tell me to stop—"

"I know."

He sends a big hand down my leg, cupping my calf, gripping an ankle, and with his free hand holds himself to ease in again and back, an inch at a time, his jaw tight, eyes trained on the progress. West holds his breath, transfixed as he works himself slowly into me, but I'm gasping; I've never felt anything like this, never been so excessively full. I reach back, flattening my palms on the counter so I can lift my hips and help him get there, working my body around him. With a bursting exhale, he groans, pulling me back to his chest, and he's all the way in, finally. I wrap my arms around his neck, silently asking for a minute to figure out how to fit these deep, gasping breaths and him inside me at the same time. But then the tension leaves my body and all I know is the blinding need to feel him moving.

"You okay?" he asks, his lips to my jaw.

"I just need—"

He covers my mouth with his when my voice breaks off, pulling out in a slow drag, pushing carefully back in, and out, and in, and out, again and again, deeper on each pass until he's thrusting in earnest and I'm positive I've never felt anything so consuming in my life. My skin is fire, brain haywire as he bends, licking a long streak of heat up my neck, stopping at my ear. "Wrap those long fucking legs around me."

Delirious with need, I do what he says, sliding my thighs around his hips, locking my ankles behind his back. Instinct tells me to squeeze hard and I'm right; he is overcome, thrusting rougher with the constraining grip of my thighs.

I reach down, feeling where he's moving, feeling the heat and slide, and he encourages me with a quiet "Yeah," moving faster, watching my hand as I touch myself. I'm torn between chasing this sensation and giving him everything I can: those sharp tugs on his hair that seem to unravel him, the scrape of my nails down his back. But when I move my hand, he catches my wrist, protesting. "No. Don't stop."

I meet his eyes, but they fall closed when he leans in to kiss me, messy and wet. "I liked the way your nails felt." He laughs quietly, somehow both wicked and shy. "The way they—"

"Tell me."

"The gentle scratch. On me."

I've been right there, right at the edge of falling, and the spiraling heat of his words sends me closer, my fingers moving even faster, not only chasing my own pleasure but *trying* to reach him now, to tap against him as he moves, to give him the tiny, delicious licks of pain. He nods, wordless, lips soft and parted as he fucks me and I have the thought that he's the most amazing combination in one man: gentle and rough, intuitive and steely, grounded and broken, but before I can look at this more carefully— before I can put the pieces together about why I'm thinking more about the man than about the pleasure he's giving me—my orgasm blindsides me, a wrecking ball flung violently sideways. I cry out in sharp surprise, clinging to West with my free hand, cupping his neck and holding his head to mine as it tears through me.

He works me through it, fast and hard, and only when I fall forward, clinging to him, does he slow to take my face in his hands, kissing me with velvet seduction, sucking on my lips, licking at me, inhaling my jagged, panting breaths. He whispers into my mouth, "You good?"

I laugh in response, euphoric.

"Sore?" he asks.

I shake my head in his cupped hands, and he releases me, gently pressing a palm to my breastbone, coaxing me to lean back onto my elbows. With leisurely shifts of his hips, West fucks me slow while his big hands roam all over me, caressing my breasts and throat, lips and cheeks, stomach and hips and thighs. But eventually, I feel the urgency rise in him, the growing tension of his torso. Setting one hand gently at the base of my throat and using the other to grip my dress around my waist, he begins in earnest again, eyes fixed on the most perfect coordinate in the world, the place where he disappears inside me.

It's the kind of raw, honest sex I've never had before and will want desperately again, but I'm too distracted to commit to the mental focus I'd need to come a second time. Instead I watch, rapt, as his pleasure plays across his features, watching the way concentration pinches his brow, watching the sheer power of his lovemaking. I am a starving dragon, deprived and obsessed, inhaling every one of his tells: his grip growing tighter, forming a fist around the fabric of my dress; his jerking, rough breaths; those rare seconds he squeezes his eyes closed, wincing in pleasure. And when he makes a sound—a new one this time, deep and warning—a desperate, aching awareness rises in me. I gasp out a pleading *yes* and West's eyes turn up to my face, his focus on my lip trapped tightly between my teeth, his pace turning furious for a blurred, euphoric handful of seconds. With a groan he drops his gaze again, sending his hand between us as he jerks out of me and sends his pleasure pulsing across my skin.

Wild victory tears through me as he stares down at my stomach, gasping, and then bends over me, resting his sweaty forehead to my chest. "Holy shit."

I dig one hand in his hair, dizzy with relief and lust and infatuation, scratching lightly at his scalp while he heaves in sharp, jagged breaths. Finally, he tilts his face up, stretching to kiss me, slow and adoring.

"You okay?" he asks.

I can only tell him the truth. "That was the best sex I've ever had."

He smiles, kissing me again. "Yeah?"

I nod, and for a few perfect seconds, we share the same breath, kissing like we've done it for centuries.

Pulling back, I reach up, pushing his sweaty hair off his forehead. "Definitely worth burning the shit out of the pizza."

I'M STILL A LITTLE shaky and jelly-limbed, so even though he just did the bulk of the work, West handles the task of tossing the first pizza and getting a second one started. I tiptoe into the banquet room and feel around the dark walls for an entrance to a ladies' room where I can clean up a little.

The entire thing feels like a sexy *Scooby-Doo* episode, and I continually expect to be busted by the mysterious owner of the island walking in with a group of goons brought to arrest us for the crime of Countertop Fornication. But in reality, it's all fine. I find a bathroom. I use it. I make my way back to the kitchen where West is still in there, alone, and his smile is more relaxed than I've ever seen it.

I laugh down at our now-clean sex counter. "You're the best guest. I swear that didn't occur to me." Apparently while I was gone, he graciously went digging for cleaning supplies and found a clean rag and a bottle of Lysol.

"Stealing a couple pizzas is one thing," he says, turning with an oven mitt and pulling the pizza out. "Leaving your gorgeous ass print on the counter is another."

We slip out to the covered patio, where we find a rolled-up rattan mat, set ourselves down, and eat pizza off paper plates, staring out into the darkness at the wild surf crashing on black sand in the distance.

I have no idea what time it is; West's phone is dead and mine is back at the bungalow, but we guess it's a little after one in the morning. It's warm and humid, the perfect temperature for a walk across a quiet island, but I'm tired enough that the trek all the way back to our bed feels impossible.

"It's maybe twenty minutes," West says, pushing our plates away and lying on his side facing me, propped on an elbow. He reaches with his free hand, walking two fingers up my back as I hug my knees.

"I want to stay here a little longer."

"Think of how comfortable the bed will be."

"Think of all the snakes in the grass between here and there."

"I'll protect you."

"But who will protect you?" I ask, looking at him over my shoulder. "That's what I worry about."

"I can see that," West says softly, with a meaning that's not so hidden anymore. He reaches up, brushing my hair off my shoulder. "Come here," he says, coaxing me down beside him, pulling me into his arms. With a shift of our bodies, he rolls me to my back.

He hovers over me, sending a hand over my hip and up to my breast, kissing me with the kind of command and tenderness that had me digging into his pants the first time. But when I reach for him, he shifts his hips away.

"Don't tempt me again, Green. I barely pulled out in time back there."

I laugh, cupping the back of his head. "You know that doesn't work anyway."

"It felt like an important compromise." He pulls me into his chest, letting me have one firm arm for a pillow, the other as a blanket.

"Liam?"

He goes still. "Yeah?"

"I had the best night of my life tonight."

He's silent in response for a few seconds, and then I feel the lingering press of his lips to the crown of my head. "Me, too."

The chorus of nighttime rises around us: waves and insects, wind rustling through trees.

"Anna?"

Goose bumps spread down my arm at the quiet intimacy in his voice. "Yeah?"

"You called me Liam."

"I did."

"I liked it."

"Good." I tilt my face to his, silently asking for one more kiss. He delivers it and then some, before tucking my head beneath his chin.

And outside, in the warm circle of Liam Weston's arms, I fall asleep.

Twenty-Six

LIAM

'm not sure whether I ever fully fall asleep, but I'm not suffering. For a few hours I'm in that syrupy, hazy place, with waves crashing nearby, cool, humid air pressing on my overheated skin, and Anna warm and asleep in my arms. Dreams flirt with the edges of my mind: mouths coming together, her soft cries, the wet sounds of our sex, the feel of her beneath me.

Even when I slowly rise to full consciousness, I stay motionless, listening to her quiet sleep noises, squeezing her when she murmurs, wondering whether I could carry her the entire way back to the bungalow. Lying for hours on a rattan mat on a wood-plank patio isn't awful, but this very same position would be so much better in a bed.

Anna sleeps facing me, both her arms tucked against her chest and by default against my chest, too. She barely moves once her face is firmly pressed to my neck, almost like a button has been pressed in her brain that lets her fully power down. Has she slept like this with someone else? She must have, of course. The thought lands with a slice, a quick, sharp paper cut, and I have to shove it away. To me, everything with her is so raw, so candid; that transparency in both conversation and sex is new to me, almost embarrassingly so. I want to lie to myself and think it's the same for her.

"I can hear you thinking," she mumbles sleepily into my throat. "But if you're going to freak out, can you do it later? You're so comfortable."

I laugh, kissing the top of her head. "I'm not freaking out. Just listening to the wilderness wake up."

Insects and birds are coming to life, whirring, chirping, calling to each other from every measure of distance, and at the suggestion of creatures out in the darkness, Anna goes rigid in my arms. And then she presses forward, curling inward, like she's trying to climb into my clothes. "Oh God, please don't mention wilderness."

I lift my head, scouting the immediate vicinity. "Doesn't seem like anything out there is very close to us."

"Not helping!"

"I do think we should head back, though. We might want to slip into the bungalow before anyone happens upon us." Specifically, my father. Nothing would more effectively kill the vibe than hearing his voice right now.

Anna wiggles some more, but this time it seems to be less about escaping from bugs and more about finding ways to create friction between our bodies. "I don't want to get up." Her wiggling turns into grinding, and she sneaks a hand between us, palming my erection. Warmth bleeds into my limbs, and I press forward, dizzy with a rush of desire.

She kisses up my neck. "I like your morning boners."

I groan, but not out of pleasure. "Green, I think I need to tell you: the word *boners* is . . ."

She pulls back to look at me. "You don't like 'boners'?"

"I enjoy *my* boners. I like the word less."

"What's better? 'Hard-on'? 'Woody'? 'Stiffy'?"

"These are all terrible."

A frown line forms on her forehead. "Devastating."

"Then I may as well get it out there that 'horny' can also go in the bin."

"You've just ensured that these words will now be staples in our marital relationship."

"I think I can handle hearing them for another four days." As soon as I've said it, we both go silent. Me, because an image has suddenly invaded my thoughts—dropping Anna off at her apartment in Los Angeles, seeing her figure shrink in the rearview mirror—and I don't like the brief shadow it sends through me.

I'm not sure what brand of quiet she's experiencing, but Anna tucks her face back into my neck, mumbling a "good" after what feels like an eternity.

Her hand slides up to rest on my waistband, and I hate that I've just cooled the moment when all I want is her touching me.

The horizon has a telling glow to it, the lazy prequel to a sunrise, and I suspect it's probably sometime just after five. Dad will be up and out soon, and what I want to do to Anna will take much, much longer than we have.

"Three hours is barely enough sleep," I tell her, reaching to tilt her face to mine. I kiss her, resting my lips against hers. "Let's head back and be lazy today."

"Do we have to be lazy?" she asks.

"No . . ." I pull back so I can get a better look at her expression. The heat in her eyes sends fire licking across my skin. "But if you're going to look at me like that, we do have to be alone."

Anna stretches, kissing my chin, my jaw, my neck. Her hand slides down again, gripping me through my pants, teasing me with a tight squeeze. "We *are* alone."

"For now." I tilt my chin up so she has better access to my neck, mindlessly hoping that she'll leave another mark. Her lips feather over my jaw, and then she bites. "My father gets up at sunrise and every morning has run along the trail that passes about fifteen feet from where we are right now."

This has the effect I'd hoped, and Anna peeks past my shoulder at the band of light just at the horizon. With a reluctant groan, she shifts her hand from me and slowly pushes up onto her side, bracing back on a palm as she sleepily blinks out at the cornflower-blue darkness all around us. "Are we going to be able to find our way back?"

"Let's take the shorter path. We haven't walked it together, but it's through the garden cabin area and I'm pretty sure there are lights."

She nods, sitting up fully and rubbing her eyes. I take another long, appreciative look at her back in this dress; even though the cream satin is rumpled from dancing and walking and fucking and sleeping, it still gleams in the moonlight against her smooth skin.

But there's also something vulnerable about her that has my chest constricting. She's hunched over, hugging her knees, and her spine presses against her skin, sharp little points all the way down her back. Her personality is so big, her confidence so solid, that until I had my hands all over her last night, I didn't fully realize how slight she is in more tangible ways. The view of her from behind in the blue-black darkness sends something inside me emerging protectively. It's easy to forget, while she's here and dressed in designer clothes, overfed at every meal, and basking in sunshine, that her life back home is hard, that she's barely scraping by. That this trip is a break from her reality, and when she returns to Los Angeles, she'll become that other version of Anna Green, the underemployed one, the one with food insecurity and unpaid bills, the one with responsibilities she's hinted at but never fully detailed.

She has money now, I remind myself. *You're paying her more than many people make in years. You can give her more. You can ensure she never has to worry about money again.*

Leaning forward, I press my lips to her shoulder blade, and kiss halfway down her spine, feeling my desire for her rise like the tide, mixing with this unexpected vigilance wrapping steel around my veins. I send an arm around her middle, hand sliding up over her breast, pressing my palm flat over her heart.

The words slip free in my thoughts—*Please be okay after this*—and I squeeze my eyes closed, pressing a final kiss to her back, not sure whether I'm making the wish for her or myself.

"Should we go?" she asks, setting her hand over mine on her chest. "This feels like the start of something we don't want Ray to see."

Laughing, I push myself to standing, extending a hand to her. Anna stretches, wrapping her arms around my neck. "I'm sad to leave the spot of the best night ever."

"You still feel that way after sleeping on the ground?"

"I had a comfy pillow." She steps back, taking my hand, and we start the trek back to our bungalow.

Twenty-Seven

LIAM

I suspect the only thing that would tip my family off to our scheme more than Anna and me appearing to know nothing about each other is how we suddenly seem like newlyweds, blocking out everything else on the island.

But there's nothing to be done. For the next two days, we rarely leave the bungalow. And when we do, I can't keep my hands off her.

We get back that first morning, drop our clothes, and finally get in the shower together. Messy, wet kisses, soapy, roaming hands work us both into a fever. It's not fully light out yet; we have all day. But we must forget all of that because we don't take the time to dry off; I set my hands on her hips, walking her backward to the bed, where I coax her down and beg my way between her legs, promising to make it good, nipping at her stomach, across her hips, until I tease her with a finger, and then my tongue, watching up the length of her body as she arches and presses into my touch. It's only the first time I've done this to her, but the shape of her is familiar; she tastes like something I've always known. With my arms around her thighs, hands clamping her knees open, I lose myself, ravenous for her silk and sounds, the scrape of her nails in my hair, and the wild, clawing stretch of eternity where she comes against my tongue.

Drunk with lust, Anna drags me up her body, flips us over, and sinks down on me, seeking, it seems, every possible way to drive me to madness: fingernails digging into my chest, teeth scraping my neck, the way she lifts her hips just as I think I might come, teasing and withholding her slick heat, giving me only the barest friction until I feel like a barbarian, rolling on top of her and pinning her wrists over her head, fucking her with a desperate fury that leaves me gasping and astounded and leaves her poured like warm honey across the sheets.

We fall asleep in a breathless stupor, waking hours later, exhausted and starving. I don't think either of us cares for one second what we look like emerging from our bungalow, but Anna looks stunning anyway. Her hair is in a messy bun on top of her head, her face free of any makeup, and the glow of pleasure lights her skin from beneath. She walks beside me along the beach to the café for lunch, her legs long and bare in cutoff shorts, arms supple and tanned in a simple white tank, and I slide my hand into her back pocket, relishing the way she fills my palm as she walks.

I can't resist reaching across the table while she spears a bite of fruit, or touching her bottom lip as she chews. She laughs at me as I move to the chair beside her so I can lean closer, press my nose into her neck, and inhale the way her sweat and my sweat together mix with the soap from the shower we took earlier. She smells like sex and sugar and me.

My hand finds its way to her thigh, my food forgotten. Her skin is satin on my fingertips, and I think about kissing it not three hours ago, think about how hard I took her after, and the way the mess of her desire spread down her thighs, right where I'm touching. She turns to capture my mouth in a kiss, her sweet pineapple tongue sliding with mine. Anna reaches with one hand to dig into my hair and I don't care who's there, who might be watching. I don't think about anything but her.

"I need you back in bed," I tell her. "On your hands and knees."

We take the rest of the food to go.

WHAT WE DON'T DO is talk out what collaborators with benefits should look like. We never stare directly at any of it, and nothing about this feels simple anymore.

Starting that first day after we make love, it might as well be just the two of us on the island. While everyone else is at a sunset game night, Anna and I hike to a secluded cove where we skinny-dip and then collapse on a blanket where she shimmies down my body, teeth dragging down my abdomen, teasing my cock with her kisses and tongue under the moonlight. The following morning, we wake slowly, lazily, making languid love with me curled behind her, my hands roaming the warm front of her body. We book a private boat to take us to a reef a few miles offshore where we snorkel and enjoy lunch on the deck, and I trace patterns on Anna's stomach as she sunbathes topless on the bow. Later, we tumble into our bungalow, where I finally play out the fantasy that looped in my mind for hours: straddling her ribs, roughly stroking my aching length, spilling on breasts still warm from the relentless sun. We have dinner that night at Jules Verne, at the table in the most private corner, hidden by the branches of a giant mangrove, and I have no idea whether anyone looks our way; all I know is no one dares to join us.

It's only later that second night—after we walk back to our bungalow, after Anna wraps her legs around me and I take my time feeling every inch of her, after I hold her boneless, sweaty body in my arms while she comes down—that we finally, truly talk.

Pushing up onto her elbow, she looks down at me. "Liam?"

"Mmm?" I reach up to stroke her jaw with my thumb.

"What are we really doing here?"

"What do you mean?" My voice comes out gravelly, my throat accustomed for the past several hours only to the hoarse, unfiltered noises she drags out of me.

"What's the loophole in the trust?"

I smile, pushing the mess of hair out of her face. "I was wondering when you'd ask."

She curls up on her side facing me and reaches beneath her head, adjusting her pillow under her cheek. "I figure we're past the point of pretending to be surface-level bros."

This makes me laugh. "Yeah?"

"Yeah." She stares at me, brown eyes luminous in the moonlight streaming across the bed. Anna traces a finger down my throat, bringing her hand to rest over my heart.

I lift it, kissing her palm, before putting it back where it was. "We leave soon."

"I know."

"And if it's okay, I'd like to keep seeing you."

She laughs. "I know you didn't mean to, but that's almost word for word what Richard Gere says in *Pretty Woman* before everything goes to shit."

"I think there are some important differences here you may be overlooking."

Anna squints at me. "Are we sure?"

Laughing, I reach around her back, pulling her flush to me. "I want to keep this going, whatever it is."

"So maybe you fly to LA and take me on a date sometime."

I lean in, resting my lips against hers, swallowing down the absurd, impulsive thought that wants to shove its way out of my throat: *Come live with me.* Instead, I say, "Anytime you want me."

She pulls back, ruthlessly biting her smiling bottom lip. "Okay."

And that easily, something ancient inside me settles.

With a deep breath, I reach forward, running my thumb over her lip, freeing it. "You know I was close to my grandfather."

She nods. "He was your favorite."

"Right. But he was also . . . a little unorthodox."

"Another word only rich people use."

I roll to my back, tucking a hand behind my head, and stare up at the ceiling, mentally sifting through what I can tell her. "Family was very important to him."

"Yeah. You mentioned that to me the first day you came over—sounds like there's a lot more buried in there."

I laugh quietly. "Yeah."

She reaches forward, tracing my Adam's apple with her fingertip. "Like what?"

"The thing about legal trusts is you can put whatever you want in them. Any stipulation." She waits for me to say more, dragging her hand down to rest over my sternum. I set my own hand on top of hers.

"I was only fifteen when Grandpa died. We were all at the reading of the will, but you can imagine in a situation like that, especially for kids, a lot of the details sort of go over your head. The reading took hours. I understood, basically, that he was leaving us each a very large sum of money. I understood that it was contingent on us being married. At the time, it didn't seem so weird that he would want that. Kids sort of take those adult directives as law."

"I can see that," she says quietly.

"About three years ago, pretty soon after I moved out of our apartment, I created a foundation. The annual deposits from the trust go directly to this fund."

"Like a charity?"

"Sort of, yeah."

"So—wait—you're not keeping your inheritance money?"

"No, like you said, I have a job." I grin at her, continuing, "With the approach of our five-year anniversary and in anticipation of the full balance of the trust coming into my name, I asked my attorney to clarify a few details about the inheritance. Whether there were any limits on its application, stuff like that."

"You mean," she cuts in, "like rules about how you can spend it?"

"Exactly." I shift, rolling to my side to face her. "You know most of the important details, like how the trust stipulates a marriage to trigger the inheritance, and if there's a divorce before the fifth anniversary, we forfeit the remaining balance."

Anna huffs out a laugh. "It's so wild."

"Well, what I didn't know, and what I'm guessing none of my siblings know, is that if the estate attorney—in this case, the firm that represents the money held in my grandfather's trust—finds evidence of artifice or fraud—"

Her eyes widen. "Like marrying someone to get student housing?"

I nod. "Yes. If they find evidence of fraud in the five-year window, the clause makes the fulfillment of the trust null and void."

"Even though we're *legally* married? You'd lose everything?"

"I'd lose everything, yes, but there's more." I trace the line of her collarbones from one shoulder to the other. "I can't say whether it was my grandfather's intention, because of course he's gone, and the attorney who drew up the documents has also passed away. But it appears that my grandfather wanted to find a way to bind the siblings together, to inspire us to support and confide in each other. He was always encouraging me to be kinder to Alex, to come from a place of understanding and empathy. In hindsight, I realize that he knew how much of a wedge our father drove between us, but he could never have anticipated how little any of us, as adults, actually disclose to each other at all."

"What are you saying?"

"I'm saying that the way he worded the clause in the trust concerned with our inheritance, legally, if one marriage is deemed fraudulent, the entire clause is nullified. The legal interpretation seems to be that it wouldn't be one sibling's inheritance but the entire balance of the account—nearly half a billion dollars—going to charity."

Anna stares at me.

"If one falls," I say, "we all fall."

I see the moment it fully lands. Dread washes her out, and she pushes to sit, the sheets falling to her waist. "You're telling me that if we get busted, Jake could lose the possibility of an inheritance? Charlie?"

"It appears so."

"What about Blaire and Alex? They've been married for over a decade."

"It doesn't seem to matter. The money was put into an account for each of us. It is my and my attorneys' understanding that access would be cut off—at the very least it would be restricted until the wording could be clarified in court. But this is the leverage I mean: my father wants me to come on as CEO. He's looking for leverage. Don't you think if he knew he could hold my siblings' inheritances over my head, he would?"

"So if he finds out, it's your life or their money?"

I nod.

"And you don't think your siblings know?"

"I can't imagine they do. Otherwise Alex would be doing everything he could to not sabotage this."

Two furrowed lines appear between her brows. "I don't understand. Why didn't you just tell them?"

"I only got clarity a couple weeks ago," I say, shrugging. "I thought I would be able to come here alone. I didn't think I would have to involve you in it. I didn't think it would turn into a circus. But then my mom implied that my father was getting suspicious about us. I don't know if he's aware of the loophole, but I'm sure his lawyers are. Or will be."

"Now if you tried to tell your siblings while we're here, you'd have to admit to Alex that we're lying," she says, nodding in understanding.

"And he'd either want his lawyers to confirm, or—more likely, since his lawyers would take weeks to do that—immediately go to Dad and ask if I'm telling the truth."

Anna exhales a quiet, "Fuck."

"Yeah."

"Why didn't you tell me?"

I blow out a breath, closing my eyes. "I didn't want you to feel the enormity of it. The pressure is . . . intense."

"You didn't have to handle this alone."

"We barely knew each other. I was just trying to get through every event without catastrophe."

Anna settles back down beside me. "We just have to get through the next few days. We can do this."

I pull in a deep breath. "We can."

"This was a lot to carry, Liam."

"It was." After a beat, I look over at her and smile. "You called me Liam again."

"I did."

Our gazes lock for several quiet beats and then she leans forward, pressing her lips to mine. When she pulls back, I ask, "Do you look more like
your mom or your dad?"

"My dad, definitely. My mom is short, has blue eyes and blond hair. My
hair is naturally brown, eyes brown." She laughs. "I used to want her eyes,
but now I'm glad that I got everything from him. He's the shit."

"I'd like to meet him."

She nods. "Yeah. I'd like that. I think you two would get along."

I smile, opening my mouth to say something about not being sure about
meeting Vivi again, though, but Anna speaks first, grinding my thoughts to a
halt: "He was diagnosed with lung cancer a few weeks after you moved out."

I roll to my side again to face her. "Oh shit. Is—is he okay?"

"Well, the lung cancer is gone—for good, I hope." She smiles weakly
at me. "But one of the possible side effects of the type of chemo he had is
what's called secondary acute myeloid leukemia."

I go still, heart dropping. "So his cancer is cured, but he got leukemia
as a result?"

Anna nods. "Before you worry too much, his prognosis is good. I
wouldn't be here if it wasn't. But at first, we didn't know. The prognosis for
this type of AML usually isn't great. So the past six months have been . . .
yeah." She reaches up, tucking a strand of hair behind her ear. "His oncologist and hematologist both think he's going to get through it. I really do
think we're on the other side, but it's been hell."

"I can't even imagine."

"I wish all of my research had been more useful to Jake's jellyfish sting,"
she says, laughing. "I know more about topoisomerase II inhibitors and myelo-
dysplastic syndrome and doxorubicin than I ever imagined I'd have to learn,
and there's not a lot approved for secondary AML, but what there is, is—of
course—also chemotherapy, which is just . . . *fuck*," she says, exhaling sharply.
"Just a type of drug that kills the cancer a little faster than it kills you."

"Anna—"

"He has insurance, but because our health care system is a nightmare, he's underinsured. And he's a mechanic, you know, so even though he owns his own shop it's not like he has a pension or paid medical leave."

It hits me so hard. Of course. *This* is why she needed money. She's been scraping her bowl just to cover her expenses *and* his. And she's twenty-five.

"Anna, you could have asked me for money anytime."

She laughs at this, the true, round sound filling the room. "I assumed you were as poor as I am." Anna tucks her hands beneath her chin. "Besides, I have enough now. It feels weird to take the money from you after everything, but—"

"No. You're taking it."

"Unless they figure out we're lying."

"Even if they all figure it out, you're taking it."

She gazes steadily at me and then nods against her hand. "Okay. I can be selfish when it comes to my dad."

"It isn't selfish. It's a business arrangement, revised verbally just now."

"Still," she says, and our gazes snag and hold. "It's different now."

It's my turn to laugh. "I can't believe it's only been a week." Reaching forward, I stroke my thumb over her cheek. "And . . . whatever happens between us after, I mean who knows . . . but I'll make sure you're taken care of."

Her eyes widen and she shakes her head. "No way. You're not responsible for me."

"I know." I nod, even if it's not entirely true. "Let's just take it one day at a time."

Anna leans in, kissing me. "One day at a time. That's all I've ever really been able to afford anyway." She grins, but then her smile turns mischievous as she rolls me over onto her, saying, "Let's see how it all feels in a few months."

I tilt my head, looking down at her, knowing I will never tire of this view. "Why in a few months?"

"I've heard divorce sex is hot," she says, and cackles in delight as I dive for her neck.

Twenty-Eight

ANNA

Of all the sounds I dislike in this world, the blare of the alarm at seven this morning takes the top spot. (We set it on the off chance that our all-night bangfest would prevent us from waking in time for the wedding day family breakfast at eight.) (And yes. It absolutely would have). But second only to that noise is the cracking squelch of an incredibly hungover Blaire Weston breaking raw eggs into her coconut water.

"Blaire," Janet says without looking away from where she's primly cutting a slice of mango into tiny, Barbie-sized bites, "you really shouldn't eat raw eggs." She's in her standard Janet Weston finery: a soft pink linen lounge set with the word *Dior* stitched into the breast pocket, and matching Dior sandals.

"Well," Alex says, and his eyes flicker to me, "correct me if I'm wrong, soon-to-be-Dr. Anna, but I believe eggs contain high amounts of cysteine, an amino acid that helps break down acetaldehyde, which causes hangovers."

I lift my coffee to him. "Well done." Apparently while Liam and I were re-creating most of the Kama Sutra, our big brother was studying medical texts.

"Yes, thank you, dear," Janet drawls. "I'm less concerned about her well-earned hangover and more concerned that she'll get salmonella and vomit all over Charlie's couture wedding gown."

Reagan gags and gets up from the table, GW giggles and begins mimicking the sound, and Alex takes an aggressive slurp of his coffee.

And across the table from me, Liam looks up, already smiling. His hair is a little wild—there was no hope in taming it after last night—and I'm not sure if he's noticed there's another small bruise under his ear. Our eyes lock, and I hope he's thinking the same thing I am, which is that the thing I did with my mouth very, very early this morning was born from pure, divine inspiration and given the sound he made when he came, he really owes me that perfect bite of pineapple on his plate.

With a laugh, he spears the fruit with his fork and drops it on my plate.

"How did you know?" I ask, amazed.

He rests an elbow on the table, setting his chin on his fist. "Because you've been staring at it for about five minutes and only just looked up with pleading in your eyes."

I pop it into my mouth and smile as I chew. "Thank you."

"No, thank *you*."

I was right. He's definitely thinking about the blow job.

Blaire groans. "The pheromones are so strong at this table, it's like living in a *Teen Wolf* fanfic." She turns a head that looks like it weighs twenty pounds to glare at Alex, who in turn is watching Liam with narrowed beady eyes.

"Liam, darling, no elbows on the table," Janet murmurs.

Unfazed, Liam straightens, pulling his elbow away and going back to smiling at his breakfast.

Charlie and Kellan arrive, their "we're six hours away from being newlyweds" glow firmly in place, but the moment Charlie sits, Janet leans over and launches into Defcon One Wedding Day Preparedness mode. A warm ocean breeze flutters the gauzy sleeves of my sundress. Blaire sips miserably at her hell juice; even her hair looks hungover. Jake helps Nixon cut his pancakes while also schooling him on the superiority of coconut syrup over maple, and Alex resentfully cleans up some milk little GW spills across the table. It's chaos, and stress blankets the air like a haze of bug spray, but there's something . . . sort of wonderful about it? I always imagined what it would be like to be part of a big family, and here I am in the thick of it, warts and all. Even with the looming threat of the loophole, Liam and I are optimistic that everything will be okay. We're falling for each other; we're not faking a thing.

It's my turn to rest my chin on a fist and gaze in adoration at him.

"I don't have any more pineapple," he murmurs, peeking up at me through his lashes.

I grin back, about to open my mouth and let some drippy, infatuated words fall out, but my phone buzzes on the table with the first call I've received in days.

It's Mel.

My manager never calls just to check in.

And I realize with a jolt that the art exhibit must have opened, and not only had I not been obsessing about it, I hadn't even *remembered*.

I throw Liam a nervous smile and stand without excusing myself, answering the call before I've even made it past the hostess stand near the entrance.

"Hi."

"Are you sitting down?" she asks, and a vibration spreads through my blood at the smile I hear on the other end of the line.

"No, in fact I essentially just hit the eject lever and launched myself out of a chair. What's going on, Mel?"

"Your paintings sold," she says.

Her words bounce around inside my ears before landing. "Which?"

A pause. "All of them, Anna. And they went for *a thousand dollars each*."

I stare out at the beach, unseeing. "What?"

"Your paintings sold," she repeats, laughing. "All three of them. Snatched up." Mel waits for me to say something, but my entire vocabulary is stuck in a traffic jam in my cranium. "Anna?"

Finally, I become unstuck, and it sinks in. I sold my work. I, Anna Green, sold *three* paintings. This might be the start for me. The path to a career I chose and trained for, a following—even a small one. Hope makes me feel weightless. "This is—this is amazing, Mel, oh my God." I walk in a small circle in front of the restaurant, my free hand in my hair, and when I look over, I see Liam at the table on the patio, craning his neck to watch me. I beam at him, lifting my hand to give him a thumbs-up.

And only a man worthy of these enormous feelings ballooning in my chest would smile in sun-bright relief back at me like that. Holy shit, I am so gone for him.

"Is there anything you need from me?" I ask.

"Not yet. We'll touch base when you're home, but for now, I'll get to work on finding some more openings for you. Congratulations, Anna."

We hang up and I stare at my screen for a few astounded moments.

And then, in my palm, the phone rings again.

But this time it's Vivi. And Vivi never calls.

Panic spreads in an icy chaser, and I let it ring twice, three times, wondering whether I'm hallucinating this or whether the universe really is this fucked up. The best news ever followed by the worst. If something happened to my dad while I was here, sunbathing and fucking and drinking—

"Hey," I answer just before the fourth ring. "What's going on?"

"No emergency," she bursts out, immediately. "My texts weren't going through, and I had something time-sensitive to run by you."

I fall gracelessly onto a bench outside the restaurant, relief making my head swim. I drop my head into my hand, willing my heart to start beating again. "Jesus Christ, Vivs."

"Sorry. Your dad is okay. He's kicking my ass at chess right now."

"Why didn't he call instead of you?"

"Because he won't pressure you into this like I will." She laughs.

"Pressure me into what?"

"So—okay, he mentioned that the oncologist recommended some in-home rehabilitation care?"

I nod, still shaking. "Yeah, um, a few weeks ago they gave us the order, but we were waiting for insurance to approve it while we sent out some requests to different agencies."

"Insurance didn't approve it," she says bluntly. "The letter came yesterday. Which is very unfortunate, since we heard back from one of the agencies and they have someone who can start now. But she isn't cheap."

"Oh." I take a deep breath. "I mean, that's okay, right?"

"That's what I thought you'd say," Vivi says, and in the background, Dad calls out, "No way, Anna. There is no way you're doing this."

"He's worried about the money," Vivi says with a meaningful lean to her words.

"Well," I say, "I just sold three paintings."

I hear footsteps, like she's moving to another room. A door closes and her voice comes back as a whisper. "Like really? Or as in, you want me to tell your dad that version?"

"Really." I turn my face to the sun and feel its warmth spread through me. Residual panic drains away and I feel only contentment. I have money from West, I have the start of a potential—maybe, let's hope—career as an artist. I might be falling in . . . I cut the thought off. "Mel just called me. Tell Dad I can cover it, absolutely no problem."

Vivi screams out a happy "Congratufuckinglations!" and I hear her jog back to the other room where I get to eavesdrop while she tells my father. He shouts in disbelief and then celebration, and the two of them do what sounds very much like dancing.

My dad, dancing.

"Here he is," Vivi says before passing the phone to my dad.

"Kiddo!" he shouts. "This is fantastic news!"

"Can you even believe it?"

"I can absolutely believe it. I am so proud of you, honey."

With a smile, I ring off and stand in place, letting it all sink in. I do the math, at which I am terrible, and realize that even if I pay off all of Dad's medical debt and his future treatment co-pays, with the money from Liam and the sale of these paintings, we can afford two months of daily physical therapy to get him back to health.

It isn't forever, and it's insane to me how fast the money goes, but it's enough. It's all we need.

EVEN THE NEW PRESENCE of Ray at the breakfast table when I return isn't enough to dim my elation. And since with this crowd I am supposed to be better at dissecting cadavers than at wielding a paintbrush, I can't burst into song about how, for the first time in my life, I sold not one but three actual paintings. But I do try to communicate as much of my joy as possible when I look at Liam across the table.

"What happened?" he mouths.

"I'll tell you later." My foot finds his leg under the table, and he captures it between his calves, squeezing, looking at me with curiosity and adoration. We get lost into a spiral of eye contact. I'm not in his brain, obviously, but I'd bet my next three orgasms that we're thinking the same thing, which is exactly how much time he plans to spend with his face between my thighs when the wedding reception wraps up tonight.

The sound of a fork dropping onto porcelain breaks through my trance, and I blink over to where Ray is now impatiently wiping his mouth on a napkin. "They just canceled now?"

Charlie, looking miserably down at her phone, nods. "Apparently a pipe burst upstairs, and the entire house is flooded."

"Surely there's something else nearby." Janet, ever the placater, pulls out her phone, too, and begins searching.

Ray looks over her shoulder and swipes it out of her hand. "Why are you looking at rentals?"

"Because it's only two weeks, Raymond. It's just a honeymoon."

"It's her only honeymoon, and the same shit could happen. I told you: it never works to rent." He leans forward, looking at Charlie. "If we bought instead, would you two use it?"

Charlie and Kellan grin at each other. "*Of course!*" she sings.

I look around, trying to figure out what the fuck is happening. Are they really talking about buying . . . houses? Liam is in his own little world, frowning out at the surf behind my shoulder. Blaire leans over, her ketone-warmed breath sour on my cheek when she explains, "You are hearing this correctly. Ray is suggesting they buy a house for Charlie's honeymoon."

I swallow around a rapidly swelling cork of "what the fuck" forming in my windpipe.

Ray slams the phone down on the table with a note of smug finality. "Done."

"Ray," Janet says quietly.

"What?" he says, waving to one of the waitstaff and snapping at his empty glass. "They needed a wedding gift. I got them a wedding gift."

"They already have one, darling. The . . ." She stares at him meaningfully.

"What?" he asks, exasperated. "I can't read your mind."

"The house we already bought them?"

Ray snaps his fingers again. "The Newport Coast place. Sure. But this is different. This is a vacation investment. Nobody seems to work here so I'm gonna find a drink." He stands, kissing the top of Charlie's head. "I'll have Terry handle it so it'll be ready for you."

I blink. I mean, I know nothing about escrows and whatnot but I'm pretty sure houses aren't bought in a day. "Isn't their honeymoon, like, tomorrow?" I ask.

No one pays me any attention, and Ray turns to leave and barrels right into a woman carrying a tray of mimosas. Glasses sail through the air, crashing with bright chaos onto the patio; one lands on Janet's lap, and Ray is absolutely doused in orange juice and champagne.

"Are you fucking blind?" he roars, and the woman falls to her knees beside Janet, scrambling for napkins to mop up the orange lake on the lap of her Dior loungewear. Waiters rush over with brooms and mops, sweeping up the piles of broken glass, cleaning the floor.

"Hello?" Ray booms, throwing his hands up. "Does anyone have a towel for *me*?"

Charlie and Kellan rush to stand, handing him their napkins as another waiter comes over with a towel that Ray snatches from his hand and uses to mop at his shirt, a polo with the logo of some corporate golf tournament printed on the pocket. His eyes are the color of a muddy puddle and just as deep, as he stares down at the waitress still trying to help Janet dry off.

"Oh just . . . let it go," Janet seethes before standing and storming out of the restaurant.

The waitress slowly rises, turning to face Ray. "Sir, I am so sorr—"

"What's your name?" he barks, ice in his voice.

"Thuy."

"Thuy, do you want to hear what I have to say, or would you prefer to bring me your manager?"

Her neck flushed, chin shaking, Thuy jogs off, and I look around as Alex, Charlie, Jake, and Kellan return to their breakfasts. Blaire sits back in her chair, her jaw tight, eyes fixed at a point in the distance. I glance at Liam, who is staring with fire up at his father. "Dad," he says steadily, "you ran into *her*."

Ray waves a hand. "It's fine."

Reagan catches my eye and panic consumes her expression. This isn't only embarrassing for her, it's probably terrifying. I give her a reassuring smile and mouth, "It's okay."

But I've lied. It isn't okay. The manager comes out, listens as Ray quietly enumerates the many transgressions this poor woman has made upon him and his family, and then shakes Ray's hand saying, "I'll handle it."

Ray sits back down in his seat, lifts his napkin, and lets it float down over his lap, picking up his fork like nothing has happened.

"Tell me you didn't have that woman fired," Liam says.

Ray stills, a bite of caviar-topped poached eggs hovering on the fork in front of him. "You think someone like that should be working in a Michelin-starred restaurant?"

"Maybe a one-star, definitely not two," Jake jokes with mock serious-
ness, and Charlie and Kellan exhale quiet, courteous laughs.

But Liam remains undeterred: "*You* collided with *her*, Dad."

"Do you have any idea how much I'm paying for this wedding?"

Blaire stands up, dropping her napkin on the table and walking away,
tilting her head for Reagan to follow. Ray doesn't even seem to notice.
Around us, the three other Weston siblings and Kellan eat in silence, pretending they don't hear any of this. Only the three little boys look around
in confusion, trying to read the cues.

It's for them that I speak up: "Whatever you're paying, it isn't enough
for you to treat a waitress like that."

Ray turns his stony gaze to me, and it takes everything in me to not
look away. "She's in the service industry," he says flatly. "It's her job to be
invisible."

Liam cuts out a sharp *"Dad."*

Ray continues to stare at me for a handful of seconds before slowly
blinking his gaze over to Liam. "I need you to give Ellis some time at the
reception today."

He's just made his point: *Anna, too, should be invisible.*

"Ellis Sikora?" Alex asks, while Liam and Ray have a silent showdown.
"From *Forbes*?"

I pull a deep breath in through my nose, turning my attention to my
plate. My heart rolls violently, a catfight in my chest. In my peripheral vision, I see Liam's hands curled into fists on either side of his plate.

I feel when he turns to look at me and meet his gaze. I'm relieved to see
the same horror I feel reflected back in his eyes. Yes, this morning has been
an amazing smorgasbord of sex, and perfect bites of pineapple, and smiling
whiskey eyes, and good news, and even better news. But reality washes over
me like ice water. This dynamic isn't kooky and wonderful. This family
isn't a charming group with a few warts. This family is gross. Liam is paying me a sum of money that I wouldn't earn in three years working two
jobs and yet, with Dad's medical expenses, it won't even last me the rest of

the year. Meanwhile, these assholes are buying a house for a honeymoon and firing a waitress Ray basically tackled for spilling mimosa on a shirt he got for free. I feel like sweeping my arm down the table and sending all the fancy crystal and porcelain crashing to the floor.

I drop my napkin on my plate and stand. Without a word, Liam does the same, and we walk together out of the restaurant.

Twenty-Nine

LIAM

Anna's strides are so long, I have to jog to join her at the transition from restaurant steps to beach sand, where I catch her wrist but don't use the contact to slow her down or try to bring her back. I wouldn't dare. Instead, I slide my hand a few inches down her arm, entwining her fingers with mine.

It's awkward walking on sand with our hands joined, but neither of us loosens our grip. Honestly, I feel sick. Sick over how entitled my parents are, sick over how silent Alex, Jake, and Charlie remained throughout all of it. Sick over that level of flippant privilege happening in front of the children. Sick over being a part of this family at all anymore.

And sick with worry that this was a bridge too far for Anna. That I'm too closely associated with something so horrible. When I glance over at her, her nostrils are flared, jaw tight, and I see the way she swallows, like she's fighting tears.

"Almost done," I tell her. "We'll be home soon."

"There are people out there who have to choose between buying food and getting their prescriptions filled because money is so tight, and your family is buying an entire house because a pipe burst in the honeymoon rental. It's gross," she gasps, looking away so I won't see her lose the battle against crying.

"It is. I'm so sorry I brought you here."

"I'm not. Or . . . I am?" She lets out a coughing laugh, wiping her nose with her free hand. "I don't even know what to feel after that. I want to have met you again. I want whatever this is between us, and we wouldn't have it if we hadn't come here. And truthfully, I let myself enjoy the fairy tale of this. Everything about this experience is seductive—the island, the food, the parties, the spa, these clothes. But is it worth it?" She shakes her head. "I don't think so. I feel like I lost some innocence here that maybe I shouldn't have held on to, but even if it made me naive, I'll miss it. I wish I could still believe somewhere inside me that terrible rich people like this didn't *actually* exist. That they didn't view people like my father and me with such disdain. They would have gotten along swimmingly with my mother."

This lands a crushing weight in my chest. "I'm sorry."

Instead of turning toward the bungalow, Anna lets go of my hand and walks straight out to the water, wading in a few yards, until the gentle waves reach her knees. I'm not sure if she needs a moment alone or not, but when she speaks again, it's quietly enough that I have to follow, letting the water wash over my shins.

"What did you say?"

"I sold my paintings," she says.

Warmth bleeds into my limbs. Holy fuck, I'd wondered if that had been the call that had sent her up and away from the table. "Anna—yes!"

"All three of them at the exhibit."

Her joy is palpable, and if it were any other moment, I would be lifting her in the air, spinning her in my arms, joking that no virgin sacrifices were required. "That's—that's *amazing*."

"Yeah."

A gull calls overhead, and at the sound of her flat, defeated tone, I lean forward to get a good look at her face. "You don't look happy."

"I am. I'm thrilled." She turns her watery brown eyes up to me. "But it's depressing, you know? To feel such a victory over a few thousand dollars. The champagne at breakfast was probably more than that."

I shake my head. "That isn't—that's not the point." Stepping in front of her, I cup her face. "Your paintings—"

"No, no, don't get me wrong. I'm *so* happy. It means something huge for me. Even if it's just a start, it's wonderful. And I'm not so naive as to think there aren't enormous divides in income around this world, but I've never been so squarely confronted with it. The past three years have been so *hard*, not knowing, with all the bills. . . ." She swallows, shaking her head and giving me a weak smile. "I just needed a few fall-apart minutes."

I nod and bend, resting my lips on hers. When I pull back, it's only so I can meet her eyes. At this moment, we are the only two people on the island. Does she feel that, too? I want to transport her away from here. "Take as many fall-apart minutes as you need."

"I really do want to enjoy the wedding today," she says, wiping her face and working to compose herself. "I want to finish what we came here to do. I want to absorb the beauty of this amazing place. I want to let myself enjoy whatever else it has to offer before I leave and return to a life that is wonderful even if it's sometimes hard."

I kiss her again. "This is a perfect goal. We're almost done. We'll go relax in the bungalow, get changed, attend the wedding, and duck out as early as we can. Tomorrow we can skip the brunch. Tomorrow afternoon, we head home. We'll leave this beautiful island and the mess of my family behind."

Anna nods in my hands and stretches to kiss me. "I adore this island. I hate the mess. But I really, really, really like you."

I smile against her lips. "I really, really, really like you, too."

IN THE FINAL FEW minutes before we leave for the wedding, I walk out to the balcony, wanting to soak up the view. For as mortifying as my family has been, the island truly is paradise, and being here with Anna has been one of the most wonderful experiences of my lifetime. After breakfast, we napped for a few hours, then lazily roused ourselves, making love and showering. But our mood dipped again as we began the slow march toward today's main event. I know I should be happy—it's my sister's wedding—but mostly I just want to get it over with. And when I hear Anna's footsteps approaching, my first thought is that it didn't take her very long to get ready. My second thought is that I'm glad; she should treat today as a formality.

My third thought . . . well, actually, I don't have a third thought. Because when I turn and see her, my brain empties, my body ignites.

Anna has worn tiny minidresses, slinky silk gowns, and low-cut evening dresses that sent my mind racing down filthy tracks. But this dress isn't anything like that. While other women will likely be wearing muted lace, beachy neutrals, conservative chiffon, Anna's dress is a statement. The one-shouldered silk gown is softly pleated, with bright teal at the top that transitions into blue, then purple, then into a flowing skirt of pink and orange, ending at her feet with a brilliant, flaming crimson.

Go ahead and look, it says. *Stare.*

Speechless, I approach, cupping her shoulders and sending my hands down her long, soft arms. I bend, kissing her bare shoulder. When I close my eyes, I feel momentarily dizzy. It's too soon to feel what I'm feeling, but I let it wash through me anyway, because it solidifies my resolve to get this precious woman out of here as soon as humanly possible.

I KNOW HOW MUCH money my family has. In abstract terms, at least, I know that it is in the billions. Alex got a Lamborghini Gallardo for his eighteenth birthday; Charlie got a Friesian horse from the tooth fairy. Hell, she got two whole houses as wedding gifts. And without really batting an eye, I agreed to pay Anna a hundred thousand dollars to tell a lie.

I know the absurdity; I can see it, even if sometimes only in theory.

But the scale of this wedding is unbelievable even to me. Along the path to the black sand cove, every tree drips with garlands of pearls, crystals, and tiny twinkling lights. Delicate glass chandeliers tinkle from the branches of mangrove trees that sway along to the ocean's gentle rhythm. Swags of bamboo and layers of lush greenery drape every chair; columns

are topped with towering vases of white king protea, cream roses, and orchids, more strands of sparkling crystal spilling from their lips.

And there is an aisle, not just a demarcation with petals or branches: a
stretch of pure white marble has been meticulously set in the black sand.
It's lined in flickering candles and ends with three wide stairs, which lead
to a raised circular stage that will function as the altar overlooking the
waves crashing against the shores of the cove. Guests won't be sitting in
folding chairs during the ceremony; there are rows of neatly aligned vintage armchairs with fluted wood frames and tufted linen upholstery. A selection of antique gilded mirrors are propped in the sand, reflecting the
entire, glittering scene back to us.

Not wanting to mingle, we'd waited as long as we could before arriving, and now, from inside the pavilion, Jake furiously waves me over. I
squeeze Anna's hand, checking her face before I have to leave her to join
the groomsmen.

"You good?" I ask.

She lifts her chin and nods but I see my own disbelief echoed in her
eyes. It's so much. Weddings are supposed to be celebratory and grandiose,
but this is bordering on grotesque.

I wait until she's comfortably seated in the front row beside Blaire before walking away.

The minute she's out of my sight, I enter a bit of a trance, wanting to
get this all over with. Yes, it's beautiful; in fact, odds are good this is one
of the most beautiful weddings ever. But after this morning's drama, it's
hard to completely enjoy it as I walk down the aisle with one of the Leighs
on my arm. Of course, there are moments of perfection that follow. Like
when the live orchestra dips into motion, and Linc, Nix, and GW walk
in tiny suits down the aisle. Or the delighted coos of the gathered guests
when GW veers off the path, determined to sit on Anna's lap. Or Reagan,
following with a basket of petals, looking beautiful and so grown-up. (She'd
been nervous about walking alone, so Anna drew her a portrait, of Reagan
glowing and confident with her chin in the air. She had stared at Anna with

hero worship in her eyes. I see the sketch at the bottom of the basket when she reaches the altar.)

And of course, the appearance of Charlie in her wedding dress does something to me, something choking and instinctive, the most bittersweet moment of my life so far. At her side, Dad looks smug and dickish, but my baby sister is a vision, more beautiful than I've ever seen her. As Charlie nears, though, my eyes turn to Anna in the front row next to Blaire. The two women clutch hands as they watch Charlie walk down the aisle toward Kellan. The pink of Anna's hair has faded from so much time in the ocean, leaving it the same blush as the blossoms strewn down the aisle.

I'm between my brothers at the altar, with my sister taking her careful steps up to the stage, and I can't stop staring at Anna. I feel the longing solidify into realization: I want our marriage to be real. Marrying her for student housing was the most impulsive thing I've ever done, and it turns out it might have been the best thing that's ever happened to me.

The sunset washes her skin in gold and our eyes meet. She smiles, laughing through her tears, and just like that, I know. I'm going to ask her to move in with me. I'll move her father close, too, if that's what it takes. She can paint all day, every day, for the rest of our lives. I'm so swept up with this version of forever that I'm startled when the audience breaks into applause and Kellan steps forward, lifting Charlie's windblown veil and kissing her with sweet reverence.

The standard wedding mayhem follows: photos with the blazing sky as a backdrop, flutes of champagne passing from hand to hand, greeting everyone as if we haven't all been together on an island for nine days. The party moves to a gossamer tent with the moon and stars visible overhead; the orchestra plays gentle renditions of pop songs, letting the crash of the waves take center stage. Everything is lit by candlelight and the chandeliers overhead. A six-tier cake is carried in, smooth with white fondant, a brush of gold leaf and an asymmetric swag of sugared orchids. Guests mingle and sample caramelized figs with bacon and chili, roasted oysters, and crème fraîche tarts dotted with caviar. They drink champagne by the gallon and talk about the splendor of the event, but I'm not interested in any of it. I have Anna Green in my arms.

I'm sure I look like a lovesick idiot, but I truly do not care. How did I not notice this perfect woman years ago when she was just across the hall?

"That wedding was beautiful," she says now, looking up at me. Half of her hair is pulled back, loose and wavy from the salt air. Her skin is warm in the humidity, her cheeks pink after two glasses of champagne. "And absurd."

"It was absolutely both."

"You know, you were supposed to be paying attention to the bride."

"Then you shouldn't have worn that dress."

She laughs and threads her fingers into the hair at the nape of my neck. "I think this dress is the most inexpensive thing Vivi packed, and yet it's my favorite."

"I can see why. You look like a sunset."

Emotion swells in my chest, eager and demanding. I should ask her to move in with me now. It's sudden—it's crazy—but it's right.

"Anna."

She turns her eyes up to me. "Mmm?"

My heart speeds up, not because I'm nervous, but because I'm ready. "There's something I need to—"

"Mr. Weston? Excuse me, Liam?"

We both turn at the sound of a voice to my left. Ellis.

Anna and I step apart a little. "Oh. Ellis—this is Anna. My wife. Anna, this is Ellis Sikora from *Forbes*."

I don't miss the way her expression crashes, and I feel it, too, the unwelcome invasion of reality into our night. "Hello."

"Sorry to interrupt," he says, but he doesn't leave. An empty apology.

I lift my brows, waiting.

"I was just speaking to your father." Ellis looks to me, then to Anna, and back to me again. "I hear congratulations are in order."

My first thought—an insane one—is that he somehow knows I'm going to ask Anna to move in with me.

"Congratulations . . . ?" I ask.

"Your father mentioned that he'll begin the three-year transition process to retirement. And that you'll be coming on board, eventually taking over as CEO."

Anna's attention presses like a red-hot iron rod to the side of my face.

"He said this?" I ask.

Ellis nods. "It's unconventional. But I think your education and in particular your focus on corporate microcultures is exactly what Weston's needs. A positive step toward a modern workforce. I'd love to dig into that, how you plan on amplifying employee engagement and shaping the corporate culture under your leadership. Do you have plans to transition back over the next few months?"

I scan the room for my father. He's standing on the far side of the tent, surrounded by his sycophants, but the moment I spot him, our eyes lock. He'd been watching, waiting for this. With a small smile, he raises his glass to me.

"We haven't discussed a plan," I say, and then clear my throat. "There are a lot of steps we've skipped here."

"Your father is confident the board won't present a problem," he says. "And I understand why you had to play coy. Can't let this kind of thing out early, can we?"

I glance to Anna. She looks as annoyed as I feel.

"I knew your grandfather," Ellis adds, jerking my attention back. "He would be proud to see you at the helm, Liam."

This feels like a dagger. I swallow, and then have to swallow again to get past the clog of anger and sadness. "Right."

"I'd love to have some time to talk to you, to perhaps plan the exclusive interview for once we return."

"The exclusive—?"

"Yes. Your father and I have set an agreement that *Forbes* will have the exclusive. Does tomorrow morning work?" he asks, smiling warmly.

I am numb. "Tomorrow . . ."

"Congratulations again, Liam." With a pat to my shoulder, Ellis nods to Anna and leaves us to return to our dancing.

But instead, Anna pulls me off the dance floor, resting a hand on the side of my neck. "Hey, sweetheart?" I blink down at her, unseeing. "Are you okay?" she asks, searching my eyes. I have no idea what she finds there.

This is a mess. It's one thing to flirt with the idea of me coming on, to let Ellis dig around a little, but this is an announcement. Turning the message around now would be a public nightmare for the company.

"Shit." I look up and, as it sinks in, begin searching for someone else now. "*Shit.*"

But he's already on his way. My eyes lock on Alex's as he approaches, cutting across the dance floor, eyes burning. Jake is jogging to catch up to him. "Alex," he says. "Slow down."

"Liam." When Alex reaches me, he roughly pushes Anna out of the way and all thoughts of Weston Foods, my father, and whatever *Forbes* might have to say about it vanish as a bubble of hot rage explodes in my chest.

"*Hey.*" My voice is a knife's edge, and I shove Alex backward. He stumbles. "I don't know what the fuck is going on here, but if you ever touch her again, I'm putting my fist through your jaw."

Alex ignores this, coming right back up in my face. "You don't know what's going on here? Really, *brother*?"

"I don't want this," I say, low and seething, protectively shifting Anna behind me. "I've told Dad a hundred times I'm not interested in that job, or any job in this company."

"So you said," Alex says, face crimson. "And yet here we are."

"Come on, man," Jake says, pleading, pulling Alex's arm to get him to step back. "Let's go outside."

Alex shakes him off. "Right here is fine."

We aren't exactly the center of attention, but we aren't incognito, either. Alex's march through the party drew some eyes. My violent shove to his chest drew even more.

"Alex," I say, inhaling to calm myself down. "No one here is trying to fuck you."

"Then why am I standing here with your goddamn dick up my ass!"

"Whoa, graphic," Anna says, coming around to stand between us. She sets a hand on my chest and another on Alex's. "Okay. Everyone take a breath. I know this feels huge. It *is* huge. But so is tonight. This is your sister's wedding reception." She looks at each of us in turn, though Alex never takes his gaze from my face. "Do this tomorrow," Anna says. "You'll get this sorted."

It takes a beat, but Alex's face relaxes. And then he nods. "You're right."

"See?" she says, exhaling a shaky breath. "Later, okay? Sort it later."

The problem is, Alex is still nodding, still staring at me. "You're right," he says again. "We'll get this sorted."

And then he turns, stumbling away.

"It's fine." Jake gives my shoulder a squeeze and tosses back the rest of his drink. "He's upset now but he'll get over it. He always does."

"Right," I say, but I'm not so sure. Despite his posturing, Alex isn't one for public confrontation. That he approached me here at all shows how blindsided he was. How reckless this has made him.

"Wait," Anna whispers, her hand clenching mine. "What's he doing?" I follow her gaze to where Alex is now on the stage with the orchestra, wrenching a microphone free of a stand near a violinist. That's when I know.

Jake exhales a quiet "fuck" as dread sends ice water through my veins.

"Alex," I call out, taking a step forward. "Brother, trust me. Don't do this."

He taps the mic and the sound reverberates through the room.

"Alex, don't," I warn again as Anna exhales a quiet curse. "This won't go the way you think it will."

He looks at me with such fury that hope sinks like a stone in my gut. I turn my head, meeting my father's eyes across the room, and the way his glimmer in the strung lights tells me he's led us straight here. We walked directly into his trap.

Alex waves an arm overhead. "Could I—?" The speakers squawk sharply with feedback, and Alex clears his throat before leaning back in, breathing heavily. The force of his exhale echoes all around the tent. His hand is shaking. "Could I get everyone's attention?"

Slowly, with the tinkling of glasses and the decrescendo of conversation, the room stills. Eyes turn to my brother, sweaty and pallid up at the front of the room, and quiet murmurs pass in a concerned wave. Anna presses into my side, and I send an arm around her waist, holding her close.

"Hello, yes, up here, hello everybody." Alex waves to a passing waitress carrying a tray of champagne flutes. "Could—excuse me, could you bring me one of—yes," he says, taking a glass. "Thank you. I wanted to make a toast." He laughs, sending a loud puff of air into the mic, and a few people around us exchange uneasy glances. "I know the toasts come later, after we all eat, but I suppose I couldn't wait." He stares down into his glass for a beat before he looks up with a smile. He seems the slightest bit calmer now, more collected. "My name is Alex, for anyone out there I haven't had the pleasure of meeting. I'm Charlie's oldest brother, and CFO of Weston Foods." Another sharp laugh, and he shakes his head.

Near the edge of the stage, Charlie and Kellan look on, trusting, curious, and a little confused.

"Well, anyway, it's my baby sister's big day and it was absolutely gorgeous, wasn't it?" He nods encouragingly at a smattering of unsure applause, and the clapping intensifies before Alex cuts it off abruptly. "Nice to have a family wedding. Isn't it? I told my brother Liam—where are you? Ah, right there." He points to me. "I told my brother Liam that he deprived us of all this." Alex sweeps his arm, gesturing around the room. "A similar day of gathering, a day to celebrate his wedding to his lovely wife, Anna, five years ago."

Beside me, Anna goes still. I blink down at her, and she looks up at me, bleak with understanding. Tears fill her eyes. "I'm so sorry," she mouths, soundless.

I bend, kissing her forehead. "None of this is your fault."

Jake leaves my side and approaches Alex on the stage, reaching for the mic. "Come on, man."

Alex jerks it away, pushing him. "I got this," he says, too loudly, and a few people near him wince. A feeling works its way through the room, like the calm before a storm, the sea pulling away from the shore before a tsunami builds. "Liam and Anna . . . see, their wedding was fast. *So fast*," he continues, laughing, as he begins to pace. "One minute Anna Green is just a friend of Jake's from UCLA, the next she's married to my private, somber, golden-boy brother who never did an impulsive thing in his lifetime."

In the distance, my mother's voice rises up. "Alex. *Stop*."

"No, Mom, this is okay. I'll bring it all back, I promise." He reaches up with the hand holding the mic and uses the back of his wrist to push his sweaty hair off his forehead. "My brother has spent the past five years telling us about his wife. A med student, excelling in her studies, wowing every professor she meets. A medical doctor in the family! Can you believe it? Every parent's dream. But you see . . . the only Anna Green I could find at UCLA switched to a fine art major her junior year. There's no Anna Green attending Stanford medical school." He frowns in feigned confusion.

"Alex, stop it," I call out, my voice deep with warning.

"There *is* an Anna Green who attended UCLA around the right time, but she recently worked as a convenience store clerk and rents an apartment in Los Angeles. That seems like it'd be a pretty nasty commute to northern California, where Liam lives, but what do I know?" He taps his chin thoughtfully. "Though I guess, if I've got the right Anna Green, she'll be able to move back in with him now that she's lost her job at the Pick-It-Up on Pico Boulevard." He cups a hand to the side of his mouth and fake-whispers into the mic, "You never want to congratulate someone for getting fired, but in this case I can't help but think it will be good for the marriage!" He stops and turns to walk the other way. Eyes follow his path, but many also flicker back to Anna, who's gone as white as a sheet against me. With the guise of her pedigree slipping, their gazes turn harsh, judgmental, and they look at her with the disdain she'd expected all along.

"Oh, come on, friends! Who are we to get in the way of love? Who cares if she doesn't really go to medical school? Who cares that she doesn't even know what fork to use?" Alex huffs a laugh into the mic and a soft smattering of laughter drifts through the tent. "As long as my brother is happy, right?" He looks squarely at me. "At least, you *look* happy, Liam. It's hard to know because we never see you. I mean, we wouldn't have even seen you together here if that little scam artist right there hadn't agreed to be your fake wife."

I stare at him with thunder in my eyes. I want to destroy him.

Voices break out all around us—surprise, protest, speculation—but Alex quells it with a hand. "Sorry. I guess *technically* you're married, right? Until . . ." Alex glances at his watch. "August fifth? Or was it the twelfth?" He turns his eyes back to me at last. I feel movement at my side, when Anna breaks free of my hand and turns, running out of the tent. "After all, being married was the only requirement for you to inherit your money. What admirable behavior for the man our father wants to be Weston Foods' next CEO." He lifts his glass aloft and smiles warmly, no idea that he could be destroying his own life right along with mine. "So thank you, Charlie and Kellan, for having this wedding so we could have some time together with Liam before he conned us all and disappeared forever."

$\mathcal{T}$hirty

ANNA

I burst outside, into air that is humid and thick and cloying with the perfume of flowering trees. I have loved this air with every breath I've taken on this trip, but right now I want nothing more than the foggy marine layer of Los Angeles in May. I want the sound of traffic and neighbors arguing and the smell of food trucks. I want to teleport myself off this island, back to my shitty apartment and my old couch where I don't have to pretend to be anyone but Anna Green: Aquarius, cheese lover, and Enzo's Pizza VIP customer discount card holder. I don't know what's going on back in that tent, but there's no way in hell I'm staying to watch the rest of it.

Am I okay? No.

But will I be?

Probably also no.

I mean, Liam is still in there being humiliated by his brother, but I feel like I was *decimated*. Alex exposed Liam by destroying me.

My optimism about the world and the people in it has been ripped wide open, exposing the stain of humanity underneath it; I can't unsee that. And I won't ever forget this bone-deep feeling of humiliation, either, especially when there's no way for me to exit this island before someone who witnessed that garbage diatribe sees me. This is very much a "never show my face in this establishment again" kind of situation, and yet I am unable to exit said establishment, being that it is an island in the middle of an ocean. Maybe I should raid the Old Hollywood costume stash and be Elvis until I can get on a fucking plane out of here.

I press my hands to my ribs, trying to pull in a full breath as I pace. The tide rolls toward the shore, water lapping at my feet and darkening the hem of my dress. I barely notice. I don't know if this feeling is anger or sadness or humiliation, but I do know that when a hand comes around my arm, all I can see is Alex's pinched, vengeful face, and for the first time in my life, my instinct is to react with violence.

My hands come up to a chest before I've taken the time to look at a face, and I shove, hard.

Liam stumbles back, his hands up. "It's me."

With a sob, I dive into his arms, and he holds me, his lips pressed to the top of my head. Several long seconds pass where he just rocks slightly, cradling me to him. Down the beach, in the tent, noise rises again. Music, voices, the clinking of glasses and silver on porcelain.

The show must go on.

Liam's voice rumbles against the crown of my head. "Are you okay?" he asks.

"No. Are you?"

He steps back, taking my chin between his finger and thumb. "I'm more worried about you. I thought he was going after me. He didn't. You took a real beating in there."

My "yeah" comes out a little soggy. I don't want to care what Alex said or what anyone else in that tent thinks of me. Would I care what they thought of my clothes or my hair or my job if I saw them on the street? No. They're just like the people I serve at Amir's Café—some of them are good, some of them are awful—none of them are better than me or Vivi or her parents or even *Ricky* in any of the ways that count. Well . . . maybe better than Ricky. The thing is, I don't *want* to care. But I do.

"This is all my fault," he says.

"It's ninety-five percent your fault," I tell him, sniffing. "I take five percent responsibility for agreeing to come. But this is what you're paying me for, I suppose. For the odds that something like tonight happened."

He stares miserably down at me. "I'm so sorry, Anna."

"I know." And I do. Regret is written all over his face, but so is the adoration he's been wearing for days. We may have started with a crazy lie, but this much, I know, is real. "I don't belong in this world, Liam, and everyone has always known it." Humiliated tears surface again and I irritably swipe them off my cheeks. "I never fooled anyone."

He shakes his head, swallowing thickly. "Anna, I want you to know that it was never my intention to set you up like that."

"I know."

Liam searches my eyes. "When I was dreaming up our story, I chose the path I genuinely thought you were taking. And at the time, it didn't matter what the fake you did or who the fake you was, not really." He swallows again, his eyes growing pained. "I want you to know—I *need* you to know—that I am not ashamed of your path as an artist. Not for one second. I think the real you is wonderful, exactly the way she is. You are funny, courageous, creative, and silly. You are honest and vulnerable. You are forthcoming and self-reliant. You are sexy as hell and amazing in bed." I laugh, and he smiles. "I am well on my way to falling for you, and fuck anyone who makes you feel small. *Fuck* them."

I let him pull me into his arms again, resting my cheek on his shoulder. A part of me really needed to hear him say that.

"I just want to get home," he whispers. "But this is such a mess. Fuck. Alex doesn't even know what he's done."

I lean back, looking into his eyes, searching. "What happens now?"

"I'm not sure yet," he admits, shaking his head. "Dad got up in there and tried his best to make Alex look drunk and unreliable, and everyone wants to keep eating caviar, so it seems like most guests are laughing it off and planning to gossip their guts out later." He inhales, steadying himself. "I'm sure they're all still in there. And when the guests are gone, that's when the real shit will go down."

HE'S NOT WRONG.

The guests drift back to their villas, cheerfully drunk and sated in both caviar and gossip. Once everyone's gone, and the staff has mostly cleared the tent, Liam and I link hands, exchange a brief kiss of solidarity, and walk inside to find a miserable assortment of Westons. Alex is slumped in a chair, his elbows on his knees, staring grimly at the floor. Ray stands near the bar, face red and neck veins bulging. Next to him is a man I don't know. They talk quietly, each slowly spinning a highball glass filled with what looks like whiskey. Jake leans against a tent pole on the far side of the room, scrolling on his phone. Janet fussily tidies while Charlie whispers angrily to Kellan in the corner. Only Blaire, who I'm guessing has gone to get the kids to bed, is missing. Lucky her.

The chandeliers are still lit overhead, Charlie's elaborate cake, half-eaten, sits on a heavy crystal stand, waiting to be boxed up. Gold streamers litter the floor. It's a beautiful mess and we're walking right into the middle of it. How fitting.

As we enter, all eyes turn our way.

"Nice of you to join us," Alex mumbles.

"I'm surprised they even came back," Ray says. "That little stunt was un-fucking-believable."

Alex looks up in surprise, as if trying to read his father's tone. "Which one?"

Ray laughs humorlessly, pushing off the bar to walk over. "Which one? Your speech, you moron."

And I truly *never* imagined a situation in which I'd ever feel bad for Alex Weston again, but this manages to penetrate my anger. Yes, Alex is annoying and intense and an enormous asshole and I suspect not very effective at his job and, while we're at it, probably a terrible lay, but objectively Ray deserves a majority of the blame.

But Liam steps deeper into the room and addresses his father. "Don't blame him. Blame me."

"I'll blame whoever I want," Ray says, still staring at Alex. "Clearly Alex thought I didn't know about Liam and Anna and decided sharing it with the world at the same time he was telling me was the way to go." My jaw ratchets slowly open. *He knew? This whole time?*

"At my *wedding*," Charlie sobs. "*My* wedding, Alex."

Alex looks around, incredulous. "Does no one care that Liam has been lying for years? That he brought a literal gas station attendant to your wedding, Charlie?"

Oh, fuck him. "I think you mean a former gas station attendant," I say, giving him the finger. Liam turns to look at me, laughing despite himself.

"You think this is funny?" Ray asks Liam. "You think this is all a game?"

"No, Dad." Liam turns back, sobering. "I think this is a very serious, very aggravating situation, and one entirely of your own making. I've told you in every way I can that I didn't want to be part of this company. And still, you keep pushing, you led us right here, when Alex is standing there, wanting this."

"He's a finance nerd," Ray says, exasperated, like he's said this every day of his adult life. "It's not a good fit."

"If you didn't think it was a good fit, you could have trained him to be a better one. You could have sent him elsewhere to gain the experience you thought he lacked. But you didn't do that."

"Because it makes sense for you to take over."

"*And I don't want the job!*"

"Because of the fucking Pisa nonsense?"

Pisa. The word sparks a memory: Ray and Liam shouting that word on the trail the day of their groomsmen fitting.

I feel the room go still, and everyone looks at Liam, who very slowly walks closer to his father and calmly says, "Because of a lot of things. But yes, Dad. Because of the Pisa *nonsense*."

I glance around the room, looking for a clue as to what Pisa is. Everyone is pointedly looking somewhere else. Charlie lets out a frustrated growl that mirrors the confused aggravation building in my chest. "What *is* that?" she yells. "What is Pisa? Just tell me! I've been hearing about this stupid thing for years!"

"Not now, Charlie," Ray says with seething quiet, his eyes never wavering from Liam.

"Why?" she says, standing in her beautiful wedding gown on what should be the most magical night of her life. Her new husband sits at her side, and I wonder if Kellan had any idea what he was getting into. Are all those houses and private islands worth it? "Why not right now?" she presses. "It feels like everything else is coming out tonight so why not—"

"*NOT NOW, CHARLOTTE!*" Ray roars, turning his eyes to her.

Charlie, bursting into tears, runs out of the tent. Kellan follows.

Liam sighs, wiping a hand over his mouth. "Well done, Dad."

Ray's jaw clenches, and he pulls a sharp breath in through his nose. "What'll it be, Liam? The company and your inheritances, or your pride? I want you to think long and hard about what this could mean."

All motion inside me stops. It's the four-hundred-million-dollar question. I look around, wondering if anyone else caught his wording.

Inheritances.

But neither Jake nor Alex seems to have registered it. They simply watch Liam. So maybe they didn't hear it? Is it possible they have no idea what Alex has done?

Just walk, I plead silently to Liam. *Walk away from all of this. None of you need that money. And frankly, none of them deserve it.*

With a sigh, Liam looks over at me. But before he can speak, Jake steps forward. "He's married, Dad. That's the rule. And look at them. No one can tell me they're not in love."

Alex shakes his head. "Maybe they're just fucking."

"Who's fucking?" Blaire says, choosing this moment to return to the tent. Her timing really is impeccable.

Alex deflates, cupping his hand over his forehead. "Jesus Christ."

"Doesn't matter," Jake says. "They're married. Legally. I was a witness. In three months, it will be five years and the balance of the trust will officially be secured."

Ray snaps his fingers. "Peter? Want to weigh in?"

The stranger I'd forgotten about pushes off the bar, stepping forward and clearing his throat. He slides one hand into his pocket like he's addressing a jury, and immediately I know he must be a lawyer.

"The clause in the will stipulates that the grandchildren are required to enter into a marriage based on mutual admiration, respect, love, and devotion," Peter says. "Your grandfather put that stipulation in because he wanted to encourage happy, secure marriages, which in turn would ensure a happy, secure company. A marriage in name only goes against the very core of what he wanted, and in my legal opinion would void the fulfillment of your trust." He looks over at Liam. "Your current affections could be argued in court, of course, but it would be very easy to prove that you and Ms. Green have not been cohabitating or, indeed, very familiar at all until recently."

Liam's looks over at me and I try to tell him with my eyes: *Walk away. This isn't only up to you. Your father has a choice here, too. He doesn't have to screw his children out of money his father left them.*

"So I'll ask you again, son," Ray says, lifting his chin to the side, toward Jake and Alex. "What'll it be? You or them?"

At this, Jake frowns, something landing wrong to his ear, and I know for certain that he doesn't understand the full scope of what's at stake here.

I hate everything about this moment so much that not even Liam's giant hands over my mouth could have kept me from losing it. "Are you fucking kidding me?" I seethe at Ray and try to not cower as the room turns to gape at me. "Seriously, is this a joke? Am I part of a documentary about how the proletariat reacts in the presence of insanely rich assholes?" I look over at Alex, who gapes at me. "Yes, and fuck you specifically, Alex, you enormous shitstain. I know what *proletariat* means, and I know what fork to use. I googled it before I got here, you dick."

Jake barks out a laugh. "Damn, Alex, she's—"

"Not now, Jakey," Janet murmurs, and then looks at me, brows raised expectantly.

Expectantly . . . like she'd love to see me try to fix this. Me, a veritable stranger. Janet could end this in an instant but she never would.

What a coward.

Rage makes my blood sublimate into smoke, and I take a deep breath, turning to face the toxic patriarch. "Ray, you are without question the big-gest asshole I have ever met in my life, and I used to work the overnight shift at the lost-baggage counter at LAX. You are a random dude, not a king. You treat people in your life like they are bargaining chips, trophies, or minions." I gesture around the room. "These are your sons, not chess pieces. You treat Alex like he's no more valuable than some dirt on your shoe and treat Liam like he's a Lamborghini you can drive wherever you want. I don't know how you treat Jake because I'm not sure you even notice him. Do you not see how horrifically poisonous you are? Or how much your children are hurting? How on earth do you sleep at night? Honestly, tell me."

Blaire lifts a tipsy hand. "Two trazodone and a big glass of red wine works for me."

Ray tilts his head at me. "Who the fuck are you to come here and talk to me like this?"

"I'm Anna Green. I'm a painter and a daughter and a former conven-ience store cashier and part-time waitress and I'm lucky to be married to your son. I don't know what choice Liam is going to make, whether he'll agree to your truly fucked-up terms or whether he'll choose himself for the first time in his life, but I can tell you this: no matter what happens tonight, it's only a matter of time before every single person in this room leaves you, and I think you know it."

Thirty-One

ANNA

We find ourselves on a plane about two hours later, headed back to Singapore. Apparently, when he's mad enough, Ray Weston can pull some very large, flight-capable strings, but I tell you what: if he thinks banishing us immediately will discourage me from future castigation, he's sorely mistaken. I am delighted to be getting the hell away from that island and everyone still on it.

I think the man beside me is also pleased, although it's hard to tell. There isn't a lot of room for personal space onboard the amphibious plane, but Liam has wedged a bubble of silence between us anyway. We silently watched the dark jewel of Pulau Jingga get smaller and smaller behind us in the night sky and then he turned forward, leaning his head back against the headrest and closing his eyes.

I meant every word I said in that tent, but the ones that stick with me right now are the ones about Liam and how I don't know what he's going to do now. Yes, he's been very clear that he didn't want to come back to the family company, but I have no idea whether he'll put his happiness above his siblings' financial interest.

And when Ray stormed out of the tent, yelling for island staff to "get me a fucking plane this instant," and the rest of the family had scattered to their various lodgings, two people hung back: Peter and Liam. I'd tried to stick by his side, but Liam had kissed my forehead and told me he'd meet me back at the bungalow.

I packed up our suitcases and waited on the balcony, not at all sentimental about leaving that cursed place. But it wasn't Liam who walked toward me from the jetty, but Gede, telling me that Dr. Weston would meet me onboard. My man ducked in through the low plane door after I'd been waiting nearly fifteen minutes, and I felt a nearly blinding relief. But then he wordlessly sat beside me, took my hand, and turned to look out the window.

The desire to know what had gone on in the hour we'd been apart is nearly killing me. But when his breathing evens out and his mouth goes soft, I know he needs sleep more than I need answers.

RAY EXPELLED US FROM the island, but unfortunately, even he lacks the power to change the Singapore Airlines schedule, so our flight to LA remains the same. With nearly eighteen hours before we depart, Liam gets us a hotel room in the airport, and I take what has to be one of the most glorious showers of my life. When I emerge, he's standing at the window, staring out at the dark skyline. He doesn't look over when I approach in a bathrobe but twines his fingers with mine when I take his hand.

I tug him toward me. "Hey."

A frown flickers across his brow and he squeezes his eyes closed, but he doesn't immediately answer.

"Liam."

At this, he slowly turns his head to look at me. I think I know the answer. The second our eyes meet, I think I get it.

"You're taking the job, aren't you?"

This time when he blinks, his lashes are wet with tears. He shrugs, and something inside my chest cracks. I move to stand between him and the window, facing him, cupping his jaw in my hands. "Isn't there another way? Do you have to go work for him?"

Liam doesn't answer but takes a long, defeated breath.

"*No one* needs that much money," I tell him. "Your siblings definitely don't."

He nods in agreement. He swallows thickly, pursing his lips to get his emotions under control. "He'll retire soon. I'll only have to deal with him for a few years."

"What did he do to you, Liam? Is that this mysterious Pisa thing?" I admit, I googled it, and found nothing. At least, nothing that sounds like a scandal. Pages and pages of information on the Leaning Tower of Pisa or an international student assessment exam, and nothing about an American family scandal. Whatever it is, it's been buried online. "I know your dad screwed you over somehow. I know you took the blame for something, and that it was bad enough for you to want out, but I have no idea what it was. Why won't you just tell me?"

He shakes his head, bringing his hands up to my wrists to gently guide my arms down. "Pisa is . . . it's just a stupid fucked-up thing in the past. It's what caused the rift with us, but it's only one of many reasons I don't want to work with him." He inhales deeply and then blows his breath out. "I have to talk to my lawyers. I have to figure it out. When we get back to California, I'll bring you to my place. We'll sit down and I'll tell you everything. But right now, I just need figure out what happens next. Can you trust me?"

Words bubble up in my throat. *I can't go back to your place; I have to find a job. I don't want to sit with this until we get back. I want to know now.* I swallow them down, wanting to do and be whatever he needs right now, but inside, I am a mess. I hate this. And as much as I hate to admit it to myself, I'm deeply uneasy. Uneasy with the thought of remaining connected to the Westons via Liam. Uneasy with him making such a terrible decision all in the name of money. Uneasy with the intrusive feeling that maybe I don't know him at all.

"I can," I say carefully, "but I don't like this."

He nods, never once looking away. "I know."

Across the room, my phone vibrates with an incoming call. "I'm going to get that. I'll be right back."

It's Mel. "Hello?"

"Hey, lady! I have some amazing news."

I close my eyes, turning to sit at the edge of the bed. I look down at my pink-tipped toes on the cream carpet, trying to anchor myself. Emotional whiplash is the name of the game these days. "Yeah? What's up?"

"Two things: one, the gallery wants another five paintings from you."

I straighten. "Oh my God, what?"

"And two, there's a gallery here in Los Angeles that also wants to feature two of your pieces."

I cup a hand over my mouth, squeezing my eyes closed. It must be the cocktail of emotions in my meager body, because it's my turn to cry. I feel tears rise up and spill down my cheeks.

"Anna?" she asks.

"I'm here," I choke, and at the sound, Liam whips around, coming to kneel at my feet.

"What happened?" he mouths, his light brown eyes round and worried.

I shake my head, mouthing back, "It's okay. It's good," and then say to Mel, "I'm just a little in shock."

"I bet you are," she says, laughing. "This is how it all starts."

"So seven in total?" I ask, and Liam leans in, mouthing more insistently. "What is it?" His fingers absently skim up and down my legs.

After Mel answers yes, I cup a hand over the phone and whisper to Liam, "The gallery wants more paintings. And there's another gallery in LA that wants some, too."

He beams up at me, squeezing my calves in his hands, and it feels so good to see that smile on his face. I reach forward, tracing his lower lip.

"When do you get home?" she asks.

"Like in an hour," I say, laughing, "because the math involved in traveling to and from Asia is make-believe."

Mel laughs at this. "Okay, well, call me as soon as you're settled so we can get this sorted."

"I will."

"Hopefully people will get to *see* them this time," she says, laughing.

"Right?" I say, laughing back, and then my joy is turned briefly on its side. I think I've misheard her. "Wait—what do you mean?"

"Oh, you know, because the original three were purchased before the show even opened."

I blink. "Before the show opened?" I ask and then I understand: I hadn't spaced the gallery opening; it hadn't even happened yet. With a sinking feeling in my gut, I ask, "Who was the buyer?"

"Anonymous."

I stare at Liam, kneeling in front of me, so happy for me. So proud. So unsurprised by all of this. "Anonymous buyer," I say quietly, and his smile falters for just a breath. "At five times the sticker price, too."

"Amen," Mel sings. "Okay, sweets, I'm hopping on another call, but we'll talk soon."

"Absolutely." Numbly, I press End Call and stare down at the phone in my hands.

"So?" Liam says, tracing his fingers up and down the back of my calves. "Tell me the good news."

I turn my face up to him. "It was you, wasn't it?"

His expression freezes, and then he tries on another smile. "What was me?"

"The buyer," I say. "The person who bought the first three paintings."

Liam's eyes flicker back and forth between mine. I silently beg him not to lie. "Yes," he admits, finally.

A stone drops in the hollow of my chest. "Why?"

"Because you wanted it so much," he says. "Because this is how these things work—buzz builds."

"You've never even seen my art."

"I saw it in your apartment before we left. I've seen your drawings on the island."

I move to stand, and he has to shift back, standing, too, reaching for my hands, but I pull them up to my chest, curl them into my body. "I feel . . ." I shake my head, out of words. Honestly, I'm gutted. "I feel so incredibly stupid."

"God, why?"

"Because I thought the person who bought the paintings had seen them and loved them."

"I have seen them. I will love them because you made them."

"This isn't a third-grade art project, Liam. That's not how it works."

He steps closer, but I turn and walk over to the dresser. "Anna. Getting noticed in the art world is—"

"Are you really going to explain this to me? Because you've spent so much time in art circles?"

He frowns. "Well, I do know a bit—"

"Because your family is wealthy, and you know a lot of patrons?"

Liam steps back, sits at the end of the bed facing me. He's still dressed in his suit from the wedding and I'm suddenly so happy that I showered, that I washed every trace of that place off me. "Okay, stop," he says. "It was only a few thousand dollars."

"Only a few—" I cut off, so irate that I'm shaking. "Do you realize that for someone like me a few thousand can feel as impossible as a few million?"

"This isn't about our backgrounds," he says steadily, so calm. "This isn't about money. This is about helping you build a name for yourself."

"This is *only* about money," I tell him, feeling the tight strangle of tears in my throat, the weight of his necklace against my skin, the ring on my finger. "You lied to me."

"I didn't."

"You absolutely did. When Mel called the first time with the news that the paintings sold, you could have told me it was you. Better yet, you could have told me before you did it. You could have run it by me." I stare at him, devastated. "How long were you going to let me think that someone else bought them?"

Liam sits up and runs a hand through his hair. "I thought it would be romantic if you saw them for the first time in my house."

I'm so exhausted, I just want to get off this roller-coaster ride. "Liam, that's what happens in movies."

He nods, his posture deflating. "Yeah."

"But in reality, what it feels like is you just using your money and influence to direct the path of my career because you think you know what's best for me, and I'm not sure, but I think that exact same situation is why you've been frowning out windows for the past six hours."

"Anna, that's not—"

"It *is* the same."

"I'm not doing what my father did," he says, jaw tight.

We stare at each other, suffering through the fucking brutality of this moment. Nothing feels lonelier than fighting with him right now.

"You're right. You bought my paintings out of love—or something that looks like it. Your father's actions aren't motivated by that. Intent matters." I take a steadying breath, nostrils flared. "But you can't buy my love. That part of me wasn't ever for sale. I gave you my body and my heart because of what you make me feel, not because you're rich. Your money is the thing I like the least about you."

"I know."

I search his eyes, trying to understand him. "And if the distinction is so important, if what your dad is doing is so abhorrent, tell me why you're going along with it. Jake, Charlie, even Alex—they'll be *fine*. Who needs that much money anyway? It's clearly made you all miserable. Do you see that? You're all rich and completely miserable, and yet you want more?"

He exhales in frustration. "I don't care about the money. But it isn't just about me."

Inside I am restless. I know I won't like where this is going, but I can't stop. "You're sacrificing your happiness to protect the rest of your family? Admirable, yes. But come on, Liam."

"Let it go, Anna."

"Charlie will be fine," I say. "The McKellans are *loaded*."

He pinches the bridge of his nose, frustrated.

"Alex and Jake have enormous salaries. They're never leaving the company. Even if Jake never marries or never has access to his inheritance, he's still richer than almost every other person on this planet. And your mom, should she ever wise up and leave her sludge goblin of a husband, will be fine. There's no way California law would leave her with no alimony. So she goes on one cruise a year instead of owning the yacht. People live with much, much less."

He lets out a humorless laugh. "You don't know my father."

"You're right, and I mean, what I do know is horrifying, but I also think your worldview is totally broken if you think any of you with your very legitimate careers are better off sacrificing your happiness to that man just to make sure you can still wear Gucci to take the trash out."

"Anna, I can't unilaterally decide to alter this huge aspect of their lives," he says, his voice hoarse with frustration.

"But it's not you!" I cry. "It's Ray. *Ray* has made you think the responsibility lies with you. *Ray* is the one who's threatening to challenge the trust so you'll do what he wants. Ray doesn't have to take this to the courts. What he's doing is emotional manipulation, Liam. You don't have to fall for it."

"Whether they need the money or not, whether it's fair or not, whether or not I'm being manipulated, at the end of the day, our marriage *is* a fraud. We *did* lie. I'm the reason my siblings are in this situation. Choosing to protect myself in all of this, despite all of that, is exactly what my father would do. I have to make the other choice."

Oh. Oh, Liam.

"But would your siblings choose *you*?" I ask, feeling disgusted by all of them. "You know they wouldn't, Liam. Maybe they love you, but they're broken." I take a step closer. "How many of them spoke up to protect Thuy at the restaurant? How many of them blinked about buying a house because Charlie's rental flooded? They brought who knows how much crap and garbage to a protected island in the middle of the ocean. If you ask them to pick between you and money, they will choose money every time."

"You don't know that," he says quietly.

"Maybe not," I say, "but I think you do. I'm the only one here offering you unconditional support and love—and I'm not even asking you to choose me. I'm asking you to choose yourself. Because they won't."

Liam's expression shuts down, and I know I've gone too far, but I don't care.

He walks back to the window, looking out over the Singapore skyline. "Well, luckily," he says, voice barely audible, "I'm not forcing them to choose."

Thirty-Two

LIAM

Anna and I break up about sixteen hours before a fifteen-hour flight. Which, I'm sure I don't need to say, is pretty fucking awful. I've been seated beside strangers on a plane dozens of times, but never has that stranger been someone I shared a bed with. Never has that stranger been someone who looked at me and saw all of the good things I want to embody. Never has that stranger been someone I thought was on the way to being the most important person in my life.

We land in Los Angeles, and once we're off the plane, I can tell Anna is dead set on getting the hell away from me, but we still do have some business to wrap up.

"Anna, wait," I say, catching her wrist just before she manages to get on the escalator down to baggage claim. We step out of the stream of traffic, walking to the side of the no-man's-land area of LAX customs where she stares up at me with red, blank eyes.

Had she been crying the entire flight?

"We have the issue of the wire transfer to settle."

She blinks away, and for a beat I fear she'll tell me she doesn't want my dirty money after all, that she can't stomach taking it. But then she inhales a steadying breath, and nods. "What information do you need?"

"Your routing number," I tell her. "And your account number."

"I can text it?"

"I think it's better to write it down."

Of all of the painful moments in the past twenty-four hours, this is the worst, I think. Both of us awkwardly searching for a pen, for a scrap of paper to write on. Anna shifts her purse onto her knee, digging around. "I got it," she says, pulling out a pen from the Crowne Plaza Hotel at Changi Airport and a receipt for something she must have bought to eat after she left me alone in the hotel room. I stare helplessly as she swipes her phone awake, opens her banking app. I stare down at the screen, blankness washing through me as I realize her checking account has about twenty dollars in it. She's already used the ten thousand dollars I sent her to pay her father's medical bills.

Anna writes down her account number, the routing number. She straightens and hands it to me, not meeting my eyes.

I glance down and my chest twists as I realize it's on the back of a receipt for a cheap hot dog. "I'll send it tonight."

"Don't send more than we agreed on," she says.

"Anna—"

"I know you, Liam. I don't want you to send more."

I nod, miserable. At this moment, I truly hate my father. I also hate myself. I hate the mess this has made, and how many lives will be affected if I don't figure this out. Not just my family, all of them. I realize she's waiting for me to break the tension, release us both; that it probably feels impolite to just turn and walk away after someone has assured you that they'll be sending ninety thousand dollars to your bank account. So I gesture for her to lead us back to the escalator, where Anna collects her bags and wordlessly disappears into the crowd headed to the taxi line. I watch her until I can't even see the pink of her hair anymore, knowing it's entirely possible I will never see my wife again.

I MAY NOT SEE her again, but she'll still be everywhere I look; while I was away, her three paintings were delivered to my house. I avoid unpacking clothes that likely smell of Anna by meticulously hanging her paintings instead. *Freesia 2* goes on a wall in my living room, a blast of cardinal, coral, and a yellow so electric it seems to vibrate. *Dahlia 4* goes on the wall in my study: concentric rings of soothing puffs of pinkish-white petals with a shock of pink in the center set against a delicate green backdrop; individual petals look nearly conical, their tender centers hiding a thousand shadows that reveal the true magic of the painting. And *Three Zinnias* goes in my bedroom, on the wall opposite my bed. When I first see it, it takes my breath away—a meticulous close-up of three overlapping flowers I assume are zinnias, one a brilliant green, one a shocking tangerine, and one a scarlet so vivid it seems three-dimensional. The energy, the colors, and the sequence of them reminds me so acutely of the dress Anna wore to the wedding that for a few minutes I can only stare at the painting, barely able to breathe. The paintings I'd assumed were her hobby in college were good, but now I see those were simple tunes, "Chopsticks" played on the piano with novice fingers. These pieces are her symphony, the result of natural talent and years of honing her craft.

Truthfully, all three are amazing. I wish I *had* seen them before buying them, only so she would have seen the honesty in my expression when I told her I loved them, that I believe in her talent.

I'm drained, but I can't sleep. Haven't eaten all day, but I'm not hungry. Collapsing on the couch, I stare at *Freesia 2* until my eyes lose focus and I have no more mental defenses left. Thoughts pummel me.

I have to agree to my father's demands. I'll have to let go of my faculty position. I'll have to let go of Anna. My brain makes these depressing rounds over and over.

My phone buzzes on the couch beside me and I pick it up, staring at Jake's profile photo. For a few rings, I consider letting it go. I'm pretty sure Blaire and the kids left early, but the others have just left the island for Singapore, which means Jake is with Dad. Maybe—just maybe—something has happened to get me out of this.

"Jake."

"Hey."

The second I hear the frustration in his single syllable, I know nothing has changed.

I press the heel of my free hand to my eye. "What's up."

"Was just calling to check on you. You and Anna get back safely?"

"Yeah. She left for her place straight from LAX. I caught a flight to San Jose. Just got home."

He pauses. "You guys leave things in a good place?"

"Not particularly."

"Dad wants to destroy her."

"She's your friend," I remind him with a trace of sarcasm. "I'm sure you've been defending her."

He's quiet on the other end. "You know I don't fucking bother getting into it with him, Liam. I know it isn't your way, but we all do what we have to do. Don't start with me right now."

"Yeah, well," I say with a sigh, "it doesn't matter anyway. I'll give him what he wants."

My brother falls quiet again for a few seconds. "What does that mean?"

"It means I'll come on board."

"Does he know that?"

"I haven't officially confirmed it yet." I frown down at my watch, trying to do the time zone math. "Where are you?"

"Singapore. In the lounge. He and Mom went to get a drink. I'm sure he'll call soon."

I close my eyes. Talk to Dad, make him a deal; my freedom for theirs. "Okay. I'll be here."

Jake blows out a breath. "Liam. I really don't want you to have to do this."

"I know."

Jake swears quietly. "So just say no."

"I can't."

"You can, though. You've said no to him a hundred times. What's he gonna do? Yell?"

I send a hand into my hair. "If I say no, it fucks us all, Jake."

The line goes quiet, and then he carefully asks, "What does that mean?"

I take a deep breath, resigned to doing this now. "It means that in Grandpa's trust, we're all linked. If one marriage is fraudulent, we all lose our inheritance."

"*Are you fucking kidding me?*" my brother seethes, voice strained.

"I wish. And Dad knows. He and I haven't solidified an agreement, but it's clear to me from my chat with Peter back on the island that if I come on board, Dad won't enforce it. If I say no to him, I get the sense that he'll challenge the trust in probate."

Anna was right. It's so manipulative. My stomach rolls, nausea washing me out.

"He really wants you that fucking bad."

"More likely he wants to win the battle," I say, exhausted. "Wants to prove to me that no matter what he put me through with PISA, I can't just walk away from him without screwing my family out of money."

Jake exhales a long, shocked breath, and in the silence that follows, my thoughts turn down a different path. When I say it out loud, it sounds insane. It sounds pathological. Maybe I should have told my siblings earlier. Maybe I should have looped them into the conversation.

Because maybe Anna was wrong. Maybe this is where Jake puts his foot down and comes to my defense. Instead of panicking, maybe this is where my little brother tells me to tell Dad to go to hell.

Maybe this is where Jake finally stands for something.

"Man," Jake says quietly. "That sucks but . . . I get it. If we'd all lose the money, I guess it makes sense. Thanks for taking one for the team, Liam."

I squint at the wall across the room as his words land.

Thanks for taking one for the team, Liam.

And this, right here, is why I didn't tell Jake. This is why I didn't tell any of them. Because I didn't want confirmation of that crystalline truth Anna articulated so easily:

They love you, but they're broken. They will choose money every time.

There's shuffling on the other end of the line; Jake's voice is muffled, almost like he's holding his phone against his chest. But I hear him say my name, and then "yeah," and then he's back. "Liam? Dad's here. Okay if I put him on?"

I sigh, leaning my head back against the couch. I thought I had another day or two before doing this but fuck it. "Why not."

"What time is it there?" Dad asks, no greeting.

"Around one in the morning."

"Well, it's four p.m. tomorrow here, and I gotta tell you: The future's pretty bright, kid."

I squint into the darkness of my living room. Is he . . . making a joke right now? "Yeah?"

"Yeah," he says. "We take off in a couple hours. Are you going to give me an answer before I come home?"

"I want you to promise me something first."

"I'm not sure you're in a position to make any demands. But shoot your shot, kid."

"I want you to step down immediately."

His laughter carries over the line. "That's not happening. There will be a three-year transition period."

"You'd force me to do this?"

"I'm offering you the company on a platter, and you call it forcing you. Unbelievable."

"Unbelievable? You're *blackmailing* me with my siblings' inheritance."

"Leverage, Liam. It's an important distinction." He laughs again. "And how's this: I'll put in writing that I won't release the remaining PISA documents in return."

My thoughts stutter. The remaining PISA documents?

The ones that leaked years ago tell a story of a teenage boy building a technology for his family company and ostensibly using it to spy on employees. The remaining, confidential documents tell a story that is much, much worse. "What are you talking about?"

Dad laughs once, delighted. "I had you either way, kiddo."

I stare, unseeing, at Anna's painting as it all sinks in. If Alex hadn't melted down in public and revealed that my marriage to Anna was bullshit—conveniently taking himself out of contention for the CEO position at the same time—then Dad would have threatened to release more PISA documents, knowing I'd lose my faculty position, knowing I'd struggle to find a job anywhere.

He would have used leverage no matter what. He had me completely cornered, and he knew it this whole time.

"Do you even want me in the role?" I ask him. "Or did you just not want to lose?"

"Come on. Don't be dramatic."

"Dramatic?" I ask. "If you pin the full truth of PISA on me, I'll be ruined."

"At worst you'd have to do some damage control."

"At worst? At *best* I do damage control. At worst I'm *destroyed*, Dad."

"What the fuck does it matter, Liam? I'm not releasing PISA because you're going to be the good brother and protect the trust. You've already said yes."

I blink into focus, looking up at *Freesia* 2. I see Anna in every single stroke of the paintbrush, every wild, vibrant streak of color. When I close my eyes, I hear her infectious giggle, remembering the way her eyes shone with victory every time she made me laugh. . . .

Is your name really West Weston?

That diamond is the size of my nipple.

I swear I blacked out after one particularly delicate part of the Brazilian. At one point they had me get on my hands and knees . . .

I let my mind wander away from my father and back to that moment of unbridled joy when Anna slapped her silicone bra onto the shoulder of my jacket. When she looked me in the eye and told me our night in the pavilion kitchen had been the best night of her life. When she stared up at me with infatuation and lust in our bed, as the hours blurred past . . .

And I remember how she looked answering the door that morning barely two weeks ago. Pantsless, baked, a rumpled mess. She was stressed, but she was glowing. She was unemployed, but she was still fighting. She was penniless, but she was *living*.

She wasn't ever afraid to start over, again and again.

I'm your ride-or-die, West Weston.

I am the only one here offering you unconditional support and love—and I'm not even asking you to choose me.

She wanted me to choose myself. Because we both knew—and I did know, deep down, no matter how hard I'd deny it—that no one else in my family would put me first.

I open my eyes, electricity shivers through me, and I find myself saying aloud, "My answer is no."

There's a shocked pause. "What did you say?"

"I said no. Unless you resign immediately, I'm not coming on."

"You're choosing this path? You're choosing to be obliterated?"

"If you genuinely wanted me as CEO for your father's company and not for some power porn bullshit, then you wouldn't obliterate me."

He laughs once, knife-sharp. "This is the biggest mistake of your life."

For a reverberating second, terror washes me out, makes me feel light-headed. But whatever instinct kicked the words out of me takes over again. "Do your worst, Dad. It won't change my mind."

Thirty-Three

ANNA

Dad has gained a few pounds. Even though I couldn't tell just by looking at him, I can feel it when I lean on his shoulder—something I haven't done in what feels like an eternity. But by the time I reach the part of the story where we're at LAX and Liam pulls me aside, making our last interaction also a transaction, Dad gusts out a breath and urges me to rest my head there while I finish the whole saga.

It feels amazing to physically lean on my dad again.

"This was quite a trip, kiddo," he says.

"No kidding."

"I wish you had told me the truth, but I understand."

"I know. It just sounded so sleazy."

"Well, did you fall for him?"

I shrug, but my heart wails out a soggy yes.

"He doesn't sound evil," Dad says quietly. "Just broken."

"Very broken. I keep thinking about how he didn't grow up with a David Green, and how incredibly lucky I am that I did."

Dad's hand comes to my knee, squeezing, and I look down at the scars there. So many IVs have gone into the back of his big, strong hand that it looks like a battlefield even though it's been forever since anything went in that way. His central port now lives on his chest, and I learned about an hour ago that we have a tentative date for its removal—six months from now. It's a hard-fought victory. Vivi even put up a countdown calendar on the wall.

"You think he's *too* broken?" Dad asks.

I run my fingers over the back of his hand. "Too broken for what?"

"Too broken for you to love him, dummy."

I tilt my face to look up at him. "You want me to stick with Liam? After he secretly bought my paintings?"

Dad shrugs like he doesn't agree with my level of offense over this. "When we care about someone, they deserve the benefit of the doubt. We have to consider not only what they did, but also *why* they did it. Intent matters," he says, and the wisdom he's shared with me my entire life yanks me right back to Singapore and that cursed hotel room and the anguish in Liam's eyes when he insisted that he and his father were not the same.

And only now does it occur to me that my suggestion that they were probably pushed him even further toward his shitty decision.

I growl out a frustrated breath. "He took a job with Mephistopheles," I say. "Literally the worst possible choice."

"He's backed into a corner, Annie."

I narrow my eyes. "David Green, are you Team West?"

Dad shakes his head, laughing. "I just want what's best for you, and when you were talking about your time on the island, you had that Anna Glow. You never talk about guys this way with me."

"It's awkward, huh?"

He laughs again. "It's not awkward. I like it." He kisses my forehead. "It's possible that he has some family stuff that is more complicated than you realize. It sounds like he grew up with money, but not much else. It doesn't have to stay romantic between you, but you are legally married to him and will have to deal with that eventually." He smiles at my groan. "I just think, give it a few days and then reach out to him. See if he's okay."

"Okay."

It's where we leave it for the night.

"Mind if I crash here?" I ask.

"Course not."

I took a cab directly from the airport to see him and unload to my safest of safe spaces. It's restorative, being back in my childhood home, but it's after one; I'm exhausted and Dad is up later than he probably has been in two years. Standing, I help him up, get him sorted through his nighttime routine and tucked in like a kid instead of a grumpy fifty-year-old swatting me away. I kiss the top of his bald head through his ever-present beanie and linger at the door. "I'm glad to be home with you," I tell him.

"Vivi's a better cook," he answers, and smiles at me just before I turn off the light and do everything I can to not worry about Liam going home to an empty house, Liam not having a David Green, Liam facing all of this alone.

VIVI A BETTER COOK than me? Yeah, right!

I've planned to have pancakes, bacon, and scrambled eggs ready for Dad, and when he walks into the kitchen around nine the next morning, that's exactly what he gets.

Mostly.

"What's this?"

"Breakfast," I say, offended.

Dad sits at the breakfast bar, pulling the plate closer and sniffing it.

I used up all the eggs for the scramble that I overcooked and had to toss, and then forgot baking powder entirely in the batter, so without both ingredients, the pancakes are a little thin but obviously recognizable as pancakes. I huff out a breath.

Dad points at the bacon, looking up at me. "What happened?"

"I thought you liked crispy bacon."

He grins. "This is bacon?"

I pull the plate away, saying, "Okay, Mr. Picky," and pull out plan B: the doughnuts I DoorDashed from Winchell's right after I burned the first batch of bacon.

"Now we're talking." Dad digs into the box and takes an enormous bite of a maple bar. I'm so happy to see him with an appetite that I can't even pretend to be offended anymore. He glances down at the counter and then nods to me. "Viv's calling," he says through a mouthful. "Probably to tell you that burned food will give me cancer."

"Oh my God," I bark, horrified, snatching the plate and dumping everything into the trash. "That's not funny!"

Dad laughs anyway and I give him the finger (my ring finger! It's my dad!) and pick up the phone, swiping to answer. "Vivs! Hey!"

"Turn on the news," she says.

Humor drains out of me at her flat tone. "What?"

"Turn it on. Turn on CNN."

I jog into the living room, digging through the throw pillows on the couch to find Dad's remote. "Dad, how do I turn on the news?" I ask, flailing.

"What?" he calls.

"The news! I don't watch news! I just watch clips like five days later on Twitter. Help me!"

"Just turn on the TV."

I hit a few buttons, finally ending up on an Apple TV menu that has nothing that looks at all newsy. I let out a garbled roar.

He walks in, taking the remote from me and laughing. A few seconds later, CNN is up and I'm staring in shock at the headline on the chyron:

Breaking News: Weston Foods Heir Apparent Liam Weston Stalked and Harassed Female Employees.

I don't realize I'm sitting until the coffee table is beneath me. "Vivs, I gotta go," I say, and drop my phone somewhere beside me.

"What's this?" Dad asks, as Liam's photo from the Stanford faculty website appears.

"Your son-in-law," I say, and turn up the volume. "And . . . I don't know."

"Just eleven years ago," Victor Blackwell is saying, "Liam Weston was embroiled in a scandal centered around the technology he developed for the company, called PISA, or Product Inventory Surveillance and Alignment. And now," the anchor says dramatically, "it appears the scandal went deeper than anyone knew. We'll get into it, after the break."

I lean in, shouting at the TV. "What? No! This is no time for commercials!"

"Wait . . . I remember this," Dad says quietly, and I look over at him while sports heroes enthusiastically crunch Doritos on the television. "There was some genius kid who created a program that was meant to keep track of inventory within the grocery network, but he programmed it to track employee activity, too."

"What?" I ask. "That *Liam* programmed?"

"Yeah. If I remember correctly, the program started combing emails or something? I think there was some big employment lawsuit, but I don't remember the details."

I wave him to shush as the anchor returns on-screen, and the panel splits to show a woman standing outside a giant Weston Foods gate.

"We're going to CNN's Stephanie Elam now, who's covering the story for us in Irvine, California. Stephanie, what can you tell us about the situation?"

"Well, Victor," she says, "the details are still emerging but here's what we know: Back in 2013, a lawsuit was brought against Weston Foods by a regional manager named Kasey Bellingham, who alleged she had been unlawfully passed over for promotion. Bellingham—a model employee by every internal metric—claimed she was up for promotion and denied at a performance review where her pregnancy was mentioned by her manager. According to Bellingham, she had never told anyone at the company that she was pregnant but had sent an email to a personal friend using her private email account on a work computer. The matter was settled out of court, and a legal spokesperson for the family explained at the time that the PISA software, designed by the son of CEO Raymond Weston, had been improperly used to track employee communications. This son, a minor at the time of the software launch in 2010, has been identified as William Weston, currently a professor of economics and cultural anthropology at Stanford. What we've learned today from an anonymous series of documents leaked to CNN is that the surveillance went much deeper than emails and was, in several cases, used to stalk and sexually harass female employees at the company."

I press my hand to my mouth, shaking my head. Everything about this feels wrong. "No way. No way." I look up at my dad, my heart sprinting out of my chest. "That can't be right. Dad, this isn't Liam, there's no way this is right."

Dad lifts his chin for me to keep watching, but I'm already dialing Liam's number. It immediately goes to a message saying the voicemail is full. Hanging up, I start scrolling, stopping on the only other Weston I have. But it's not Reagan who answers, it's Blaire.

"Hello?"

I launch myself from the table, pacing the room while this local correspondent continues to discuss the terrible, impossible, devastating things Liam is accused of doing. "Oh my God, Blaire. What the hell is happening?"

"Well, hello, pretty little liar." There's a smile in her voice, no heat, but I can picture the sharp, teasing glint in her eye.

"Okay, listen. I wanted to tell you everything. I really did, but for reasons that I think are now incredibly obvious, I couldn't."

"Oh, honey, I think you mispronounced 'I was paid to lie my ass off.'" She laughs. "Which, honestly, I can respect. But goddammit, Anna, I was excited to have a friend in this mess of crazy."

"You do have a friend," I promise her. "I'll take you out for a full margarita bar, Taco Tuesday, whatever, as soon as humanly possible, but you have to tell me what's going on."

She pauses. "I take it you're watching the news."

"Yes! What is this?"

"This, sugar, is Raymond Weston going for blood."

"But why Liam's blood? Didn't he take the job?"

"Alex isn't home yet, so I'm not sure, but I presume this means he did not," she says.

I stare at the television, digesting this while my heart crawls into my windpipe. Another photo of Liam is shown on-screen, this one from when he's younger; he looks barely out of his teens, but the chyron reads, *Female Weston employees pressured into sharing personal photos.*

"What?" I ask, reeling. "He *didn't* take the CEO position?"

"Based on your question, am I to understand that you aren't with him right now?"

"No. We had an argument and I think we ended things." I feel the lump in my throat expand. "And now his phone is going straight to voice-mail, and he won't reply to my texts."

Blaire lets loose a long sigh. "All these years and I knew this would come back around."

"Will you tell me what it is, Blaire? Is this how Ray screwed Liam over?"

"Were you so busy fucking that boy six ways to Sunday that he never told you about the shit Ray pulled? Damn," she says, smacking her lips. "This tastes like envy."

"Can you please just . . . focus? I'm standing here watching the news say that Liam used software he created to spy on and sexually harass female Weston's employees and I cannot believe he would ever do that."

"Well," Blaire says simply, "then don't."

Relieved, I crumple down onto the couch. "Okay."

"I'm really not supposed to be talking about this. Ray paid a shit ton of money to have it scrubbed from Google searches, but I guess the talking heads never forget." I hear the click of spiked heels against tiled floors, and the soft sound of a door being closed. "So, if someone asks, you didn't get this from me, but here we go: PISA—it's an acronym for the program Liam built while he was in school—was only ever meant to monitor inventory across stores," she says. "It was a great idea, really. The entire goal of it was to reduce food waste." My chest seizes at this, an inward, protective growl. "But when Ray wanted more 'transparency in his employees' activities,'" she says, and I hear the leaning air quotes in her words, "Liam did what Daddy said and modified the software to not only track ordering systems, but to log specific keywords in *all* of the programs, including emails. Kasey was just the start of it." She hums, as if thinking this through. "Really, Kasey was the most minor of all the cases. But she was the first and went public before they figured out how to keep it under wraps. At the time, it was easier for the stockholders to forgive a reckless teenage boy for being naughty than a CEO for being a letch."

"So it was never Liam doing this, right?"

"Oh God, no. Liam just handed the program over to IT and went away to college. Ray was the one spying. Ray was the one starting up conversations with employees, making them feel special for becoming friendly with the CEO, and eventually pressuring them to send him photos or share personal information."

My stomach sinks. "How old was Liam when all this happened?"

"Let's see. He developed the software when he was fifteen to maybe seventeen? And the scandal broke about three years later. I think he was twenty. Twenty-one. Thereabouts. God, he was gorgeous. All that pent-up—"

"Blaire."

"Sorry," she says, and laughs. "He was a minor when he created it, so it's why his name generally wasn't used in any of the stories. After Kasey came forward, all hell broke loose behind the scenes. God, the number of lawsuits they must have settled out of court. I can't even imagine."

"If they're settled, why did Ray even do this?"

"Because he's pissed as hell and a lunatic," she says, like I'm very stupid. "I bet that fucker dumped a ton of stock so he won't feel the pain of this in his portfolio, either."

And I guess I am very stupid, because I cannot fathom a human this petty and terrible. I feel my jaw slowly drop. "I'm sorry, you mean he really did this because he's mad Liam won't do what he says?"

"Ray is a first-class narcissist, Anna. Are you just now figuring that out?"

"But Liam is his *son*."

Blaire barks out a laugh. "It's honestly sweet the way you think that matters at *all*."

"In most families, it matters a lot," I reply.

"Janet always says Liam was her thinker. Imagine a boy who, at fifteen, conceives of a system that could be successfully implemented for a NASDAQ-traded company. If I'm honest, I think it intimidated Ray a little. God knows Liam intimidated me." She lowers her voice. "You've seen the way Ray is with the guys. He's always been like that, thinks he's toughening them up. It works with Alex, but Liam never fell into line. If you ask me, that's what Ray hates and respects the most in Liam. He doesn't bend. And if Liam turned him down for this job?" She whistles.

I look back at the television. The chyron has been updated again—*Stanford University releases statement: "Liam Weston is a promising young professor. We are launching a full probe into these allegations."*

What a mess.

I start pacing again. "Why doesn't Liam just come out and tell the truth? That it was Ray behind all the messages?"

"Because all of the communication was sent from an admin account. Ray can easily shrug and say he's an old grocery man who doesn't even know which button turns on the monitor. And Liam did create the software. He did enable the surveillance."

"Fuck," I whisper.

"Between you and me," Blaire says, "I wasn't one bit surprised when he started that foundation."

"Oh, right. He mentioned that. What is it exactly?"

"He set up an endowment for Weston employees."

My gaze locks, unseeing, on the television as I process this. "An endowment?"

"Yeah, so anyone at the company can apply for a grant to take a class, go to college, travel, or purchase a home. Basically, he's trying to rebuild the culture in his own way, on the outside." While my mind blanks of everything but overwhelming adoration for Liam, Blaire cups her hand over the phone and hollers out to the kids in the background. When she comes back, she says, "His entire inheritance is going into it. It's all anonymous, as far as I know, but he's had IT put the link to the application right on the website. Drives Ray fucking crazy, but of course Ray takes credit for it anyway. We all know it's Liam."

And at her mention of the trust and what Liam's doing with his, I realize what this means. Liam said no to Ray. He chose himself. Ray could and will challenge the inheritance.

An idea sparks, sending hope spreading warm and electric through my veins. I think I know what to do. It's going to be a gamble, but I *know* I wasn't wrong about Liam's siblings: they will always choose the money.

I reach for my purse and mouth to my dad that I have to go but I'll fill him in as soon as I can.

"Blaire," I say, opening my Uber app, "I need to tell you something, and you're not going to like it. But first . . . do you know where Liam lives?"

Turns out, Blaire only vaguely knows where Liam lives, and after I fill her in on the situation with the loophole and the trust and how she and Alex and all the Weston children could possibly lose all their money, she's screaming too much to be very useful anyway.

Jake is more helpful. He replies to my text saying he has no idea what Liam's address is, because every time he's visited, Liam has picked him up at the airport.

> Do you just float through life completely oblivious?

I mean yeah. Sort of

Wait—ok there's a park near his place in Palo Alto

I think it's called Hoover Park

And his house is on a cul de sac. Is that helpful?

Actually yes.

I will stop drawing this portrait of you with bad skin and a bald spot

I'm assuming some shit went down

Because when Dad got off the phone with him, he flipped

Yeah. You're on a plane?

If so, I'm sure it's being broadcast on whatever news you can get in your first-class airplane apartment

Do you know if he turned down the CEO job?

I think he did.

Fuck.

No, you know what? Good.

Fuck Dad.

I don't know if this means Jake knows about the condition in the trust, but I don't have time to worry about it, because my driver is pulling up in front of Terminal 2 at LAX.

I am insane, I know this, but I convince myself the information I have is enough to go on and buy a ticket at the Delta counter for a flight to San Jose leaving in two hours.

While waiting at my gate, I discover that nearly every residential street in Palo Alto is a cul de sac. But once I land, and once I get out of the taxi at Hoover Park, I realize with devastation how easy it will be to find Liam's house.

I only have to follow the news vans.

Thirty-Four

ANNA

They are everywhere. Bumper-to-bumper all around the park and a few side streets, but they are especially packed down Byron, where I can only assume Liam lives. Follow the chaos seems to be the rule, and I weave between bodies, ignoring the urge to photobomb the people standing with microphones in front of cameras and yell that this is all made up, that there is no way on earth William Albert Weston would do any of this. But I resist because the last thing I want is for someone to ask whether I know Liam personally, and have a horde of reporters shoving microphones in my face.

A large cluster of journalists crowd around a dove-gray house with neat white trim. And there it is: Liam's beat-up old Honda parked in the driveway. My heart does a painful kung fu move inside my chest.

He's home.

I move with renewed determination through the crowd.

"Where does she think she's going?" someone behind me asks with a snotty laugh.

"You can't approach the door!" someone yells to me. "It's considered private property!"

Another voice shouts, "We all have to wait for him to come out!"

But as I continue to walk, the tenor changes. I feel the wave of awareness move across the mass of bodies, hear a few people murmur my name, and I register my enormous mistake: I haven't put my hood up. I didn't hide my hair.

I haven't been on Instagram in days, but everyone else at the island was posting constantly, and given that I am legally married to the hottest Weston sibling and given that the Westons were the celebrities of the entire vacation, it's one hundred percent assured that my mostly inactive account with fifty-two followers has been tagged in many, many photos. Any journalist worth their salt knows everything there is to know about Liam, and that now includes me, and the shitstorm that happened at the wedding.

"Anna!" a man yells. "That's Anna Green! That's the wife!"

And from there, everything devolves into chaos. My name is shouted in a cacophony of voices so earsplitting it triggers a strange instinct to cry in panic. Mics are shoved in my face; hands come up to my shoulders, my back.

Do you have any comment about the scandal?

Can you tell us what you think about Alex Weston's statements?

Have you and Liam consummated the marriage?

Have you spoken to Ray Weston?

Anna, is it true you and Liam are expecting a baby?

Jesus Christ.

Arms try to guide me this way and that, journalists step in my path, blocking me in so I have to Tetris my way through the narrow path of bodies. There are so many people around me that I don't know which way I'm walking until I suddenly find myself in the middle of the street and have to redirect back over toward Liam's house. There are a few nice humans who are trying to help me, but most are hoping to get a photo, a word, anything out of me.

Do you know if Liam Weston has any comments about what his brother said?

Anna, over here, one photo, please!

Is your marriage to Liam Weston legitimate?

"Please," I say. "Please just let me through."

A murmur rises up farther away in the crowd, and all hell breaks loose. Just beside my ear, one of the helpers yells, "*Over here! Over here!*" The crowd screams, "*Liam!*" in unison only seconds before an arm comes firmly around my shoulders and I'm pulled into a solid chest and ushered through the crowd.

Liam.

I gust out a sob, wrapping my arms around his waist.

"I got you," he says. "I got you."

My face is pressed to his shoulder and his voice vibrates through me as he calmly says, "Let us through. . . . Excuse us. . . . No. . . . Excuse us. . . ." And when a strange hand comes around my forearm, Liam's voice turns deep and sharp: *"Do not touch her."*

Finally, we break through and reach his front steps, where he pushes me up to the porch, swings his door open, and slams it quickly behind us.

The chaos seems to melt away outside, and Liam and I stand facing each other for a few breathless seconds before I burst forward, throwing myself into his arms.

"I didn't know!" I sob.

"I know." His arms come around me, his hand cupping my head, smoothing my hair.

"You didn't tell me!"

"I'm sorry, I—"

"I know you didn't do any of this, Liam, I know what happened." I step back and he looks down at me with confusion. "I talked to Blaire, and she explained everything. We have to fight this! You have to go out there and say that you absolutely did not do any of the things they're saying."

He frowns down at me. "I don't need to—"

"You *do*," I insist, sucking in a very ugly, very wet breath. "*I* need every-one to know that you would never, not in any universe, do these things."

His eyes soften. "Anna."

"Were you afraid of telling me?" I ask. "Were you afraid that I wouldn't believe you?"

"Anna," he says again, bemused.

I push on, twisting my fingers into the fabric of his shirt. "I know we only just reconnected, and I know we're still new—wait, I think we broke up but can we get back together?"

"Anna," he says more firmly, and I panic because what if he doesn't want to give this a go anymore?

"No, Liam, let me say this, because with context all of it makes sense now. I get why you almost took the job. But then you didn't?" I ask. "Did you decide it wasn't worth it? Because I fucking agree! Even though you needed the money for your foundation. God, you are amazing. Do you know that?" I frown, a little. "Well . . . I still don't love that you bought the paintings but—" Liam takes one step to the side and color catches my eyes. "Oh. *Oh.*" I clap a hand over my mouth. There she is: *Freesia 2* just behind him on the wall. He already hung my paintings?

I burst into tears again. "Oh my God, okay, I forgive you. Oh my God, you were right, the movie version is actually really romantic, and you put it up there, which means maybe you still want to make a go of this?" I search his eyes, which have gone warm with amusement. "I want to be your girl-friend. Your wife." I wince at this, recalibrating. "Maybe let's date until the wife thing feels right? Whatever my label is, I would very much like to go out on that porch and tell every asshole out there exactly where they can shove their news cycle."

Liam steps forward, cupping my face and kissing me firmly on the mouth. He pulls away an inch to say, "Anna. Please shut up."

I gasp in offense and then melt into confusion. "That . . . was a very perplexing sequence of actions."

"First, I need you to know how talented you are." He looks briefly over his shoulder and then back at me. There is absolute wonder in his eyes. "Other than you, standing here in my living room, these paintings are the most beautiful things I've ever seen."

"You're really good at this flattery thing," I say through tears.

He lifts his chin to something behind me, and I turn to see—well, let me start by saying his place is fucking amazing. No wonder he didn't want his old couch. Second: he's got CNN on the screen.

"No! Why are you watching this?" I ask, bending to look for the remote. "This isn't good for you!"

But he urges me upright, leaning over my shoulder and pointing. "Anna. *Look*."

I focus on the screen and when my mind calms long enough, I'm able to register what I'm seeing.

Or, rather, *who*.

On the television is a replay of Alex, from some unknown number of minutes ago, speaking into a microphone somewhere familiar, but which I can't immediately place. Below him, the chyron reads:

Alex Weston: "My father stalked and harassed employees. Liam never engaged in any predatory or illegal activities."

"Whoa," I mumble. "That happened way faster than I expected."

Liam turns me back to face him. "What do you mean?"

"I saw the PISA stuff on the news and flipped out. The only number I had other than yours and Jake's was Reagan's, and I assumed Jake was on a plane. Blaire answered and told me everything, including about your foundation. That's when I realized I had to test my theory that your siblings would follow the money."

Liam laughs. "Well, you're right." He lifts his chin to the screen. "He's still in Singapore." That's why it looks familiar. He's outside the Crowne Plaza Changi. "He realized Dad really was going to bring me on as CEO and I think he finally snapped. He didn't get on the plane. And then, apparently, Blaire called him, screaming about the loophole. She said she'd stay married to him, but not if they were broke."

"Holy shit. And Alex gave a press conference?"

"Well, *conference* is a generous term," he says, laughing. "There were only a couple journalists nearby when he had the comms team alert the media, but it's picked up everywhere now. He said, basically, that while I did develop the software, none of the surveillance of personal data or harassment came from my computers. Dad had his shady lawyer drop the news before Dad got on the plane. But Alex responded by having the tech team release the IP logs."

"That was a big gamble for Alex," I say. "Your dad won't react well to this when he lands."

"I don't think it matters. The board knows. And soon the Fed will know that Dad dumped a huge amount of stock just before he did this. Dad is out as CEO, and in a shitload of trouble."

I stare up at Liam and he gazes down at me, his amber eyes gleaming. "How do you feel?" I ask.

His face moves through a few expressions—a smile, a wince, and then he closes his eyes and my heart twists painfully when his face just . . . breaks. He cups a hand over his brow, shielding his eyes, and his voice comes out thick. "I feel really fucking relieved." He pulls in a jagged breath. "This has been my biggest fear for years. That Dad would drop the worst of it, that it would leak, that it all would get pinned on me again and it would destroy everything I've worked for."

I don't know what to do with all of these emotions, but some bodily instinct does, because I step close, wrapping my arms around his waist and pressing my face to that perfect space between his neck and shoulder. "Oh, sweetie."

"I knew there was more, you know?" he says, and folds me into his arms. "My family didn't talk about it specifically, but I always knew there was much worse stuff out there. He used me the first time and it was just horrible. My name was kept mostly out of the press, but everyone in our circle knew who it was. Professors in my business program looked at me differently." He swallows. "I switched majors. Decided to turn to academia. I knew my dad could totally ruin me again, and worse, but I never really thought he *would*. I just thought, 'If I can keep my distance, if I can find another career, if I can be married, settled elsewhere, he'll move on. I can do good from the outside, with the foundation. He won't expect me to come back.' I realized at the wedding that I was wrong. He hadn't moved on, and he still had that leverage."

"Not anymore," I say.

He exhales a huge breath and laughs through tears. "Not anymore. Because of you."

"And the trust?"

"Dad might want to get the lawyers involved and make things messy, but something tells me he has much bigger problems. He's going to want his kids on his side, and that won't happen if he challenges Grandpa's trust."

I am so happy for him. So relieved, so grateful that Alex—someone I'm sure to feel conflicted about for the rest of my days—actually did something brave and useful. For money, sure, but credit where credit is due.

Liam leans our embrace to the side so he can reach for the front curtain and peek out. The reporters are all still there.

"Are you going to go out there and talk to them?" I ask.

He turns back to me. "Probably."

"What are you going to say?"

"That it's true I created the software and modified it at my father's instruction, but I wasn't behind the surveillance activity. That I hope the family company can move on from this and I know that we'll be doing everything we can to handle it in a way that feels transparent. That we plan to immediately hire a consulting firm to conduct an internal culture assessment."

" 'We,' huh?"

"My grandfather founded this company because he loved his family," he says. "I'd like to think we can make something good of it."

"I hope that includes finding a way to disconnect love from money," I tell him. "Your grandfather tied the two together with good intentions, and your father with terrible intentions, but in the end it doesn't matter what the intentions were: It has made everyone in your family devalue love. It has made loyalty and servitude the bargaining chips that keep the money flowing."

Liam cups my face and bends to kiss me. I leave my eyes open for just a beat and catch the way his fall closed and the utter devotion on his face when our lips meet. "I want to deserve you," he says when he pulls away.

"You already do."

"I want all of you. I want to give you everything I have." His lips linger on mine one more time. "There are no strings attached to what I'm offering," he tells me. "I just want you. I just want to love you."

"Unconditionally." I wrap my arms around his neck and pull him into a hug. Liam holds me for several minutes while the reporters mill around outside, the TV drones in the background, and our hearts slow to a steady, tandem beat. I pull back and stroke his jaw with my thumbs. "I'm sorry for what I said in the hotel. Even if I was right, it was harsh."

"You had to stand up for yourself and that's what you did. I'm sorry I didn't tell you about the paintings. You were right. It was controlling."

"Someone wise taught me that intent matters."

"Someone?"

"David Green. Mechanic and therapist, apparently. Also, your father-in-law." I stretch to kiss his smile, and when I pull back, his eyes do a careful circuit of my face. It's the same way he took me in that morning, so many days ago now, in my apartment, like he's slowly scanning, taking me in one feature at a time. I know I look like a mess again, but this time, his expression isn't trying to mask panic. This time, he's looking at me like he's seeing everything he wants all wrapped up in a pink, harebrained package.

"Is it weird seeing me in scrubby clothes again?" I ask, gesturing to my plain blue tank top, Cookie Monster pajama pants, and sneakers.

"Not even a little. I prefer this version of you."

"The real version."

"The real Anna," he says. "The real Liam."

He gets another smooch for that. "Okay, go take your victory lap and I'll be here for when you come back inside and want some celebratory horny boner banging."

He laughs. "Holy fuck, I'm so happy you came."

"Same."

Liam gazes at me with what looks a lot like the L-word. "When do you have to fly home?" he asks.

"I bought a one-way ticket. So, technically never."

He smiles. "So you can stay tonight?"

"I may have to call my dad," I say with a wink. "But I can, I want to, and I shall."

"And then every night after that?"

"Let's start with the one," I say, kissing his chin. "And see where it takes us."

Epilogue

LIAM

Where it takes us, immediately, is our first night in my bed.

The chaos up and down my street continues long after I make a statement to the press, but even with the flash of cameras and a swarm of incessant questions being shouted my way, it's easy enough to leave the stress of it all outside knowing that Anna is waiting on the other side of the door for me.

I could probably do anything with Anna waiting for me.

Our time on the island together was sexually adventurous, but there's a new wildness, a raw openness to our lovemaking this first night home. As I push into her again and again, her limbs loose from exertion, skin damp with sweat and flushed from yet another orgasm, I let myself forget about the decisions that still have to be made, the complicated conversations that lie ahead, and give myself over to the realization that there's nothing left for me to hide. Anna knows every secret I've tried to keep buried, every insecurity and shameful moment from my past; she knows the mess that is my family, and she accepts it anyway—accepts me. It's a mental freedom I've never experienced before. I give myself over to her completely.

For a week, my phone buzzes constantly; reporters linger on the street. And for a week, we shut out the world. We order groceries and cook together; we watch movies and play board games. She buys us face masks and we wear them while trading foot massages. She makes me teach her how to dance the jitterbug; I let her paint on me with a set of body paints she orders from Instacart. Most of all, we make love, any and every way we possibly can.

But eventually, real life pushes back in. We both have a lot to figure out. In our quiet moments, lying face-to-face in my bed, we try to plot out what the next page looks like for each of us: Do I retain my faculty position or step into an executive role at the company? Does Anna return to Los Angeles to pursue the promise of these gallery showings or do I convince her to move here and pursue her art closer to me?

My biggest regret is that because of my actions, Anna questions whether she deserves any of the success her art is finding. But she can't hold on to this insecurity for very long in the face of the true sincerity of my awe. She is a massively talented painter. In the end, we agree to take some time to tie up the loose ends of our lives outside of this burgeoning relationship. She will return to LA; I will meet with my academic higher-ups to forge a plan. And, at least for now, we'll do the long-distance thing.

ANNA

LONG DISTANCE TURNS OUT to be good for us. It's devastating to be separated for days at a time from Liam and his glorious Goddamn, but the miles between Palo Alto and Los Angeles also mean we get to know each other in different ways. Long-phone-call ways, and letter-writing ways. Constant-texting ways and "send me a picture of what you're doing right now" ways. We have dirty phone sex nearly every weeknight, and dirty real sex as many weekends as we can manage.

Like this, we thread ourselves into each other's lives so completely that there's no question how or whether we could fit together for more than a luxury vacation. I've only felt really seen by two other people—Dad and Vivi—and as the months fly by, there is a new, indelible Liam-shaped imprint in nearly every part of my life. In my confidence when I paint, and in my vision of a future where my art blooms into a full-fledged career; in my new financial security, and my dissipating worries about Dad's health and his hospital bills. Liam's impact is present in my mood, my sleep, my sexual satisfaction, my outlook on everything. *He* becomes my everything.

I finally tell him as much, on a sweltering day in August at my local tiny bakery.

"You see that right there?" I say, and nod to the pink-wallpapered wall where a framed print of one of my favorite paintings in the world hangs. "I'm going to see the real thing one day."

He follows my gaze and then looks at me over his coffee cup. "What's it called?"

"*Dance in the Country* by Renoir. It's one of the Dance series he'd been commissioned to paint, and of the three I love it the most. It's at the Musée d'Orsay in Paris. Have you ever been?"

"In high school." My expression must give away exactly what I'm thinking—how outrageously fancy he continues to be—and he playfully nudges my foot with his under the table before trapping it between both of his. "I remember seeing *Starry Night*," he says. "*Whistler's Mother.* A lot of Monet. A lot of Van Gogh." He studies the piece again. "What is it you love about this one?"

I turn my attention back to it. "It's the feeling I get when I look at it. The details. Some might just see two people dancing, but . . . look at his hat on the floor—it's like he was so swept up in the moment it fell to the ground, and he couldn't be bothered to pick it up. The forgotten table, the spoon still in the cup, her fingers barely grasping her fan, and he's holding her so close, completely unconcerned with the people behind them. See the way he's gripping her waist?" I say, pointing. "And is he nuzzling her cheek? Smelling her hair? Whispering something naughty into her ear? Is that why she's smiling with that look of absolute bliss on her face? She's so in love."

His chin rests on his hand and butterscotch eyes gaze at me instead of the print, so full of lust and devotion and wonder it feels like the room shrinks down to a satin-lined shoebox, and we're the only two people inside. "I know how she feels."

My heart pounds against my rib cage when I meet his eyes. I know Liam loves me; it's always there, barely contained beneath the surface. It's visible in everything he does; it's obvious just by the way he looks at me. But he's never said the words.

Never wanted to push me, I know.

"So do I," I say now.

His gaze drops to my lips. "Are you saying you love me, Anna Green?"

"I'm saying I love you madly, West Weston."

Liam stands from his chair, unconcerned with the tables of people around us as he pulls me into his arms, just like the man in the painting. "I love you, too," he says against my cheek. "I have been aching to say it for so long."

ONLY A MONTH LATER, September tiptoes in and we're too busy banging each other on a Labor Day weekend getaway in Cambria to realize what it means: Liam has gained full access to his trust. Surprising no one, the We Can Safely Divorce date comes and goes and there is zero talk of divorce. Divorce would feel like breaking up, and I have a hard enough time saying goodbye at airports; no way would I let this man say goodbye on paper.

But I guess that means there's also no talk of marriage, either, even though we both know that, hello, we are very much still legally married. I took off my ring and gave it back to him on the flight back from Singapore all those months ago; Liam never wore one. So when he climbs out of my bed one Saturday night in October, digs in his suitcase, and then sets the iconic turquoise box on my rumpled bed between us, I feel unprepared for the complicated emotions that smack me right in the face.

"What is this?" I ask carefully.

"It isn't what you think," he says, taking my hand. "I mean it is—it's your ring—but I'm not asking you to put it back on."

"Is this you admitting that the nipple-sized diamond is real?"

Liam laughs. "Yeah. It's real."

"Fuck me," I say on an awed exhale.

Smiling, he looks down at our joined hands. "This ring is yours, Anna. It's yours whenever you want it. Or we can sell it and get a different ring, a more Anna-appropriate ring, a ring a Muppet would wear, with gemstones of every color or a chain of diamond daisies. Whatever engagement ring you want is yours. As is my grandmother's wedding band. I can't tell you how happy it would make me to put that on your finger."

He takes a breath, puffing out his cheeks as he exhales, as if he's not getting this quite right. He's so fucking cute I want to lick his face.

"I know it's soon," he says more earnestly, meeting my eyes. "I know we've been married for five years but only together for five months. I know our lives are complicated and we don't live near each other, and we're still figuring out what we each want. But I love you. So much. I can't fathom wanting someone else, *anything* else, the way I want you. There's a ring in that box for me, too, when you're ready for me to wear it. Whether it's a month from now, a year. Shit, I'll put it on tonight if you tell me to." He frowns. "'Never' wouldn't be my preferred answer, but I'd take that, too." He winces at his sweet rambling. "When you're ready—if you're ever ready to be my wife for real, I'll be here, ready to be your husband for real."

I was joking on the plane months ago when I talked about the proposal of my dreams because to be honest, I never thought much about how that might look. The world tells girls we should want romantic, flashy grand gestures, and those can be great. But if I *had* given it deeper thought, I know I'd have dreamed up something just like this—an offer given with honesty and communication and mutual respect—over anything showy. So I kiss him. I keep kissing him until we're both lost in it and push him back and sink down on him and tell him over and over as I move that I love him. I know someday I'll be ready to wear a ring again, but right now, what we are is perfect.

The ring box goes in my dresser drawer for the time being, but the man and his love stay right at my side.

BY JANUARY, DR. WILLIAM Weston is no longer the only professor in this relationship!

Well, technically, I'm an instructor, and it is at a local city college, but it is a dream job. Teaching art to college kids on the path to figuring out what they want to do is amazing, as is being able to speak to that fear in them that they've chosen something impossible and elusive and will end up homeless eating apple cores out of the public garbage cans. I love, too, the older adults returning to school—the mom of newly graduated triplets finally finding time for herself, and the thirty-five-year-old dude raised by a shithead dad, who's only now realizing that loving art won't make him weak. My favorites are the two women in their seventies who met in a research lab years ago at Caltech and have a bet over which is the worse painter, so they took a class to find out.

I'm also painting like I've never painted before. Unless Liam and his Goddamn are around to distract me, or I am teaching, painting consumes my every waking moment. Which is good, I suppose, because after the two successful art shows last spring in Laguna and LA, more galleries want my work. Galleries in Berkeley and Santa Barbara. Galleries in San Diego and even Seattle. Galleries in San Francisco and Dallas. In February, I get a request for a solo showing at a small gallery in Boston, and Liam and I celebrate with a fancy dinner out in San Francisco when I'm up for the weekend . . . my treat.

I'm not the next art scene It kid, but it's a start.

Liam decides to stay on as faculty at Stanford for the time being but takes a seat on the Weston Foods board to help guide the corporate culture overhaul. The current COO will be CEO in the interim—a woman who is apparently a badass with silver hair and balls of steel (a Capricorn, of course)—with the idea that when she retires in five to ten years, Liam will take over. Everyone seems happy with this plan, and although I know nothing about business culture of any kind, I can appreciate that Liam, at only thirty-one, didn't feel entirely ready to step into the role. Look at that: a circumspect, mature Weston man. There may be hope for them after all.

And speaking of the Weston men, Alex and Jake remain where they are—as CFO and CMO, respectively—but have added twice-weekly therapy and intensive management training into their schedules. As of last summer, Ray was officially booted out of any role at the company. He's been charged with insider trading for the shares he unloaded before leaking the PISA documents. His trial starts soon, and it won't be the end of the mess for him: he's under investigation for racketeering and other quasi-sports-sounding charges I only vaguely understand. When he lost his position, his power, and access to most of his money, he also lost his current mistress, who took her story straight to Janet. Yes, it's wild that this is what it took for Janet to finally leave Ray, but we celebrate all the wins, even the bittersweet ones.

LIAM

IF IT HAD BEEN up to me, Anna would have spent that first night in Palo Alto and stayed for every single night after. If it had been up to me, Anna would never have taken off the ring. But it wasn't up to me, and thank God, because where we landed is so much better than anything I could have imagined.

To my absolute delight, once Anna has her first few shows in the Bay Area, she admits that the Northern California art scene suits her much better than the one in LA. The more time she spends up near me, the more friends she collects: at a local studio, at the coffee shop, at a park when she's walking my neighbor's dog. Gradually, all of these people become my friends, too, until we have a full, lively, and interesting community all around us.

By the time the following May rolls around, and we celebrate one real year together, Anna tells me she's ready to move in with me. It takes every bit of willpower to not call my Realtor the second the words are out of her mouth. To quote a movie my girlfriend has made me watch at least five times, "When you realize you want to spend the rest of your life with someone, you want the rest of your life to start as soon as possible."

When the inheritance came into my name last September, I dedicated eighty percent to the foundation and put the rest in various savings and investment accounts. Which means, of course, that with my salary from Stanford and my Weston board duties, I can buy us any house we want. But at Anna's insistence, and with her art career growing quickly, she contributes a chunk toward the down payment on the four-bedroom home we close on in July. It's somehow both polished and funky, with an asymmetrical, trilevel architecture that pleases Anna's need for nonconformity and contemporary accents that please my need for clean lines and modern decor. There's an office on the first floor for me, a small art studio in the backyard for her, a room upstairs with two sets of bunk beds for my niece and nephews, a master suite with space for a giant bed, and a room right down the hall for whatever comes next.

Anna does make one financial concession, however. Sticking to her rule that she can be selfish for the people she loves, she lets me buy her father a house nearby, a small two-bedroom bungalow with a giant garage, so that David Green can retire, tinker with cars, and enjoy the life he fought so hard to live, and his daughter never has to be more than five minutes away from him again.

BUT WITH DAVID MOVING close to us, my expectations about what a family can be shifts, too. He is everything Anna said and more; David is warm and affectionate, proud and loyal, devoted and protective. The first time we met over a year ago, I went to shake his hand and he pulled me in for a long hug, thanking me for making his daughter so happy. I was overcome; his easy acceptance and affection hit me in a surprisingly tender place, and I spent the entire next day feeling out of sorts and like I'd messed up somehow, realizing only later when I talked it out with Anna that I'd never been hugged like that by a father figure before. I hadn't known how to respond.

Over time, I figured it out. Hugging David when he walks into our house feels completely normal now. His hand warmly cupping my shoulder when I'm stressed about work is calming, reassuring. I no longer stare at Anna chatting obliviously at the ceiling, with her head in her father's lap on the couch and think it looks a little weird. I think if I watch David Green and his daughter enough, I might not make a terrible father myself one day.

I want that same closeness with my family, but we're all broken in similar but opposing ways, and I have to be realistic about what that means for forming bonds of trust and vulnerability. We have group therapy every other month or so. I have lunch with Jake and Alex the first Tuesday of every month; I talk to Charlie frequently. I see my mother every other Sunday. But the night that Anna invites everyone over for dinner at our new house is the first time outside of group therapy that the whole family will be in one room since our time on the island.

Not the whole family, I mentally amend. Because only a month ago, in July, just over a year after everything blew apart, my father was sentenced to eleven years in prison and fined five million dollars for dumping stock before going to the press. There are more charges coming—not to mention whatever the IRS finds when they finish combing through his finances. It wasn't the maximum sentence, but it wasn't far off, and the severity of it took the business world—and our family—by surprise. As part of our deal with Dad not to challenge the terms of Grandpa's trust, I was present in the courtroom, along with Jake and Charlie. Alex was noticeably absent, and I was deeply proud of him for that.

I always knew our father was toxic, but even I didn't realize how his behavior colored every one of us until he was excised like some kind of festering tumor. Mom is newly divorced, and less passive-aggressive. With access to most of their accounts frozen, she also has considerably less money now but seems happier for it. Jake and I are slowly finding our way back to each other, and it's taken work on my part not to let that final thing he said to me before PISA hit the fan reshape our entire relationship. Without Dad bankrolling his life, Jake has learned to live on what he makes as CMO, which is fucking plenty. He also seems to have zero interest in getting access to his trust. A part of me wonders if it's a form of personal penance for the mistakes he's made, but he'll have to work through that on his own.

But the idea of having everyone over . . . of letting them into our new home that feels warm and safe and light and *ours* is suddenly terrifying. Anna watches me arrange and then rearrange and then re-rearrange fresh veggies on a platter and moves to wrap her arms around my waist, resting her head on my back.

"It's going to be okay, you know."

"Is it?" I ask. "Alex and Mom aren't in a great place. Jake still gets weird around me. Charlie doesn't really articulate any feelings about anything."

"Even if it's awful, it's going to be okay," she says. "You know how I know that?"

I turn in her arms, leaning back against the counter and loosely wrapping my arms around her. "How?"

"Because even if it goes off the rails, even if everyone ends up shouting and crying and accusing, they'll still leave at the end of the night, and we'll still have our house and our life and this love that nobody can touch."

I stare down at her. "You're right."

"We get to decide how much of our hearts we want to give them." She stretches, kissing me, her lips passing slowly over mine, her tongue drifting teasingly over my bottom lip. "Now tell me you love me."

Something inside me melts, and my "I love you" is thick with a desperation I can't mask. I want to lock the doors and take her upstairs and spend the night showing her my devotion.

"I love you, too." Anna smiles and stretches to peek over my shoulder out the kitchen window behind me. "Now prepare to answer the door. Alex and Blaire just pulled up."

The arrivals are loud and chaotic; everyone immediately gets a drink in their hand and is blessedly loose by the second. By the time we sit down to eat, we are a noisy bunch. Our table growing up sat sixteen, and nobody but my dad ever spoke much at mealtimes. This table seats eight and there are twelve of us with extra chairs from the kitchen carried in, sitting crammed together, knees knocking, some of us straddling the corners, everyone bumping elbows. We're occupying the same space; we are making room for each other. There is not a single break in the conversation all night.

My mother's only passive-aggressive comment—"Anna, darling. You look so *comfortable* in that outfit!"—earns only a hearty "I am!" from my beloved. Blaire is just as loud as always but seems to drink less. Charlie is newly pregnant with twins and she and Reagan practically glow under Anna's attention. Jake and Kellan have Mom screaming with laughter while they do the dishes. Alex is calmer out from under our dad's shadow, more attentive with his kids. He ends the night being GW's fire engine, walking on all fours around our living room while GW puts out "fires." Alex and I don't exchange a single sharp word all night. There's no need for us to compete because there's nobody to impress. It gives me hope that he'll be okay. That we'll be okay.

ANNA

ON THE NIGHT OF August 12, officially our sixth wedding anniversary, Liam works late. It's been a big day: With his foundation fully funded as of last year, he spent today awarding tuition and grant money to this year's 250 Weston employee recipients. If, like me, you're delighted by the idea of a proud Liam Weston handing out giant paper checks, prepare to be disappointed. Liam *was* proud, but each person who walked up to the lectern received a leather-bound certificate of appreciation, a heartfelt handshake, and a discreet but impressive automatic deposit into their bank account. Still, even without the magic that would have been confetti and giant checks, the ceremony was wonderful. I sat in the audience beside Janet and Alex, with tears in my eyes, watching Liam fulfill a dream he's had for almost a decade. It might seem strange to those of us who grew up without money to imagine wealth ever being a burden, but Liam saw the people he loved do terrible things with those resources, and I can only imagine the weight that's been lifted for him by seeing those same resources used for good.

I left Liam a few hours ago, and when he gets home, he calls up the stairs for me.

"Up here!" I tell him, listening to the clunk of his shoes coming off one by one near the back door, the sound of his keys dropping into the bowl on the counter, and his footsteps on the wood stairs.

"You're never going to believe what happened after you left," he says, his voice growing louder as he makes his way down the hall toward our room. "Alex stopped by my office and asked to be more involved with the selection process next year. I'm telling you; he's grown into his position so much. It's like he's a di—" He stops just inside the doorway, hand caught in midair as if he were about to loosen his tie. "Well, hello." He eyes the scene before him, a distinct glint of interest already darkening his amber eyes.

The scene before him is me, completely naked and waiting for him on the Hungarian goose down and Egyptian cotton dream that is our giant bed. *Our* bed, in *our* bedroom, in *our* house. Fuck, I still love saying that. On my finger is the ring. It isn't the first time I've put it on since Liam gave it back to me—I'd occasionally take it out and try it on for a minute or two and then put it back—but today is the first time I've left it on. Today felt different. Today felt right.

"Hello, Dr. Weston," I say. "How was your day?"

"Pretty good, but I'd say it's improving by the minute." He pulls off his tie with a grin. "What's happening here?"

"Oh, you know, it was such a big day I thought we could keep cele-brating." With my legs stretched out in front of me and crossed at the an-kles, I place my palm on my chest, wiggling my fingers. "Notice anything different?"

His gaze slides up my body, from my toes to my breasts, and I know when he's spotted the diamond—I mean how could he not, it's *huge*—because his tie falls to the carpet at his feet. He meets my eyes again and I wonder if he sees the ocean of words there, all of them for him. "Anna . . . what are you saying?"

I'm so fucking happy, I can't keep the grin from my face. "I'm saying I'm ready to be your real wife."

He clears the distance between us in a few steps, and I squeal when he wraps me in his arms and pulls me from the bed, my toes barely skimming the carpet. He huffs a heavy breath into my neck. "Fuck yes."

"I love you, too." I laugh.

"I meant what I said," he says quickly, breathless. "You don't have to keep this one. I'll exchange it for any ring you want."

"No way. I love it. There are a lot of memories attached to this thing. Besides, if we ever get stranded somewhere I can use it to signal planes overhead."

Liam pulls my arm from around his neck and looks at my hand, at the delicate platinum band encircling my finger, at the ginormous diamond twinkling in the fading sunlight. "Maybe we could do it over, though?" he says. "A real ceremony with everyone there. It can be as fancy or not fancy as you want."

I can feel the heat of his clothed body against my naked skin, and I wonder if anyone has ever felt luckier than I do right now. "Let's do it," I say. "But only a little fancy. Not too fancy. Not private-island fancy."

He smiles against my mouth. "We'll save that for the honeymoon."

"Yes, but let's discuss it later. We failed at divorce sex, but I've heard engagement sex is top tier, and you're wearing way too many clothes."

Liam kisses me, taking small, stumbling steps until the bed presses against the backs of my knees. Together we undo his shirt, smiling into kisses and laughing as we pull the fabric free from his pants. The sight of his shirt falling to the floor is a starter pistol to my pulse, and I don't stop until he's naked and on the bed—broad chest, long athletic legs, and . . . other things, all gloriously in proportion.

It doesn't matter how many times we've done this—my married-people sex math checks out, by the way—I still never know where to start. His neck? His chest? His legs? His cock? Liam's body is a landscape of hard lines and sharp angles, and I climb over his legs, wanting to devour every bit of him. Greedy palms map the thick muscle of his thighs and up to the flat plane of his stomach. Once I decided to wear the ring, I also made a nail appointment, wanting to surprise him. Not only will my nails look great in the 387 braggy engagement pics I plan to take, but they have an added benefit. Liam sucks in a breath when he realizes it, too, and I drag my pink-tipped fingertips over his stomach, not hard enough to hurt him, but enough to leave four tracks of flushed, pink skin behind.

"Fuck." He hisses. "It's going to be like that tonight, is it?"

I nod, making my way down his body to take him in my fist and then in my mouth, my hair falling around his hips. He gathers the strands in his fingers, forcing my chin up. "You going to hide that pretty face the whole time?"

I groan around the length of him and look up his body. I could get drunk on those eyes, on the hunger there, his focus torn between my mouth on his cock, and his ring on my finger. I suck and taste, savoring the weight of him against my tongue, not sure if I want to finish him this way or feel him inside.

He decides for me, his voice a gravelly "Come here" when he cups my elbows, dragging me up his body, and settling me over his hips. His mouth finds mine again, his kisses a distraction for us both as he sits up beneath me and pushes his hands into my hair. Each kiss is punctuated with soft sighs and grunts as I slowly rock above him, the length of his cock sliding forward and back. His hands move to my ass, and he moves me over him in long, slippery slides. Aching want settles low in my stomach, between my legs. He lifts me onto my knees, and it changes the angle just enough that the blunt head of him catches me where I'm wet and open and so, so ready. Liam stills me with a hand to my hip before reaching between us, holding himself at the base and guiding me while I sink down, inch by inch, until I'm not sure where he stops and I begin.

"That's it," he says, gripping my ass again in both of his palms. "Just like that." He kneads the muscle there, pulling me open until he's seated inside me, and I gasp at the sensation of being so full in some places and so empty in others. I ride him like this, losing track of time as he kisses and fucks me, his hands setting off small explosions along my skin. His mouth finds my neck, my nipples. His groans grow louder in my ear. My orgasm flickers just off in the distance, close enough to reach out and grab, and when he flips me over, hooking an arm under my knee and bringing me closer, fucking me harder, it's finally there, spiraling through me in shimmering lines and sweeping brushstrokes. A work of art, a masterpiece, finally complete.

Wild now, he bends me nearly in half, each thrust sending me into the mattress and farther up the bed until he's coming, his helpless grunts heavy in my ear.

When he finally stills, I am melted sugar poured across the bed, I am a spent storm cloud slowly drifting apart, I am the quiet decrescendo of a frenzied concerto. With his lips pressed to my neck, Liam pulls out and then collapses at my side, his chest heaving, skin wet with sweat.

"Holy shit," I say, pulling in a shaky breath. "Honeymoon sex is going to be unreal."

With an exhausted laugh, he rolls to face me, taking my hand in his and looking at my ring again. "We're getting married."

"We *are* married," I correct. "We're just . . . getting a do-over. Happy anniversary, by the way."

He kisses me, humming against my mouth. "Happy anniversary." Considering something, he pulls back to meet my eyes. "Do we start counting from one?"

"No way," I tell him. "I want credit for all six."

"Then I have a lot of anniversary presents to catch up on."

"You do," I say. "But that's a lot of pressure. Let's make a deal."

He pushes himself up on his elbow, gazing down at me as he twists a curl of my hair around his finger. "What do you want, then? Name your price."

"What number would make you sweat a little?" I ask, grinning. "What would be just on the border of you saying no, but you'd still say yes? How about loving me for another six years, times ten?"

He does his best to look serious, but the smile never leaves his eyes. "Yes, sixty years is a very long time."

"Then how about forever?"

"You're a tough negotiator, Green-Weston."

"I learned from the best."

Liam grins, and there in his eyes is adoration and lust and promise and everything else I ever wanted. "You've got yourself a deal."

$\mathcal{A}$cknowledgments

WHAT A JOY THIS one was. Hopefully this book felt like it was written happily during a continuous stretch of warm summer days, because it absolutely was. In fact, this book was pure sunshine, an easy draft that took only four weeks to complete.

Just kidding! That's only if we don't mention the three other terrible attempts we wrote first because we couldn't get the idea right. An idea is always perfect; it is shiny and fresh and flawless. It will appear in your head fully formed and, as writers, we know that our only job is to put it down on the page. Easy! Alas, it isn't always easy to translate that shine into a full manuscript, and sometimes a draft comes out looking like you've just thrown a dart at a dictionary 90,000 times. So, for any new or aspiring writers out there, please know this: thirty books in and we sometimes still fumble the ball (that's a football reference, but we all know that now—thanks, Taylor). The two of us are somehow still learning the lesson to trust our gut and to be fearless: sometimes starting over is painful but correct.

Holly Root is usually the first person to hear all our crazy ideas, and that's because she is both our biggest cheerleader and unafraid to tell us when an idea is Not It. We heart you, Holly. Our PR rep, Kristin Dwyer, puts up with us every day; when we say we're a handful, we mean that we text a lot of questions that should probably be emailed and sometimes forget that we are in the Precious's box and start talking about BTS. But we love her more than Daenerys loves Drogon.

Jen Prokop is a freelancing editorial genius. She finds all our weak spots, guides us in a way only someone who lives and breathes romance can, and does it all with superhuman speed. You are an absolute treasure.

We were there for the Simon & Schuster 90th anniversary and we can't wait to be there for the 100th and beyond. Not many authors are lucky enough to feel like they have a true publishing home, but we do. Jen Bergstrom, we could not love and respect you more. The team you have built at Gallery is the best because that is what you inspire in people. You are wise and fierce and kind and hilarious. Thank you for always being our champion.

Abby Zidle, we have thanked you in so many books and finally, finally we get to thank you for being our editor! It took us playing the long game, but we are nothing if not persistent. We value your romance brain, your strategic guidance, your hard work, and your wisdom. Thank you for being our voice in the room and the jokes in our inbox.

WE LOVE YOU, GALLERY BOOKS: the wizardess behind the curtain Jen Long, editorial Yoda Aimée Bell, whip-cracker Frankie Yackel, brilliant hype woman Lauren Carr, whiz kid Eliza Hanson, marketing genius Mackenzie Hickey, social mastermind Abi Cardello, savvy badass Anabel Jimenez, our personal goddess and savior Christine Masters, and of course John of the Mustache Vairo—we adore you all. Sales folks, we owe you dinner and drinks, but especially Leora Bernstein for the hype, always. Thank you, Sally Marvin, Paul O'Halloran, Fiona Sharp, Lisa Litwack, and Anne Jaconette. Audio division, imagine us speaking sweet nothings into your headphones: Lara Blackman, Sarah Lieberman, Gaby Audet, Louisa Solomon, Taryn Beato, Sophie Parens, Chris Lynch, Tom Spain, and Desiree Vecchio. Last but not least, Jonathan Karp, we know you're the big boss and we're sorry we got so intense when we found out you also love BTS. But what can we say? When we love something, we go hard.

Thank you, Heather Baror-Shapiro, for getting this book into the hands of readers across the globe. Mary Pender-Coplan, you are an actual unicorn. Matt Sugarman, we never want to sign anything without your eyeballs on it first. Thank you both for always looking out for us.

Maria Hardjanto, thank you for naming our fictional island. We hope you can easily imagine Pulau Jingga nestled in the gorgeous archipelago of Indonesia. Martha Henley, thank you for the information about post-cancer rehabilitation, ports, and recovery milestones. You will always be our hero and Bombshell. If we got any details wrong in either case, the errors are ours and ours alone.

Thank you, Kate Clayborn, for being a pillar to lean against and the source of many of Lo's most restorative mantras. Thank you, Susan Lee, for your generosity of goodies and energy, and for always being down to commiserate, cheerlead, and celebrate; 2024 is your year. We couldn't do this without you both.

To our best friends, whose memes, playlists, and concert companionship got us through the adventure of this book—please never leave us. Ha-ha but no really: Erin Service, Katie Lee, Ali Hazelwood, Sarah MacLean, Jen Prokop, Rosie Danan, Julie Soto, Jess McLin, Jennifer Carlson, Brie Statham, Amy Schuver, Mae Lopez, Alisha Rai, and Christopher Rice. We love you all!

Our gorgeous, wonderful readers! We saw so many of you this year and we still have so many hugs to give. Thank you for reading, for coming to events, for waiting in lines, for shouting about our books, for sharing your stories and experiences with us, and coming along on this ride. Whether you read, blog, make TikToks, record podcasts, have a book club, leave reviews, ask for our books in stores, or just talk about them with your friends, we couldn't do this without you.

Booksellers and librarians, you deserve front row seats at your favorite shows, green lights at every intersection, only good hair days, and three wishes per calendar year. Thank you for all your work and helping get our stories into the hands of readers.

Our seven favorites are all enlisted, but we'll see you soon. Kim Namjoon, Kim Seokjin, Min Yoongi, Jung Hoseok, Park Jimin, Kim Taehyung, and Jeon Jungkook, we've said it before, but we'll say it again: ARMY will always wait for you.

Our families aren't surprised that our acknowledgments get longer with each book because they listen to us talk about how lucky we are all the time. Our kiddos were much smaller when we released *Beautiful Bastard* in 2013; now they are in college or driving and even the youngest, who was three when our first book came out, is taller than Christina. Our husbands have survived many, *many* deadlines and somehow still smile when we talk about our newest book. Thank you, K, R, C, O, and V, for being the beating heart of CLo.

My sweetest Christina, this was the year that taught us when we thought we were already flexible, something would come along and bend us in half. Thank you for doing this with me, for always putting in the work on the page and across the table, and for trusting me with your words and heart and hopes. I cherish you.

To my favorite face, my Lolo, thank you for always being the person I look up to the most. I've said before that the best part of being half of CLo is getting to read your words first, and it's truer now than ever. Thank you for your patience and encouragement and for believing in me when I don't. You are Xanadu-level magic and I love you more than I have words to say.